# WHEN THE MUSIC DIES

To Jim

# WHEN THE MUSIC DIES

A Novel

## KEN VANDERPOOL

TWIN
OAKS
PRESS

ISBN 978-1-937937-00-3

Printed in the United States of America

Twin Oaks Press
twinoakspress@gmail.com
www.twinoakspress.com

Cover and Interior design
By Sandra Vanderpool

## Dedication

For my brother, Edward Neal Vanderpool (1948-1992), and for all the brave officers of the Metropolitan Nashville Police Department, past and present, who have traded their days and nights to protect us and provide us with one of the safest of America's most beautiful cities.

You all have our unceasing respect and appreciation for a job well done.

# WHEN THE MUSIC DIES

Life is our gift from The Holy One;
His design for us all is the same.
After creation, the challenge is ours,
to give back a life lived in His name.

The love we show for our fellow man
writes the background music for our lives.
So, love your neighbor as yourself,
and live—so the music never dies.

*Ken Vanderpool*

# Prologue

*Clarksville, Tennessee*
*June 4, 1994*
*Saturday Late*

He approached Ryan Wilson from behind. Ryan and his fellow neophyte paratrooper Dave Coleman sat on limestone boulders, pulling their clothes on over bodies still damp from the midnight swim they'd shared with their dates. The splash of the spring-fed waterfall on the surface of the lake helped to shroud the intruder's advance. In one skillful motion, his arm encircled Ryan's head and covered his mouth so he couldn't speak. He jerked Ryan's head up tight against his own and through clenched teeth, whispered his tequila breath. "Was she worth it, you cheatin' son of a bitch?"

Before he'd completed his question, he opened Ryan's throat with the seven-inch KA-BAR blade. He restrained him until Ryan's body grew limp, and then lowered him to the dirt. The killer stepped behind the rocks and crept toward Dave, who was seated no more than twenty feet away, tying his running shoes.

Dave stood, fastened his jeans and was buttoning his plaid shirt when he turned to shout at Ryan over the roar of the falls. As his eyes were deciphering the shocking image before him, the crouched killer rose up. The tempered steel of his guilty blade found the small depression below the young soldier's Adam's apple, and he thrust it until the honed tip struck the vertebrae at the back of Dave's neck.

The killer's hand braced the hilt of the knife. As he skillfully fended off Dave's waning attempt at self-defense, he watched the panicked soldier's mouth flexing, searching for air.

He clutched a fistful of Dave's shirt and pulled him closer. Staring into his victim's watering eyes, he tilted his head and slowly twisted the knife. Blood leached from both sides of the blade.

"There's a price to pay for adultery, you bastard, and you're paying it."

Dave fought to steal another breath, but there was none. Life left him there.

The killer jerked the knife from the soldier's throat and shoved him. Dave's body collapsed across the large rock where he'd been sitting. The killer kneeled and wiped each side of the black carbon steel blade across the leg of the dead man's jeans. He glanced in the direction of the girls, and moved behind a large tree near the edge of the woods to wait.

It was now twenty-eight hours since he'd stepped into the stale darkness of the small apartment and found her note on their kitchen counter—not the loving welcome he'd anticipated for more than a year. Her guarded words didn't explain. His wife had left that to the neighbors.

"I saw them leave together late that night," the E-4's wife from next door had told him. "I was up watching a movie. They'd left together before, but they were loading bags in his car this time.

"I remember when I first saw him. He wore a single chevron—only an E-2. I wondered who he was. I couldn't figure why, with you on deployment, she was allowing a man inside her house, unless ..." she stopped, and then looked away.

As the killer concealed himself at the base of the tree, thoughts of his wife's infidelity fed his anger. He had no idea where she and her adulterer had fled, but he needed to kill them ... now.

*I gave my life to this country—and to my wife. But, the ungrateful bitch couldn't keep her pants on until I got home. While I'm deployed, honoring my commitment, she's enjoying herself and breakin' her damn vows.*

As Connie Neal and Heather Lawson finished dressing in the woods, he could hear their high-pitched laughter over the roar of the falls. It reminded him how all this had begun earlier at the saloon.

The irritating date-night banter from the two couples in the booth next to him was overpowering the heartrending country and western music he'd selected at the jukebox. His plan for musical solace wasn't working. These people didn't get it. There was nothing left that called for laughter. Their loud-mouthed babble had confirmed their plans. He was familiar with the old quarry.

"You'd better be dressed," Heather shouted, as the girls moved along the bank toward the clearing and the campfire. "We don't want to see those shriveled up packages again." The girls laughed.

The killer worked his way through the woods so he could get behind them. The girls stepped into the clearing.

"Oh, my God!" Connie screamed.

A muscled arm tightened beneath Heather's chin and pulled her backward. She stumbled, struggling to regain her balance and her breath.

Connie couldn't believe what she was seeing.

Heather's face reddened as she pulled at the man's arm and screamed, "Help! Help me!"

Connie looked for a weapon, anything to use against the attacker. She grabbed a limb, and swung it at the man's head. With Heather's neck wrapped in his left arm, he turned and the limb missed his head, striking his right shoulder. Connie lost her grip on the limb and almost fell.

Searching for another weapon, Connie failed to see his fist coming at her head. She dropped motionless to the dirt.

Connie awakened, unsure of how long she'd been unconscious. Her clothes were in shreds and the full weight of his body was on top of her.

"No! Please. No!" she screamed.

He ignored her pleas, slapped her and continued his sexual assault, shouting, "Whore. You unfaithful whore."

Still dazed from the blow to her head, Connie tried without success to push him off. Thrashing in all directions, she looked to her left for maybe a rock to .... She stared into Heather's bloody face, her throat as wide open as her eyes, looking back from the plum colored dirt where she suffered, and lost her fight. Connie was stunned. Her fear overwhelmed her. But, her increased struggle only served to irritate her attacker more.

"You adulteratin' whore." He hit her again. "I go off to fight for this country; you ignore your vows and start screwing some damn ranker behind my back."

"What are you talking about? Who *are* you?" Connie screamed.

"I'm your husband, damn it. And you won't be fornicatin' no more. You hear me? No more."

"I'm not your wife!" Connie screamed through her last tears.

"No—but you'll do."

She never saw the blade.

# Chapter 1

*Nashville, Tennessee*
*April 14, 2003*
*Monday Morning*

**Nine Years Later**

Metro Homicide Detectives Mike Neal and Norm Wallace were sitting in the empty retail parking lot gulping down a hasty breakfast and trying to come to grips with facing another day on the back of two hours sleep. They worked into the early morning investigating a murder outside the Sandstone Apartments in the southern part of the city. Two hours and a shower was not a fair exchange for normality, but then what was normal anymore?

Both detectives jerked their heads from side to side, attempting to locate the source of the screaming tires as the sound wrapped around their cruiser. From the passenger's seat, Mike caught sight of the multi-colored clunker in his peripheral vision as it bucked to a smoking stop.

A man tumbled from the driver's seat and wobbled toward their car. Mike could see he was unkempt. He appeared to be unarmed and from the looks of him, recently unconscious. Mike's reflexes caused him to react from the sound of the man's dirty hands slapping hard against the passenger side window.

"Damn," Norm mumbled through a mouthful of bagel. He fumbled the white paper around his breakfast, and a glob of warm cream cheese oozed from his bagel and landed on his sport jacket.

"Shit."

Gravity had already begun to lengthen the oily mess by the time he retrieved the lid to his coffee cup and scraped the glob from his stained lapel.

Outside, the agitated man yelled an obscure threat that sprayed his anger in spittle across the car's side window. His face was contorted and his hair tousled, but Mike thought he looked familiar.

"Wha tar you doing?" The English portion of the Latino's mixed-language rant was at last understandable.

Mike recognized Gabriel Sanchez from the homicide he and Norm worked last night. He was the young victim's older brother.

"This jerk's attitude needs a tune up," Norm said, as he yanked his door handle.

Mike parked his half-eaten yogurt on the opened lid to the glove compartment. He threw his notepad on the dash and kicked open his door, driving Sanchez backward and causing him to fall.

At thirty-seven, Mike Neal was six feet tall and just under two hundred extra-lean pounds. His light brown hair was maybe a half inch longer than his 1990's Army buzz. He'd been told that when he smiled he looked like John Bon Jovi after a four dollar haircut. He wasn't sure it was meant as a compliment.

"What the hell's wrong with you, Sanchez?" Mike yelled as he stood over the scruffy man.

Sanchez lurched to his feet.

"Wha tar you two doing sitting in your damn car? You are supposed to be looking for the gang-banging bastards who killed Tony." His wide-eyed stare exposed a thousand tiny blood vessels that confirmed to Mike—Sanchez was drunk.

Sanchez made these same expectations clear to the detectives late last night at the Davidson County morgue after identifying the body of his brother Anthony, dead at eighteen. Tony was robbed and shot while delivering for Pauletti's Pizza.

"Sanchez," Norm said, "we're all trying to find your brother's killer, but Tony's murder isn't the only homicide in Nashville this week. We have other distraught families with murders that also have to be investigated. You need to chill out before you get *your* ass in trouble."

"I don't give a damn about nobody else's problems. I want you two looking for *Tony's* killers. Don't you understand?" he screamed then clenched his teeth as he lunged at Mike.

Mike side-stepped and pushed him away. Sanchez stumbled, caught his balance and then took a swing at Mike. Mike blocked the weak attempt with his left forearm as he grabbed Sanchez's shirt and rotated him so he could get behind him and gain control of his arms. Norm reached for his cuffs and stepped forward, but Mike's compassion caused him to shake his head. Norm backed off.

"Calm down, Sanchez," Mike said. "You're not helping Tony, or yourself."

As Mike continued to restrain him, he could tell by the stench from Sanchez's clothing and his breath, he'd consumed more than his share of beer and tequila since last night's incident.

"It is too late to help Tony, thanks to you cops. If you had locked up the gang-banging bastards, Tony would still be alive. Now, let me go. Let—me—go!" He jerked his arms, attempting to free himself.

Mike pushed Sanchez away. He stumbled, turned and swung wildly at Mike again. Mike grabbed his wrist mid-swing, twisted it and then moved behind him once more. Irritated with Sanchez's attempts to fight, he locked him in a rear-naked choke hold, a hold he'd performed countless times during hand-to-hand combat training and afterward while serving with the Army Criminal Investigations Command. The maneuver was designed to restrict blood flow to the brain if maintained for a few seconds. It began to render Sanchez powerless.

Norm came closer to help.

"He's done," Mike said, squinting in response to Sanchez's disgusting odor.

As Sanchez's resistance waned, Mike released the hold and eased him down to the pavement next to their car. He rubbed Sanchez's neck to stimulate his return to awareness.

"Grab a blanket," Mike said.

Norm pulled a blanket from the trunk, rolled and placed it under Sanchez's head.

"Gabriel, you'll need to lie still for a while," Mike said, happy the man was now quiet.

Some locals had gathered near the cars. Witnessing the confrontation, they offered their bold judgment on how the situation was being handled by the detectives.

"Man, you kill dat dude," one of the young men shouted, then laughed. "See—you done choked him. Damn."

"He looked dead to me, already," The other teenager said. "Call Five-O." They both laughed, then gave each other a high five.

Steamed by the free-flowing criticism, Norm walked over to the young men announcing, "Okay, it's time to move on."

Most of the group turned, mumbled, and walked away, but a couple of them just stared at Norm.

"Wha? Chu gonna choke us too?"

"I suggest—you take this opportunity to leave," Norm said as professionally as he could.

"Zat a threat?"

Norm's eyes opened wide as he gave each of them his most intimidating stare. He took a deep breath. "I don't make threats—I predict the future."

Norm glanced back at Mike, who rolled his eyes knowing well what was coming. Norm stepped closer to the two and leaned his large frame forward.

"If you don't leave—right now," Norm put his fingertips to his temple, squinted and spoke slowly, "in the future ... I see you ... lying there," Norm pointed to the pavement, "in handcuffs ... looking up at me through black eyes with multiple lacerations and colorful contusions. And, I see me ... looking down at you ... wondering why you didn't leave when you had the damn chance. Do you understand, or do I have to use *body* language?"

"Chill out, Po Po. We out-a-here." The twosome offered their confident swagger as proof of their machismo.

Norm watched them walk away then returned to Mike and Sanchez.

"I called for EMS to check Sanchez and patrol to take him and his car back home," Mike said.

Sanchez, finally docile, sat leaning against the Crown Vic. He batted his eyes, still clearing away the stupor.

In minutes, the medical techs arrived and checked his vitals. Sanchez appeared to have regained some self-control.

"Detective," Sanchez said to Mike, in a calmer tone. "Remember what I told you last night. The family of the man who died in that bar fight in Escondido got their justice when I was sent away. I paid my dues. Now it's *my* turn. You people find these thugs and get me my justice, or I *will* do it myself."

"You're making some damn poor decisions, Sanchez," Norm spoke up. "You might want to rethink that one."

"Then do your damn jobs, so I don't have to," Sanchez shouted. "I promised my mother when I brought her and Tony to Nashville that the move would save him from the same San Diego gang-hell that cost me seven years of my life. Now I got to face her every day, both of us knowing I failed, again. I don't care any more."

"Give us a chance," Mike said. "We'll find them."

"You'd better," he demanded.

Mike and Norm left Sanchez with the EMTs and returned to their car.

As soon as he fell into the driver's seat, Norm jerked down the visor mirror and craned his neck to inspect the stain on his lapel. "Do you know how hard it is to find a decent Fifty-Four Extra Long sport jacket? Cheryl is gonna shoot me for sure."

Mike leaned forward to grab his notepad off the dash. He looked at the dark spot on Norm's lapel and said, "And you've given her a target, right over your heart."

Six feet-four, three hundred and fifteen pounds; the only thing slight about Norm was his level of patience. At forty-eight, Norm wasn't anywhere near his partner's physical conditioning. But then who was? Each fall, Norm made sure he was able to meet the department's minimum physical training requirements. That was good enough for him.

Norm flipped up the visor. "Do you ever want to knock the hell out of somebody when they go off on you like Sanchez? I don't see how you keep from it."

Mike smiled. "No, not really. I remember how I felt after my sister Connie was killed in '94." Mike hesitated. "When I flew home from Iraq, I was crazy too—almost like Sanchez. All I knew was somebody had to pay for my sister's death. I wanted it to be her killer, but I was prepared to make life miserable for everyone involved if it would get her some justice. I gave the detectives in Clarksville hell for months. They hated to see me coming, and they saw me much too often."

"I can't imagine how you must have felt."

"I was so mad; I beat the hell out of the heavy bag at the gym every day for three weeks." Mike looked out the window at nothing. "I couldn't hit my father. I had to hit something."

"Are you and your dad talking?"

Mike hesitated a moment, looked down at his note pad, and then shook his head without answering.

"Geez, Mike. Can't you cut your old man some slack?"

"If he'd looked after Connie like he promised me, like a father is supposed to do, my little sister wouldn't have been at that old quarry. She would still be here. I was on the other side of the planet serving my country; dealing with Saddam Hussein and all the other fanatical crazies." Mike looked at Norm. "All he had to do was take care of a seventeen-year-old girl, and he blew it. She was his daughter, for God's sake. If he'd paid as much attention to her as he did everyone else's kids on his damn high school baseball teams, *Coach Neal* might have noticed his child was in danger. I have trouble with that."

"Has there been any progress in the case lately?"

"I haven't heard anything from the Clarksville detectives in months," Mike said. "I think it's just another cold case to *them.* I keep hoping something new will surface there, or here, that will rekindle the investigation, but so far there's been nothing."

Norm nodded his head.

Days were rare when Mike failed to make some type of personal effort toward the resolution of his sister's murder. Mike vowed that this was one case *he* would never allow to become cold.

Mike sat quietly for a few minutes staring out the car window. "Even after all these years, I still feel like something will happen to point us in the right direction. I need to be able to close this chapter in my life—and in my father's life too. If I can, then maybe he and I can find some common ground."

Norm and Mike had previously discussed their dissimilar relationships with their fathers. Norm and his dad had been close, up until the elder Wallace's passing five years ago. Mike hoped, at some point, he and *his* father could reconcile and find peace.

Mike's cell phone rang.

"Mike Neal."

"Mike? Lou Nelson."

"Hey, Sergeant. What's up?"

"I'm sure you know Crime Stoppers has received dozens of calls from alleged witnesses to the shooting last night at Sandstone."

"There are a lot of folks who'd like to claim that reward," Mike said, "but they haven't been offering up anything new."

"No," the Sergeant said, "until now."

# Chapter 2

*Hubbard County, Tennessee*
*Monday Morning*

Brad Evans sat motionless at the base of a large oak tree. He'd been in position since before first light.

Brad had been through his alertness routine already, but his muscles were telling him it would soon be time to repeat the procedure. The drill included the flexing of muscle groups and breathing control exercises. Meant to keep an aging shooter sharp during his wait, Brad developed the ritual for himself when he turned fifty and began to feel the effects of age. It worked to delay the dulling of senses and the numbness of muscles from prolonged inactivity.

He never had this problem in his younger pre-arthritic years, perched in the trees of Vietnam waiting for unaware Viet Cong to stroll into his kill-zone. His youthful conditioning throughout his twenties aided his ability to stay in the trees for days. The North Vietnamese placed a heavy bounty on all of America's snipers who were captured alive. The chance to torture American snipers to death was of high value to the vicious enemy.

Only Brad's eyes were moving; surveying for signs of activity around him. The polished senses of an Army-trained sniper, although learned thirty-plus years earlier, still provided him the focus he needed to block out all else, excluding his current objective.

He detected a faint rustle in the distance at his nine o'clock. Maintaining his body's position, he gradually rotated his head toward the sound. Not yet able to confirm the source, he listened. He detected the faint crack of a branch as it was bent and then released, followed by the almost inaudible sound of dew-covered spring leaves slapping against each other. All sounds, his and the target's, were magnified in the damp morning air.

Still tracking on the sound, Brad caught sight of his quarry as he turned abruptly. Stock-still, the target waited. His eyes were doing double-time, checking the area. Brad's icy stare gave him no reason to suspect danger.

The target continued slowly along his path, then froze. Only his dark eyes were moving.

Brad elevated his Tikka T3 rifle the last few inches until the pad on the ultra-light polymer stock met his shoulder. Gradually, he brought the barrel above parallel with the ground. In the same motion he tilted his head and maneuvered his right eye into alignment with the rear lens of the scope. He centered the magnified image on the reticle. No adjustment needed. Target at twenty yards.

*Point of aim equals point of impact.*

The only thing between Brad's right eye and the target's left eye was the glass-etched crosshairs on the lens.

The high-pitched report of the small-bore rifle raced through the woods and echoed across the valley. The target dropped. Brad stood.

His eyes still on his victim, Brad cradled his rifle across his left forearm, grunted and stretched, attempting to recover from the period of immobility.

Brad stepped cautiously through the previous year's slick decaying leaves and empty acorn shells. As he reached the kill, he smiled. He bent over and inspected the entry wound. Blood trickled from the left eye socket and the exit wound in the rear of his head.

"Center of the eye; one shot—one kill," Brad said.

He picked up the large amber-colored fox squirrel and finagled it into his game bag at the rear of his hunting vest.

"That ought to keep Rocky busy for about five minutes."

Rocky was Brad's Rottweiler; his friend and the hungry beneficiary of all Brad's target practice kills.

As soon as he heard Brad's footfalls nearing the house, Rocky began his raucous welcome ceremony. It was rare when Brad's homecoming failed to deliver Rocky a fresh breakfast. His barking and jumping against the chain link fence grew more energetic once he caught sight of his benefactor. Brad chuckled, then reached back into the game bag, extracted the rodent and hurled it up and over the fence. As always, Rocky was ready. It appeared he was killing it again, the way he pounced on the bushy feast, holding it with his paws and tearing at its body with his huge canine teeth. Brad could hear the bones break as fur flew in the wind. Rocky's bark was now replaced by a satisfied low-pitched growl.

As he reached the house, Brad removed his hunting vest and draped it over a hook on the screened-in back porch. Julie would have demanded he remove his boots before entering the ceramic-tiled kitchen, but she wasn't there to remind him. He laid his rifle across the top of its hard composite case and grabbed the cold pot from the coffee maker. After pouring the remainder of his 4:00 a.m. coffee into his mug, he stuck it in the microwave for a minute and fifteen. He stepped to the sink, rinsed the coffee pot and gazed out the window at his buddy who was finishing his morning snack. It was just him and Rocky now. It wasn't the same.

Four months ago, Brad's wife Julie was returning from a trip to Nashville to see her doctor when her car was struck by another driver who ran a stop sign. She was killed. Just that day, Julie had been diagnosed with stage-four breast cancer. She didn't get the chance to share her fear or her depression with her husband. Brad found out about the cancer a few days after the funeral when Julie's doctor called, concerned about why she'd failed to make her next appointment.

"Realistically, she had maybe three to six months," the doctor told Brad.

"That was three to six more than we had together, thanks to the son of a bitch that hit her," Brad told him, wishing he'd been able to help her through what was to be a short period of grief and pain.

The time following Julie's death was dreadful for Brad. He had difficulty keeping his mind focused on anything.

Brad was a self-employed gunsmith who worked out of his home. He was also an independent contractor working as a wildlife exterminator. Brad's sniper training made him the perfect choice for the duties involved in varmint removal. The task called for someone to either trap or exterminate persistent pests such as beaver, raccoon, or coyote who were infiltrating the world of the humans. Many of his referrals came through his gunsmith customers.

Brad enjoyed the independence that came with being self-employed and self-sufficient, but that was when he had motivation at home. He spent much of this time now sitting in his rocking chair on the front porch, staring at and talking to Julie's empty rocker next to him. So many times they spent their evenings there talking, laughing, sharing today and planning tomorrow.

Brad wanted justice for Julie and for himself, and he was becoming less and less concerned about how he got it. He knew enough about the legal system to know the guilty seldom reaped all they sowed. He'd been told very little about the driver who struck Julie's car, but one of the witnesses told him the man was a Latino. It would be months before the man would be tried for his crime, assuming he didn't plea it down to a lesser offense or dash back to Mexico. Brad prayed that some silver-tongued defense lawyer wouldn't be able to prevent this killer from paying for his crime.

"There is something seriously wrong when a person can just kill one of us and walk away like nothing happened," Brad told the assistant DA. "What's happened? Where's our protection?"

*I'll tell you. It's in my holster.*

# Chapter 3

*Crimnal Justice Center*
*Homicide Unit*
*Nashville, Tennessee*
*Monday Morning*

"Hey, Wolfe."

"Yeah, Lieutenant?" Detective Doug Wolfe rode his desk chair from his gray cubicle out into the aisle, so he could see Lieutenant D. W. Burris.

"Have you seen Neal or Wallace this morning?"

"I haven't seen either one. Aren't they working the Sandstone shooting from last night?"

"Yeah, but we had an update scheduled at ten." Burris looked at his watch. "Obviously, they're late—again."

Burris was painfully punctual. The pain was all his. He tried to demand the same respect for promptness from his detectives, but he was convinced by each of them daily, it was pointless. His men had an unstructured job, and they always had an excuse for being late. He made an effort to tolerate it.

At forty-seven, Burris had spent half his life with the Nashville Police Department. When he saw fifty sneaking up on him, he decided to reject the idea of getting old. He was determined to stall it, or at least give it one hell of a fight. He worked out faithfully at the department gym. He played racquetball with a passion and made it a habit to defeat all comers, regardless of rank.

Burris's desk was positioned so he could see through his office door and down the rows of matching cubicles to the entrance at the opposite end of the large room. It wasn't that he had to monitor the comings and goings of his team, but this way his booming voice was better able to reach all the ears that needed to hear it. This morning most of the detectives were where they should be, on the streets conducting interviews and following up on leads.

He heard movement at the far end of the room and looked up to see Norm Wallace's bulky form fill the doorway. He watched Norm trying to prevent the heavy metal door from clanking shut behind him, announcing his arrival.

"Did you lose your Rolex, Wallace?" Burris shouted as Norm turned and aimed himself toward his boss.

"Uh—no, Lieutenant," Norm said. "Sorry we're late. Didn't Mike leave you a voicemail?" Norm said, preparing his defense as he strolled to the door of Burris's office.

"I haven't had time to pick up voicemail, Wallace. I have been working."

"Lieutenant, we were sort of attacked while we were eating breakfast," Norm said, as his ample girth stressed one of the cheap metal-framed chairs in front of Burris's desk.

"You were *what*?" Burris leaned forward, dropping his forearms on his desk pad.

"Gabriel Sanchez is the older brother of the victim from the Sandstone shooting last night. He saw us having breakfast, drove up behind our car and took issue with the fact we were feeding our faces instead of searching for his brother's killer."

"You've got to be kidding."

"Kinda what I thought at the time. The goofball even took a swing at Mike. That was a bad idea."

Hearing the door as it closed, Burris looked up and watched Mike approach his office. "Detective Neal. Glad you could join us."

"Morning, Lieutenant." Ignoring the sarcasm, Mike took the chair alongside his partner.

"Norm tells me you had a confrontation this morning?"

"You could say that," Mike said, preparing his folder for their discussion. "Nothing like starting your day with a little hand-to-hand combat."

"What happened?"

Mike shared the details of their morning adventure and assured Burris that the EMS team cleared Sanchez, confirming he was okay after his brush with forced unconsciousness. Burris admired Mike's skills, but he hated it when the detective used combat moves he'd learned in the Army. Some were capable of injuring people, and most were against departmental policy.

"Okay, what have we got so far on this Sandstone shooting?"

"Victim was nineteen," Mike said, "male Mexican-American. He was delivering pizza—worked for Pauletti's off Nolensville Road. He was robbed and shot. Three nine millimeter brass were found at the scene; no prints. Victim took two in the chest and one under his eye which left a large exit wound in the back of his skull."

"What's the medical examiner's schedule?" Burris asked.

"I put that call in on the way here," Mike said. "I left her a message. I know she's short-handed now and blitzed with work."

"Do you expect any revelations from the autopsy?" Burris asked.

Mike looked up. "I can't imagine what they would be."

"I'd say the nine was the cause of death," Norm said, shrugging his shoulders and offering a faint smart-ass smile as he glanced up at Burris, and then at Mike.

Burris looked over the top of his reading glasses at Norm. "No shit?"

"I know." Norm exchanged solemn looks with Mike, "This stuff comes to me all the time. It's a gift."

Mike turned his attention back to his notes, refusing to comment on Norm's weak attempt at humor.

"We spoke with four witnesses who admitted they heard loud talking, gunshots or both," Mike said scanning his notes. "Our most confident witness is a single black female, forty-seven. Her apartment is on the second floor facing the common area from the shooter's right. Says she turned off her lights when she heard the shouting. She went to the window and looked out the edge of her mini-blinds. Said she saw muzzle flashes—couldn't remember how many. She said she saw Sanchez drop, then she witnessed three men run to a dark colored car at the end of the parking lot. She let us know she's tired of all the violence and wants to know why we can't do something about it, so she and her neighbors can live in peace."

"That's quite an observation from a civilian," Burris said.

"I thought so. I asked her how she was able to see and remember so much. She said she watches all the cop shows on TV."

"Seriously?"

"Yep," Norm said. "That's what she said."

"You think that taints her recollection a little?" Burris asked.

"I don't know," Mike said. "She didn't appear to be embellishing the story."

"I don't get the idea she's been at Sandstone very long if she's still griping about the area?" Burris asked.

"No," Mike said, "she didn't give the impression she was aware she lived on gang turf."

"If she watches the local news like she does the network, she'll get educated real soon," Norm said.

"We also have a single Mexican-American male witness, twenty-six, asleep at the time in a first floor apartment and woke up to the shots. Says he jumped up and looked out the window in time to see two, maybe three men get into a black Chevrolet. He says one of the men had a green bandana and baseball cap in his hand."

"Two men?" Burris asked.

"Yeah, maybe three," Mike said.

"Green, huh?" Burris leaned back in his chair and ran his fingers through his wavy salt and pepper hair.

"Yes, sir."

"Does this witness know he lives on gang turf?" Burris asked.

"I got the distinct impression he knew," Mike said. "He was wearing a black and gold cap during our interview."

"Hmm. You think he was lying about the green bandana to throw us toward his rivals?"

"I didn't get that from him. He said nobody in their right mind wears green around there. He said green is the color of a target in that neighborhood, and he was surprised these dudes made it out alive. He seemed like he was being honest, but you can't tell."

"Interesting," Burris said. "What about your other witnesses?"

Mike flipped the page. "One is a married, looked to be mixed-race, male, thirty-five. He said he saw the victim get out of his car and approach the building. I asked him what caused him to notice Sanchez. He said he heard his car sputtering when he parked, and then saw the clip-on pizza flag on top of his car. That's all he admitted to seeing. He said he didn't see the other men, but for the record, the look on his face and his body language said otherwise. He knew the environment where he lived. He had two young kids at his feet."

"Another concerned citizen," Burris said. "Okay, what else?"

"The last one is a female," Mike said. "Widowed, white, no age given. I'd say late fifties to early sixties. Claimed she heard the shots and called 911. Said she was watching the news when she heard the commotion. The call was registered by 911 dispatch at 22:20, so that appears to match. She said this wasn't the first time she'd called 911 since moving to Sandstone."

"It won't be her last," Norm said.

"Is that it?" Burris asked.

"Yes sir," Mike said. "Everything that's meaningful so far."

“What about the people in B-26 who ordered the pizza?”

“Well, we talked to two couples there. They said they didn’t hear anything suspicious. In their condition, and judging from the volume of their music, they may not have. They were barely coherent when we talked with them. The place was in a fog and smelled like a rock concert. They asked if we’d seen the pizza man; they said they were starving.”

“Cannabis,” Burris shook his head.

“That was all we had, until Lou Nelson called us while we were wrapping up the fiasco with Gabriel Sanchez this morning. It looks like out of all of the bullshit calls to Crimestoppers since last night, there was one caller who wanted to meet with detectives to discuss what he saw.”

“Really?” Burris said.

“He asked if he could meet with us during his break. He works downtown. He said he’s the assistant manager for one of the tourist shops on lower Broadway.”

“I’ll expect an update from you two afterward.”

“You’ll have it,” Mike said.

The detectives stood and headed for their desks.

“Good morning,” Carol Spencer said, as she saw the partners.

“Hi, Carol,” Norm said, searching for a bare spot on his paper-covered desk.

“Hello, there.” Mike stopped to face Carol.

The thirty year-old MNPD crime scene photographer was delivering copies of photographs to the detectives’ desks. Her shoes had a military shine and her perfectly pressed criminalist uniform was dark navy blue like the patrol officers. According to Detective Neal, few of the female officers filled out theirs in quite the same manner as Carol. Mike often thought Carol’s ex-husband must have been blind and stupid.

“Do y’all have any of the photos back yet from the Sandstone Apartments shooting last night?” Mike asked.

"I don't know," Carol said. "That one wasn't mine."

"Yeah, I know. I didn't see you there."

"I'm headed back to the lab now. I'll check and call you. Okay?" Carol smiled.

"Works for me." Mike returned her smile and added a wink, then watched her walk away.

Carol was an aerobics nut, and the three classes she attended each week kept her body firm, flexible, and flab-free. She wore her thick brunette hair in a tight braid that dropped halfway down her back. Carol wore little make-up since she never knew what crime scene environment she would be thrust into next. She carried no more girly tools than necessary.

As she reached the door, she pushed it, then turned, glanced back at Mike and smiled. These two had been covertly nurturing their mutual attraction for several months. Captain Moretti's Law kept the liaisons infrequent and undercover.

"There will be no intra-departmental fraternization allowed," Moretti said. "Find your *amore* outside this department—*capisce*?"

Mike dropped his eyes from Carol and turned away, trying not to be seen scrutinizing her ... exit. He opened and laid his folder on Detective Vega's desk. He was about to sit when Norm spoke up.

"Uh, did you decide to change desks?"

"Huh? Oh," Mike said. He scanned the desktop and picked up the folder. "I was uh, going for coffee. You want some?"

"Yeah—sure." Norm chuckled and nodded his head. "Two creams and lots of," he made a kissing sound, "sugar."

# Chapter 4

*New York City*
*Monday Mid Day*

He paced the hardwood, and from the thirty-sixth floor of the rented New York City flat, Abdul Malik Kadir contemplated the movement of the minuscule masses below. As always, the infidels walked the streets comfortably oblivious to what was taking place around them.

Abdul maintained the small apartment as a base of operations in the United States. Even after the devastation of the towers, the presence of Arabs in this huge melting pot caused less alarm than in any other city. This was true, most especially with those Arabs who, like Abdul, spoke excellent English and were seldom seen out of a tailored Italian suit and crocodile shoes. Abdul's gold Rolex offered an affluent touch that helped to sell his deception.

A well-heeled business professional in appearance, Abdul's true nature was brutal and malicious. Trained in the terror camps of Afghanistan, the thirty-five-year-old Syrian was a lieutenant with pretentious aspirations. Farid al-Rishari was his sovereign; the ultimate fearless jihadist. Few had failed him, but only once.

The ashtray on the end table was filling with unfiltered attempts to calm Abdul's anger. Enraged that his deadline was in jeopardy, Abdul could wait no longer. He was about to break one of his own security rules by placing a satellite phone call to Indonesia. He felt he had no choice.

Mahmoud Zahar was jeopardizing Farid's plans as well as Allah's will, and that was intolerable. If this mechanical engineer caused all the work that went into this operation to fail, Farid would be furious, and Mahmoud would be the one to pay the final price.

Abdul attached the encryption device to the satellite phone and placed the call. He listened as numerous tones established his connection and finally produced a ring. Abdul identified himself, and Mahmoud was called to the phone.

"Yes? This is Mahmoud."

"What is wrong? Why has the device not arrived as I specified?" Abdul said, containing his rage.

Recognizing Abdul's rant, Mahmoud answered, "We had difficulty. Completion of the unit was delayed."

"Difficulty? I am not interested in your problems. I made it clear to you what was required. Do you not understand the significance of this plan?"

"I understand the plan. It took longer than we expected to perfect the mechanism."

"You were given ten weeks to complete the project. You said you could—"

"I told you," Mahmoud interrupted, raising his voice, "I could make you no promises. The apparatus took longer to develop than I expected. The metering valve seals failed to prevent release of the test material numerous times. I had to seek another solution."

"You were chosen because of your advanced training and creativity as an engineer. Why do you insist on explaining failures?"

"We have developed our skills and found our voice with explosives," Mahmoud said. "Who do you think wrote the manual used to prepare the October attacks in the Philippines, the consulate in Denpasar, and Bali?"

"It is true. The accomplishments of Jemaah Islamiyah are well-known," Abdul acknowledged.

"Yet, we have never constructed a device such as this."

"And, our people have never faced this mounting attempt at the destruction of Islam," Abdul said. "As I stand here in the midst of our enemies," he stopped at the oversized window, "I can hardly breathe. The Americans have begun to recruit our own and turn them against us. The Iraqis have grown weak under Hussein and now many are following the American invaders like underfed dogs.

"The American Senator Callahan is speaking at this conference. He is determined to guide the Kurds to sovereignty. Before Callahan and his advocates can use this conference to work the Kurds into fervor, they must be stopped. Our benefactors insist that we eliminate this attempt to form an American-driven satellite republic aimed at seizing control of northern Iraq's oil resources. We cannot fail. Killing a room full of Kurds in the process will only underscore our commitment."

"I know the battle well," Mahmoud assured him. "Let us get back to the device. When you came to us, you demanded this apparatus contain no metallic components."

"Yes," Abdul said. "There will be much security and many metal detectors at this gathering."

"The non-metal parts that were available to us in Asia were inadequate. Other solutions had to be explored. If my construction of this apparatus had been rushed and thrown together like other of your past plans, you and your group would be the first ones to die as the result. My delay was saving your ungrateful life."

"Hold your tongue while you still have one, engineer." Abdul was sensing a side of Mahmoud not yet revealed. He appeared less intimidated than before. Possibly, the ten thousand miles between them was feeding the engineer's courage.

"We depleted all of our available options," Mahmoud explained.

"We had to order the new valves and seals from the United States. It took almost a week to locate them and get them to Indonesia. We completed the re-tests. The seals held. We shipped the package to the United States, March eighteenth on a cargo ship."

"You did what?" Abdul exploded again. "Why did you not ship it via air freight so I would have it now?"

"The completed package cannot move via air due to its contents being under pressure. It is not able to withstand the temperature and pressure changes in the cargo hold of an airplane. Did you want it to explode over the Java Sea?"

There was only silence in response to Mahmoud's rhetorical question.

"Your package will arrive at World Spice Company, outside Nashville in LaVergne, Tennessee."

"Where? Why was it sent to this place?"

"Relax. Your lack of faith is disheartening."

"Do not challenge my loyalty to Allah, EVER!" Abdul shouted.

"Like *your* cadre, we have people in place where we need them throughout the United States. We have a man at Long Beach harbor who has already verified the cargo ship's arrival. We have an experienced man at World Spice Company who has confirmed the container is in transit, and he is awaiting your package. He will remove it from its secure storage within the container and contact you for delivery instructions."

"What about customs? Are you sure it was not detected?"

There was silence on the phone line. Mahmoud decided not to criticize further Abdul's incessant challenges.

"World Spice receives a container shipment of bulk spices from Asian Herbal Export on the fifteenth day of each month. They are one of the largest bulk spice shippers here in Jakarta. This monthly shipment has taken place for so long the customs inspectors in both Indonesia and Long Beach no longer give it a second look."

"How do you know this?"

"I know this. That is all you have to know." Mahmoud's words were growing bolder. "You demanded delivery by the third week in April. Yes?"

"Yes," admitted Abdul after an irritated pause.

"And you will have it on the night of the fifteenth, which meets your requirement. Now—my money?"

"After I receive the package," Abdul said.

"No," Mamoud said. "You will exchange the payment with the courier at the time the package is delivered to you.

"I do not have the payment with me."

"Then I suggest you get it by tomorrow night if you expect delivery of your package."

"Do not threaten me."

"No threats. I am explaining to you the simple logistics involved in you obtaining what you want. Exchange the payment for the package at the time of delivery—or there will be no delivery. This is clear, is it not?"

Abdul was silent; his blood pressure was building. He was not accustomed to relinquishing control.

"I am sure," Mahmoud said, "that a package as valuable as this would be useful to others with similar aims. Or, maybe I should contact Farid directly, to determine *his* desires for the package."

Mahmoud waited. "I am sorry. You will have to speak up. I did not hear you."

"So be it!" Abdul shouted. He killed the connection and threw the phone across the room.

# Chapter 5

*10-7 Bar & Grill*
*Nashville, Tennessee*
*Monday Mid Day*

The 10-7 Bar & Grill was a favorite spot for many of Music City's men and women in blue. The tavern was owned and operated by Hubert "Hub" Teer, a retired twenty-two year veteran from the Patrol Division. Hub was shot in the ass, or lower back as he preferred to call it, in 1988 during a domestic call. He was forced by his injury to take disability retirement. Hub still walked with an exaggerated side-to-side limp that, along with his low-riding pot belly, made him resemble an Emperor penguin.

Known by the officers simply as Hub's Place, the restaurant was located down the street from the Central Precinct on Broadway, less than two blocks from three of the city's busiest entertainment and convention venues. This remodeled adult book store stayed busy feeding the masses year round. If it wasn't packed with tourists, it was full of off-duty officers enjoying a well-deserved break.

Mike and Norm arrived early for their meeting, hoping to get a chance to visit a few minutes with Hub. Their work had kept them so busy; they hadn't been in the place in months. Mike wondered how the jovial old cop was holding up. He missed hearing Hub's embellished stories about the old days, back before Nashville "got screwed up by all these damn Yankees and aliens from all over creation," as Hub claimed.

Mike parked in a space that was a block east of the restaurant. He knew both he and Norm could use the exercise; especially after one of Hub's giant Steak 'n' Cheese sandwiches.

"Smell it?" Norm asked as soon as he opened the cruiser door. "Man, now I'm about to starve."

"You're always about to starve," Mike said. From the looks of you, it wouldn't hurt you to fast for a few months."

"Gimme a break," Norm said as he drew in more of the aroma. "You can smell those onions and peppers all the way to the Titans stadium. How can anyone resist that?"

"Yeah, Hub was a genius putting in the little exhaust fan that pipes the kitchen aromas out onto Broadway."

"Hey, buddy," A tattered old man said, as he stumbled up to Norm. "You got any change?"

"Beat it, dude," Norm said. "I'm working this side of the street."

Mike laughed and shook his head. "Oh, that Milwaukee charm."

Norm grinned and jerked open one of the ten-foot tall mahogany doors which welcomed patrons to the 10-7 Bar & Grill. The detectives moved from the bright sunshine into the shadowy tavern.

Once inside, they had to pause for their eyes to adjust to the cavernous atmosphere. The restaurant's fifteen-foot ceiling was painted matte black to camouflage it along with the pipe and ductwork from a more recent time. The burgundy brick walls sported almost a century's patina of experience.

Mounted on the brick at the rear of each booth, were a half-dozen thin black frames displaying glass covered photos of Nashville's police force over the years. The city's officers from years past were memorialized in photographs throughout the eatery. Most of the photos from the last three decades were in color. Some, like Hub and his tavern, reflecting their advanced age.

Hub's Place was not one of the classiest spots in Music City, but it was the safest. When you left Hub's Place, you knew you had been protected, and your stomach knew you had been served.

The sound of cooks yelling "Order up," the register ringing, the loud talking and laughter all told the detectives their old friend's restaurant was still a big hit.

Mike and Norm took seats at one of the high-backed hardwood booths and grabbed menus, though they knew well what they would order.

Still as sharp as ever, the old cop didn't miss a trick. Hub had caught sight of Mike and Norm as they crossed in front of the bar. He threw together two Steak 'n Cheese Combos and was on his way to their booth with the platters in the air when he shouted, "Two Hub combos for two of Nashville's finest." His raspy voice, a product of too many years of cigarettes, could be heard over the restaurant's noise.

"Hub. How's it going, you old fart?" Norm said.

Laughing, Hub sat the platters on the table then took a boxing stance and punched Norm in his right arm.

"Damn," Norm grabbed his arm.

"It's all good." Hub shook hands with the detectives and they all laughed. "Hell, if business was any better, I'm not sure we could handle it." A waitress appeared from behind Hub with two extra-large sweet teas.

"That's great," Mike said. "How's the family?"

"Working their butts off in the kitchen, like me. It's good to see you boys. How's your duty?"

"It's getting worse," Mike said. "I'm afraid the city's growth is bringing with it more of the bad to go with all this good."

"Too many damn foreigners, like I been sayin' for years. Everybody's got to get a taste of Nashville. One of these days we're gonna explode from all these people movin' in here."

"Hub, all these people are making you successful," Norm said.

"Bullshit. Most of the people I'm feedin' are tourists. They're eatin', lookin', listenin', and leavin'. And, that's a good thing." Hub laughed. "It leaves some room for the rest of us."

"Hey listen, it's great to see you two. I've gotta get back in the kitchen before Marge comes out here and kicks my ass, and my old ass has seen enough damage for one lifetime. Don't stay away so long next time." Hub leaned over putting his hands on both men's shoulders. "Don't try to pay for these combos either or I'll have your asses arrested."

"You don't have to do that, Hub. We can pay," Mike said.

"Oh, no. This one's on the house. But, I better see you both back in here next week, and payin', or I'll have you picked up. You got that?" Hub acted as though he was going to punch Norm again.

"We got it, Hub," Norm said, laughing and throwing up both hands as a defense.

Hub waved as he waddled back toward the kitchen.

"Look," Mike said, tossing his head, "standing at the door."

The young man was alone. He shielded his eyes with his hand and scanned the restaurant. Convinced this was their Crimestoppers witness, Norm stood and waved the young man over.

Weaving his way between the crowded tables, he arrived at the detectives' booth. His employer's name tag introduced him, but he still said, "Hi, my name is Derek Snell."

"I'm Detective Wallace. This is Detective Neal," Norm said, as he reached for his sandwich.

Mike rose halfway from his seat to shake the young man's hand and then moved his platter to the back of the booth so Snell could sit. Mike knew from experience that there was a flying elbow danger zone on Norm's right side that few had survived.

A waitress arrived at the booth soon after Snell sat. He gave her his order and looked from Norm to Mike and back.

"Why don't you start at the beginning?" Mike removed his pad and pen from his jacket and laid it next to his plate.

"Okay." Snell inhaled. "I was coming home from work around ten. I worked over a little because we were real busy. I work down the street here at one of the tourist shops." Snell looked at Norm, then at Mike. "You already know that, right?"

"Yeah—go on," Norm mumbled, through a mouthful of steak.

"I pulled into the complex. I live in building number eight, by the way. I was driving up the entrance lane toward the apartment sign when this car came around the corner on my side of the drive almost on two wheels. He had to swerve to get back on his side."

"Did you see the driver?" Mike asked.

"Yeah, sorta. He was dark-skinned. I think black. I couldn't be sure. The dash lights were on him, so he was a little easier to see than the passenger. He looked black too, though. It was hard to tell."

"Was there anyone else in the car?" Mike asked.

The waitress arrived with Snell's cheese-fries and cola. He thanked her and waited for her to leave.

"I'm not sure. I couldn't see the back seat. It happened pretty fast."

"Describe the car," Mike said.

"That's what I saw best. You see, I used to have a '77 Chevrolet Caprice Classic Landau, and this car was the spittin' image of the one I owned. Same color, four-door, vinyl half-roof, everything. Mine was stolen in the summer of 2000. I was so pissed. I only had liability. I didn't get anything for it."

"What color was the car?" Mike asked.

"Oh, sorry. It was Midnight Blue Metallic. Well, mine was. I'm pretty sure this one was too."

"What else can you tell us about what you saw?" Mike asked.

"I noticed when my lights hit the car as he made the curve, the windshield about halfway across had a nasty crack like somebody hit it with a brick or a baseball or something. You know, one of those spider web cracks where the breaks in the glass are circular?" He held his hands out forming a large circle with his index fingers and thumbs.

"I wondered if the car was mine. It didn't look like mine did when *I* owned it. My Caprice was in good shape." Snell looked at Norm. Mike was writing, and Norm was inhaling fries.

"Why didn't you call the police last night?" Norm asked, dunking a cluster of French fries into a large puddle of ketchup.

"I didn't know anything happened at the apartments until this morning."

"You didn't associate the sirens last night with the car speeding out of the complex?" Mike asked.

"I live in the back of the apartments, and in South Nashville we've got sirens twenty-four seven. They all sound like they're out on Nolensville Road to me."

"Can we have your phone numbers, at home and work so we can get in touch if we have any more questions?" Mike asked.

"Sure." Snell gave Mike his numbers and ate more of his cheese fries.

"You gonna eat that?" Norm asked Mike while grinding the final bite of his sandwich.

"Why? You want it?" Mike asked what he knew was a dumb question.

"Well, there's no sense in letting it go to waste."

"Geez, Norm," Mike handed the plate across the table.

"Well, if there's nothing else, I gotta get back to work," Snell said.

"Derek, thanks for your help," Mike said. "If we make any headway with your information, Crimestoppers will be in touch."

Snell scooted out of the booth and stood. "Let's hope so. I could use the funds, and I'd like to think it might help you catch that boy's killer."

"Me too," Mike said. "Thanks."

Norm tossed his head and grunted a goodbye.

As Snell walked toward the door, Mike watched Norm vacuum the remains of the second sandwich and fries.

"Man, you have got to rein in that appetite. You're gonna have trouble hitting your numbers on the POPAT in September." Mike knew how taxing the Police Officer Physical Abilities Test could be for an officer who was accustomed to the exertion. Someone who was essentially sedentary and carrying Norm's load could easily fail to meet his minimum limits and end up on suspension.

"That's five months away." Norm wiped the melted cheese from the corner of his mouth.

"Yeah," Mike said, "and about thirty pounds."

# Chapter 6

*White Tail Lodge*
*Hubbard County, Tennessee*
*Monday Afternoon*

"Damn it, Richard. I don't care what it takes. Listen, you've got to use this opportunity to ramp up our image and our exposure. With a vehicle like the Internet available to us, we have a unique means to market our organization, and our beliefs. We have to seize it," Carl W. Garrison III explained to Richard Hopkins, Director of Public Relations for The Alliance for the Racial Purification of America.

"TARPA's image is critical." Garrison stood. He began to pace behind his desk as much as the coiled phone cord would allow. "If we are going to fight this war, we have to have soldiers—battalions of soldiers. As you and I have discussed before, too many of the members we've been attracting over the last few years aren't arriving with the skills we need for the coming battle."

"So true. But we do need numbers," Hopkins said.

"I understand we need numbers." Garrison waved his arm in the air. "But, first we need strong, impressive and committed recruiters we can send out to enlist others like themselves; others who believe our country is headed down the road to hell, and that somebody has to have the balls to step up and save it, before it's too late. These engaging and intelligent people will then be able to clone themselves and grow our numbers with folks armed for the conflict."

As the charismatic leader of TARPA, Garrison practiced the television evangelist brogue that captured and held the attention of so many supporters. Garrison, like his father before him, worked hard to maintain an impressive appearance. His hair received a conservative cut every two weeks, and American-made suits were the only clothes he purchased. You would never see Carl Garrison in an Italian suit, or one made anywhere outside his country.

He knew one of the main reasons his father's philosophies on race and religion had been so difficult to promote was centered on the number of less-than-impressive individuals who had flocked to their cause over the early years. Garrison made strides in improving TARPA's image in the years since his father's passing, but there was much work still to be done before people of influence could ever bring themselves to go public with their support.

"The time is right," Garrison said. "The good people of the USA are tired of these foreigners coming in here from all over Central and South America, and these camel drivers from the Middle East taking jobs away from our people. Our citizens are fed up with the federal government's failure to close our borders. They're ready to see somebody take charge and change things. That's where we come in. I've got a few congressmen on a leash, and with some quality people on our front lines, we can start to garner some positive attention from the media, and make some of those changes."

"Yes, sir," Hopkins agreed.

"But Richard, you have to make this clear on our website, in our brochures and in all of our promotional materials. You've got to present TARPA as the attractive and practical solution that it is; the place for people to turn who are tired of seeing their hard-earned tax dollars spent to feed and care for all these illegals. It's all in the wording,

Richard. Use your marketing degree, son. Reel them in."

"I understand, Carl. This is an overwhelming responsibility we have."

"Absolutely, and you're the front man. It's your job to make sure they know we're here for them, and that they see us as a viable option for dealing with this crisis. They must understand it is *indeed* a crisis, and they must believe we are worthy of their endorsement, and more especially their financial support."

Garrison looked across his expansive office to see his two deacons at the doorway. He smiled, motioned for them to come in and then looked at his wristwatch. He waved his open hand toward the burgundy leather sofa and chairs.

"With the growing volume of these aliens pouring into Middle Tennessee," Garrison said, "if we don't act fast, we'll all be speaking Spanish, or even worse, Arabic by the end of the year."

The deacons chuckled quietly, not sure who Garrison was talking with.

"Now get those promotional materials edited and the website prototype finished, so we can get them in front of our prospective members. Are you with me?"

"I'm with you," Hopkins assured him.

"Good. Send the new copy for my approval the moment you have it ready."

"Yes, sir."

"Talk with you soon."

Garrison hung up the phone.

"Gentlemen." He spread wide his arms, smiling. "Welcome."

The men stood as Garrison approached. He shook hands with them like he hadn't seen them in months; it had been only a week.

Howard Hall, rotund senior deacon and close ultra-conservative friend of Garrison's for over twenty years said, *"Buenas dias, amigo."* Hall maintained a sober gaze.

Rod Justin stared at Garrison who was solemn at first, then he burst out laughing along with his old friend, allowing the younger Justin the comfort to follow.

"That was Richard Hopkins, our young public relations guru," Garrison said as the deacons removed their suit coats and took their seats at the conference table. "He's having some trouble executing our plan to present TARPA as the solution for a confused and racially misdirected society."

"Is he back on track?" Hall asked.

"He'd better be. I don't have the time or the inclination to babysit his young ass while we construct this societal washing machine. We cannot afford to have the people of America continuing to perceive us as another Klan. They've got to see clearly, and be able to embrace the positive differences between us and that old gang. I've talked with a number of people about this during my recruiting efforts. They still see the Klan as a bunch of hardcore, right wingers living in the past. We must be recognized as the people's champion; the preferred new alternative for today's ethnically conscious Americans."

"Absolutely," Justin said. We could influence so many more people if we could get them to see past their paradigms and hear our message."

"Too often," Garrison said in his exaggerated drawl, "I think the public's focus on what they know is God's will, gets stolen away by the dramatic and sensational trash delivered to their living rooms by the media. We have to be prepared to thrust ourselves in front of that drama in order to intercept the spotlight."

"We can do this," Justin agreed.

"We may even have to *create* the drama that becomes our stage," Garrison said.

"Amen," Hall said.

"We have to make it clear to the unaware that equality doesn't exist except in the minds of the weak. We have no business mixing with the A-rabs, the Jews, or the Jig-a-boos. All that integration hogwash does is to further weaken the white race.

"Too many Americans today agree with our values, but don't feel comfortable opening up and making that fact known. Public association with ultra-conservative groups such as ours could be detrimental to the lives and careers of certain folks who are in positions of influence in our country. That's okay. If their anonymity is all they require in order for them to continue supporting us financially, then so be it. We'll make that trade. We will always have advocates who cannot occupy the front lines."

"God bless them," Justin said.

"Yes, and God bless their money," Hall added.

"Amen," Garrison said.

The men laughed.

Garrison's desk phone rang.

"Excuse me, gentlemen." Garrison walked to the desk. "Carl Garrison."

"Carl, it's JD."

"Hello, Jimmy Dan."

"Turn on the television sir; Channel Four. They're on commercial right now, but there was a teaser before the ad about an upcoming story I think you'll want to see."

"What's it about?" Garrison picked up his remote and turned on the large screen TV in the corner of the huge office.

"One of your favorite subjects."

"Really?"

"Yes, sir. Middle Eastern aliens."

"Here it is. It's on now. Thanks, JD." Garrison hung up the phone and turned the volume up as he walked back toward the conference table.

A graphic of the Kurdish national flag came up on the screen to the right of the middle-aged anchorman's graying pompadour. He began to speak.

"The Sixth Annual Kurdish-American Conference will be held here in Nashville this year."

Video from last year's conference in San Diego began to play on the screen as the anchorman continued.

"This Thursday and Friday, April seventeenth and eighteenth, an estimated four-hundred plus attendees from around the world will convene at The Centurion Hotel for two days of meetings and speeches aimed at the promotion of Kurdish sovereignty and regional stability in Kurdistan, as well as the progress of hundreds of Kurdish families now making their homes in Middle Tennessee. Spokesperson from Nashville's Kurdish community: Dr. Asad Zana."

A video clip began.

"Our mission here in Nashville is to promote the cultural, educational, and socio-economic development of all Kurdish people as well as refugees and immigrants from other nations. We also seek to facilitate their increased contribution to the Nashville and Middle Tennessee communities where they live and work."

"Oh, bullshit," Garrison said.

The anchorman returned to the screen.

"In addition to Mayor Burleson and Governor Duncan, local governmental and religious leaders are expected to attend. Kurdish leaders in Nashville plan to welcome large numbers of dignitaries from their native Kurdistan and Iraq as well as numerous religious and political leaders from across America.

"Keynote speaker for the international conference will be the six-term Democratic Senator from New Jersey, Raymond Westbrook. Senator Westbrook is the Ranking Member of the Senate Subcommittee on Immigration, Refugees and Border Security. Westbrook has received significant criticism from his right-wing opponents over the past year for what has been termed his 'porous border' approach to homeland security.

"Rumored to be one of the conference's guest speakers is the controversial Republican Senator from Texas, Charles Freeman Callahan. Senator Callahan is a member of the Senate Subcommittee on Near Eastern, South and Central Asian Affairs. Callahan has been a staunch supporter for an autonomous and democratic Kurdistan since serving the U.S. Central Command as Brigadier General during Desert Storm."

A file video of Callahan speaking to the media began to play.

"The citizens of Kurdistan with their steadfast support of the United States, their longing for freedom and their abundant natural resources are a fertile field for establishing a lasting foothold for democracy and a strong U.S. ally in the Middle East. I intend to support these courageous people until they have achieved their autonomy."

The anchor returned stating, "Since Turkey's Parliament made their decision just over a month ago to prohibit the U.S. from utilizing Turkish bases to launch attacks on Iraqi forces, Senator Callahan has not been shy in his ardent criticism of Turkish leadership or in his support of the Kurds."

Callahan's video returned to the screen.

"The Turkish government has frequently threatened military intercession based upon suspicions that an economically autonomous Kurdish entity in Northern Iraq could negatively impact the stability of the Kurdish minority within Turkey. An intrusion of this nature cannot be allowed."

"The timing of the senator's speech here in Nashville," the anchor said, "seems ironic as only this past Thursday April tenth, Kurdish Peshmergas arrived in Kirkuk replacing Saddam Hussein's vacating army and creating one more dilemma for Turkey's frustrated leadership.

"There will be more on this international gathering later tonight on the Scene at Six and Ten.

"In other news today, ..."

Garrison shut off the television. He began to pace the room, nodding and rubbing his jaw.

"Well, well," he said as he stopped to face the deacons. "Gentlemen, this little rag-head shindig with the Kurds looks to be a lot bigger than we thought."

There were tentative looks from the deacons. They could see he was scheming. Garrison turned and continued to pace the floor, rubbing his hands together.

"Not only are we being delivered the entire leadership of this local throng of foreigners, we've been granted the unique opportunity to effect some much needed change with some of the self-serving bullshit mongers from Washington and the Middle East."

"Outstanding." Hall nodded, seeking to be supportive of his chief.

"We're gonna take advantage of this herd of rag-heads," Garrison's animated hands accented his words, "and while the cameras and the world's curiosity is focused on them and their bizarre way of life, we'll demonstrate how to handle the immigration problem." Garrison produced a devious smile. "The opportunity is here my friends—our guns are loaded—our aim is true, and it's time to pull the trigger. We're going to send some of these aliens back home and the rest of them to hell."

Garrison stood erect and reflected as he gazed across the room at an imposing life-size full body color portrait of his deceased father that was positioned between two floor-to-ceiling oak bookcases.

"My daddy—would be so proud."

# Chapter 7

*Criminal Justice Center*
*Homicide Unit*
*Nashville, Tennessee*
*Monday Afternoon*

"Okay, listen up," Burris yelled over the chatter. "Some of you may have seen the memo the chief posted on the board yesterday. It seems we have yet another convention at The Centurion Hotel with a large number of dignitaries, beginning on the seventeenth."

"Oh, great."

"Just what we need."

Numerous mumbled moans came from across the room.

Burris lowered his brow and waited for quiet. "Patrol and Events Traffic have been on this for a month or so, but they have recently asked for those of us who are available, or could be available for overtime, to assist where needed. This duty is expected to be higher level personal security for some of the elevated risk dignitaries when they arrive at BNA and then while they're at The Centurion. All of you have been through this before, so gimme a break. Occasionally, we're asked to help out."

"Hey, Lieutenant," Dennis Bolton shouted. "Are there any female dignitaries? Say mid-thirties, brunette, maybe a little top-heavy?" He cupped his hands at his chest. "If so, I'm available."

Laughter broke into more chatter and derogatory comments about Bolton's social calendar.

"Hey, Bolton," Detective Cris Vega shouted. "You need to get a life, dude. While you're at it, get rid of the blow-up doll I saw in your cruiser. That's not considered a ride-along." She shook her head. "Tacky, very tacky. Try to find yourself a *real* woman."

The room exploded with laughter.

"You volunteering, Vega?" Bolton yelled.

"Not on your life, detective. I'm not that hard up."

"That's not what I heard," Bolton shot back with a laugh.

Vega elevated her right arm and middle finger as high as her small stature would allow.

"Okay, Bolton has signed up for security detail," Burris said. "Anyone else?"

"Hey, Lieutenant," Bolton said. "I was just kiddin' around."

"I'm not." Burris stared at Bolton. "You're first on the list. I suggest you be there, Detective."

"Shit," Bolton said softly, so as not to get any other surprise assignments.

"Any more smart asses stepping up?" Burris asked. There was silence. "Okay—"

"What organization is this, Lieutenant?" Norm Wallace interrupted.

"The event is the Kurdish-American Conference. I'm told the dignitaries will be here from all over the U.S. as well as a few foreign countries. Those on security detail are to report to a planning meeting at sixteen hundred hours tomorrow. See Lieutenant Armstrong to confirm your dates of availability. See me with the same info by tomorrow morning, first thing. Any questions?" Burris waited.

"I promised the Captain at least three of you would be able to help out for a day or two." He looked up and scanned the room over the top of his glasses. "I know who's available. Do not make me a liar, people."

He paused. “Dismissed.”

As the collection of detectives funneled themselves through the conference room door, Jack Hogue couldn’t hold back.

“A-rabs.” He shook his head.

“The Kurds aren’t Arabs, Hogue,” Mike Neal said.

“I don't care what you call ‘em. They're a bunch of camel-chasin’ towel heads like all the rest of ‘em over there in that big cat box.”

“You are such a bigot,” Norm said. “When is your Klan membership up for renewal, Hogue?”

“Make your jokes.”

“How many Kurds do you know anyway?” Mike asked.

“I don't hang with the A-rabs, Detective.”

“What about Hispanics? Do you know any Hispanics, Hogue?” Norm goaded.

“Of course, we got dozens on the force. Carlos Guzman and Victor Rosado are detectives. They’re cool. They’re hard-working, honest, church-going folk.”

“That’s right,” Norm said. “You liked them from the beginning, right? As soon as they got here back in the 80s, you welcomed them with open arms when they entered the academy.”

“Well, not really.”

“What? You weren't suspicious and distrustful?” Mike said. “You didn’t call them names like taco cops? You didn’t talk about them like you’re talking about the Kurds now?”

“I don’t remember.”

“Bullshit, Hogue,” Norm said.

“Well, maybe I criticized them a little. Everybody was doing it back then.”

“No. Everyone wasn’t,” Norm said. “But, you and Gil Murdock were giving them hell.”

“Hey, we didn’t know them then.”

“Yeah, and you don’t know the Kurds now,” Mike said. “But, that isn’t keeping you from despising them.”

"Give me a break," Hogue said.

"Let's go, Norm." The partners headed for the interview rooms.

"Hey, Marty. Where did you put the Davis brothers?" Norm asked.

"Two and four, but you may want to talk with the 'Yo' in room five before you see those two."

"Yeah?" Mike said.

"Officer Russell from the gang unit said you need to hear this one's story on what went down at Sandstone."

"Really?" Norm said. "I love a good story teller. Don't you, Mike?"

"Yep, as long as some of what he's telling is the truth."

"Who is it?" Norm asked.

"Orlando Reese."

"You're kidding. Reese?" Norm looked at Mike and laughed. "Well, he has been known to tell us the truth on occasion."

"By the way," Marty said, "the younger Davis brother hasn't spoken a word yet. He looks like he's scared to death by the isolation. The officers that brought them in said Troy, the older one, appears ready and anxious to talk. He's already rolled on a Demetrius Brown as the doer and a few minutes ago, he requested that he and his brother be tested for gunshot residue to prove their innocence."

"Confident, huh?" Norm said.

"And knowledgeable. Have we found Brown yet?" Mike asked.

"Patrol picked him up over on Buchanan a half hour ago and they're on their way in now."

"Tell me they located the weapon," Mike said.

"Not yet. They're towing the car in for the search. It belongs to the Davis boys' mother."

Norm walked through the door to Interview Room Five and held it open for his partner.

"Wh'sup, Gents?" Reese said.

"Hey, Lando," Mike said, taking a chair. "Tell us what you heard about the shooting at the Sandstone Apartments."

"What, no small talk? No 'how ya been doin', Lando? No catching up?"

"Lando?" Norm said, as he delivered his *that's enough* stare.

"Alright, alright. You know my brother Twan, right? Sorry. *Antoine*."

"Go ahead," Norm said.

"Well, he's the one that knows a bunch of the AJs—Arm of Justice, ya know?"

"We know what it stands for," Norm said. "Get on with it."

"Okay, so he heard 'em talkin' bout one of theirs doin' a dude at Sandstone. You know Sandstone is Los Punzados territory?"

"Yes," Mike said. "We're aware."

"Tell us something we don't know yet, Lando," Norm barked.

"Hey, man. I'm tryin' to explain, okay?"

"Okay. You've explained," Norm said. "Now spill it."

"Geez, how come you big dudes are so hostile?" Reese asked. "Hey, Mike. What does Los Punzados mean anyhow?"

"It translates to *the stabbing pains*," Mike said. "You were saying?"

"Wow, I guess that fits. Anyhow, Twan told me he heard that D-man took a couple of AJ wannabes—"

"Who's D-man?" Norm interrupted.

"Brown, D-man Brown. Real tough son of a bitch. Anyhow, Antoine said he took these two wannabes with him to scare the pizza boy. I'd say he wanted to impress these two with his macho and his nine millimeter."

"Let's curtail the editorials," Mike said, "and move ahead with the facts as you heard them, okay?"

"Sure. Okay—Twan said the pizza boy had X'd one of the AJ's tags, and he'd been braggin' about it. Said he was some kinda ex-gangster from San Diego before he moved to the musical city a few months back. He was dissin' the local colors like they wasn't real gangsters. I guess he missed the Southern Cal street action and wanted to stir up some shit here. Might have been a bad idea, huh?"

"Ya think? Facts, Lando," Norm shouted.

"What else did your brother tell you?" Mike asked in a milder tone.

"That's about it. He said they didn't take D's car 'cause D was afraid that drivin' into South Nashville, somebody might put some holes in his Navigator."

"Brown drives a Lincoln Navigator?"

"Yeah, that's what Twan said. I don't know what color or anything. They was in a Cap Classic at Sandstone. Belonged to one of the young dogs, I guess."

"Well, if you've started guessing again—I guess—we must be finished," said Norm.

"Thanks, Lando," Mike said. "We appreciate your help."

"No pra, gents." He stood and puffed out his chest. "Anything I can do to help out the PD."

"Right. We should have more stand-up citizens like you, Lando," Norm kidded.

"Yo, uh—who do I need to see—to, uh—get my, uh—you know?" Reese said with both hands actively assisting with his request for money.

"I don't know, Detective Neal, do you know who he needs to uh, see to get his uh, you know?" Norm mocked Reese.

"I'm not sure, Detective Wallace," Mike said. "Isn't Detective Jack Hogue in charge of the Confidential Informant Compensation Program?"

"Why, yes. I think you're right," Norm said, turning to Reese. "Lando, see Detective Hogue for your payment."

"Thanks, gents. Later on."

Lando strutted from the room while Norm worked to suppress his laughter. "Detective Neal, I'm surprised at you."

Mike smiled.

Norm made his usual bold entrance into Interview Room Two with Mike trailing. The older Davis brother was sitting slumped in the straight-back chair, arms folded, chin in his chest and both legs bouncing. He sat up in the metal chair.

"Troy Davis? My name is Detective Neal. This is Detective Wallace.

Can we get you anything, a soda, some coffee?

"No, sir. The officer gave me one already."

"We're here so you can tell us what happened at the Sandstone Apartments last night," Mike said. "You don't mind if I record our conversation do you?" He placed a small recorder on the table.

"Uh, yes, sir. I mean no, sir. I don't mind. I'm gonna tell you the truth." Troy Davis looked down at his folded arms.

"This is Detective Mike Neal, Detective Norm Wallace, and Mr. Troy Davis. It is April 14th.

"Telling us the truth is a very good idea, Troy," Norm said.

"Relax and tell us what you remember," Mike said.

"Have you talked to my brother yet?" Troy asked.

"Not yet," Mike said.

"Is he okay?" Troy asked. "I don't think he's handlin' this very well."

"I'm sure he's fine," Mike said. "He's in another room like this down the hall. The officers are keeping an eye on him like they did with you."

"Okay." Troy took in a large breath. "Me and my brother Robert—we live with our Mama, our Grandmama, and our Auntie. We got two sisters too. We're the only men in the house. Lately, I guess for the last few weeks, we been hangin' with some dudes on the street. Listenin' to music, smokin', drinkin', and all that. We kinda got wrapped up with 'em. You know, they was strong like real men. Like the men on TV, know what I'm sayin'?"

"How old are you, Troy?" Mike asked.

"Nineteen."

"How old is Robert?"

"Seventeen."

"Go ahead." Mike looked at Norm and then back at Davis.

"They asked us if we wanted to hook up with them. You know, join their gang. You ever heard of the Arm of Justice?"

"Yeah, we've heard of them," Norm said.

"Last night, D-man came to me. He's one of the AJs. He asked if we wanted to ride with him to scare a boy who X'd one of their tags. He said all he was gonna do was scare the shit out of him so he wouldn't even think about doin' it again. I thought sure, why not, we're three on one. We're gonna scare a dude. You know? It could be fun." Troy took his eyes from Mike, looked down and hesitated, appearing to realize how that sounded from this perspective.

"Go on," Mike said.

"D told me to drive. He said he was low on gas. So, we got in my car."

"What kind of car do you have?" Mike said.

"It's a blue 1977 Caprice Classic. It's really my Mama's car."

"Did she know you were in it last night?"

"Yes, sir. But, she thought we was surfin' the mall at Hickory Hollow."

"Okay, continue," Mike said.

"We got in my—my Mama's car and D told me to go to Pauletti's, over on Nolensville Road. When we got there, he told me to turn around and park on the side street and turn the engine off. He said the dude we was lookin' for delivered for Pauletti's Pizza. So, we waited. Pretty soon the dude drove into the back lot. He parked his car and went inside. D told me to start the car and be ready. He came back out in a few minutes with some pizzas. We followed him."

Reliving the night was making Davis even more nervous. He was sweating and his breathing rate had escalated.

"You okay?" Mike asked.

He nodded and kept looking down. "I screwed up, didn't I?"

"Well," Mike said, "you have an opportunity to try and at least repair it a little."

He looked at Mike. "I didn't shoot nobody, and my brother Robert didn't either. We went along for the ride. D lied to us. He said he was gonna scare the dude, but he robbed him and then he shot him—right there. He shot him three times." Davis shook his head. "It was bad."

"What kind of gun was it?" Norm asked.

Davis wiped his eyes with the back of his hand. "A nine millimeter.

That's what he said it was."

"Then what happened after Brown shot the boy?"

"We ran back to the car, and I drove outta there as fast as I could. I took D back to his car, and then me and Robert went home. I didn't sleep all night. I could hear Robert cryin'. He had his face in his pillow, but I didn't tell him I knew. He's so scared. I gotta get him outta this. He didn't do nothin'. This is my fault. He wouldn't been in it if it wasn't for me. I don't care about me, but I gotta get him outta this. Mama's gonna die when she hears, and she's gonna kill me first. What can I do?" He held his head in his hands.

"You're doing it, Troy," Norm said. "The one who did the shooting is the one who should go down for it. Your testimony will be necessary in order to put him away."

"No problem. I need you to promise me Robert goes free. He ain't done nothin'."

"We can't make a lot of promises," Mike said, "but the more you and Robert help the District Attorney, the better your chances."

"What else do I need to do?"

"Do you know a lawyer?" Mike asked.

"No, sir."

"Listen," Mike said, "we're going to have to place you under arrest—"

"What?"

"Hang on. Listen to me."

Troy's lips tightened along with his forehead, and he battled back his emotions as best he could.

"We don't have any choice, but to place you under arrest," Mike said. "We'll get a public defender down here for you and Robert before you leave this room."

"You gonna arrest Robert, too?

Mike nodded.

"Does my Mama have to know?"

"I'm afraid so," Mike said. "I think they may have already called her. Robert is still a minor, you know."

"Oh, shit," Troy said, dropping his arms and then his head onto the table.

"Troy, sit tight and we'll be back in a little while," Norm said. "If you need anything, just knock on the door."

Outside the door, Mike turned to Norm and said, "He's telling the truth."

"Yeah, I think so too."

"Marty, you got Demetrius Brown yet?" Norm asked.

"Yeah, he's in number three."

"Keep an eye on this kid for us?" Mike pointed toward room number two. "He's upset."

"Sure," Marty said.

Mike opened the door to room number three to find Demetrius Renaldo Brown in his best bad-ass gangster pose. He was slumped down in the straight-backed metal chair with his arms pulled back inside the arm holes of his dark green XXL hoody. He had a low-brow tight-lipped screw you gaze on his face, and he avoided acknowledging the detectives' arrival with as much as a glance.

Brown's file had cautioned Mike he was no virgin in the interview room. His gang attachment guaranteed he'd been coached on how to deal with the police. Rookies talk; veterans listen. Find out what the cops know and what they think they know. Gather information, then exercise your rights and tell it all to your lawyer.

Mike clicked on his recorder and laid it on the table. "Demetrius Brown? I'm Detective Neal. This is Detective Wallace. I see from your sheet you've been through this exercise quite a few times," Mike said flipping through Brown's file. "So, I'll assume you have no problem with us recording our discussion today?"

Brown offered no response. Mike took it as his approval.

Mike read the Miranda card. He was confident they had Brown with the Davis brothers' testimonies and those from the neighbors, but he was concerned that if he didn't read it, they could lose him.

"Do you understand your rights?"

There was no response.

"Mr. Brown?" Mike asked again.

Norm stepped forward from his position at the door. He jerked the hood off Brown's head and kicked the chair with his 15EE causing it and Brown to rotate facing him. Brown tried to stand as he extended his arms back through the sleeves, but Norm forced him back down into the chair. Norm leaned down, hovering over him. In his deepest voice, Norm said, "Answer the detective."

"Yeah," Brown said staring up at Norm with gritted teeth and clinched fists.

Norm gave Brown a self-confident smile and back-stepped to the door.

"Would you like to tell us your side of what happened last night at the Sandstone Apartments?" Mike asked.

Brown kept staring at the table. He said nothing.

"Would you like to tell us anything at all?" Mike waited.

There was no answer. Mike and Norm had seen this game played countless times before.

"You know, Brown?" Mike said. "You don't look stupid."

Brown lifted his eyes briefly.

"Anyone," Mike paused, "who would shoot another man in front of this many witnesses has got to be disturbed—or high. Wouldn't you think? Were you high?"

Brown appeared to be ignoring Mike.

"I mean—if I was going to cap some dude, I would plan it out so nobody saw it happening, but him. Right? He's not gonna tell anybody. So, what made you pop a kid three times with a nine millimeter in front of an apartment building full of people who were watching you do it through their living room windows like it was going down on HBO?"

Brown glanced up at Mike. The idea there could be so many witnesses seemed to arouse a modicum of concern.

"Yeah, at least a dozen witnesses," Mike said. "You gotta admit it,

Brown, this was not your best move."

"You know, Brown," Norm spoke up, "the funniest thing—well, you won't think so, but the funniest thing to me is we don't even need the testimony of those brave, observant South Nashville citizens."

Brown's eyes shot up at Norm without raising his head.

"No, we don't," Norm said. "You see, we have something even better." Norm smiled. "That's right. We have your young companions; your new *homeys*, both rolling over on your ass. Isn't that amazing? You not only whack a nineteen-year-old kid for some pizza pocket change, but you take along two impressionable teenage witnesses to watch you do it from ten feet away. What the hell were you thinking?

"Your young gangster wannabes have just arranged a nice deal with the Davidson County District Attorney," Norm lied, "that will allow them both no more than probation in exchange for their testimony as eye witnesses to the first degree murder of Anthony Sanchez. You are screwed, Brown. This is a classic dunker."

Brown's chin jutted forward and his breathing became exaggerated. He said nothing.

"So, Brown," Mike said, "as you can see, with this many witnesses we don't have to have a confession. But, if you were feeling remorseful, and would like to motivate the District Attorney to reduce your inevitable and lengthy sentence, we'd be glad to accept your confession. Besides, I believe like your young friends said, you may have gone to Sandstone to scare the Sanchez boy and then emotions caused things to get crazy. It happens. If you were to own up to what we already know took place, there is a good chance the D.A. would take that into consideration. What do you say, Brown? Just get it off your chest? Lessen your sentence?" Mike nodded, attempting to solicit a positive response.

Brown's mouth opened.

Mike felt optimistic.

"I want to see my lawyer," Brown said without looking up at either detective.

"What? Damn. Really? After all that, and you still aren't gonna confess? If this goes to trial, your ass will be parked in Old Sparky," Norm said, referring to Tennessee's electric chair.

"Okay," Mike said. "Your lawyer it is. But, he's not going to be very happy with the case you're handing him."

"I know the D.A., Brown. He's hungry on this one," Norm said. "If you don't own up, you're going to make some muscle-bound butt buddy at Riverbend a very happy man."

Mike stood. He looked briefly at Brown, hoping to add some pressure and elicit a change in his decision. He turned, opened the door and stepped into the hallway. Before following Mike through the door, Norm turned back and stared at Brown.

"Hey, Brown."

Brown cut his anger-filled eyes toward Norm.

Norm winked. "Thanks for the slam dunk."

# Chapter 8

*Mike Neal's Home*
*Nashville, Tennessee*
*Monday Evening*

Mike Neal's duplex was a two-story stone bungalow with a detached garage. He converted the half-basement of his Green Hills home into his personal gym where he spent at least one hour each evening toning his body, purging his stress, and for a brief time, escaping his death-filled world.

He'd been home just long enough to change into his workout clothes, and was in the process of hydrating for his treadmill run when there was a knock at the kitchen door; then another—and a third.

"What the hell?" As he got closer to the door, he heard the little voice and the scratching.

"Mike. Mike. Come quick. Hurry."

Mike increased his pace. He opened the door to see all thirty-four inches of Mason Holliman standing next to his perpetually excited stubby-tailed Jack Russell terrier, Tag.

"What's wrong, buddy?

"Mike, come quick," Mason begged. "Hurry. Hurry." The boy turned and ran toward the outdoor staircase to his second-story apartment.

Afraid there might be something wrong with Mason's mom, Mike pulled his door closed and jogged after the boy. On the sixth step of the metal staircase, he caught up with the five-year-old. Tag was already on the landing at the top of the stairs, barking. Mike snatched up Mason and held him close for the rest of the climb. On the upper landing, Mike jerked the storm door open and shouted. "Jennifer?" There was silence, during which Mike realized he wasn't armed. Then he heard her voice.

"Hi, Mike." Jennifer walked through the kitchen doorway into the living room with a dish towel in her hand and a big smile on her face.

Mike gave a relaxed sigh. Still holding the boy, he looked at her and said, "What's wrong?"

"Mike, let's go," Mason said as he wiggled, sending Mike the message he wanted to get down.

Mike lowered Mason to the floor, his eyes still on the boy's smiling mother. Mason took hold of Mike's fingers with both little hands and began to pull him.

"Hurry, Mike. Hurry." He yanked several times on Mike's hand then bolted toward the bathroom with Tag whose legs were moving much faster than his body on the slippery hardwood floor.

Mike looked back and shrugged at Jennifer who seemed to be enjoying the expressive display of her son's excitement.

Mike stepped into the small bathroom where he found Mason on one side of the toilet and Tag standing reared with his front paws on the opposite side of the wooden seat. Both were looking down into the bowl. Tag was barking and Mason was still shouting for Mike. His little voice rang as it bounced off the porcelain and echoed through the old tile bath.

Conditioned already by Jennifer's smile, Mike readied himself. "What is it, buddy? What's wrong?"

"Mike, it drowned-ed."

"It what?"

"It drowned-ed. My ship—it drowned-ed. It's down there." He pointed toward the water.

Tag barked twice in agreement.

"Mom said I can't get it. She said you would help."

"What happened?"

"I put my ship in the water. Then, it fell over and it drowned-ed. I tried to get to it, but I accidently pulled the handle and it flushed-ed." He paused and lowered his head. "I didn't mean to do it, Mike. I'm sorry."

Mike placed his hand over his mouth like he was contemplating how to help, but he was simply trying to hide his laughter.

"It's okay buddy, I think I can fix it."

"O-kay." Mason smiled nodding his head.

"Does Mom have any wire coat hangers?"

"Huh? I don't know. I think so. Mom. Hey, Mom." He ran to the kitchen, shadowed by the dog.

Mike lifted the seat. Leaning back, he looked down into the toilet as far as he could. He could see the gray stern of the shipwrecked plastic vessel. Mike sat on the edge of the tub smiling and waiting for Mason's return. He heard the little tennis shoes slapping the hardwood and Tag's claws clicking on the floor.

"Hey, Mike. I got it. I got it."

"Great. Thanks, Mason."

"You're welcome," Mason said with both hands on his hips. Then he and Tag assumed their spectator positions on either side of the toilet bowl.

Mike pulled the coat hanger with both hands until it stretched into a two foot long deep-sea crane ready for the recovery of the sunken battleship. Mike dramatically slipped the coat hanger into the water, hooked the plastic ship and gradually brought it to the surface, as water poured from the ship's bow.

"Yea. Mike, you got it." Mason clapped his hands and Tag barked his support.

Mike allowed the toy to drain and then tossed it into the sink. He washed it with hot water and hand soap before drying it and giving it back to the boy.

"Mason," Mike said calmly.

The boy looked up at Mike. "Huh?"

"Don't sail your ship in the toilet, okay? Do it in the sink or in the tub when you take a bath."

"Okay, Mike." Mason smiled up at him and then he grabbed Mike around both legs and squeezed him hard. "Thank you for saving my ship, Mike."

"You're welcome, buddy." Mike rubbed his hand through the boy's hair and considered what it might be like to have a son like Mason. He was such a great kid. Mike wondered if Mason's dad had any idea what he was missing, or if he cared. Mike looked up to see Jennifer standing in the doorway, staring at the two of them.

"Well men, mission accomplished?"

"Aye-aye captain," Mike snapped to attention and saluted. Then Mason mimicked him.

"Thanks, Mike."

"No problem. Glad I could help raise the ship."

Jennifer smiled. "Have you had dinner?"

Mike thought. "No, I guess I haven't."

"Would you like to join us?"

"We're having chili dogs," Mason added, "and Fritos."

Mike laughed then hesitated. "I can't stay long, but sure, I'll have a dog with my buddy."

"Yeah," Mason cheered.

Mike smiled at Mason and patted him on the back as they walked into the living room.

"Hey Mike, watch this." Mason bent forward, tucked his head and pushed himself into a forward roll across the rug, barely avoiding Tag.

Mike applauded. "Bravo, Bravo."

"What's that mean?" Mason said with wrinkled forehead.

Mike and Jennifer looked at each other and laughed.

"It means you did that very well," Mike said.

"Yes, I did," Mason said proudly.

"Okay, boys," Jennifer said, "let's eat."

After dinner Mike said, "I hate to eat and run, but I've got work waiting downstairs."

"Do you have to?" Mason whined.

"Yep, I sure do. Sorry, buddy. But I'll see you again later in the week." Mike stuck out his hand and Mason shook it.

"Ooo—kay, if you have to." Mason hung his head and marched into the living room with Tag trailing behind him.

"Thanks for helping Mason," Jennifer said as she took a stack of dirty dishes from Mike and placed them into the sink.

"It's my pleasure, I assure you." He stood staring through the doorway at Mason and Tag.

"What?" she asked with a smile.

"I was just thinking. I wonder if Carson has any idea what he's missing with his son? He's such a great kid, and you're doing a good job with him."

"Thanks, Mike. But, I don't think he knows or cares. Rick Carson is a very self-absorbed ..." she mouthed the word *prick*. "He didn't care much for anything during our short time together except himself and his drug money. I honestly believe he seduced me into thinking he was in love, when all along, I was only a pawn in his plan."

"Did he think having a Texas State Police investigator as his wife would somehow protect him from the cartel?"

"I don't know what he thought, but I wish I'd met the real Rick Carson before I married him. The whole episode was so embarrassing for me and the department. I can't believe how he played me."

"Luckily," Mike said, "his plan and his guilt became clear during the trial."

"If he had not been afraid of the repercussions from his drug connections," Jennifer said, "the DA may have been able to plead him down and secure indictments on some of the cartel leaders as well."

"Rick was smart to keep his mouth shut and spend a few years locked up rather than assure his prompt demise at the hands of the Mexican cartel."

"Yes, thank God," Jennifer said. "The jury saw him for what he was and not what he advertised himself to be."

"He got what he deserved. I'm thankful you and Mason are safe here and a long way from his clutches and those of his ugly friends."

"Me too. By the way, any changes in your sister's case?"

"No, nothing new."

"Mike, I meant it when I told you I would be glad to help you if there is research you want me to do. Murph wouldn't mind. Why don't you send me the names of the suspects you told me about and I'll run some fresh traces? We recently installed new software, and now no one can hide from The Daniel Murphy Agency."

Mike smiled. "I don't want to impose. You haven't been with him long enough to take advantage. Murph was kind enough to give you a job. I'm sure you've got other investigations he needs you working on."

"Well, I'm going to ask him about it, whether you like it or not. He's your friend. If there is something I can do to repay your kindness to me and Mason, I'm going to make it happen," Jennifer insisted.

Mike nodded. "Thanks. You get Murph's blessing, and I'll email you the data."

"Good."

"Have the Marshals checked on you lately?" Mike asked.

"Yes, Amanda Dodd called the day before yesterday. You two have made our transition into this new life much smoother than it could have been. You're a great friend, Mike, not to mention landlord."

"Well, let's hope the witness protection folks continue to fulfill their side of the deal. Be very careful and call me anytime. Okay? I mean it."

"I will; especially when we have more sunken ships," Jennifer said.

"No," Mike corrected her, "Drowned-ed." They both laughed as they walked to the front door.

Jennifer took his hand and kissed him on the cheek. "Take care, Mike."

"You, too." Mike looked over Jennifer's shoulder and shouted, "See ya, buddy."

"Bye." Mason waved.

# Chapter 9

*Mike Neal's Home*
*Nashville, Tennessee*
*Monday Evening*

Mike regretted missing his cardio workout, but the chance to spend time with Mason was a treat, and his schedule seldom allowed for it.

He turned on his desktop computer, and then retrieved the battered vinyl binder from the shelf above his PC's monitor. He leaned back in his chair and opened it across his lap. Mike had most of the data from *this* murder book memorized, but he continued to review it frequently. He searched for that one unforeseen something that would click and cause almost nine years of concentrated effort to produce anything that would make it all fall into place. So far, the years had netted little in the way of solid suspects or solutions.

The label holder on the spine of the binder was empty, but the original, still in the possession of the Clarksville, Tennessee Homicide Squad, read: Case #94-078, Wilson - Coleman - Lawson - Neal. It was his sister's murder book.

The cracked corners of the blue binder reflected the years since he met with Clarksville Detective Alfred Ellis. Almost a month into the case, and with it still unsolved, Mike convinced the seasoned detective to put his job on the line and loan him the murder book so he could review the facts of the case for himself.

Ellis was adamant at first, stating he could not even consider such an idea. A former 1st Lieutenant with the 101st Airborne, he felt a sensitivity for his fellow soldier's situation that otherwise would not have existed. He told Mike he could imagine how *he* would feel if it was *his* sister, and their positions were reversed.

Mike finally talked the detective into taking a controlled risk. Ellis side-stepped departmental policy by loaning the book to Mike for "One hour—no more," he said.

Mike's six years as a criminal investigator with CID convinced Ellis to trust him. Grateful for that trust, Mike agreed to honor Ellis's conditions which included keeping this breach of policy from the detective's partner, Felton Sinclair.

The first time he opened the binder, Mike prayed he could handle what he knew would be shocking photos of his little sister's murder. All photos taken at the quarry and during the autopsy were included for Connie's three young friends, but Ellis had thoughtfully pulled all the photos of Connie from the murder book. He also placed a note on the front cover with the address of the closest copy shop. At the bottom of the note, it read: "Ask for Billy Joe and remember; this did *not* happen. Hurry."

Over the years, Mike frequently reviewed the detectives' interview notes from discussions with Stampede Saloon employees, managers and customers, as well as friends of the four young victims. These notes were added to the detective's conclusions based upon the accrual of all their investigations.

Often, as Mike examined the murder book, he thought of how limited it was to represent four such horrific homicides. He knew, had this carnage taken place in Nashville, each of the four murders would have a book at least this thick and there would have been two homicide teams assigned to the aggregate investigation. Mike prayed that the limited scope of the murder book did not represent a tenuous investigation.

The night Mike returned with the copied pages, Detective Ellis shared information Mike recalled each time he opened the book.

"You have to wonder," Ellis told him, "if that old man hadn't decided to go fishing early the next morning, how long would it have been before somebody came across the crime scene? The first officer said the old guy told him he was standing in the middle of it all before he even realized it was blood.

"When Sinclair and I first arrived at the scene, it was—disturbing," Ellis said. "Fortunately, we don't experience crimes of this magnitude here very often. The scene and the mode of the murders told us the killer was enraged. We could never figure what this group of kids could have done to cause this much anger in someone. We still can't."

Mike's experience told him there was something here, within these few pages, to help him find Connie's killer. Since he was not involved in the investigation, Mike had not been able to decode it all. He tried to remain confident, reminding himself, some cases take more time. He knew the odds. Few cold cases which remained unsolved after nine years were ever cleared. But, that was true of other cases. Those cases were filed away—in a box.

The first page protector in the binder contained Mike's own notes from his discussions with Ellis. As he reviewed his remarks, he recalled more of the Clarksville detective's words.

"Entirely too many people were at the scene when we arrived." Ellis paused. "You've got to remember this was our biggest murder scene of the last decade. All the forensic folks were there. We don't have that many. We get help from the TBI when we need them. We needed them.

"The criminalists were waiting for us to arrive and do our thing, so they could do theirs. Much of the scene was already contaminated by the Rescue Squad whose divers were already in the water. The dirt and rock around the site were splattered with considerable amounts of blood dried in place. Some was contaminated and some was washed away by the actions of the divers, the EMTs, and the Rescue Squad as they removed the bodies from the water." Ellis shook his head. "Most of these folks didn't have a clue how to handle a crime scene of this magnitude."

"The precise location of each of the four murders was fairly obvious from the concentration of blood on the rocks and the ground. Based upon the footprints, drag marks, and other evidence at the scene, we determined the killer attempted to re-dress the bodies. One of the girls was wearing what had to be one of the boy's shirts.

"It appeared the killer dragged them to the water's edge where he collected flat limestone rocks. We found the rocks crammed inside their clothing, and after securing the rocks in place by tying their shirttails and tightening their belts around them, he rolled each body into the water and dragged them out to the lake."

Ellis continued. "One of the too few pieces of meaningful evidence collected at the scene was multiple common shoe casts and photos of shoe impressions taken from near the murder sites. Some of the victim's shoes were on their feet and others were found in the lake. Impressions made from the victims' shoes were later used to eliminate many of these prints. There remained several common impressions of a man's size ten boot with a deep hiking tread. This same boot impression was found numerous times around the lake's edge and also tracked back toward the access road away from the quarry. None of the victims, or the old man, wore boots that matched these prints.

"The location, freshness and number of these common shoe prints was significant. The fact they appeared to move repeatedly between the concentrations of blood increased their importance and likelihood they belonged to the killer. Alone, these prints are of limited value, but they could be used to confirm a suspect, assuming we secure one and assuming he's dumb enough to still have the boots in his possession."

Mike's computer desktop came to life and grabbed his attention. He clicked the Internet access icon and the modem responded with the expected series of tones. Once online, Mike opened his email. He was hoping for another Iraq status report from his mentor, Colonel Wm. T. Lee. It had been almost a week since his last. Mike scanned through a list of over two dozen emails. There it was.

*Hey, soldier. What's shakin' in the Music City? Sorry I haven't been able to write in a few days. We've still got our hands full here in beautiful downtown Mosul—the jewel of Mesopotamia. Wish you were here to share the load.*

*We're starting to receive quite a number of requests for investigations into assaults on, and mistreatment of, detainees, even in the prisons. We're getting similar complaints of abuse from some Iraqi citizens while their homes are being searched, as well as grievances claiming property theft by our soldiers.*

*Last week we had a Corporal who fired his weapon into the floor of an Iraqi family's home because they weren't being as cooperative as he thought they should be. He said he was trying to get their attention. Can you believe this shit?"*

"Yes, unfortunately," Mike said out load.

*Some of these young men have so much repressed anger and so few options on how to release it—they're looking for payback. They've witnessed their best friends get shot or blown apart by IEDs and RPGs. Then, they watch as the boys that survive the attacks are sent home to face their future with broken bodies: missing arms or legs or eyes. It's troubling.*

Mike knew too well what the Colonel was talking about. His

thoughts momentarily turned to his friend and fellow CID investigator Ron Kremer.

*Over here, the ones that aren't scared shitless should be. They don't have a clue where the next attack is coming from. They know it's coming. The knowing serves to strain every nerve and prime them for their out-of-control anti-social behavior.*

*Enough with the bad news. How's the world of the homicide detective? Hopefully, it's at least more colorful than this place. As you well know, the only colors we get to see over here are sand beige and blood red.*

*Let me get out of here and get some sleep. Maybe I'll be back in my old skin tomorrow.*

*Oh, before I forget. There's a group that's been formed to replace the United Nations inspections teams. It's being called The Iraq Survey Group and they've been mandated to search for weapons of mass destruction. I told my buddy Lieutenant Colonel Rob Vaughn, who's assigned to the group's North Sector, about your theory on Sinjar Mountain being Saddam's storage closet. He laughed, but I told him you spent considerable time in that area in '91 and may have a unique perspective. I asked him to give it some consideration as a favor to me. He said they'd already done that dance.*

*Don't worry. I'm not gonna give up. He'll listen.*

*We miss you, buddy. Take care. - Tim*

Mike responded to the Colonel's email with some current information about his life and his job which, after writing the email, seemed more like one and the same than he realized. He also offered Lee some additional data on Sinjar Mountain and his suspicions on the significance of its proximity to the Syrian border.

Before shutting down his computer, Mike finished his PC session the same way he had every one since his sister Connie's death, nine years ago. Over the years that he spent away from home, he saved all of Connie's email to a file that he had intended to give her when he returned. He created a diary of sorts for that purpose.

Since her passing, his ritual included bringing up her last email, dated 6/3/1994 and reading it—again.

*Hey, Big Brother. How's Sand Land?*

Mike could hear Connie's voice saying the words.

*Caught any camel killers today? I wish that was all you had to do. I hope your corner of the world is getting safer. I watch the news every day to see the endless footage of that sand colored hell you guys are living in—if you call that living. I sure hope this doesn't turn out to be Vietnam Vol. II.*

*Michael, I miss you so much. Please come home soon. Mom's death is draining the both of us. Dad might as well be gone too. He's no help to me, or even himself. He's a vegetable. I can't talk to him like I can with you. We share no interests, nothing. He sits in front of the damn TV trying to stay distracted from thoughts of Mom. I guess I can understand that, but he's like a zombie.*

*You are the only family I have left. I felt so safe when you were here. I'm proud of your work to try and make the world safe for all of us, but I'd rather have you home. I need you here. Why don't you see if you can get one of those special discharges? You know, a hardship discharge to care for Dad and me. God knows I'm a hardship case, having to tolerate Dad.*

*Hey, do you remember when we were kids? Well, at least I was a kid. We used to sit in the porch swing and talk? I crawled up in the swing, hugged your arm and leaned on your shoulder as you kicked the floor and kept the swing moving. You told me stories about all the people and places you'd read about in school. I remember closing my eyes and telling you that your words were like music that took me away to those places. Remember that? I was just thinking about that today and wishing we could relive those days. I was wishing your words could take me away from all this and deliver me to where you are, so we could swing on the porch again.*

*Mike, your email is therapy for me. Your words are still music to my ears. Every day, I rush to get home, praying you've written. I read your email over and over again. I really do. I guess I sound silly, but I can't wait until you are home, even if it's just for a visit. Michael, please come home, as soon as they'll let you. And write as often as you can. I'm serious. I need to hear from you as often as possible. It really sucks here!*

*I miss you so much, and I love you. Please come home.*

*Your Sis, Connie*

"I love you too Sis," Mike whispered, "and I miss *your* music."

Mike leaned back in his chair and called up memories of the hundreds of conversations he'd shared with his little sister. Always the manipulator, she had a way of getting him to do almost anything for her. Mike smiled.

The metallic click of Carol unlocking the deadbolt on the kitchen door brought him back to the present.

# Chapter 10

*Mike Neal's Home*
*Nashville, Tennessee*
*Monday Late Night*

"No—No!" Mike's screams jolted Carol from her sleep. She sat up in bed.

Mike was tossing his head side to side, groaning, sometimes talking, but his words were unintelligible. His brow and jutted jaw told her he was mad at something or someone. The violent shifting of his body had pushed the blanket to the foot of the bed. His hair and pillow were soaked with sweat. Carol placed her hand on his chest; his body was clammy.

"Mike. Wake up. Mike. You're having a nightmare. Carol patted his cheek. Wake up. Mike?"

Mike's eyes opened abruptly and he sat up. In the same motion, he grabbed Carol's wrist jerking her arm away from his face. He pulled her to him and wrapped his arm around her neck. Carol screamed and after a brief moment Mike, realized where he was, and released her. He fell away from Carol and sat leaning back with his hands behind him, propping him up. His chest still heaving; he continued to exhale forcefully. Carol sat staring at him, petrified. His rapid blinking verified the nightmare was over, for now.

"Mike, are you okay?"

He turned toward her, wide-eyed and still not breathing normally. He stared at her face.

"Mike?"

He took in another large volume of air and blew it out. "I think so."

"What was that all about?"

"What?"

"You know what. The nightmare."

He shook his head. "I don't know."

"Don't give me that."

He closed his eyes and prayed something intelligent would come to him which would appease Carol without his having to tell her the truth. Nothing came. He had awakened from the same distressing nightmare for the sixth, maybe the seventh, time. But, this was the first time for Carol, or anyone else, to witness it.

"Mike, talk to me. I want to help you."

He sat unresponsive for a moment, looking down and away from Carol. "I can't."

"What do you mean, you can't?"

"I can't talk about it."

"About what?"

He turned to her. "About the nightmare."

"This isn't the first time is it?"

Mike looked into her eyes knowing they would force him to be honest. "No," he said at the end of another deep exhale.

"What is it, Mike? What's haunting you?"

Mike had never told anyone. Only *he* knew the facts. It seemed like a mistake to even consider sharing it now. He trusted Carol, but sometimes people knowing things—changed things; sometimes knowing things changed people. Maybe things were best kept as they are.

"I need something to drink," Mike swallowed.

"At this time of the morning?"

"I mean, like hot cocoa."

"Oh, sure. I'll fix you some." Carol laid her hand on Mike's cheek.

Carol took Mike's t-shirt from the chair where she'd tossed it last night after she yanked it over his head. She pulled it on over her naked body as she walked to the kitchen. Mike followed her and sat at one of the bar stools.

He pointed to the cabinet with the cocoa and watched as she nuked the water and mixed two large mugs. She came around the bar, delivered the steaming chocolate and sat on the stool next to him. He hoped she knew enough to practice patience. She had worked around Mike long enough to know he didn't like being pushed.

After a few minutes, Mike began to open up.

"Did I ever tell you about Ron Kremer?"

"Hmm, I don't think so. Who is he?"

"He was my best friend at CID when we were in Iraq."

"Really? I guess you've never told me much about Iraq."

Mike nodded. "He was great. He saved my life once after a fire fight near the Turkish border. He kept me from bleeding to death the day I got all these." Mike pointed to his scars. "He was so worried about me." Mike smiled. "I could tell how much he cared. It was all over his face while he was patching me up. I knew then—I had a real friend."

"Sounds like it," Carol said.

Mike sipped his chocolate and took his time before speaking again.

"We were a good team and Captain Lee, who's a Colonel now, knew it. So, he kept us working together on a lot of investigations."

"Ron was from Chattanooga, East Ridge actually." Mike chuckled. "I remember the day when I first saw him. We were gathered outside the mess tent and I heard him answer when the Captain was questioning some of the transfers. I remember telling one of the other investigators, "Man, with an accent like that, he's gotta be from Tennessee."

Mike stared at his hot chocolate as he swirled it around the mug, smiling.

"He was so funny. He was always up; always in a good mood, a real joy to be around." Mike nodded again. "I remember once when we were in Mosul on leave. We walked up to these two beautiful American nurses.

Ron said, 'Wow. This is amazing. You look just like my third wife.' The girls smiled at each other and the one he was targeting said, 'How many times have you been married, soldier?' Ron leaned close to her with his sexiest look, winked and said in a soft voice, 'twice.' I about lost it. The girls did too."

Carol laughed out loud. "Did he go back to East Ridge after Iraq?"

Mike's joyful expression fell from his face, and he was quiet. He looked up at Carol, took a long breath and said, "Yeah—but he had to go home in a box."

Carol gasped. She saw tears collecting in his eyes as he swallowed hard.

"I'm sorry, Mike."

Mike's lips tightened and he closed his eyes, forcing the tears down his cheeks.

"He was such a great guy." Mike turned to Carol. "Why? Why?" He asked Carol the question he'd been asking himself for ten years.

Carol leaned closer and wrapped her arms around his neck. She kissed him on his cheek and held her face hard against his. "We don't know, Mike. We never know why."

After a few minutes, Mike gathered his thoughts and began again.

"We talked about getting together; going fishing and hunting. He was gonna teach me to fly fish in the Hiwassee River. Living so close, it would have been easy to stay in touch after the Army. We even discussed moving him to Nashville. We were looking forward to life after CID." Mike shook his head. "It's been ten years ago this month. When I recall it, the pain still feels the same."

"What happened?"

Mike knew it was time. It was time to get it out. He stared into his mug.

"Ron and I took two of our team and left for Tal 'Afar. We were going there to investigate the alleged molesting of an Iraqi girl by an American soldier. We arrived at the location and split into two teams in order to canvas the area. We spoke with some of the neighbors and confirmed the location of the family's home.

"Ron and I entered the building and as Ron turned the corner to our left, he walked into it. It was a single shooter with an AK47. Ron was hit three times in his vest and once in his neck. The bullet struck his carotid and blood exploded out of the right side of his neck."

"I dropped back behind the corner and radioed the other two investigators with our location. I guess when the man realized he'd shot Ron, he threw his rifle down and began to shout. When I heard the weapon hit the floor, I came around the corner with him in my sights. I told him in Arabic to shut up, but he kept shouting. I kicked the rifle out of his reach and went back to Ron. He looked bad. His blood was spreading across the floor. I tried to put pressure on the wound and stop the flow, but it was no use. The whole side of his neck was torn open.

"I turned back to the man and shouted over his ranting again for him to shut up. I wanted him quiet and honestly—I wanted him to die for what he had taken from me.

"I guess adrenaline was flooding my body. I was overwhelmed with anger. I couldn't help myself." Mike stopped talking and looked at Carol.

"I saw him make a move in my peripheral vision. He was already on his knees. He leaned out in the direction of the rifle. I think now he may have been begging for his life or praying, but at the time I was looking for an excuse. I was looking for a reason to kill him. That was it."

"I shot him four times, center mass. I went back to Ron. It was too late. He was gone."

Carol pulled him close and held him.

"I devote my life to try and find people who commit the ultimate human crime and bring them to justice. I myself have killed, and not met justice."

"Mike, it was war. It's not the same."

"He was unarmed."

"Yeah, he'd been unarmed for what, maybe five or ten seconds? You thought he was going for the rifle again. It's not the same. It's war. It changes everything."

"But, I lied about it."

"What do you mean?"

"I didn't say anything about him dropping the weapon."

"Mike, you didn't lie about it. You knew no one else was there to corroborate and they wouldn't understand."

"I don't expect anyone to understand, who hasn't been there."

"Absolutely," Carol said. "How *could* anyone understand who hasn't fought in a war dodging bullets at every turn, or had to watch his best friend bleed to death in front of him."

Mike looked into her eyes.

"No one else alive knows about this—no one." Mike paused. "Now, *you* know."

"It's safe with me, Mike. You know this. But, you can't look at it like it was a homicide."

"When I came back in '94," Mike hesitated, "my mind was still on Connie and the trauma caused by my father's failures. Then I tried to start a normal life, whatever the hell that is. I guess I was able to force this into my subconscious.

"The nightmares started almost a year ago; right after Norm and I took a domestic call and found a Middle Eastern man on his front porch over in South Nashville. He'd been shot in the chest with a large caliber weapon. He looked a lot like the Iraqi who killed Ron and I guess the resemblance must have triggered it."

"Mike, you're not at fault with this. You thought he was going for his weapon. You had to stop him. It was you or him. You've got to let this go. You have nothing to feel guilty about."

"Then why after ten years is it still haunting me?"

"After what you've told me tonight, I'm not sure it's the killing of the Iraqi man haunting you as much as your difficulties letting your friend Ron go. Are you feeling responsible in some way for Ron's death?"

Mike was quiet. His face began to tighten. "He saved my life." Mike hung his head in his hands.

Carol gave Mike some time before she spoke. "Mike, you can't blame yourself for Ron's death."

Mike sat mute for a while.

"Through my entire life, I've had a difficult time trying to love." He paused. "And for some reason—I cannot understand whether it's destiny or The Wizard behind the curtain, but somebody's got a grudge. All I've got to show for my efforts is a long line of deaths and relationship failures."

"What do you mean?" Carol asked. She knew some of Mike's past from their discussions, but she also knew, right now, he needed to talk.

"First, it was my Dad. I could never satisfy him. He could never bring himself to be pleased with me or anything I did. Then Mom, always the great mediator, passed away so early. This caused my father and me to grow even further apart.

"Then, Ron. Ron was my brother—truly my brother. I owed him my life and I lost him. I was supposed to repay the debt. I was there, but I failed.

"Connie. God, help me. I lost my baby sister; my friend. I swore to her when she was twelve years old and scared, I would always be there to protect her. I let her down and my father, once again, let me down." Mike wiped his eyes with his napkin.

Carol listened patiently, wanting to console him and tell him he was wrong. She wrapped her arm under his, and laid her head on his shoulder.

"I've always heard 'time changes things'," Mike paused, "but so far, if anything gets changed, I have to do it myself."

Mike drained his mug.

"For me, time hasn't been a lot of help." Mike locked on Carol's eyes as he brushed a lock of brunette behind her ear. "Are you sure you want in on this dysfunctional mess?"

"I'm sure," Carol said without hesitation. She kissed him.

# Chapter 11

*I-65*
*South Nashville*
*Tuesday Midnight*

He pressed the cruise control as the speedometer of his pickup reached seventy, then shifted his body into a more comfortable position for the long drive home.

Brad Evans chuckled as he thought of the cash he'd pocketed during this week's poker marathon. The beer-buzz from the six-pack he'd disposed of during the games was gone. He was feeling quite pleased with the evening and his display of Texas Hold 'Em skills.

The long drive up to Nashville from his farm in the southern part of the state was worth it to spend a little downtime with old friends. These get-togethers were even more important to him since Julie's death.

Brad enjoyed recalling the memories of their happy years, but he tried not to think of Julie's death. Thoughts of her passing fed feelings of hatred for the gangster that ran the stop sign and slammed into her car, ending her life and ruining his forever.

"If the son of a bitch gets his due, I could at least have a chance to find some peace," Brad professed to the Assistant District Attorney. "But, no. The liberal laws of our democracy will allow some simple procedural mistake to wash away the sins of the guilty bastard, and he'll get off with a hand slap. The court knows he killed her. What's the problem? Hang his ass, now."

In the weeks following the wreck, Brad came close to a nervous breakdown. Had it not been for the support from his friends, he was sure he would have lost all control. For a while, he was obsessed with thoughts of killing the man who destroyed his life. It seemed fair at the time. Brad's friends convinced him to drop the idea and focus on what Julie would have wanted for him and his future.

That perspective and the generous support from his friends served him well for a time, but recently, he'd started missing Julie more. Maybe it was the lonely nights at home without the warmth of her touch, or the sound of her soft and comforting voice as she sang and played the upright piano he'd bought her for their fourteenth, their ivory anniversary. And maybe it was the fact he felt robbed and thought that he deserved compensation for his enormous loss.

Traveling Interstate 65 at this hour, Brad focused on driving safely and within the speed limit knowing most people out at this time of night are under the influence of something, or they're up to no good, or they're cops. He wasn't in the mood to encounter anyone on this list.

He was still inside Davidson County when the light from his truck's bright beams illuminated a blurred movement at his two o'clock. He glanced in time to see a figure in dark clothes wearing a black & gold cap climbing the embankment with a bag in his hand. Looking back to the road ahead to check his path, he again jerked his head to his right and rear to verify his suspicions.

*That black and gold head gear; those were the colors of the gang banger that killed Julie. These thoughtless asocial punks are painting up the highways and defacing buildings with their damn gang symbols.*

Brad's moonlighting job involved removal of destructive nocturnal animals. He knew his rifle was there, but he reached behind the seat with his left hand to confirm it. His adrenaline pumped his heart rate up with the acceleration of the truck and the anticipation of some justice. The next exit was less than a half-mile away and fortunately the banger had not yet begun his vandal's craft. There was time.

Brad scanned from left to right for signs of potential witnesses or law enforcement as he coasted to the top of the exit ramp. He pushed down the left-turn signal and came to a complete stop at the top of the ramp. He accelerated across the overpass, continuing to scan the roadways.

Driving past the northbound entrance ramp, he took the industrial road that paralleled the Interstate highway. He chose to risk a bit more than the speed limit in order to arrive before the gang banger was finished. With no other vehicles in sight, he turned off his lights before cresting the hill and then slowed to a stop across the freeway from the retaining wall. He was right. The little shit was already at work spraying the wall with his gang symbols.

Brad pushed himself across the truck cab to the passenger side as he looked back at the freeway and the dark figure who was now busy with his work. He'd chosen his concrete canvas thoughtfully. He was painting in an area between the highway lights and one which was shadowed by the overpass of a perpendicular bridge.

Brad calculated the distance at just over one hundred yards. Shifting forward to the edge of the seat, he pulled the seat back forward and reached behind it to grasp the handle on the polymer gun case. Lifting the case and easing it onto the seat next to him, he popped the four latches and raised the lid. The rifle with its ultra-light stock and mounted optics was suspended securely between two thick layers of foam cushioning. The foam protected the match grade marksman's instrument from shock.

Brad removed the rifle, its sound suppressor, and one round of .223 caliber Remington Soft Point ammo. He closed one latch and placed the case on the floor in front of the seat. He carefully rotated the suppressor until it grabbed the matching threads at the business end of the rifle's barrel. Brad opened the chamber and inserted the cartridge. He shoved home the bolt.

A distant flash of lightning caught Brad's eye as it crawled the horizon breaking itself into a dozen electric cracks across the sky. The prolonged rumble of the trailing thunder, his adrenaline, and the rifle in his hands called up Brad's memories of Vietnam. Earlier in the evening Brad watched the weather girl on Channel Four as she predicted that the approaching cold front's progress would slow, and its arrival would be delayed until the hours near dawn.

Brad's training told him that the current weather conditions and the distance to target were acceptable and there should be no concern, other than discovery.

He lowered the power window on the driver's side. He repositioned the truck's rear view and driver's side mirrors so they could alert him to the lights of approaching traffic. The roadway was clear.

From the passenger position, Brad stretched out across the seat, allowing his left elbow to rest on the cushion of the center armrest and the rifle barrel to gently meet the window frame of the driver-side door. Only the suppressor was exposed outside the window.

Brad rotated the MOA (minute of angle) turret four clicks on the Leupold VX-3 scope in order to achieve the elevation correction needed for the distance to target. The surface target area was the black and gold pattern on the rear of the gangster's cap. The true target, the medulla oblongata, was now centered on the scope's reticle. Brad controlled his breathing.

The gangster appeared unconcerned about detection. Focusing on his work, he stepped back from the wall.

Brad hugged the trigger with his index finger. He deepened his breath for a count of three, and then held it as he gradually brought the trigger toward him. *Pfft.* The rifle spat out the traveling end of the cartridge with almost no sound.

The gangster was shaking the stirring ball in his aerosol can when the 3.6 grams of lead entered the rear of his head at three thousand feet per second. On impact with the base of his skull, the lead began its tumble. Fragmenting as it raced through the man's brain, pieces of jagged lead burst from his face. His head fell forward as he collapsed to the ground.

Brad checked his mirrors for headlights, and then sat up in the seat. He pulled the gun case from the floor and onto his lap. Removing the suppressor from the barrel, he placed it and the rifle back into their protective foam recesses.

As he lowered the gun case behind the seat, Brad glanced across the highway for a last look at his target. He cranked the engine, repositioned his mirrors and drove away.

Somewhat content, he knew he could never feel any satisfaction until the body belonged to Julie's killer.

# Chapter 12

*MNPD Gym*
*Nashville, Tennessee*
*Tuesday Morning*

Mike was invigorated by his workout with free weights and the heavy bag. He was not a pretentious man, but he paid attention to his health. He maintained his conditioning with twice-weekly visits to the MNPD gym and nightly cardio sessions at home. The workouts were a priority, begun during his years in the military, and now they were even more crucial to ward off the life-eating stress monsters that came with his job. Near the end of each cardio session, while assaulting the suspended leather bag, Mike visualized the image of the monster that killed his sister. This always prolonged his workouts.

As he walked from the steamy showers back into the locker room he spotted Tom Sanders and a man he didn't know. They were pulling on their gym clothes. Tom was one of the Narcotics Section's senior detectives.

"Hello, Mike."

"Tom," Mike said, towel drying his hair. "How's the drug biz?"

"We're snowed," Tom replied, laughing at his own pun. "Mike, have you met Chuck Kelsey?"

"I don't think so." Mike turned toward the stranger and offered his hand.

"Chuck—Mike Neal," Tom said. "Mike's with Homicide. Chuck just recently joined us."

Mike dropped his towels on the bench and reached for his boxers.

Chuck winced as he spotted Mike's assortment of scars up and down the right side of his body. He gave Tom a questioning look.

"Those are his souvenirs from Iraq," Tom said. "Mike was with Army CID."

"I didn't mean to stare," Chuck apologized, embarrassed by Tom's statement.

"I'm used to it." Mike half-smiled.

"CID, huh?" Chuck asked.

"Yeah, '89 to '94."

"So, how did you get the scars?" Chuck asked.

"From a rocket-propelled grenade in April '91. The Iraqis fired into a group of Kurdish Peshmergas while they were talking with us near Zakhu in the northern part of Duhok province."

"Peshmergas?"

"Yeah, Kurdish fighters. We hooked up with them early that morning. We were investigating information we'd received about Iraqis who were slipping onto the base at night and planting explosives in an attempt to destroy our logistic supply facilities."

"Sounds like the Iraqi army liked the Kurds about as much as they liked us," Chuck said.

"That's for sure. Most of the Kurds in northern Iraq have been pro-American for a number of years. They helped us out on several of our missions."

"I didn't realize CID got involved in that kind of assignment," Chuck said.

"Well, the overall mission of CID is to investigate serious crime wherever the United States Army has an interest."

“That’s a broad mission statement,” Tom said.

“I guess it is, but this particular task definitely fit. Based on the damage and the satellite images we reviewed in preparation for the mission, this one had to be done.”

“How bad were you hurt?” Chuck asked.

“I caught seven pieces of shrapnel that somehow found their way around twenty-five pounds of body armor. They burned like hell, and I lost a lot of blood, but fortunately they hit fleshy areas, and most importantly, missed my femoral artery.”

“Sorry to be so nosey, but this stuff is interesting. I was never in the military.”

“It’s okay,” Mike said. “It *was* exciting at the time.”

“How did you get away?” Chuck asked.

“With the four of us and the six Kurds, there was enough firepower to repel the assault and take out the attackers.”

“Were these Kurds seasoned military?” Chuck asked.

“Yes. They were all skilled and well-armed. They insisted on traveling back to our base with us after the attack, in case we were hit again. During the return trip, our guys were able to stabilize the two of us who were wounded.”

“That sounds pretty scary,” Chuck said.

“I assure you, it’s as close to death as I want to come,” Mike said as he continued to dress.

“Were the Kurds always so supportive?” Tom asked.

“I think so, and they still are. I’ve done considerable reading about the Kurdish people since that incident, and gained even more respect for them. They went through a helluva lot even before they suffered under Saddam Hussein.”

“Interesting,” Tom said. “We have a sizeable population of Kurds here in Nashville.”

“Yes, that’s true. Our patrol officers have told me that based upon their experiences with the Kurds here, most of them—at least the adults anyway—seem to appreciate being in America and they can’t wait to get their citizenship."

"We know a few who are having some violence and drug issues with their teenagers," Chuck said.

"None of the ethnic groups, or for that matter white kids," Tom added, "are exempt from the influence of the gangs."

"At least the adults can relate to their past and know they have it a lot better here than in Iraq," Mike said, grabbing his bag. "Tom, I gotta run. It's good to see you again." Mike offered his hand. "Chuck, good luck cleaning up our streets."

"We'll need it, Mike."

"Tell Norm hello for me?" Tom said.

"Will do." Mike started toward the exit. His cell phone rang.

"Mike Neal."

"Mike, it's Cheryl."

"Hey, good looking." Mike glanced at his watch. "Are you up early or just now coming in to work?"

"I had to work a double last night. The ER was chaos."

Norm and his wife Cheryl, a seasoned cardiac nurse, became Nashvillians when, in 1998, a cardiologist who had relocated to Nashville, came through on a promise. He offered to double Cheryl's salary if she would leave Milwaukee and follow him to the premier cardiac facility in the South, Nashville's Saint Thomas Hospital. Norm and Cheryl agreed on the lucrative change while gazing out their kitchen window at more than three feet of white winter.

"I'm heading home," Cheryl said. "I figured you would be at the gym about now."

"Good guess. I'm just leaving."

"So, to what do I owe the pleasure of this call, Mrs. Wallace?"

"I called to invite you to dinner tonight."

"Really?"

"I'm preparing your favorite: my three-meat, three-cheese lasagna."

"Wow, that's good stuff, but isn't that fattening?"

"Not so much the way I make it; whole wheat pasta, low fat cheeses and extra-lean meat."

"Is the big guy so socially unskilled he couldn't manage his own partner's dinner invitation?"

"No. I told him I wanted to invite you myself."

"Why?"

"Why what?"

"Why did *you* need to invite me?"

"Michael, why do you have to make this so difficult?"

"I'm not making it difficult. It's my job to ask questions and gather information. It's what I do. I just don't understand why Norm didn't say anything about it."

"I asked him not to say anything. Like I said, I wanted to invite you myself."

"Okay, so who's going to be there?"

"What makes you think someone's going to be there?"

"Cheryl—I know you. You've been trying to set me up for the last two years."

"I have not. Besides, what's wrong with me being concerned about you? You're my friend and I love you. I want you to be happy."

"Thank you, but you don't have to take it upon yourself to try and make me happy. I am happy enough."

"Mike, you know what I mean."

"Yes. I'm afraid I do."

"Thank you."

"Okay, I may accept your invitation, but under one condition."

"What?"

"You tell me who is going to be there in addition to me, you and the big one."

"Michael," Cheryl hesitated. "It's a surprise."

"Cheryl, you know me. I do *not* like surprises. Who is it?"

"You are hopeless."

"Thank you. Who?"

"A fan."

"I have a fan?"

"She likes the way you look, and I told her what a great guy I think you are."

"Two fans. Now, I have *two* fans. We could start a club."

"Michael, give me a break. Are you coming to dinner or not?"

"Who?"

"Okay. Carol Spencer."

"Carol? *Our* Carol?" Mike acted surprised. He knew that Norm suspected his connection with Carol, but he'd always been tactful enough not to bring it up. Obviously, Norm had also not divulged his suspicions to his wife.

"Yes, Carol."

"She likes the way I look?" Mike asked.

"Yes. Mike, you need to open up to potential relationships."

"Cheryl, are you forgetting about Captain Moretti's Law? Carol is a co-worker."

"Screw Moretti," Cheryl said. "He doesn't have to know everything."

"He thinks he does."

"We'll make this our little secret. It's only dinner. Okay?

"I—don't know."

"So, are you coming?"

"Let me think about it."

"Michael?"

"Of course, I'll come."

"Well, why don't you say so?"

"I just did."

"Remind me to punch you out later."

"Oooo. Sounds like fun. What time is dinner?"

"I'd like you to arrive about eight o'clock."

"As long as our neighbors don't interfere by killing each other, I'll be there. I'll bring a couple bottles of that Arrington Vineyards Cabernet you and Norm got me hooked on."

"Great idea."

"Cheryl."

"Yeah?"

"Thanks."

"I'm looking forward to it, Mike."

"Me too. See ya later."

Mike closed his cell and thanked God for his friends.

# Chapter 13

*Quick Market, Hwy 64*
*Hubbard County, Tennessee*
*Tuesday Morning*

Brad Evans stopped at the market to fill his truck with gasoline and pick up a few groceries. He was confident no one had witnessed the shooting of the gangster artist last night, but he was still a bit hyper-sensitive to his surroundings. It had been many years since he'd killed another man. It had been that long since Brad was motivated to take a life.

As he walked through the door, he heard his name and jerked his head to locate the source.

"Brad—Brad Evans?"

Brad saw a familiar, but older, face.

"Arnie Nicholson," the fifty-something man said.

Brad's former neighbor extended his hand and smiled.

"Arnie. How've you been?" Brad grabbed Arnie's hand. "I haven't seen you in ages. How long has it been?"

"Twelve, maybe fifteen years," Arnie said.

"How's your Mom and Dad?"

"Dad passed last summer," Arnie said.

"I'm sorry to hear that."

"Mom was diagnosed last year with Alzheimer's. I've got her living with me and Sheila, so we can keep an eye on her," Arnie nodded. "I heard you bought the old Melton farm."

"Yeah, I bought it almost ten years ago."

"So, how's your wife? Any kids?"

"I—lost Julie last December."

"Oh, Brad. I'm sorry." The excitement drained from Arnie's face.

Brad nodded his appreciation.

"So, are you still on the farm?"

"Yeah, me and Rocky."

Arnie tilted his head. "Your son?"

"No," Brad smiled. "Rocky's my Rottweiler."

"Oh, cool. I've got a couple of Redbone Hounds I hunt coon with."

"I'll bet that's fun."

"It is," Arnie said. "I love to hear 'em howl when they've got the scent. Sheila hates it. She says it bothers the neighbors. Hell, nobody lives within half a mile. I think it bothers *her*."

Brad smiled thinking how much he'd like it if Rocky's barking could be bothering Julie again.

"Hey, man. Are you busy later today, around lunchtime and later on?"

"I don't know," Brad said. "Why do you ask?"

"We're having a barbeque at the lodge today. I would love for you to come. You could see Sheila and meet a bunch of the guys at the lodge. You may know some of them. They're a bunch of hunters from around here. What do you say? You wouldn't have to stay all day unless you wanted to? Hell, you may have so much fun you'll want to stay."

"I don't know, Arnie." Brad wasn't sure he was up to meeting a mob of new people.

"Hey, do you still shoot as good as you used to?"

"I hunt frequently, and I built a target range on my place. So, yeah.

I stay in practice."

"Listen, part of the festivities is a bunch of shooting contests. There'll be rifle and shotgun competitions, and one for handguns. There're prizes too, *cash* prizes. My guess is you'd win something if you're half as good as you used to be. And I won't say anything to the competition about your—uh, 'training'." Arnie laughed.

Brad thought for a moment. Maybe this was a good thing. Maybe he could pick up some new gunsmith customers and even pocket some prize money.

"Where is this place?"

Arnie explained how to find the lodge. "You can come anytime you want after 10:30. It would be great to have you with us."

"Maybe I'll come by for a short visit."

"Great. Sheila will be excited. Man, it's really good to see you again. I thought maybe you'd moved away."

"I considered it after I lost Julie, but I enjoy my place. I like the solitude."

"Sounds great. Well, I can't wait for you to see our lodge."

"You never said what the name of the lodge is."

"Oh, I guess I didn't. It's the White-Tail Lodge."

"A bunch of deer hunters, huh?"

"Yeah well, we say *that* isn't the reason for the name."

"Oh?" Brad asked.

"Yeah, it really means you got to have a white tail to get in." Arnie laughed and slapped Brad on the back. "We'll see you in a few hours, buddy. Don't forget your guns."

# Chapter 14

*Mustafa's Restaurant*
*Nashville, Tennessee*
*Tuesday Morning*

"Excuse me, Mr. Mustafa. There is a Mr. Daran Hamid here to see you in the lobby," the young waitress said.

"Thank you. Tell him I will be right there."

The round restaurateur shuffled from his office in the rear of his Middle Eastern eatery and up the main aisle to greet his visitor.

"Mr. Daran—welcome to Mustafa's. I hear you are about to celebrate a glorious event." Mustafa grabbed Daran's hand in both of his.

"Yes," Daran stood a little straighter. "Today, after eight long years, I become an American citizen."

"Congratulations. I too, realized that honor almost twelve years ago. This is a happy day. How can I help you to enjoy it?"

"My supervisor and your friend, Mr. Zaid Zebari recommended that I ask you to prepare the food for my celebration."

"Yes, he told me. I would be honored. What can I prepare for you and your guests? Is the celebration this evening?"

"Yes, if it is possible, I would like to pick up the food at seven."

"That should be no problem." Mustafa pulled a pad and pen from the pocket of his white shirt. "Now, what would you like to serve?"

"Do you have a specialty?"

"Oh, yes. We have many, but our Mixed Grill is our most popular selection for groups.

"That sounds good," Daran said. "I am expecting twenty people, maybe a few more."

"Very good." Mustafa made notes. "If you can wait here, I will return with the ticket for your food. You can pay tonight when you pick it up."

"Thank you." Daran glanced at his wristwatch.

After a moment, Mustafa returned with a white bag. "Here you are. This is my gift to you, to honor you on this important day in your life. This is more than enough Baklava for your guests tonight. You can take it with you now. You will have enough to carry this evening with food for twenty-five."

"I do not know what to say."

"Say nothing, but promise me you will enjoy Mustafa's creations and then tell everyone you meet." Mustafa laughed.

"I promise. Thank you very much for your gift." Daran dropped the ticket into the bag.

"You are most welcome. I will see you this evening."

"Yes," Daran said. "I will be here."

Daran smiled as he jogged to his car in the light rain, thinking of how memorable this special day was going to be.

As he backed from his parking space, he paused to allow a large green delivery truck to pass by. Checking his watch, he still had plenty of time to get to the ceremony.

Once out of the parking space, he accelerated around the building to see the truck stop abruptly in front of him. He stomped on his brakes. That's when he felt the jolt from behind.

# Chapter 15

*I-65 South*
*Nashville, Tennessee*
*Tuesday Morning*

The rain was steady and had been since before daybreak.

"I got the worst damn luck," Detective Jack Hogue mumbled as he stared through beaded raindrops on the passenger side window.

"Now what's your problem?" Cris Vega asked.

"We ain't gonna find zip for evidence in this shit."

"Hey, it rains this time of year," Cris said. "You ought to be used to it. There's not a lot you're going to be able to do about it, you know."

"It still pisses me off."

"Everything pisses you off, Hogue. Maybe you should have been on your knees this morning asking God to postpone this mess."

"I get tired of these high maintenance calls. You'd think we could draw a simple, indoor domestic shooting with the wife sitting with blood on her hands and a smoking .38 in her lap. But no, we got flood duty."

"We all get tired of it," Vega said. "I'm tired of people blowing each other's brains out and expecting us to create some sense from what happened and then make it all better, but so far it hasn't stopped too many of them. Until it does, we got a job to do partner, rain or shine."

Detective Cris Vega was small compared to most of the men in the department, but even at five-foot five, she exhibited a presence respected throughout the department. Short black hair in a shag cut with a mocha complexion that required no makeup; she was both physically and emotionally strong. Her confidence was fortified by her years as a Mexican-American growing up on the streets of Houston, Texas, where even the boys hesitated before crossing her. She was a cop's kid; straight by the book, no bullshit and intolerant of incompetence and stupidity. Both of the latter were specialties of her new recycled partner.

Jack Hogue was a crude and opinionated thirty-two year veteran of the Nashville Police Department who spent much of his tenure riding the coattails of his friend, and partner of twelve years, Detective Gilbert Murdock. Now that Murdock had taken his retirement, Hogue's bigotry and his questionable performance were primed for exposure.

"Why are you parking up here?"

"Hogue, look down at the Interstate. Do you want to try and climb that embankment in the pouring rain? Or, would you rather slip over this railing, jump down three or four feet and be thirty seconds from the crime scene?"

Hogue grunted, knowing his agility level at such tasks.

"Thanks for your vote of confidence, *partner*. I didn't start this line of work yesterday, you know."

"Really, Vega? I took you for a rookie." Hogue couldn't resist being a smart ass.

"I got your rookie right here, asshole." Cris saluted Hogue with her middle finger.

"Let's go." Cris turned up the collar of her trench coat, grabbed her umbrella and charged into the downpour. With the umbrella over her head in one hand, she resembled a circus act as she stepped up onto the railing and then down on the other side. Using one hand to steady herself, she paused a moment squatting on top of the short wall. She jumped and landed next to the base of the wall.

Hogue watched her athletic display from the comfortably dry sedan and rolled his eyes. It took a bit longer for him to leave the car and longer still to negotiate the railing. When he finally scooted off the top of the wall, his umbrella was in the grass, and he was soaked to his shorts.

"What do you have so far?" Cris asked as she held up her shield to Officer Richard Rollins who identified himself as the first officer on the scene.

"I arrived at 0615. I got a call from dispatch saying someone spotted a body here on the west side of Interstate 65. Honestly, I figured it was a homeless guy passed out under the bridge. I've seen them near here before. When I got here, there were two cars parked down there. One was a citizen, trying to help. I thanked him and asked him to leave the scene. The other was Jason, over there." Rollins pointed. "He's an off-duty EMT on his way home. The Isuzu is his. He checked the victim with me and agreed he was deceased and had been for a few hours. The victim is a white male, about five feet nine or ten and one-seventy to one-eighty. He looks to have a small caliber entry wound at the base of his skull."

"How long ago did the criminalists arrive?" Hogue asked, trying to become part of the investigation.

"Maybe ten minutes before you guys; they've not been here long."

"Do we have an ID?" Cris asked.

"This wallet was in his left rear pocket," Rollins said holding up the bagged wallet. Tennessee operator license states his name is Shawn Parsons. He's nineteen and lives at The Berry Hill Townhouses near Melrose.

"Just to confirm," Cris said. The body has not been moved at all?"

"Correct. All we did was check for a pulse, grab his ID from his hip pocket, and then I got Jason to help me throw the plastic sheet over him to try and preserve what little evidence might still be here after the downpour."

"Thanks." Cris looked around in all directions for possible points of origin for the shooter. "Has the Medical Examiner been called?"

"Yeah. They were notified about twenty minutes ago."

Cris stepped over a can of red paint and squatted down close to the body. She pulled up the plastic and examined the back of the victim's head where there was a hole that looked to be a bit smaller than the diameter of a pencil. The victim's Pittsburgh Steelers cap was in the grass between his head and his right hand. His right index finger was stained with a rainbow of colors.

"How long before you're finished with your photos?" Cris asked the crime scene photographer as she replaced the plastic.

"About five minutes," the tech said. "Do you need some special shots?"

"Did you get shots of the body already?"

"Yes, I did those as soon as we arrived because of the rain, but I shot them with the plastic sheet in place."

"When you're done, I need to turn the body so you can shoot frontals."

"Sure. I was waiting on the medical examiner's team for that."

"Normally, I would wait too," Cris said. "But, at the rate we're losing evidence in this rain, I don't think we can afford the delay."

"Give me a few minutes," the photographer said, "and I'll be with you."

"Thanks," Cris said.

Cris bumped umbrellas with Hogue who was standing close behind her. She turned to face him. "Well, what do you think, Jack?"

"I think we got one more dead dumb ass gangster that's consuming valuable time we could be spending on an important investigation of somebody who's worthy of it."

"Well, I guess that explains the redneck perspective. What makes you think he's a gang member?"

"Normal people here don't deface public property by spraying their gang tags all over the city."

"I hate to be the bearer of enlightenment for such a committed and narrow-minded viewpoint Hogue, but this victim was not tagging his gang's ID."

"Then what do *you* call it?" Hogue asked.

"The unfinished artwork on the wall is no gang tag. It's just that: artwork. This young man was simply practicing his misdirected craft. This untouched public canvas was for him a place to display his talent. Now, taking that into consideration, who the hell pops a graffiti artist in the back of the head from what? At least a hundred—hundred and fifty yards away?" Cris said as she pointed across the freeway.

"Is that the only scenario you've got?" Hogue asked, anxious to offer up his two cents worth of possibilities.

Cris hesitated, then stopped herself from saying what she wanted to. She motioned for Hogue to follow her to a spot away from the others.

"Jack, if you have one that works, please—be my guest."

"It could have been a ricochet. It could have been a shot from a half-mile away that found an unfortunate home. It could have been someone he pissed off who was following him, then came up behind him with a Saturday night special. It could have been a homey who was with him, planning to paint the wall, and they got into a fight. It could have been a rival gang member who was driving by and thought the same thing I do; this idiot is taggin' the wall with his gang's ID and that homeboy decided to punch his ticket."

"What the hell have you been smoking?" Cris asked. "There is one thing for sure. Murdock must have been the expert in your partnership. That's the craziest bunch of hypothetical bunk I've ever heard. Do you really believe any of that crap?"

"It's all possible," Hogue said.

"Yeah, and it's also possible all this is a dream, and I'm going to wake up at any minute. Please, Burris—wake me up." Cris shook her head as she walked toward the photographer.

"Detective?" One of the criminalists shouted from near the victim's artwork.

"Yeah," Cris said.

"You got a minute?"

"Sure, what is it?"

"Look." He pointed to the bottom of the retaining wall.

In the grass, at the base of the wall, was what looked like a piece of raw turkey meat with a small army of ants beginning their own investigation. Cris dropped to her knees in the wet grass for a better look.

"You got a paper evidence bag on you? And tweezers?"

"Sure," the young man said, reaching inside his kit.

Cris took both from the tech, rested her opened umbrella on her shoulders and picked up the specimen. She shook it to encourage some of the ants to abandon their discovery, then bagged it.

"What do you think it is?" He asked.

"I'm not sure, but I've got an idea." She closed the bag and the clasp. "Here take this and be sure you document where you found it."

"Are you ready to shoot the frontal?" Cris asked the photographer.

"Sure."

"Jack, give me a hand over here," Cris shouted.

Hogue joined Cris and while Officer Rollins and the young EMT held the plastic above them, the two detectives rolled the body.

The photographer emitted a gasp like someone had doused her with a bucket of ice water.

As the body was rolled face up, it was evident *all* the face wasn't up. A good portion of the man's nose and upper lip dangled onto his left cheek. The rest was in a paper evidence bag.

# Chapter 16

*Hubbard County, Tennessee*
*White Tail Lodge*
*Tuesday Late Morning*

The morning rain moved out of Middle Tennessee and was replaced with mostly sunny skies. Brad checked eastbound Highway 64 in his mirror and slowed his truck. The red and white sign on the chain-link fence was right where Arnie said it would be, and Brad turned onto the narrow limestone gravel road.

Brad had driven no more than fifty feet before the transition from the bright sun to the darkness of the dense woods, limited his eyesight. He stopped his truck and turned on the headlights. Even in the middle of the day, the canopy of trees was so dense, the few laser-like rays of sunlight that shot to the floor of the woods failed to light the roadway. Once his pupils adjusted to the darkness, he continued his drive.

The gravel road slalomed around aged trees whose canopies bore much of the spring leaves darkening the woods. The huge Southern Red and Willow Oaks created the thick woods along with Ash and Elm trees.

In the distance ahead, Brad saw a brightly lit area he suspected must be his destination. He wasn't sure what he expected to find there, but as he drew closer, what he saw was something else. He observed what appeared to be the entrance to a fortress. An eight-foot tall solid wooden fence ran from the roadway in both directions as far as he could see.

His attention was arrested by numerous flashes of sparkling sunlight reflecting from the razor wire running in continuous loops above the top of the fence line. Another wire ran the length of the fence, mounted so that it stood out from the top of the enclosure. It was anchored every six feet by black ceramic insulators.

"Electrified? What the hell is this place?" Brad asked aloud. He was beginning to question his decision to visit the lodge when he spotted two video cameras panning to observe his arrival. The huge double-doors where the roadway met the fence opened away from him revealing two men, each sporting a Heckler & Koch MP45 on a black canvas sling and semi-automatic pistols holstered at their belts. Brad lowered his window for the larger of the two men who had a clipboard in his hand and a questioning look on his face.

Brad nodded his head once.

"What's your name?" The man said with a gruff expression.

"Brad Evans."

"Your sponsor?" The guard said without looking up from his clipboard.

Brad wrinkled his brow. "Sponsor?"

"Yeah. Sponsor. Who invited you?"

"Oh, Arnie Nicholson."

"Arnie?" He looked at Brad then down at the paper.

"Yeah."

"You got any weapons on board?"

"Arnie told me there would be some shooting contests. He said I should bring them."

"We log in all weapons brought onto the grounds."

"You want to see them now?"

"If it wouldn't be too much trouble," the guard said with a sarcastic tone.

*Friendly asshole.* Brad opened his door and stepped out of the truck. He pulled the seat back forward and reached for the Starlight cases that held his guns.

"Open 'em."

Brad wanted to say 'No shit', but thought better of it.

Brad placed the cases flat on the ground, flipped the latches and lifted the lids. As he stood, he saw the other guard open his truck's passenger door and start searching through the cab of his truck.

"There's a pistol in the glovebox," Brad said, trying to prevent any surprises.

"Why do you have a suppressor for this rifle?" The big man barked.

Brad was getting his fill of this cantankerous jerk. "I do contract work–varmint removal. I sometimes work concealed in populated areas after dark. Folks tend to get a little agitated when they hear gunshots in the night, so I take out unwanted animals, quietly."

The guard looked at Brad for a minute as if to determine whether he was telling the truth or yanking his chain. Then he proceeded to log the descriptions and serial numbers from each of Brad's long guns. He stood and stepped back. He looked at Brad, still unsure of his story.

"You can put 'em away now."

Brad closed the cases and returned them to the truck.

The other guard completed his search and was hugging his H&K as he delivered his log of Brad's Sig Sauer pistol to the big guard.

"I need to pat you down," The guard said, standing poised as if ready for a fight.

"I'm not armed."

"I *still* have to pat you down." The guard stared into Brad's eyes.

Brad took a large breath and let it out. He wasn't happy about this, but he didn't want to reflect badly on Arnie. He faced the guard, and held his arms out parallel with the ground.

The guard dropped his clipboard on the ground and frisked

Brad.

"Okay," the guard said, pointing to the truck. He collected his clipboard and made another notation.

Brad climbed into the truck and closed the door. He looked at the big guard for some sign of approval to enter the compound. He was still writing on his clipboard. The man finally looked up, raised his arm and pointed.

"You see the parking lot there on this side of the old house?" the guard asked.

"Yeah," Brad said, without taking his eyes off the guard.

"That's where you need to park."

"Got it." Brad accelerated while still watching the guard. He was grateful to be finished with the less than congenial welcoming committee.

He pulled into a space close to the building and as he closed the truck's door he glanced back at the big gate and the big ass that had checked him in. He locked his truck and began his search for Arnie.

Brad had decided to wear a new western shirt and jeans with, what he referred to as his dancing boots. The shirt was one that Julie bought him not long before her death. He had not worn it before today. Brad had no plans to dance, but he felt close to Julie wearing the last clothes she had bought for him.

As he walked from the parking lot he could hear loud music and kids laughing. These were sounds he had not heard for quite a while. He and Julie used to go out for dinner and a little boot scootin' on Saturday nights. She always enjoyed those special evenings and Brad was content anytime Julie was happy. So many things in his solitary life caused him to miss her. He even missed doing his poor excuse for the Texas Two-Step, but he would never admit that to anyone.

"Brad."

Brad turned to see Arnie approaching with an attractive middle-aged lady in tow. It was Sheila.

"Man, it's great you could come."

Brad smiled and shook Arnie's hand.

"Same here Brad," Sheila said. "Welcome to the White Tail Lodge." Sheila held out both arms and gave Brad a hug. "It's been a long time."

"Yes, it sure has. Thanks for the invite."

"The competitions start at two," Arnie said. "Did you bring your guns?"

"Oh, I might have a couple in the truck," Brad said.

"Great. Come on, Brad," Arnie said. "Let's get some sweet tea, and pitch some horse shoes."

"Oh, please," Sheila said, shaking her head. "Ever since he put in those pits behind the house, he thinks he's an expert."

"Come on, babe," Arnie said. "Can't you see I'm tryin' to hustle the man? Help me out here."

Brad and Arnie both laughed.

Sheila rolled her eyes and threw up her hands. "Men," she said, shaking her head. "I'm going back inside with the girls."

"Okay, Hon, I'll come show you my winnings in a few minutes." Arnie looked at Brad as they walked away. "She's the best thing that ever happened to me."

"I understand," Brad said.

"Oh—sorry. I wasn't thinking." Arnie dropped his head.

"No, don't apologize," Brad said. "Don't ever apologize for loving your wife. You appreciate your wife. That's good. I appreciated mine. I'm lucky to have had her as long as I did."

Arnie nodded.

"So, show me your horseshoe tossing form," Brad said, trying to change the subject.

Arnie perked up. "You're on, buddy."

The two old friends had been playing about thirty minutes when Brad asked, "Arnie, what kind of place is this lodge?"

"What do you mean?"

"I don't know of any men's lodge anywhere with armed guards

watching over electrified perimeter fencing. What's the deal?"

Arnie turned to Brad with a serious look and asked, "Have you ever heard of TARPA?"

"TARPA? I don't think so."

"It stands for The Alliance for the Racial Purification of America."

"Racial purification? What the hell does that mean?"

"We believe America was founded by a group of white Christian men who intended for this country to remain for white Christians, not for every alien who wants to escape his current predicament and sponge off all our hard-working, tax-paying, and law-abiding citizens."

"I guess I can understand that perspective."

"I knew you'd feel that way."

"How else can I feel? The bastard who killed Julie is probably in the U.S. illegally. If he is, and if I know our government, he's probably getting a welfare check. He's got a public defender fighting for his freedom and both the sons of bitches are getting paid with my taxes."

"That's exactly the kind of injustice we're battling," Arnie said.

Brad nodded his head. "Good for you."

Forty-five minutes and two horseshoe matches later the reunited friends decided to grab some barbeque and prepare for the shooting competition.

"Man, this is some fine barbeque," Brad said.

"Two of our men cook it right here on the property. We've got a large pit out behind the mess hall that'll cook ten pork shoulders at a time."

"What *don't* you have here?"

"Not much. When you've got over six hundred acres to work with, there's room for everything you need."

"I noticed several other buildings, and some of them look like apartments," Brad said.

"Those are dormitories where the men sleep who are here for training."

"What kind of training?"

"We have training sessions throughout the year in various disciplines important to our cause. Our people usually spend some vacation time and weekends participating in these sessions."

"What are some of the courses?"

"Some I'm sure you've been involved in during your military career: Hand-to-Hand Combat, Survival Skills, Small Arms and Rifle Weaponry, Conventional and Unconventional Explosives, Defensive and Offensive Driving Skills. They're all pretty interesting."

"It sounds like it."

"With your Army experience, you could teach them." Arnie laughed.

"I *have* taught a couple when I was in Iraq." Brad smiled. "What time is the competition?"

"Oh shit," Arnie said, checking the time and grabbing his tea. "We gotta go."

The shotgun was not Brad's weapon of choice. Use of this gun required the shooter to be relatively close to his target—not a strong tactical position when the target was an adversary who might also be armed. However, Brad had owned a Remington Model 870 twelve-gauge pump for years, and he had done enough dove and quail hunting to be every bit as proficient as most other shooters. He felt capable of holding his own in any shooting competition.

"Anyone who can take their limit of fifteen doves can hit flying clay targets," Brad said. "Unlike doves, clay targets don't make forty-five degree turns in midair. Hell, the damn targets are red. Just watch 'em and then shoot where they're gonna be when the buckshot gets there."

When the thunderous shotgun contest was finished, Brad had grabbed second place behind Buddy Westmoreland, who'd won the lodge's shotgun competition for the last four years. Runner-up status paid Brad fifty dollars.

The rifle competition required participants to fire at twelve-inch targets fifty yards down range with .22 caliber rifles using standard long rifle ammo. All rifles used were required to have iron sights only, no optics allowed. Shooters were asked to fire ten shots each from three positions: standing, kneeling and prone. Brad won this easily by placing all 30 rounds within the fourth ring from the target's bull's eye. For his flawless efforts, he collected one hundred dollars.

The competition leading up to the handgun finals had been fierce, lasting over three and a half hours. The thirty-four contenders were required to shoot 9 millimeter or 40 caliber ammunition using a semi-automatic pistol of their choosing. All handguns were inspected by the judges.

The list was now whittled down to three shooters who were scheduled to compete in the handgun finals. The names of the three finalists had been posted and spectators were choosing their favorites. Darryl Miles, Glenn Prater & Brad Evans would be competing for the day's final prize, two hundred dollars cash.

Brad wasn't sure who Miles was, but Arnie told him Prater was the big guard who'd cleared him at the gate. That piece of news was what Brad called *motivation.*

After much anticipation by the White Tail Lodge members and their families, Ross Pruitt, Operations Director for the lodge, stepped to the microphone to explain the rules.

"May I have your attention?"

After a moment, everyone quieted.

"I hope you are all enjoying your day. We're glad you all could be here."

The crowd cheered briefly.

"This year's handgun finals competition will be unlike any we've had in past years." Pruitt smiled. "This year, the finals will consist of a series of handgun-related tasks. Performance of these tasks, as well as the accuracy of the shooting itself will be timed. Gentlemen, if you will remove your personal side arms and hand them to the judges, I'd like you all to step up to the three tables here before me."

The men relinquished the pistols which had helped them reach the top three spots in the contest and took their assigned positions behind the tables.

"The tasks involved in today's contest include the following: Each of you must field-strip a forty caliber Glock Model Nineteen down to its five basic parts and then place them on the table in front of you. Once this step has been completed and confirmed by your judge, you will reassemble your pistols, load ten rounds into the empty magazine, insert the magazine, cock the weapon, and place as many rounds as you can within the rings of a twelve inch target mounted twenty-five yards away."

The crowd moaned and chattered among themselves for a moment, then cheered and applauded.

Pruitt chuckled. "Are there any questions, gentlemen?" He checked with each contestant. "If not, we'll prepare to start the competition."

The three men stepped up close behind the tables. The tables were covered with a white cloth and each held an Austrian-built semi-automatic pistol, ten rounds of .40 caliber ammunition, a pair of shooter's safety glasses, foam ear plugs as well as shooter's noise reduction earmuffs. Each of the three contestants was assigned a judge to time their performance as well as confirm disassembly and proper re-assembly of their weapon.

"Gentlemen, if you will put on your safety equipment and place your hands flat on the table before you, we'll be ready to begin."

The shooters did as they were asked.

"Judges, are your stopwatches ready?"

The three judges lifted their stopwatches in acknowledgement.

Pruitt counted off, "Ready ... set ... go."

The three judges started their clocks as the contestants grabbed their pistols and began disassembly. It was obvious; this was no one's first field stripping.

Brad pressed the magazine release and allowed the mag to fall from the grip and onto the table. Next he grasped the rear of the Glock's slide in his right hand and depressed the slide releases on each side of the pistol with the index finger and thumb on his left. As the gun's slide moved forward, Brad inverted the gun and caught the slide as it fell from the frame. He pulled the recoil spring from its seated position and slipped the barrel from the slide dropping all three pieces on to the cloth covered table. Brad looked up at the judge who nodded his head.

Brad replaced the barrel in the slide, tucked the end of the recoil spring in place and seated the other end at the front of the slide. He grabbed the frame and pushed the slide into position over the frame and pulled it to the rear and placed the gun on the table. Ready to load the magazine, he grabbed it in his left hand and gathered about half the loose bullets in his right.

As he began pushing the bullets down onto the magazine's follower, he wondered which stage of the contest the other two men were on. He'd heard no shots. That's all that mattered. He collected the rest of the bullets and continued loading the magazine. All ten cartridges in the magazine, he shoved the mag into the grip, grasped the serrated sides of the pistol's slide and pulled, cocking the action. That's when he heard gunfire from another table.

Brad brought the pistol into firing position and caught the heel of his right hand in the palm of his left. He assumed the Isosceles shooting stance and began punching holes in his target. He didn't bother counting his shots. When the pistol's slide locked back, it confirmed what he already knew.

As he lowered his pistol, Brad heard the three last reports from Miles's gun before the range fell quiet, and the applause erupted. He looked down range, but couldn't tell, from his angle, how well the other shooters had done, but he was confident.

"Weapons on the tables, please and step back."

The smell of pork barbeque smoke that had dominated the air since Brad arrived at the lodge was now mixed with the smell of burned gun powder, two of Brad's favorite aromas.

The judges retrieved their shooters' targets and returned to the announcer's table. The three competitors removed their safety equipment and stood quiet, waiting for the results.

The judges remained huddled for no more than three minutes.

"Ladies and gentlemen," Pruitt spoke into his microphone. "In second place with nine out of ten shots inside the target, and a time of one minute and four seconds, our own Glen Prater."

The crowd applauded. Brad relaxed and gave Prater a satisfied smile.

"With a time of one minute and five seconds, and with all ten rounds inside the target—Brad Evans."

Arnie cheered, whistled and clapped his hands. Applause from the crowd began with less vigor than for Prater, but as they saw Arnie stand, applaud, and continue to shout his approval, their response grew into more worthy praise.

Brad smiled as he accepted two crisp hundred dollar bills and shoved them into his front pocket with the other bills. He nodded to the crowd wishing he could see Julie there smiling and cheering for him. He mouthed the words thank you as the people acknowledged his winning performance.

"Brad," Arnie yelled as he stepped toward Brad. "Great job, buddy. Congratulations."

"Thanks."

The two friends returned the guns to Brad's truck and Arnie kidded Brad about his success on the target range. "You could have had the decency to let someone else win a little." Arnie laughed.

"What do you mean," Brad asked, "I missed ten percent of the clay targets on purpose."

"You're kidding?"

"Of course, I'm kidding. I ain't throwing a cash prize shooting match for anybody, much less somebody I don't even know yet."

"By yet, I assume you mean you might like to get to know these folks?"

"Maybe." Brad shrugged his shoulders.

"Great. I can't wait for you to meet Carl."

"Who?"

"Carl Garrison. He's our leader. His grandfather started TARPA back in the thirties."

"Yeah?"

"Let's go. I need to show you our assembly hall. It's full of our history. It's in this building behind the old house."

They walked through a side door into a large meeting room that resembled a modern church on the inside. There were at least thirty rows of pews facing a small stage with an oak podium. The large room had been added onto the back of the old antebellum home.

The first thing to catch Brad's eye was a large black and white profile photograph of President Theodore Roosevelt under which was printed a quote.

> *There can be no divided allegiance here. Any man who says he is an American, but something else also, isn't an American at all. We have room for but one flag, the American flag ... We have room for but one language here, and that is the English language ... and we have room for but one sole loyalty and that is a loyalty to the American people.*
>
> - Theodore Roosevelt, 1907

"Wise man," Brad said.

"He didn't mince words, did he?" Arnie added.

"Spoke softly—carried a big stick." Brad held up his fists as if clutching a baseball bat.

Both men laughed like a couple of teenagers.

As they walked into the auditorium, Arnie said, "The main residence was built in 1884 by Reverend Garrison's great-great granddaddy, Captain Jefferson C. Garrison. Here is a picture of him in his Confederate dress grays taken during the Civil War."

With his thick black beard resting on the gray chest of his frock coat, his left hand on the hilt guard of his battle sword and his right hand on the grip of his cap and ball revolver, Captain Garrison was indeed a proud and impressive looking soldier.

"A striking man, huh?" Arnie asked.

"That he was."

"He was a real hero. He led a company of Confederate soldiers at the battle of Forrestown where they annihilated over two hundred Union bluecoats."

"You said he was *Reverend* Garrison's great-great granddaddy?" Brad said.

"Oh, yeah. Carl is not an ordained minister. One of his followers nicknamed him "Reverend" a few years ago and it stuck. Carl liked the moniker. He thought it suited him, so he encouraged its use."

As they ambled past a wall covered with pictorial tributes to the Civil War and other American conflicts since, Brad noticed a distinctive document framed and hung prominently on the front wall of the meeting room near a modern portrait of a man in a navy blue suit. The document and the large portrait were hung on either side of an intact but old and tattered American Flag framed in a thick shadowbox and hung as the front wall's centerpiece. Brad could read the short inscription beneath the flag from across the room.

***"The Commitments of Our Fathers are Ours to Keep."***
George W. Bush, 9/12/2001

Arnie smiled as he watched Brad viewing the treasures displayed throughout the room. He could tell the keepsakes were appealing to his patriotic pride.

Brad walked up to the large framed document and began to read:

***"The Alliance for the Racial Purification of America"***
*Founded January 1st, 1938*
*Hubbard County, Tennessee*

*This Declaration issued by The Alliance for the Racial Purification of America,*
*Tennessee Chapter, hereby bestows upon the undersigned Gentlemen,*
*the Title, Liberties and Privileges of Membership.*

*On assuming the Rule of Dominion over the Glorious Empire to them Assigned, which shall henceforth continue to be theirs regardless of dispute, they shall be Saluted and Honored with the Symbols of Dignity, and Acknowledged within the Grand National Governance and Lawful Authority of this Reputed Alliance.*
*This Declaration executed in the Supreme City of National Law, Forrestown, County of Hubbard, State of Tennessee,*
*United States of North America, on this 1st day of January, 1938*
*Confirmed with the Eternal Seal.*
*Grand Sovereign – Col. Carl W. Garrison, Sr.*

The formal declaration was followed by signatures totaling sixty-eight names. Brad was reminded of America's Declaration of Independence. As he read the list, many of the legible surnames were familiar to Brad, including Arnie's.

People began to enter the auditorium and take seats. Arnie looked at his watch.

"We'd better get a seat. It's almost time for Carl."

"He's going to speak?" Brad asked.

"Yes, he said he's got something special he wants to talk about today."

"Where's Sheila?" Brad asked, looking around the room.

"She's in the mess hall with the other women cleaning up, but they'll all be in here soon."

The room was filled by the time Arnie introduced Brad to a half dozen of his friends. Each one commented on his marksmanship.

Brad and Arnie took their seats in time to see a dapper gentleman in his early fifties, with an abundance of charisma, step into the hall to a roar of shouts and applause. Carl Garrison's navy blue suit was no doubt tailored for him, and his shirt was whiter than white. The tri-color striped tie communicated his patriotism. He was waving and shaking hands like a political candidate as he made his way onto the elevated platform. He crossed the front of the stage toward the podium, still shaking hands and talking with admirers. With a broad smile, a few finger points and head nods, Garrison continued to savor the admiration from the crowd of over three hundred. He held his hands in the air attempting to quiet the group. It was obvious; this man was comfortably in power.

He began to speak with an embroidered southern drawl.

"My fellow Americans—welcome to White Tail Lodge once again." The people applauded until Garrison raised his hand.

"I want you all to know. I admire you—I respect you—and I value your dedicated involvement in our efforts to return America to the racial purity intended for her by our founding Christian fathers."

Primed for his stirring words, the group offered up loud cheers and applause.

"However," he waited for the crowd to calm, "I want you all to understand—our past endeavors and our devotion to TARPA's goals, while admirable and for a time effective, will no longer be enough to achieve the change we seek for our beloved country."

Moans and exchanged questioning mumbles came from the crowd.

Garrison nodded his head and raised a hand in the air.

"The people of the United States—your friends and neighbors," he pointed, moving his finger across the crowd, "are not embracing the significance of our objectives."

There were more mumbled groans and negative remarks throughout the room.

Someone sitting behind Brad shouted, "Wake up, people!"

After a moment, Garrison held up his hands to quiet the crowd again.

"Our fellow Americans are proving daily, they would rather stick their heads in the sand and deny the truth than to awaken and see through clear eyes the devastation being brought upon our nation by the inconspicuous invasion of our country's borders by alien trespassers who are attempting to hybridize our Anglo blood."

The entire gathering stood in unison shouting forceful "Amens" and offering loud applause. Garrison gazed across the room nodding a furrowed forehead.

Brad hesitated, then stood with the crowd in order to see. He looked around at all the excited folk clapping and yelling their support. He was impressed by Garrison's command over the gathering.

Garrison again raised his hands. The crowd calmed and finally sat.

"The foreign influx of beggars and heathens from our so called allies and the alien influence being exerted on our country's leadership continues to increase." He paused. "Beware. Pressure is increasing; attempting to convince us to give up our God-given right to live free, segregated and protected by the principles established by our white Christian forefathers centuries ago."

"Yes," shouted several of the men and women. The crowd stood again, cheered and applauded.

Garrison took the microphone from the pulpit and walked to center stage. He allowed their consensus to build before calming them with his hands once more.

"My fellow Americans—we have got to close the door. This unbridled immigration from every nation on Earth is perverting our freedoms, robbing us of both our money, and what's left of our racial purity." He walked back to the pulpit and paused. "We have to shut the door ... *now*." As he said *now*, he slapped the oak podium with his open right hand causing a thunderous roar throughout the room.

"Shut the door now." His followers began to chant. "Shut the door now. Shut the door now."

Garrison maintained his solemn expression. He held up his hand until the people began to settle down.

"We must stand together," Garrison shouted over the microphone.

The crowd remained standing and applauded again.

"We must stand strong," he paused and waited for the response.

"Amen." Shouts of approval came from across the group.

"We must stand firm against the world's coercion to force us to melt into a global community where interracial lifestyles are openly accepted and promoted to the detriment of us all." He allowed his polished drawl to crescendo into a fevered pitch. Feedback screeched from the speakers in response to his volume.

Brad looked around the room. Arnie was clapping and yelling. He began to clap slowly himself so he didn't look out of place. Everyone in the room was standing. Looking at each other, they were nodding, cheering and applauding their collective agreement with Garrison's words.

Garrison raised his hands and as soon as the noise calmed enough for his words to be heard, he leaned forward, grabbed the sides of the podium and shouted into the mike, "We are ..." he paused to allow the congregation to join in his affirmation. "The Alliance for the Racial Purification of America," they all repeated in unison then exploded into more cheers and applause.

"Is he impressive or what?" Arnie shouted at Brad over the applause.

Brad smiled, amazed at the level of sheer frenzy Garrison had been able to invoke in little more than five minutes.

"When the crowd thins out, I want to introduce you to Carl," Arnie said.

Brad nodded.

Garrison worked his way toward the door as the applause softened.

"Let's go," Arnie said. "He'll go back to his office now, and we'll catch up with him there."

Arnie and Brad exited through the room's side door and reentered the building behind Garrison and the gathering of ladies still trailing his aura.

As the last of the flirting followers left Garrison's office, Arnie stepped into the doorway and cleared his throat, "Got a minute? There's someone I'd like you to meet."

"Sure." Garrison stepped toward the door, offering his hand and a large white smile.

"Carl Garrison, meet Brad Evans. Brad and I are old friends. I invited him out today to share in our fun."

"It is a pleasure to meet you, Brad." Garrison pumped Brad's hand. "And, it's a joy to see someone so adept at marksmanship."

"You saw that?" Brad asked.

"Brad's father raised him in the woods with a rifle in his hands," Arnie said.

"I can believe that," Garrison said as he looked Brad over.

"It's more accurate than you know." Brad smiled.

"I heard on the radio this morning," Garrison said, "there was another marksman at work early today. Seems that someone shot one of those gang-bangers last night while he was vandalizing one of our Interstate highways."

"That's one less criminal we have to incarcerate and feed for the next twenty years," Arnie said.

"Now that's a blessing." Garrison added. "From what the reporter stated, it must have been quite a shot."

"If that guy had been here today," Brad said, "I may not have as much money in my pocket right now."

The men all laughed.

"Gentlemen, I'd love to sit and talk," Garrison checked his Rolex, "but I have a meeting in thirty minutes. Brad, would you be available to talk with me later this evening? I'd like to pick your brain about something. Would that be okay with you?" Garrison nodded, attempting to elicit Brad's agreement.

"Uh ... I guess so." Brad looked at Arnie then back at Garrison. "What time?"

"Say around seven o'clock, here in my office?"

"Okay," Brad said.

"Great." Garrison extended his hand again to Brad. "It was a pleasure to meet you, Brad. I'll look forward to our chat this evening."

Brad and Arnie stepped into the hallway and out the exterior door. "What does he want to talk to me about?" Brad asked.

"I have no idea." After some hesitation, Arnie said, "But, I have to be honest with you, Brad. Carl asked me about you during the competition, and he sent word to me later that he wanted to meet you."

"Why would he want to meet *me*?"

"Carl's a straight shooter," Arnie said. "It sounds as though you may be developing a new and quite powerful friendship. There are worse things, you know."

"Okay. I guess I'll withhold judgment until tonight."

"Good idea," Arnie said. "Before you go, let's see if there's any homemade ice cream left."

# Chapter 17

*Tennessee State University Campus*
*Nashville, Tennessee*
*Tuesday Late Afternoon*

Karim al-Waleed was reading the day's assignment for his computer programming class when he checked his wristwatch. "Sajid, it is time for work." He stood and returned his books to his backpack. "We must go now, or we will be late."

Sajid Aziz closed his Thermodynamics textbook and loaded his study materials into his backpack. The two men walked hurriedly toward the exit, but as they had been trained, not so fast as to bring attention to themselves.

When they exited the building, Karim asked, "Have you heard from Abdul?"

"Not since last week. I received an email. He was confirming his arrival and the meeting with us tomorrow. Why do you ask?"

"I am growing tired of the waiting." They paused their conversation to let two girls pass on the sidewalk. "We have been here in this nightmare for over two years, and I am growing weary of studying and working—working and studying.

Sajid unlocked the car doors and both men tossed their packs into the backseat. "And," Karim paused looking at Sajid across the top of the compact car, "I am tired of being looked at by these—these arrogant self-righteous infidels like I am some kind of second class human who is here to serve at their table."

"Hold your tongue," Sajid said in Arabic as he scanned the area around the car. "Get in."

As soon as the car doors were closed, Sajid said, "People can hear you. You know how sensitive the Americans are now. I understand how you feel, but you must be more careful with your words."

Karim continued his tirade as Sajid backed from the space and drove away. "Who are we fooling, Sajid? Hopefully, it is not ourselves. Will our sacrifice here make a difference?" He looked out the side window. "I want to awaken the world. I promise my father each and every day he did not die in vain. So many of our proud Republican Guard gave their lives when these infidels invaded Iraq only to have our world overrun by these Godless pigs."

"Be careful Karim, we are too close to our destiny to allow our emotions to betray us. Try to remember, we are in preparation, and we must make sacrifices to position ourselves where we need to be in order to carry out Allah's plan."

"I understand, brother," Karim said, "but I do not share your patience. I need to see some progress—some accomplishment. I must honor my father."

The flashing blue lights arrested their attention, disorienting them both just before the short siren blast brought their adrenaline to a peak. Sajid hit his brakes hard causing the blue and white patrol car to almost strike them in the rear.

"What is wrong? What did you do?" Karim asked.

Sajid pulled to the curb, then glued his eyes to the driver-side mirror. "This is what I get for becoming lost in your complaining. I must have accelerated over the speed limit. You need to hold your tongue, Karim. I know you. We can get through this, but you *must* keep your mouth shut. Do you understand?"

As the officer walked up, Sajid lowered his window.

"Good evening. May I see your license, registration and proof of insurance please?"

"Yes, officer." Sajid removed his license from his wallet and collected the other documents from the glove box as he looked at Karim. He handed the papers to the officer.

"Thank you. Do you know why I pulled you over?"

"No, sir."

"I clocked you at ten miles per hour over the posted limit."

"I didn't realize." Sajid tried to think of an excuse.

"Just a minute; I'll be right back," the officer said.

Sajid watched his mirror as the police officer returned to his cruiser.

As soon as the officer was inside his car, Sajid asked, "Tell me you do not have your pistol with you." Sajid knew Karim liked to carry his small Beretta Cougar, but he'd promised Sajid that he never took it with him to class.

"No, it is at the apartment," Karim said.

"Good. At least we have *that* to be grateful for," Sajid said.

After no more than five minutes, a second patrol car arrived behind the first with its lights flashing also. Both officers exited their cars and spoke briefly before walking to each side of Sajid's car.

The officers stood by the doors, their left hands on the door handles and their right hands near their weapons.

"Gentlemen, we'd like both of you to keep your hands in full view and step out of the vehicle please," the first officer said.

"What is the problem, officer?" Sajid asked.

The officers opened the doors. "Please exit the car and move to the curb. Keep your hands away from your body. Extend your arms and place both your hands on the car. Now, spread your legs. Each officer stood close behind one of the students and waited for them to comply.

"Do either of you have any weapons or anything sharp on you?"

"No," Sajid said.

Karim shook his head. "No."

"We will need to check you for weapons."

Sajid looked at his friend. Karim's shallow breathing and lowered brow were displaying his feelings of outrage. Sajid cleared his throat. His eyes told Karim to contain his emotions and allow this episode to play itself out.

Sajid held the submissive position against the car and continued to watch Karim as the officers frisked them both. All the while, Karim stared back at Sajid with enlarged nostrils and hate-filled eyes. Afraid Karim might lose control; Sajid gave him a slow, almost imperceptible, shake of his head and mouthed the words "be calm" in Arabic.

Following the pat-downs, the officer who pulled them over said, "We need to see your student IDs."

Sajid knew the officer had seen the TSU student parking decal. He and Karim reached into their pockets for their wallets.

"Slowly," the second officer said.

The two handed their photo ID cards to the first officer, who went back to his car while the second officer waited with the two of them.

After several minutes, the officer climbed from his cruiser and approached the others.

"Mr. Aziz, would you mind if we searched your vehicle?"

"Why? What are you looking for?" Sajid asked.

"We have recently arrested a group of students at TSU who turned out to be members of an organized group selling illegal drugs to their fellow students and other young people on the streets. We need to be sure you are not a part of that group."

"Officer, I assure you we are not selling drugs," Sajid said. "We are students. I am studying to be an engineer, and my friend here is a computer programmer."

"Do you mind if we search your car, or do we need to obtain a warrant in order to do so?"

"So, you will be searching it with or without my permission?" Sajid asked.

The officer nodded. "It won't take long."

"This is so typical," Karim mumbled.

"In that case, officer, go ahead." Sajid elevated his voice so all of Karim's criticism could not be heard. "We have nothing to hide." Sajid gave Karim a look that told him to shut his mouth.

"Step away from the car please and stand over here." The first officer directed the men to a spot several feet from the car.

The last officer to arrive returned to his cruiser and opened the passenger side rear door. Bending and reaching inside the car, he appeared to be manipulating something in the backseat. After a brief moment, he stood back and allowed a large black Labrador Retriever to exit the car and then march along side him on a leash.

The K-9 team began their examination of the car's exterior. The dog began at the front of the car. He circled the car sniffing the front bumper, wheels and fenders. He worked his way back to the trunk, then came up the near side where the officer opened the back seat passenger door allowing the dog inside.

There was an undeniable heightened sensitivity for police officers who encountered someone with a Middle Eastern appearance, name or accent. Over the last few months there were instances where even some of Nashville's West End area residents from the Jewish community received additional attention during normal traffic stops. Some of them understood; some were angry. But, they all knew why it was being done. They were as fearful of the terror threats to the public safety as any other citizens, if not more so.

As the Retriever searched the backseat, the dog knocked one of the backpacks from the car and onto the sidewalk. The officer retrieved the bag, and as he lifted it an amber bottle fell out.

"What's this?" He asked as he picked up the bottle and read the label.

There was no response.

"What's in here? It says it's Vicodin."

Sajid turned his head toward his friend. It was Karim's backpack.

The officer dumped the contents of the bag onto the concrete sidewalk.

Karim cursed inaudibly in Arabic as some of his work spilled out and was now spotted, wet with the disrespectful slobber from the four-legged cop. Sajid became nervous and asked Karim in Arabic what was in the bottle.

"Medicine." Karim answered, also in Arabic.

"Speak English," the officer said.

Textbooks and spiral notebooks were scattered across the sidewalk.

"Which one of you is Karim al-Waleed?"

"I am," said Karim, with an irritated tone.

"Is this your prescription?"

Karim nodded. "Yes."

"Vicodin?" The cop said, remembering it was on the list of controlled narcotics he had to memorize.

"It is my migraine medication," Karim said. "There is also a bottle of Midrin in there if your dog has not yet *eaten* it."

Sajid knew Karim took medicine for his headaches, but had no idea it might be a problem.

"Call the pharmacy. Call my doctor," Karim said, with a disgusted tone. "They will confirm it. If all this keeps up, I will soon need to take two of them."

The officer pulled his cell phone from his duty belt. He held the bottle near the cruiser's head lamp and punched in the pharmacy's phone number.

Sajid looked from the officer back to Karim, whose lowered brow reflected his diminishing patience.

"Is this a valid prescription for Karim al-Waleed?" He looked at Karim as he listened. "Thank you," the officer said, then closed his phone. "The pharmacy confirmed the prescription is his." He crammed Karim's belongings into the back pack and tossed it back into the seat.

Sajid laughed inside with relief. He looked over at Karim and shook his head.

The officer and the dog explored Sajid's backpack and the rest of the car without incident.

"Looks like we're good here," the K-9 officer said.

"Okay, sign here, Mr. Aziz," the other officer said holding out his citation pad.

"Yes, sir," Sajid said.

"You're okay to go, but watch your speed." The officer handed him the citation.

Sajid and Karim returned to the car and left for Mustafa's, now almost an hour late for work.

It took only minutes to complete the trip to the restaurant, but knowing Mustafa, they suspected the explanation for their tardiness would take the rest of the night.

Sajid knocked on the rear door of the restaurant and the two men were admitted by one of the cooks.

"Where have you two been?" Mustafa shouted from the kitchen as the men opened their lockers and removed their uniforms. "I am already short one worker. Your friend, Ahmed called to say he was sick and would not be here today."

On the drive over, Sajid instructed Karim to let him do the talking with Mustafa. With no confidence in Karim's ability to hold his tongue, Sajid told him to act as though he was shaken by the incident with the police and to keep to himself the balance of the night.

"We were stopped and harrassed by the police," said Sajid.

"What? The police? Where? Why?"

"We were on Charlotte Avenue on the way here from the University. They stopped us because of our appearance, of course. We are all terrorists to them, you know."

"Surely, they would not be so bold," Mustafa said.

"Obviously, they have been instructed to detain all who appear Middle Eastern," Sajid said. "Their paranoia since the planes flew into the towers has fueled their fears and caused them to act irresponsibly."

"I have heard about racial profiling on the news, but I had no idea they would do such things here in Nashville," Mustafa said.

"It was obvious. They were harassing us because of our appearance. They were rude and disrespectful. They called us rag-heads and shoved us up against the car. I was sure they were going to arrest us. They even called in dogs to search the car. It was terrifying, Mustafa—terrifying."

"Dogs? What was their reason for detaining you to begin with?"

"They never told us why."

"Why the dogs?" Mustafa asked.

"They said they were searching the car for weapons and explosives."

"This is terrible. I cannot believe it has come to this. I am going to call my councilman now. He is a very good customer of ours." Mustafa walked toward his office.

Karim looked at Sajid with wide eyes and a questioning stare. Sajid caught up with his boss. "Mustafa wait, please."

"What?"

"I am not so sure this is a good idea," Sajid said, trying to think of a way to stall Mustafa.

"What do you mean? These men need to be reprimanded for their racist behavior, or even terminated. I know my councilman. He is a good man, and he will not allow this to go unpunished." Mustafa thumbed through his phone list.

"I understand and we are respectful of your concern, but I am afraid these policemen may not let this go. They seemed like men who would seek retaliation, and you know they are in a position to make our lives hell here in America. We want to be able to complete our education in peace. Surely you understand?"

Mustafa turned to Sajid. "If these rogue policemen are allowed to treat us this way and get away with it, they will only do it again," Mustafa said.

"I know and I am sorry, but I would ask you to allow me this. I am concerned for Karim as well as myself." Sajid glanced at Karim. "He did not handle this well. He is easily upset as you may know and is quite worried about our future. We need to be able to complete our education and return to our homeland without having to watch behind us wherever we go. Please consider this. Do not give them further reason to pursue us, or even worse. Please? Allow us this?"

Holding the telephone handset, Mustafa looked at Karim, then back at Sajid, contemplating his request.

# Chapter 18

*Brad Evans's Home*
*Hubbard County*
*Tuesday Evening*

Brad checked the clock. He was ready earlier than he'd planned and had some time to kill before leaving for his meeting with Garrison. He picked up the bundle of mail from the kitchen counter and browsed through it, tossing the junk mail into the trash and considering the same for the bills.

He grabbed the remote and turned on the small television that sat on the kitchen counter. The local news was on and a graphic of a semi-automatic pistol was on the screen next to the headshot of the anchor.

"This morning, the body of a young white male was spotted near a retaining wall on the west side of Interstate 65. Metro Police stated the young man was shot through the back of the head with a single small caliber bullet."

A video of a Metro police officer came on the screen showing him with his finger behind the small hole in the rear of the victim's Pittsburgh Steelers cap.

*No. That was one of those gangster caps.*

"Detectives determined the nineteen year-old was a locally notorious graffiti artist known as Spart. A photo of the young man filled the TV screen. "His real name was Shawn Parsons," the anchor said, "and he lived in the Melrose area off Franklin Road."

"Shit," Brad said. "You stupid son of a bitch. What were you doing there?"

A video started with a graphic at the bottom of the screen identifying the young woman speaking as Detective Cris Vega.

"Gang taggers normally paint in one color," she said. "It's the message or the marking of territory for them. The graffiti artists are focused on the colorful art itself and making their specialized artwork known to as many people as possible."

The anchor spoke again. "No suspects have been identified, but Metro Police are working to determine the origin of the shot and detectives are reviewing video recordings with Tennessee Department of Transportation to determine if the state's elevated traffic cameras may have picked up related activity in the area last night."

"Surely not," Brad said, "not from that distance and in the dark?"

"Metro Police have asked that anyone with information related to this incident contact Crimestoppers at 615-74-CRIME or 615-742-7463.

"Damn it," Brad said as he punched the power button on the remote. "That son of a bitch was still defacing public property and breaking the law," he rationalized. "Damn varmint." Brad snatched his keys off the counter and headed for the truck.

Brad drove to the lodge without a memory of the trip. His mind was dominated by last night's blunder. At the entrance, he saw Prater, now working the gate alone.

"I'm here to see Carl Garrison."

"I know. Step out of the truck." Prater stared at Brad as he moved away from the truck and stood in the place where he had waited earlier in the day. "Do you have any weapons on board?"

"No. Well, there's a forty cal in the glove box. I thought you meant long guns."

Prater looked at Brad with a disgusted look.

Brad watched as his truck was searched once again. Prater pulled the seat back forward, but Brad had cleaned the long guns after the competition and left them at home.

Prater turned to face Brad without speaking and dropped his clipboard. Brad raised his arms, stared at his Sig-Sauer which was now shoved inside Prater's belt.

"You know where to go?" Prater asked when he finished the pat down.

"Yeah." Brad climbed back into the truck.

"You can pick the Sig up on your way out."

Brad gave Prater a nod then drove toward the old house. He parked in one of the many empty spaces outside the entrance and found his way to the door of Garrison's office.

"Come in. Come in, Brad." Garrison came toward Brad from behind his massive desk and offered his hand.

"Thank you."

"Can I get you a drink?"

"Do you have Jack Daniel's?"

Garrison laughed. "I'd sooner run out of food."

Brad laughed.

"On the rocks?"

"Yes, thanks."

Garrison prepared their social lubricants and handed one to Brad.

"So, did you enjoy our community gathering today?"

"Yes. Thank you for having me."

"It appears you left quite an impression on our marksmen today."

"I tried not to ruin my welcome."

"You're quite a shot. You don't have to apologize for your talents."

"Thank you. I can use the prize money."

"Arnie seems to think highly of you."

"Arnie's a stand up guy. We've known each other a long time, but we lost touch and this morning we were able to renew our friendship."

"That's great to hear. We love Arnie and Sheila. They play a large role on our team here." Garrison paused a moment. "That's something I wanted to speak to you about, Brad. I think there is a place for you on our team, and I'd like to think you might be interested."

"What kind of place are we talking about?"

"Well, as you could see for yourself today. We believe strongly in our God-given rights as well as those promised us by our country's founding fathers. The Second Amendment to our Constitution provides us with the right to protect ourselves and our families. With this many weapons in use by one group of folks, we're always in need of the services of a quality gunsmith, sometimes on short notice. Arnie tells me you are one of the best."

"Oh, I don't know about that. I know my way around weapons. I've always been partial to guns, ever since my Dad started taking me hunting when I was three."

"Three?"

"Yeah, I was carrying a slingshot then. I shot my first squirrel from his lap with a .22 caliber rifle when I was five."

Garrison chuckled.

"He used to take me out to the walnut trees and tell me which hanging walnut to shoot with my .22 rifle."

"Sounds tough for an adult, much less a child," Garrison said.

"It was good target practice, but it got even harder as I got older. When I was ten he had me shooting squirrels, but only in the eye and *he* got to pick which eye. That's with a scope, of course."

Garrison laughed. "No wonder your skills are what they are. I wish all our dads showed that kind of interest in their youngsters."

"He was quite a role model for me in a lot of ways."

"It sounds like it. You were in the military?"

"Yes, Army. Sniper. Two tours in Vietnam."

"Ahh, that's where the talent comes from."

"In reality no, my Dad should get the credit. I had the talent when

I enlisted. It was just a logical assignment once they saw me on the range."

"We are in such need of good father role models today. Do you have children?"

Brad explained his situation, Julie's death and the Latino charged with vehicular homicide.

"I am so sorry, Brad. Is this alien paying for his crime?"

"No, not yet. His trial date hasn't come up yet."

"Do you feel confident he'll be convicted?"

"That will depend upon his lawyer and our so-called legal system. And no, those two variables offer me little confidence."

"And what about the fact he's so obviously guilty?"

"There's no guarantee he'll even show up at the trial. All he's got to do is go home."

"You mean he's running free?"

"Yeah, his public defender got him released since it was his first offense, supposedly."

Garrison shook his head. "Brad, if I could assure you this murderer will receive his just reward, what would you say to that?"

"I'd like to be sure that could happen, but I don't know how to do that."

"That shooter of the graffiti artist on the Interstate last night knew how."

Brad sat quietly. After a moment, he looked at Garrison. "Yeah, but he may have been impetuous," Brad said, taking a drink.

"Oh?"

"The news reported tonight the tagger wasn't a gang banger. He was only a young punk out to deface public property."

"Well, when you start to break the laws of the land, you have to prepare yourself for the consequences."

Brad shrugged and looked at his drink.

"Brad, I know how to make sure your wife's killer meets his justice. If you want, I can help you see that this alien pays for his sins. Are you interested?"

Brad hesitated with his response. He stared at Garrison and thought about how much he loved Julie. He could feel his adrenaline rise.

"Maybe," Brad said, unsure of Garrison's motives.

"Okay," Garrison said. "I'll get back with you on that subject."

Brad drained his glass. This much gunsmith business could set him up for life, but Brad knew that wasn't all Garrison had in mind.

Garrison stood and took Brad's glass to the bar for a refill. "Let's talk about another subject. What do you know about C-4?"

Brad was taken aback by the question. He wondered where this topic was going to lead. "I used it a little in Vietnam. I know it's safe as long as it's in the right hands. I also know pound for pound it's as potent an explosive as you can find—assuming you can find it."

"Well, I *had* a source," Garrison said. "But, it seems his supply has dried up. This has caused my plans to stall."

"Plans?" Brad repeated, wondering why Garrison could possibly want C-4.

"I have a project."

Brad listened, suspicious.

Garrison took a slow drink. "I have a family of beavers who have decided to dam up my creek. Nothing else has worked, and I'm ready to get serious." He smiled.

"Sounds like it." Brad was convinced this was a lie. "So, you're looking for a new source?"

"Yes, a quick and discreet one. I don't want to stir up any trouble with the law."

"I have a friend. He's good at acquiring—things, but he isn't cheap."

"Where is he?"

"Kentucky," Brad said.

"Can we trust him?"

"*I* do. He's a good man. I was in Vietnam with him. How much are we talking about?"

"Not much," Garrison said. "Maybe a pound?"

"A pound?"

"I'd like to get enough in case their brethren rebuild and I have to evict them again."

"Oh. I'll ask him."

Garrison handed Brad his refill.

"I appreciate your help with this, Brad."

"No problem, Carl. Can I call you Carl?"

"Absolutely," Garrison said. "To friends." Garrison clinked Brad's glass. "Now—let's talk about that Mexican resolution."

# Chapter 19

*Cumberland Plaza*
*Nashville, Tennessee*
*Tuesday Evening*

Moved by the image, he stood erect and motionless. Like a soldier at attention, he stared at the American flag in the photograph. The color guard representing all branches of military service was presenting America's red, white, and blue.

The colorful photos lined the hallways of the Nashville offices of Empire State Commercial Properties. The photos captured the April 17, 2001 dedication ceremony for The Ellis Island Immigration Museum and The Wall of Honor. Overlooking the Statue of Liberty and the New York skyline, The Wall was a unique exhibit paying tribute to America's rich cultural heritage, and celebrating American immigration from its earliest beginnings.

The framed photograph that had Daran's attention not only captured the spectacle of the day, but beyond the colorful celebration in the foreground, standing erect in the distant haze of the New York City skyline, was the haunting grey image of the World Trade Center towers that, in five months, would be no more.

Momentarily ignoring his janitorial duties, he held his chin high and his hand over his heart. Daran again recited his new affirmation aloud: "I pledge allegiance to the flag of the United States of America, and to the republic for which it stands, one nation under God, indivisible, with liberty and justice for all."

His smile, and more so his tears, relayed his newfound patriotic pride. "Liberty and justice for all," Daran repeated. "Now, it includes me too."

He swelled with pride at this morning's joyful ceremony as he was sworn in; one of America's newest citizens. The only way he could have been more proud was if his father and mother had lived to see it. Unfortunately, that wasn't meant to be. Saddam Hussein and his maniacal sons saw to that in March of 1988 when they annihilated thousands of Kurds with mustard gas in the northern Iraqi village of Halabjah. Eighteen at the time, Daran and his younger sister Zena were visiting his mother's family in Mosul.

"Daran," Tomar shouted, but Daran had already turned the volume back up on his iPod. "Daran."

"Sorry, what?" He jerked the ear bud from his ear.

"Are you going to finish with the trash?" Tomar asked, as he dusted desktops.

Daran's cousins were happy for him and even a bit jealous of his American citizenship, but not so anxious to carry his workload while he daydreamed. "If we are going to keep our jobs and celebrate later tonight, we will have to finish cleaning these offices. Okay?"

"Sure. Sorry. I saw the flag there and—well," he shrugged his shoulders, "I remembered this morning," Daran said, apologizing.

"We know you are excited." Hoshyar smiled. "Your mind is not on our work. Why not go ahead and run your errands. Tomar and I can finish here."

"I could not leave you two to do all the work," Daran said.

"It is not a problem. We can take care of it. You stop at the market and pick up the items on the list, then go by the restaurant and pick up the food. You did order the food this morning?"

"Yes, cousin. I stopped at Mustafa's and ordered the food before I left for the ceremony. I was running late, but it was done. I told him I would get the food later this evening."

"Good." Hoshyar said, as he removed his latex gloves and reached for his wallet. "Here is thirty dollars to help pay for the food. We will meet you at your apartment at eight o'clock, okay? Now, be on your way."

"Are you sure you do not mind?" Daran asked.

Hoshyar smiled and nodded. "We are sure."

Daran began to walk away and then turned back. "Thank you, cousins."

"Go," Hoshyar and Tomar shouted in unison and then smiled.

Daran laughed and waved as he left. He knew he was fortunate to have his family here in Nashville now. Over the last eight years, he helped nine members of his family to leave Kurdistan and come to Tennessee. Daran was the first to become an American citizen.

Known for its enterprising people and their southern hospitality, Nashville opened its arms and welcomed the Kurds much like it had the industrious Hispanic community. The Kurds, like the Hispanics, were determined to earn their way, working hard and contributing to the thriving Middle Tennessee economy. Many of them, like Daran and his cousins, worked more than one job and had already set their sights on starting their own business someday.

As Daran waited for the garage elevator to arrive at level six, he reached over to his iPod armband and rotated the selector to his favorite tune: James Brown singing "Living in America." He loved to listen with the volume loud. When the elevator doors opened, Daran stepped out singing a duet with the *hardest working man in show business.*

As he exited the artificial freshness of the recently cleaned elevator, the cool evening breeze took Daran's concentration from the music. The gentle mist of rain dampened his face as it drifted through the open-air garage. Daran paused and smiled to himself as he closed his eyes and took in a deep breath of Nashville springtime. The pesto focaccia from the bakery across the street stirred his hunger and made him even more anxious for the evening's celebration to begin. He was thrilled to be an American enjoying America.

As he strolled the ashen concrete structure to his car, Daran recalled the caves he and his cousins explored as children. Carefree days of the late 1970s in the mountains of Kurdistan soon gave way to the angst brought about by the tyrannical Baathist regime. Killing many of his countrymen and driving thousands more away, they ravaged his homeland. So many good people lost so much, or died trying to save it.

Daran's attention returned to the present and he smiled as he spotted his joy: his 1995 Desert Mist Acura Legend. It was four months since he made the largest purchase of his life. He worked all the overtime he could until he had saved enough for the down payment. The car had 98,000 miles, but Daran crowed, "For an Acura, it is only broken-in."

Daran's smile was dissolved by the scratch on the car's rear bumper and his memory of this morning's collision outside Mustafa's. But, he was not about to let that ruin his celebration.

Daran sidestepped between his car and the Yukon Denali parked along side. He unlocked and opened his door, watchful not to let it touch the shining SUV.

His head was bobbing to the blaring music when the long razor-sharp blade connected with his lower back and passed through his right kidney into his liver. Daran's wide-eyed gasp was followed immediately by an attempt to scream away the intense pain. Nothing came out; his shriek muffled by his attacker's hand.

As he was shoved from behind into the tight space, his car's open door slammed into the SUV. Daran's body recoiled from the searing torment, but his response did nothing to alleviate his suffering. Pushing against the roof of his car, Daran fought to resist, face his attacker and defend himself, but his efforts were futile. He felt his body weakening from the unbearable burning inside him.

The throbbing pain in Daran's lower back pulsed in time with his heartbeat and redoubled as his attacker withdrew the blade, multiplying the internal damage. Again he cried out, but the muted sound from his effort was little more than a muffled groan.

There was hardly enough time for him to form the thoughts in his mind. *Why? Somebody, help me!* An abrupt force jerked his head backward, compelling him to gape upward. Daran's pleading eyes bulged, in search of a savior, but saw only the dull expanse of the garage's cement ceiling illuminated by its harsh florescent light.

As the attacker's blade opened his throat, blood erupted from his neck and promptly beaded as it spurted across the freshly waxed roof of his car. The slash caused Daran more pain than any language could describe, but description was pointless. This anguish was to be fleeting.

Daran grabbed at his throat with both hands. It was no use. Awareness was leaving him; life ending.

Daran's attacker pushed down his head and shoved him across the front seat of his car. His blood painted the taupe leather interior as the attacker wrestled Daran's wallet from the rear pants pocket of his uniform. Daran battled without success to capture one more useless gasp and refuse death.

Beneath his head in the passenger seat laid his family's congratulatory gift, soaking in the life that was leaving him. It was the tri-folded Stars and Stripes—now his death pillow.

# Chapter 20

*Mike Neal's Home*
*Nashville, Tennessee*
*Tuesday Evening*

The soothing sound of Jack Daniel's Whiskey cascading over ice, and the plans for a peaceful Italian dinner at Norm's house, were both shattered by the irritating tones from his cell phone. He looked at the phone's display and recognized the incoming number.

"Mike Neal."

"Mike," Sergeant McKnight said, "you've got a customer."

"Where?"

"Cumberland Plaza, in the parking garage, level six."

"What happened?"

"Not sure. The killer used a knife. They said it's a bloody mess. No suspects spotted on site. The first officer has the area secured, and they're waiting on you guys."

"Have you contacted Norm?"

"Not yet."

"I'll call him myself en route." Mike glanced at his watch: 18:38. "ETA for me is gonna be about ten minutes."

"I'll tell them you're on your way."

"Thanks."

Mike flipped his cell phone closed, glanced at the sweating glass holding tonight's refreshing Tennessee tranquilizer and said, "Later, Jack."

He tightened his tie without buttoning his collar, re-belted his .40 caliber Glock and his detective's shield. He grabbed his tweed blazer and swatted at the light switch as he pulled the door closed behind him.

The less than two-mile jaunt from Mike's Green Hills duplex to downtown at this hour was a fast trip. The sixteen pulsating lights and blaring siren on his black Crown Vic Interceptor provided him an even quicker path over the wet pavement of 21st Avenue.

Mike pushed the number two on his cell phone and held it down.

"Detective Wallace."

"Norm."

"Hey, Mike."

"I hope you weren't planning on a fun-filled dinner with your wife and your partner."

"What now?" Norm could hear the siren over the phone.

"We have a deceased citizen."

"You're kidding?"

"I wish," Mike mumbled. "I was so looking forward to Cheryl's lasagna."

Norm looked at the bathroom clock. "It's almost 18:45. What's the twenty?"

"The parking garage, Cumberland Plaza, level six."

"Six? Isn't that the roof?"

"Not quite. I think it may be the last level before the roof."

"Okay—No, honey. It's Mike. Okay. Cheryl says Hi. You got any details yet?"

"Not much. The desk sergeant said it was a 10-51."

"Mike, listen. I just stepped out of the shower. There's no way around it; I'm gonna be a few minutes."

"No problem, buddy. You have a lot of real estate to dry off. I'm almost on the scene now. Kiss her for me and try to make it a quickie, okay?"

"Mike."

"Tell Cheryl I'm sorry about dinner and the blind date. See you in a few ... Honey." Mike made a kissing sound, smiled and snapped his cell phone closed before Norm could respond.

Mike's first years with Homicide had been made much more bearable, thanks to his partner. Norm and Mike got along well, and their performance was proof that they made a superior investigative team.

As he came up behind Cumberland Plaza, Mike turned off his lights and siren. He yielded to his habit of checking the building's outer perimeter so he could feel confident the first officer had secured the crime scene. Fortunately, he found no access point which wasn't marked with a police tape, sawhorse barrier or an officer and his patrol car.

Mike showed his shield to the officer at the ground level entrance, and drove into the parking garage. He wound his way up the concrete spiral, and as he reached the fifth level and the crime scene tape, he could see the EMS team had already arrived. He hoped valuable evidence had not been compromised in their attempt to assist the victim, who according to the first officer's communication was already deceased.

After parking his car, Mike opened the trunk and removed his clipboard with the graph paper pad. He snatched a couple of nitrile gloves and Tyvek shoe covers from the box and shut the trunk. His personal recorder and digital camera were his crime scene weapons of choice and were always in his sport jacket pockets.

Mike walked the ramp the rest of the way to Level Six. There, he found a young patrol officer, no doubt recent ex-military, whose uniform was so sharp it looked like he had just put it on. He was standing with an EMT near the elevators, waiting to brief the investigator in charge.

"Mike Neal, Homicide. Are you the first officer?"

"Yes, sir. Greg Curtis."

Mike glanced beyond the young officer as he spoke and spotted Steve Hill who Mike knew well, and who he guessed was the crime scene supervisor. Sergeant Hill smiled and nodded at him. Mike took this to mean he was allowing the young officer to gain some crime scene experience. Mike was willing to allow this as long as all procedures were followed to the letter. Training was necessary, but not at the expense of Mike's crime scene or the victim's justice.

"What's the status, Curtis?" Mike tucked the clipboard under his arm and pulled on his shoe covers and gloves. He was pleased to see the young officer was already wearing his. Mike began his notes as the young man led him toward the victim's car.

"Sir, it appears the victim was stabbed in the lower back and his throat was cut. There may be other wounds. I can't be sure. There's a lot of blood inside the car. I checked for a pulse as soon as I arrived, but there was none. It appeared he had already bled out."

Curtis stood back as Mike began to move. The young officer watched the detective's every step, never touching the car. Mike surveyed the inside of the car from multiple angles. He retrieved his digital recorder and began his soft-spoken personal monologue.

Whenever possible, Mike liked to give the immediate crime scene a quick review before the Crime Scene Unit arrived. Looking intently, he noted what he could see of the victim's facial features, his hair, and clothing. Mike made verbal notes of the faded burgundy polo shirt with an American flag pin, the calluses and the cut across the man's right hand and the severed white cord dangling from the left ear bud still resting in the victim's ear.

Round globules of blood in a variety of sizes dotted the top of the car. Some of the blood had collected and run down the rain trough until it reached the rear window. Then, traveling down the side of the car, it had formed a small puddle on the pavement next to the left rear tire.

The majority of the victim's blood appeared to be pooled on the passenger side carpet and in the front passenger seat. Blood spatter, pulled downward along vertical surfaces by gravity, was scattered throughout the front compartment of the car.

Mike speculated and pieced together what he thought might have taken place to create this horrific scene. Realizing the officer was monitoring his movements, Mike asked, "Did you have on your gloves?"

Curtis wasn't sure if he was speaking to him or into his recorder until Mike glanced up.

"When you checked for the pulse."

"Oh, yes sir. I put my personal protective equipment on as soon as I arrived, and I was careful not to touch anything except the victim's temporal pulse. Well, to be honest sir, I did have to touch the bottom of the power door lock on the driver's door in order to be able to get to the victim's head from the passenger side. I barely touched the lock," Curtis said. "I was also careful not to step in the blood there on the driver side."

"I'm glad you're being observant. Can I assume you've called in the plate?"

"Yes, sir. Right before you got here. The car is registered to a ..." Curtis checked his pad, "Daran Hamid, thirty-three years old. The address is an apartment on the south side of town."

"Now, let's go back to the beginning. Tell me about when you arrived." Mike's attention was split between his notes and the young officer's recall.

Looking again at his note pad, Curtis began, "I arrived at 18:24. I saw no movement in the area."

Mike listened as Curtis recounted each of his efforts since his arrival on the scene.

"Have you seen any other activity in the area?"

"No, sir. Only EMS, the other officers and then you."

"Has anyone other than you and me been near the victim's car?"

"Only EMS since I've been on site. He verified there was no pulse. The maintenance supervisor said he went over to the victim's car, but when he saw all the blood he became nauseated and backed away. That's when he made the 911 call."

Mike looked at the young man with pride. "Sounds like you've done a pretty good job so far."

"Thank you, sir."

"You know, you don't have to keep calling me sir."

"Yes, sir. Uh—okay, Detective."

Mike smiled. "I need you to make certain we don't compromise the crime scene by allowing anyone in here that isn't necessary to the investigation. You may have heard I'm a bit of a stickler for procedures."

"I've heard comments."

"I'll bet you have, and likely more than just comments." Mike smiled, realizing the officer was trying hard to impress him. "If you have any questions, see me immediately." Mike gave him his card. "Be watching for the Crime Scene Unit and Detective Wallace. Do you know Norm?"

"No sir, but I know he's your partner."

"That's right. He's a big guy." Mike held his hands out and up as though he was describing Bigfoot, "He'll have on a tie, but it will be loose around his neck. You can't miss him. He's bigger than everyone else. Let me know as soon as he arrives, and remember, no one else gets inside the first perimeter except the crime scene techs."

"Yes, sir."

"Thanks, Curtis. We'll talk again after Norm gets here."

Half expecting the boyish cop to salute him, Mike turned and walked toward his car trying not to smile. He wanted to ask Curtis how long he'd been on the force, but he had a pretty good idea he was in his first year.

Glad to have found very little to criticize about him, Mike wished for a way to capture and preserve the young officer's zeal.

# Chapter 21

*Hillcrest Apartments*
*Nashville, Tennessee*
*Tuesday Evening*

Abdul pushed in the key Sajid had mailed him and unlocked the deadbolt. He stepped into the apartment far enough to shut the door behind him. He was immediately disgusted by the smell of decayed food and the muddle the young men had chosen to live in.

He stared out the filthy front window as he waited for their return. He was becoming more and more infuriated by what he saw around him in the apartment. The young students were allowing themselves to become lazy. The apartment was a wreck. He could not bring himself to even sit on the furniture for he knew his suit cost more than the entire contents of this apartment.

Cigarette butts overflowed the ashtrays. Trash was everywhere, and the sink was full of food-covered dishes.

He stood at the window contemplating and awaiting the students' arrival.

*These immature boys may not be ready for the mammoth task facing them. I should have come sooner; I should have assumed they would need my guidance. Farid cannot know of this. This chaos would not bode well for my reputation. This must be corrected.*

He checked the time and realized he would have to leave now in order to find the city of LaVergne and The World Spice Company.

*Allah, guide me.*

He slammed the apartment door behind him and locked it.

# Chapter 22

*Cumberland Plaza*
*Nashville, Tennessee*
*Tuesday Evening*

"When the photographer and the Crime Scene Unit are finished, we'll need a few of your officers to walk the scene," Mike told Sergeant Hill. "Until then, I want you to have some of your men hit the streets to canvass businesses and any citizens within a three block perimeter. Talk to anyone who's been in the area today from about 1500 until now. We have very little to go on so far. Get us names and numbers and let them know either Norm or I will get back with them very soon. As you know, ask the officers to look for any video equipment that could have recorded anything of value."

"No problem," Hill said. "I've also got two officers documenting all these vehicles on level six, and I'll get with the print techs when they arrive and get them in the loop. What do you want me to tell the people who are waiting on these cars?"

"Let them know to stay in the lobby and we will release their cars as soon as we can get them cleared."

"Okay."

"Also," Mike said, "we need to assign a few officers to canvas the building and search for anyone who may be here with the victim's employer or anyone who might know the victim. We suspect his name is Daran Hamid, thirty-three years old. According to the building's maintenance supervisor, the victim worked for a janitorial company that cleans some of the offices here. Check with the maintenance guy; he may know which of the offices the victim's employer was contracted to clean. You might also call the janitorial company's office; they may have an emergency number since it's after business hours. See if they can tell you where the victim was supposed to be working tonight."

"I'll take care of it," Hill said.

Mike walked back to the victim's car and continued gathering evidence.

Carol Spencer was rolling her suitcase-sized bag of photographic gear up onto the sixth level when she saw the flashes. She scanned the area and spotted Mike leaning over the front windshield of the victim's car. She approached him from behind.

"Are you trying to insult me in front of all these officers?" Carol asked.

"What?" Mike shoved both hands into his jacket pockets. He prepared himself for what he knew was the impending storm. "I didn't say anything."

"You don't have to *say* anything, Detective."

"Oooo—kay." Mike knew that tone. "What did I do?"

"That." She nodded toward his jacket pocket.

"What that?" Mike turned the palms of his hands upward, knowing well she was referring to his digital camera, but trying his best to play dumb.

"In your *pocket.*" She shook her head, disgusted.

He looked down, and began to pat his jacket pockets. Then he stopped. "Oh—that."

"Yeah. *That.*"

"I've uh, always used it. I told you before."

"Yes, I know. And, you don't need to use it," Carol assured him.

"It's, uh—a habit. I need it."

"No, you don't."

"Well, yeah I do."

"No, you don't."

"No, Carol. I really do."

"Why?"

"I have to do some of my own shots, okay?"

"No, you don't. You could tell me when you want something, and I'll shoot it for you. It's why I'm here. It's my job. I'm good. I'm a pro. I actually get *paid* for this."

"It's not the same," Mike said.

"No, you are right there, Detective," Carol said, placing her fist on her hip. "My shots are a hell of a lot better than you're going to get from that $9.95 toy."

"More than likely. And by the way, I paid a lot more than $9.95. Thank you." Mike attempted to inject the most miniscule bit of humor.

"My shots are in a different league." Carol held up her weapon of choice like it was an assault rifle. "This Nikon D2X Digital SLR won't even be available to the public until sometime next year. Between camera and lenses, there's over twenty-five thousand dollars of quality in that case." Her tone of confidence elevated as she spoke. "I have a total of seven years photography training and experience. The D.A.'s office expects the best. With me—they get it. And, by the way, so do you—no extra charge."

"Okay. Okay. You're right." Mike held up a hand. "Yours would definitely be better."

Carol's speech pattern had convinced him he was chalking up a loss.

"Don't start patronizing me, detective."

"Shhhhit. I can't win." Mike knew the game was on.

"Detective, you definitely need more training." She stepped closer to him.

"I'm sure that's what half the section says behind my back," Mike said, almost joking.

"I don't mean *that*, and you know damn well they don't mean it either. You're an excellent detective, Michael. That's not the issue. Some of them are upset because you've progressed faster than they did. Your six years with CID doesn't mean shit to them. Those guys go by 'street years'."

"Yeah? Most of my *street years* were spent in the streets of Basrah, Duhok, Mosul and later in Mogadishu. We were doing the same investigations and making the same arrests in those non-English speaking hell-holes that these guys were doing back here in the so-called civilized world. But, they should know—the guns-to-suspects ratio is a bit higher there. *Everybody's* carrying, and their favorite target is American camo. Personally, I'll take Music City. It offers a much longer life expectancy."

"I don't blame you," Carol said, attempting to bring down his elevated tone. "But, I still think you need another kind of training," Carol whispered using a sensual tone.

"Yeah? What kind is that?" Mike calmed his voice.

"You need my kind of training," Carol said confidently, reeling him in. Lately, she seized any opportunity to try and elevate their relationship.

"Photography?" Mike said, with a look that confirmed he knew better.

"No, smart ass. You know what I'm talking about."

"Remind me."

"Think about it, Detective Neal. You know you need a more regular dose of my training sessions."

"Oh. Yeah. You bet I do," Mike said with a sneer. "Hang on. Let me get that cleared with Moretti and I'll get right back to you."

"You're incurable," Carol said.

"Absolutely. And by the way," Mike knew he was about to end Carol's attempt to get to him. He nodded in the direction of the uniforms on level five. “Don't tell Wendy down there that I’m taking my own photos.”

“Why is that?”

“I also do my own sketches before the techs arrive and if she suspected, it might piss her off.”

“You’re worried about what *she* thinks? But you can stand there in front of me snapping shots with that–that Brownie Instamatic without concern?”

“I didn’t mean for you to see that. I didn’t know you were here yet.”

“You don't trust us, do you?”

“That's not it. That is absolutely not the point.”

“It appears that way.”

“Well, it's not,” Mike raised his voice.

“Shhh,” Carol said wrinkling her brow and looking over Mike’s shoulder at the officers.

He took a huge breath and looked at the floor. Carol could tell he was no longer in the game. He looked up with a different face.

Straining to get it out, he hesitated then said slowly, “I’m concerned we’ll miss something.”

Carol nodded her understanding and allowed Mike to talk.

“I’m afraid we’ll miss some small piece of trace evidence, and it will end up costing us the case. I can’t ...” Mike stopped and tightened his lips.

Watching the battle with his emotions swell, Carol knew his motivation. She cared too much to let him continue. She placed her hand on his arm.

“I know–like Connie’s case.”

Mike glanced up at her. He swallowed hard, then nodded slightly.

“Yeah–Yeah.” He looked at Carol with tight lips, and then he spoke. “Sorry, if I hurt your feelings by using my camera. I can’t help it. The odds are against us, and I have to do all I can to win.” Mike looked at the floor. “I don’t need another damn cold case.”

“I didn’t mean to beat you up,” Carol said. She wanted to wrap her arms around him, but it wasn't possible—witnesses and Moretti's Law.

"Okay," Mike said as he reached into his pocket for his recorder. "Enough mutual persecution. We need to get finished before the crime scene truck get here."

Carol smiled and said, "We'll talk later, okay?"

"Sure."

Mike shook off the emotional discussion as he approached the officers gathered near the barrier next to the elevator.

"All right, everyone listen up." He waited for their attention. "Right now, I want everybody to remain outside the first perimeter on the fifth level until further notice. We're going to be shooting the crime scene, and I don't want any of your smiling faces in these shots. Understand? I'll let you know when we're finished."

Some of the officers had only viewed Mike and his work from a distance, and they saw him as arrogant and hard to please. His confidence and scrupulous ways were quite often misread as cocky. But, those who had worked with him, witnessed his focus and the quality of his work, knew otherwise. His and Norm's success rate was the best in the Homicide Unit and had been for almost a year.

Mike walked back down the ramp toward his car intending to hang up his jacket. There he was, strolling up the ramp. The smirk on his face told Mike that Detective Jack Hogue didn't care if he was violating orders from the lead investigator or even that he could be jeopardizing evidence. He was pissing off the lieutenant's fair-haired boy, and enjoying it.

Ever since Mike and Norm solved their first case in late 2000, Hogue acted like the new team was stealing his and partner Gil Murdock's thunder. Mike's CID experience, his professionalism and his by-the-book dedication made him a high caliber investigator. Hogue's brusque old-school ways didn't always harmonize with Captain Moretti's expectations. Mike's scrupulous methods presented the image the Captain wanted for the detectives of the MNPD. Hogue didn't speak the language.

Mike and Norm had encountered Hogue, his partner Murdock, and their shared aversion on too many occasions. These guys made no effort to hide it. Norm wanted to speak to Moretti about it, but Mike thought it best to ignore them and hope they would grow tired of their competitive behavior. Obviously, even with Murdock's retirement, that goal had not yet been achieved.

"What are you doing?" Mike growled. "You're not supposed to be up here. I asked everyone to remain outside the first perimeter. You *know* the procedures."

"You didn't mean me," Hogue touched his chest with both hands, "I'm here to help you, kiddo. I can be your partner." He looked around the garage. "Hell, somebody needs to be."

"First of all, I meant especially you, and secondly, I don't need your help. Norm's on his way. Hell, you're not even on duty tonight."

Hogue offered a crooked smile.

Mike could tell the aging detective had been drinking long before the stench of his breath arrived. "Step over here, we need to talk." Mike took him by the arm and even though he resisted, Mike was able to direct him behind one of the garage's large pillars and away from anyone's line of sight.

"Watch it, Neal. You're getting me riled." Hogue snatched his arm as Mike released his grasp.

"Listen, Hogue, you've been dogging me ever since I came to Homicide, and I'm fed up with it. Mouthing off around our guys is one thing, but risking the destruction of my crime scene evidence will not be tolerated."

"I know what I'm doin'," he slurred. "I'm not risking anything."

"Sure. You're too smashed to *know* what you're doing. In addition to risking the evidence, with the media here, you're risking your job and your pension. Besides, you need to understand. I'm not competing with you. The way this city is growing, unfortunately there's more than enough crime for all of us. I'm here to do my job and do it to the best of my ability. And I'm going to do that, whatever it takes."

"Oh chill out, show-off. It's only another dead Mexican. He probably got hacked by one of his pissed off amigos."

"Hogue, I can't decide what's more repulsive about you: your insensitivity or your bigotry. The man is Middle Eastern. You don't have a clue *who's* responsible for this murder, and so far neither do we."

"Mexican, camel jockey, who gives a damn?"

"Look, the fact that you're determined to get yourself fired is your problem. The issue is, on your fast trip to career hell, you take the department with you, and I'm not going to let that happen. These guys work too hard, and they don't deserve it."

"You'd do well to benefit from my years of experience," Hogue said.

"Hogue, I value a short list of people's opinions. And I assure you, yours didn't make the cut."

"You're just afraid I'll show you up."

"There are reporters and cameramen waiting a few levels down with some very expensive video equipment. They get paid to catch idiots like you on tape so the world can marvel at your pathetic behavior. If you want to trash your career in front of your peers and half of Nashville, I couldn't care less. But, I'm not going to let you soil the image of this department. I'd rather have the good citizens of this city watch me kick your drunken ass all over this parking garage on the Scene at Ten."

Hogue stood there, staring at Mike.

"So, what's it gonna be?" Mike asked.

Jack Hogue was seeing a new side of Detective Neal, and it didn't appear to be one he wanted to challenge, particularly not in his current intoxicated condition.

Mike's nostrils flared as he took slow deep breaths, trying to remain calm. He was not only surprised at himself after his rant, but disappointed as well. This asshole had taken him to the edge, and it was a long time since Mike had lost control. He could feel the bloodflow to his face increasing. He was prepared for an all out show-and-tell so this clown could see all the interesting things Mike learned in the Army. Mike had no intention of doing it with the media watching, but that wasn't the package he was selling Hogue.

"I've got to go," Hogue mumbled as he looked at his watch then turned and walked away.

Mike watched Hogue's back as he battled equilibrium on his way down the ramp. When Mike was sure Hogue was gone, his eyes went back to his work. It took his concentration a little longer.

Out of his peripheral vision, Mike saw his bulky partner climbing the ramp. Norm had to park on the fourth level due to the growing collection of law enforcement and emergency response personnel.

"Glad you could join the party."

"What's that asshole doing here?" Norm said, catching his breath. "Don't we have enough shit going on without that idiot popping up like a zit on prom night?"

"He acts like he's lost without Murdock," Mike said.

"Poor bastard," Norm said tongue-in-cheek. "Okay. What do we know so far?"

Mike brought Norm up to speed on the details. "I'd like you to talk with the two men from facility maintenance and then interview the ladies waiting down in the lobby. Their vehicles need to be the first ones we process so they can go home to their families. They've been waiting the longest. Afterward, you need to question the other car owners so when the print techs are finished with the cars, those folks can go home."

Mike walked to where Sergeant Hill was speaking with some of his men, "Steve, can you have a couple of your guys locate the head of security and check out the camera mounted over the elevator?

"Sure thing, Mike," the sergeant said.

"Detective?"

Mike turned to see Officer James Bowden approaching.

"Sorry to interrupt."

"No problem. What's up?" Mike asked.

"Ms. Spencer asked me to find you. I think she's spotted something."

# Chapter 23

*Hubbard County, Tennessee*
*Brad Evans's Home*
*Tuesday Evening*

Brad learned that not only was Carl Garrison an exceedingly influential man with countless prospective gun-totin' contacts, he appeared to be interested in helping Brad find justice for Julie. Brad felt there could be potential in this unusual relationship.

"Hello."

"Carl?"

"Hello, Brad. Any news yet?"

"Yes. I spoke with my contact in Kentucky. He can get you what you need."

"That's great. When can we get it?"

"He is receiving the delivery tomorrow morning, and he wants us to pick it up as soon afterward as possible. He also told me he has developed the ability to mask explosives and prevent detection by bomb dogs. You may want to talk with him about that, Brad said, in an effort to expose the bogus story about the beaver dam."

"That's interesting." Garrison smiled.

"I didn't realize masking of explosives could be done reliably," Brad said. "I know C4 has a pungent odor that's normally detectable by trained K-9s."

"It sounds like something we need to hear more about," Garrison said. "Who is this guy anyway? You said you met him in Vietnam?"

"Yes, I served with him. He's on a short list of technicians who are willing and able to work fast and without questions or conscience for whoever has the ability to compensate them.

"He sounds like a valuable man to know."

"Yes, and not someone you want working for your opposition."

"I'll be free tomorrow morning after nine. Does that work for you?"

"Sounds good. The drive will take between two and three hours, assuming normal traffic."

"That'll give us a chance to finish that discussion we started yesterday about your skills and some of our needs here at the lodge. I've got some ideas I think you'll like."

"I'll pick you up at your office at nine-thirty," Brad said.

"I'll be ready."

# Chapter 24

*Cumberland Plaza*
*Nashville, Tennessee*
*Tuesday Evening*

Carol was near the roof level of the parking garage when Mike and Officer Bowden approached her. Mike could see the yellow evidence markers she'd placed on the pavement at the edge of the ramp. She lowered her camera. "I thought you might want to see these."

Mike looked inside the ninety-degree angles of the three evidence markers. There were cigarette butts, wet from the misting rain. He squatted for a closer look. Finding a few butts in a parking garage was not front page news, but these cigarettes were different.

As Mike stood, Carol looked up at him, "Are those markings Arabic?"

"Yes." He paused for a moment. "I wish finding Middle Eastern cigarettes today was more unusual than it is." Mike stared at the butts, then looked around the garage. "These could be helpful, Carol. Thanks."

"No problem." Carol smiled.

"You keep those beautiful eyes open," Mike said as he and Officer

Bowden turned and began to walk back toward the victim. He loved the fact that Carol took so much pride in her work.

"Detective," Carol shouted.

"Yeah?" Mike stopped and turned around.

"What did you say?"

Mike thought for a second. "Uh, I don't know." He looked at Bowden. "What did I say?"

Bowden shrugged his shoulders.

Carol wanted to hear it again. Mike had never paid her a compliment in public.

Mike looked back at Officer Bowden, who turned up his palms.

"Oh yeah," he paused. "I said 'You keep those *dutiful* eyes open.'"

Carol squinted.

Mike looked at Bowden and tossed his head toward the crime scene. The two men turned and started back.

"Keep looking, Carol," Mike yelled without glancing back. "You may spot something else." Mike laughed to himself.

"Hey, Mike," Norm yelled as he rounded the corner, "I just spoke with Sergeant Hill and the guy in charge of the—uh ... security cameras. I use the term loosely."

Mike stopped, "That doesn't sound good. What did he say about the one over this elevator? Can he burn us a disk?"

"Well, yes and no," Norm hedged.

"What do you mean, yes and no?"

"He can't get us a disk because they still use VHS tape to record here in the parking garage."

"You've got to be kidding me. Do they know we're now in the twenty-*first* century?"

"They switched to digital video recorders in the office tower, but in the parking garage they kept their VHS recorders to save money. They're on a loop recording process that recycles the cassettes."

"Damn," Mike said, as he bowed his head.

"He said they have never had any issues causing them to need recordings from the garage."

"Well, they sure have one now," Mike said. "VHS quality sucks even when it's not recycled. Nobody's using VHS to record security cams anymore. The images are always unpredictable."

"I guess the camera is worthless," Norm said.

"We could use a break in this case, and I was hoping the camera would be it. So, are we getting the tape, shitty as it is?"

"Yeah, I took it and gave him a receipt. It's bagged and labeled. I'll get it to Dean McMurray and see if he can clean it up enough for us to see anything. I've seen him do some amazing things in the Audio/Video lab with his Mac and video software. Maybe we'll get lucky."

"Do me a favor," Mike said. "Bring the crime scene techs up to speed and tell them Carol is about finished with all the video and photos except the close-ups. They'll be able to start working soon."

Sergeant Hill stepped off the elevator with two young Middle Eastern men. They, like the victim, were dressed in burgundy shirts and black slacks, obviously their employer's uniforms.

The looks on their faces said they were clueless about what was going on and uncomfortable with their current surroundings. Being corralled by a police officer and taken through a sea of emergency responders and their flashing strobes was enough to unnerve anyone.

Sergeant Hill escorted the men to where Mike was standing. "Detective Neal, this is—uh. Your names again please."

"Hoshyar Kaman. This is Tomar, my brother."

"These men work for Z.Z. Maintenance with Mr. Hamid," the sergeant explained, making sure to use the present tense until they were given the tragic news.

"He is our cousin," Hoshyar spoke up. "Our mothers, they were sisters."

"Mr. Kaman, I'm Detective Mike Neal. When did you last see Mr. Hamid?"

"An hour ago?" Hoshyar said looking at Tomar, who nodded in agreement. "He left us early to run some errands before his celebration tonight. He became a U.S. citizen this morning, and we are going to celebrate his good fortune later tonight. Why are you asking these questions?"

Mike paused for a moment. He needed to gather more information before informing them the reason for their celebration was gone.

"Were you with him earlier today? Mike asked.

"Yes," Hoshyar said. "We went to his ceremony and reception this morning downtown at the state capitol building. Then we came home. Tomar and I had lunch, and then we met him here at five o'clock to begin cleaning the offices upstairs. About an hour later is when he left to do the errands. What is the matter? Where is Daran?"

"I'm sorry to have to tell you," Mike said softly, "but we believe your cousin has been killed."

"No," they both said, looking at each other and hoping they were right.

"This cannot be," Hoshyar begged. "We just talked to him upstairs. You must be mistaken."

"You are wrong," Tomar said. "It must be someone else."

Fear gathered in both their faces. Their eyes searched for a reason not to give in to the possibility.

"Does your cousin own a light brown Acura Legend?" Mike asked.

Hoshyar's eyes squinted and began to tear. "Yes, he bought it a few months ago."

"The victim's car is registered to Daran Hamid," Mike said.

"No, no. This is why we left Iraq." Tomar cried, covering his mouth with his hand. "This cannot be happening. Not now. Not here."

"Daran was so happy to finally become an American citizen after eight long years." Hoshyar explained, tears forming in his eyes. "He studied hard and he learned to speak English. Then he taught us. Oh, Daran—Daran."

"What happened?" Tomar asked.

"It appears he was attacked as he was entering his car," Mike said, trying to make it sound less gruesome than it was.

"Why him? Why Daran? He did not have a lot of money." Tomar cried.

"We aren't sure yet. We hope to uncover evidence telling us more about what happened and why," Mike said. "I know how difficult this is," Mike assured the men, meaning every word. This case, like so many others, dredged up Mike's own painful memories.

"Once the Medical Examiner collects the body, we will need someone to identify Mr. Hamid. Do you think one of you could do that for us?"

Hoshyar looked at his brother, and took a deep breath to settle himself. "I will do it."

"Thank you," Mike said. "It will be a big help. Now, gentlemen, if you would, wait here with Sergeant Hill for a moment. I want you to meet Detective Wallace. He will talk with you, and I will join you shortly. We need to ask you a few more questions, and then we'll allow you to return to your family."

Mike raised his hand and indicated for Norm to join them.

"Officer Curtis," Mike shouted across the garage.

The young officer hurried toward Mike. "Yes, detective."

"You did arrange for a meeting room for interviews?"

"Yes sir, the building superintendent has provided us a small conference room. It's past the coffee shop in the rear of the lobby."

"Gentlemen, Detective Wallace will escort you to the conference room. I'll join you shortly."

# Chapter 25

*The World Spice Company*
*LaVergne, Tennessee*
*Tuesday Evening*

After a two hundred and fifty-two mile journey across the western half of Tennessee, the drayage truck delivered ocean container SMNB052778 to World Spice Company's receiving dock at 5:22 p.m..

Ali Patek, the supervisor in charge of receiving and the raw materials warehouse, acquired his instructions from Mahmoud Zahar long before the container's arrival. He scheduled two of his best warehousemen to work overtime in order to see the monthly delivery was verified as accurate and put away in the warehouse. Once all barrels were confirmed against the World Spice Company purchase order, scanned into inventory, and transported to storage, the warehousemen were dismissed.

Patek noted the storage location of the specially tagged barrel when it was put away by his men. Now alone, he drove the clamp-lift to the marked location, pulled the barrel from the rack and transported it to the inbound inspection area. Again he confirmed the assigned markings and broke the seal.

Patek pulled on his respirator and his arm-length rubber gloves. Then he removed the metal ring closure from the barrel's top and raised the lid. Even with the thick inner plastic bag still closed, the pungent aroma of coriander passed through the paper element of Patek's respirator and triggered his sneeze reflex. He stepped away from the barrel, raised his mask, and sneezed three times.

Still sniffling, he repositioned the mask, and returned to his assignment. Patek was told by Mahmoud when the device was packed, the top of the plastic bag would be ten to fifteen inches below the surface of the coriander. Patek knew that rough seas could have caused settling to a lower point in the barrel, and it did. Patek dug through the seeds, removing double-handfuls until he felt the top of the thick plastic bag. After rocking the package back and forth, he was able to raise the bag to the top of the coriander.

He then lifted and placed the package onto a nearby work table. After spraying the bag with a cleaning solution, he wiped it down with towels until it was dry. He secured the device in layers of bubble-wrap, taping the edges of each layer as he went. He placed the padded device into a double corrugated carton and taped it securely, ready for transport to a delivery point, yet to be determined.

Patek removed his cell phone from his belt and dialed the number Mahmoud had given him.

"Yes?" A man's voice answered.

"The package is ready. What is the delivery point?"

"Are you at the spice company?" Abdul asked.

"Yes."

"Have you secured the package for travel?"

"Yes. It is secure; padded and boxed. To where do I bring the package?" Patek was getting frustrated with Abdul's questions.

"To your dock door number five. I am outside." Abdul hung up.

Surprised he would not have to make the delivery, Patek was grateful that the task would soon be over. He placed the package onto a two-wheeled hand truck. Before walking the package to dock number five, he removed his pistol from his pocket, pulled the slide to ready the semi-automatic, and tucked it into the front waistband of his trousers where it would be concealed by his loose-fitting shirt.

Keeping his hand near the pistol, Patek pushed the button to raise the electric overhead door half-way. As the door came up, he could see a black SUV parked near the dock with the rear door opened. A well-dressed man stood holding a briefcase.

"Your security is non-existent," Abdul said in his usual threatening tone.

"There are no longer many pirates seeking to steal spices," Patek said.

Abdul didn't appreciate the man's remark. He scanned the area around the rear of the building once more then placed the briefcase onto the metal dock ramp. He released the latches, raised the lid and rotated the case to face Patek.

"It is all there as agreed with Mahmoud. Give me the box."

"Patience," Patek said as he looked closer at the contents of the case. He fanned four of the stacks of one hundred dollar bills. He closed the case and pulled it back from the edge of the dock. He took the box and set it on the dock where Abdul could reach it.

Abdul wrapped his arms around the carton. He made a wrinkled face, released it and backed away, holding his hands out away from his body as if they were somehow contaminated.

"What is that smell?"

"It is the coriander that your item was packed in for transport from Indonesia."

"This is unacceptable," Abdul said. "I cannot use this if it can be smelled from twenty meters away."

"Relax, the smell is affecting only the outer packaging, not the contents."

"How do you know this?"

Patek sighed. "There are three separate layers of sealed four mil plastic surrounding the device. The smell cannot permeate even the outer layer. The package had to be hidden inside one of the spice barrels for the voyage. The coriander was chosen in case customs became interested and used their dogs to search the shipping container. We have done this before, you know."

Abdul wondered how many times Jemaah Islamiyah had used the monthly spice shipment as their mule, transporting explosives, and who knew what else, into the United States.

At this point, Abdul had few options. Allah's work was waiting. He picked up the pungent box and placed it in the rear of the SUV. He closed the doors and turned to see Patek holding the briefcase in one hand with the other hand tucked under his shirt. The dock door was closing.

Abdul was not in the habit of questioning Farid, but he hoped his mentor's decision to use the engineer would turn out to be a wise one. He walked to the open driver's door, stepped up into the SUV and left with his package.

# Chapter 26

*Cumberland Plaza*
*Nashville, Tennessee*
*Tuesday Evening*

Mike spotted the open door of the conference room. He could see Norm talking with the Kaman brothers inside. He entered and took a seat facing the two young men.

"Where are we?" Mike asked.

"The gentlemen were telling me about Daran's activities earlier today. Mr. Kaman," Norm nodded to Hoshyar, "suggested we also speak with Daran's sister who lived with him in his apartment. You said Zena is her name?"

"Yes, Zena." Hoshyar nodded.

"He said she may be able to add to what they know of Daran's activities in the early part of the day, as well as previously this week."

"Very good," Mike said.

"And, Detectives," Hoshyar interrupted, "if you would allow me to be the one to tell Zena, I would appreciate it and I am sure she would also. Her English is not good and I am afraid she may not handle this well." Hoshyar looked at his brother who nodded his agreement.

"She has depended upon Daran for many things since she arrived here. He is—he was her older brother. Since the death of their parents in Kurdistan, he has taken care of her like a father. She was a child when they were killed, and he has been her parent as well as her brother. I will now have to become more for her." Hoshyar looked at Tomar. "*We* will now be her brothers. It is my place to tell her."

"We understand," Mike said. "That won't be a problem, but we'll need to speak with her tonight as soon as you have told her, and she has had a brief time to grieve. You can go to her when we are finished here, and we'll follow you to the apartment."

"Thank you," Hoshyar said.

"You do understand," Mike said, "we will need to search Mr. Hamid's apartment for evidence that could help us discover who did this?"

"Yes. I will explain to Zena so she understands."

"Good," Mike said. "Now, what can you tell us about Daran that could help us discover what may have happened here tonight and why?"

Hoshyar looked at Tomar and back to Mike. "Daran was a gentle man. He was peaceful, and he knew people like us need to keep our distance from others who may not be so ... welcoming. I do not think very many people recognize what we go through, especially the hate-filled expressions we received after the disasters of September 2001."

"I understand," Mike said.

"It is rare for us to be looked upon with respect by those outside our small community. Occasionally, we still receive the uncomfortable looks. Fortunately, in America there are the police. We have you to help us feel safe, but that does nothing to stop the hate."

"I can't begin to understand the prejudice you face," Mike said. "There is still considerable fear within many Americans when they see people of Middle Eastern heritage. I'm sure this will continue for quite a while. Do you know of anyone who may have been motivated to take their prejudice to this level? Had Daran experienced any confrontations that might have escalated to this?"

"Daran and I spent much time together," Hoshyar said, "especially before Tomar came to America. We have seen many people who were uncomfortable with us, but few who caused us to fear their actions."

"Had Daran been acting strange in any way lately?" Norm asked.

"No, he was very happy," Tomar said. "He was excited about becoming an American citizen."

"Yes," Hoshyar agreed. "He worked so hard to learn everything required of him. He was ready, and he was so proud."

"Had he spoken about any confrontations he may have had with anyone?" Mike asked.

Hoshyar turned to his brother. "I do not know of anything. Do you?"

"No," Tomar said.

"Did he drink alcohol?" Norm asked.

"No. We choose not to drink alcohol," Hoshyar said. "It is actually forbidden for us."

"What about gambling?" Mike asked.

"No. He did not have money to waste."

"Did he owe anyone money?" Mike asked.

"No," Hoshyar said, "he was a simple man with simple tastes. He did not borrow. He did not even have a credit card."

"Who were his friends?" Mike was pretty sure of the answer. Most of the Kurds in Nashville kept to themselves and their families, but he needed to hear it from them.

"We were his friends and his family. There are a few people at Z.Z. Maintenance who are our friends also. Ahmad Ayala, Denise Byrd and Mr. Zaid Zebari."

"Did Daran ever have a problem with any other of Mr. Zebari's employees or maybe a customer?" Norm asked.

"No. Daran was liked by everyone," Tomar said, "especially our customers. He was a good man. He was not a trouble maker."

"Is there a chance Daran could have had a relationship with

someone you two wouldn't know about?" Mike asked.

"I do not think so," Tomar said.

"There is a girl," Hoshyar said as he looked at his brother. "Sarah is her name; Sarah Jennings. She and Daran became good friends, and they spent time together."

"Was this a romantic relationship?" Norm asked.

Hoshyar looked down then back up at Norm. "Daran did not talk to us much about her, but I am sure he talked with Zena."

Mike turned to Norm. "I think it's time we talk with Zena."

# Chapter 27

*Daran Hamid's Apartment*
*Nashville, Tennessee*
*Tuesday Evening*

As they promised Hoshyar, Mike and Norm allowed the cousins almost a half hour to share the dreadful news with Zena, and to allow her to grieve briefly with her family. The detectives knew this was not enough time to absorb the tragic event or to mourn. It wasn't fair. But, they needed to gather all the information they could while it was fresh and while it might still offer them answers to the increasing number of questions which always followed a homicide.

Norm knocked on the apartment door. The light in the peephole went dark for a moment, then two deadbolts retracted. Tomar opened the door and stepped back to allow the detectives to enter.

After nodding their thanks, they walked to the sofa where a young woman dressed in a dark floor length dress with a colorful scarf over her head, sat next to Hoshyar. Another young woman, dressed similarly, sat on her other side. Hoshyar stood.

"Detectives Neal and Wallace, this is my cousin Zena, and this is our neighbor and friend, Lana."

*"Slaaw—Tchoni?"* Mike said, looking at Zena and using most of the Kurdish language he'd learned while in Northern Iraq.

Zena closed her eyes and bowed her head to convey her silent thanks and welcome.

"Please have a seat." Hoshyar pointed to the chairs opposite the sofa.

"What was that about?" Norm whispered as they turned toward their chairs.

"I said hello, and I asked her how she was doing," Mike explained.

"Detective Neal—you are so cosmopolitan."

Mike shook his head, trying not to smile at his partner's jibe.

Mike flipped open his pad and turned to Hoshyar. "Does Zena speak English?"

"Yes, a little. She understands more than she speaks, so I may have to help her with her answers."

"That's fine," Mike said, smiling at Zena.

Zena spoke briefly to Hoshyar, but kept her head bowed.

"Zena asked me to offer you her welcome and apologize for not having food to serve you. She said she can make some tea if you would like some. It is very good."

"Thanks, I ..." Norm began.

"That's not necessary," Mike said, interrupting. "Please thank her for her hospitality. Assure her we understand your family's grief, and we're sorry we have to intrude like this. Can I assume you've discussed with her why we are here?"

"Yes, she understands you need to ask her questions to try and discover what happened and why. I told her you and your people will need to look around the apartment, but will try not to disturb anything. She has few possessions, and she is protective of them."

"Thank you. I understand," Mike said. "We will be careful, but we will need to examine most of what's here in hopes of finding something that will tell us where else to look for answers. We may also need to take some things with us for a short while, but they will be returned safely. I assure you. Is that okay?"

Hoshyar spoke to Zena, and she nodded her head.

"When we're finished with our questions, do you have somewhere for all of you to go so the physical investigation can be completed?"

"Yes. Tomar and I live here in this same building."

"Good." Mike directed his attention to Zena. "We want to thank you for allowing us this intrusion into your home. We are here to try and learn anything that might help us to find Daran's killer. We understand Daran attended the ceremonies downtown this morning to be sworn in as an American citizen. We also know he reported for work at Cumberland Plaza at about five this evening. What can you tell us about his activities before the ceremony and then afterward prior to his reporting for work?"

Hoshyar helped Zena understand the questions and then gave Mike her answers.

"She said Daran left the apartment just after seven this morning. He told her he had errands to run. We came for Zena at eight o'clock, and we know Daran was at the ceremony on time because we waved to him as the group walked in together."

"What were his errands?"

Hoshyar spoke with Zena. "She said the only thing she knew he had to do was go by Mustafa's and order the food for tonight."

"Is that the restaurant on Charlotte Avenue?" Norm asked.

"Yes, Mustafa's," Hoshyar said. "That is where Daran was going when ... ."

Mike nodded so that Hoshyar did not have to finish.

Zena spoke to Hoshyar.

"Zena said Daran was going to pick up Sarah this morning also. That must have been the other errand."

"Do you know about Daran's activities following the ceremony?"

"There was a reception at about ten-thirty for the new citizens and their families. We were all there to support Daran. He was so happy." Hoshyar's voice broke.

Zena brought her tissue to her face and patted the tears from her eyes.

"After the reception the new citizens were taken on a tour of the state capitol and then had a catered lunch with the mayor and the governor in the capitol building. They were allowed to bring one guest each. Daran invited Sarah."

"Zena, let's talk about Sarah," Mike said. "Tell me what you know about her and her relationship with your brother."

Hoshyar made sure Zena understood the request, and she spoke up with what sounded like considerable input.

"Zena said they met by accident at the international market. Daran came home that day and told Zena about how he helped Sarah when she dropped her food and made a big mess at the market."

Zena interrupted Hoshyar with more about Sarah.

"Zena told me she had seldom seen Daran so happy. Daran and Sarah spent as much time as they could talking, sometimes for hours, on the phone. Sarah seemed interested in learning about Kurdistan, Iraq and Daran's life there. She thought it was exciting. Zena said she could never understand what it was that sounded so exciting about Northern Iraq.

"Zena said she believed Sarah was good for Daran. She is convinced Daran was falling in love." Hoshyar looked at Zena. "She said she hoped Sarah was too, for his sake."

"Can you tell me more about what Daran did after the luncheon?" Mike asked.

Hoshyar questioned Zena.

"Zena said Daran returned home at about four-thirty this afternoon. He changed into his work clothes and left soon after. She said that is all she knows, but she suspects Daran spent the day with Sarah after their lunch. They were spending much time together."

"Zena, what do you think about Daran and Sarah? Was this a friendship or a love relationship?" Mike asked.

Zena must have understood Mike's question. She didn't hesitate to offer her answer to Hoshyar.

"She thinks it began as a friendship, but the longer they knew each other the closer they became," Hoshyar said. "Sarah sometimes ate dinner with us at our work in order to spend time with Daran. Sarah told all of us she had suffered through some unsuccessful and painful relationships. I think Daran was determined to see her happy. I do not believe he ever experienced a connection like this with a woman."

Zena grabbed Hoshyar's arm and spoke up.

"Zena said that Daran had never been in love. He was nervous about it."

"I understand," Mike said.

Mike paused and turned to Norm. "Why don't you call the techs and let them know we'll be ready by the time they get here."

Norm stood and stepped outside to make the call.

"I apologize for some of the questions I have to ask." Mike gathered his thoughts. "Like just about all murders where knives are involved, the suspect has to be physically close to the victim in order to complete his task. This type of violence sometimes leads us to believe the killer may have known the victim, or at least been acquainted, and likely had some degree of rage driving their actions. Zena, can you think of anyone who may have felt this level of rage for your brother, for any reason?"

Hoshyar explained and after thinking for a moment, Zena answered. Hoshyar translated.

"She said her brother was a passive man. He became upset occasionally, but the things that troubled Daran were injustices, and usually it was those involving someone else, not himself. He used to watch the news and say, 'How can people treat each other that way?'"

"Detective," Zena spoke slowly and directly to Mike for the first time without Hoshyar translating. Her dark tear-filled eyes looked straight into his. "I cannot imagine anyone with the rage for my brother, or for anyone, that must have been in their heart for them to do this."

After a moment of reflection, Mike said, "Thank you." Standing,

Mike stepped closer and addressed Zena. "Again, we're very sorry for your loss. We appreciate your talking with us and welcoming us into your home. We may have to speak with you again. We will try to disrupt as little as possible during our physical investigation."

Mike looked at Hoshyar and said, "One of the uniformed policemen will escort you all to your apartment and come for you when we're finished."

"Can I speak to you in private?" Hoshyar whispered to Mike.

They walked outside with the others, but when Tomar and the ladies left with the policeman for their apartment, Mike and Hoshyar stayed behind.

"I did not want to bring this up in front of Zena. She knows nothing about it." Hoshyar glanced back to be sure they were not being heard. "Be sure to ask Sarah Jennings about her ex-boyfriend, Jimmy Dan Mullins. This man is dangerous. He used to follow Sarah when she brought us dinner. I remember she once said she wanted to file a restraining order, but feared it would anger him more. Sarah told Daran not long ago, Mullins threatened to do something if she did not stop seeing him."

"When did he make this threat?"

"You will have to ask her."

# Chapter 28

*Dara Hamid's Apartment*
*Nashville, Tennessee*
*Tuesday Evening*

"Norm—what are you doing?" Mike asked as he rounded the corner into the small kitchen.

The big detective jerked the white bag from his face, rolled the top back down and returned it to the refrigerator shelf. "I was looking for evidence."

"Did that smell like evidence?" Mike asked.

"It smelled heavenly. It's baklava."

"I know. You're starved again, right? You can eat something later when we're finished. We've got work to do."

"Ten-four," Norm said. "I'm almost done in here. I haven't spotted anything of interest. Hell, I haven't spotted much of anything at all. They must have meager tastes."

"And a meager budget too, I'm sure. Most of us can't even relate. Why don't you give Wendy a hand in the bedroom? Maybe there's something in his personal papers that can provide us some direction."

"Sure." Norm's gloved right hand fumbled to get his pen from his shirt pocket and make some quick notes. He took six steps to get from the small kitchen-dining combination to the even smaller second bedroom.

"Any luck yet?" Norm asked.

Wendy wrinkled her nose and shook her head. "Not much. Only the basic personal stuff we all have; actually quite a bit less than we have. I've got some things there in that box that might offer some information."

Norm looked in the box at evidence bags containing a pair of off-brand running shoes with mud in the soles, personal items from the bathroom and the dresser top, and a large flat envelope.

"I found this in the top dresser drawer," Wendy said as she picked up the manila envelope. She opened the clasp and pressed the edges until the sides spread apart.

Norm peered inside to see a greeting card with a matching envelope and a flat Hallmark bag. "Is anything written on the card?"

Wendy smiled and nodded. "It must have been for his lady friend."

"Sarah," Norm said.

"He wrote some very nice words; told her how important she was to him. He said she was his 'gift from God'," Wendy quoted. "At the end, he told her he loved her. It sounds to me like it could have been the first time he'd told her. Well—would have been."

Norm blinked. "That's sad."

"It gets worse."

"What do you mean?"

"The receipt in the bag gave the date of purchase as over a month ago."

"Hmm. I guess he's been working on his English," Norm said.

"Maybe—more likely his nerve—and he never got the chance to use it."

Norm looked at his watch. "We gotta get finished here and get back to the CJC."

"Hey, Mike?" Norm took a quick exit from the bedroom and found

Mike, looking through some photos. “Have the officers located Miss Jennings yet?” Norm said.

“Yes, she’ll be waiting on us when we get to the Justice Center. You guys about finished?”

“Yeah.”

“Tell Wendy to wrap it up, and I’ll let the cousins know we’re leaving.”

# Chapter 29

*Criminal Justice Center*
*Nashville, Tennessee*
*Tuesday Late Evening*

Mike and Norm entered the Homicide Unit and spotted an attractive young woman with long blond hair sitting with Officer Tonya McCord. She was holding a steaming coffee cup and a hand full of used tissues.

"Ms. Jennings? My name is Detective Mike Neal. This is Detective Norm Wallace."

"Hi," Sarah said.

"We're sorry to have to drag you down here like this tonight, and we're also very sorry for your loss."

Sarah nodded. "Thank you."

"Tonya, thanks for helping Ms. Jennings, and we appreciate you both waiting for us. We came straight from the Hamid apartment.

"Sarah, would you like for me to stay with you?" Officer McCord said.

"Oh, no. You can go and be with your family. I'm fine. Make sure you kiss that darling little man for me." Sarah handed back the wallet photo of three year old Tyson McCord.

"I'll be glad to," she looked at the photo and then at her watch, "but it may be tomorrow. It's past his bedtime." Officer McCord leaned over and hugged Sarah. "Hang in there, honey. You'll get through this. These guys are two of Nashville's best." She handed Sarah her card. "You call me anytime if you want to talk, okay? Anytime."

"Thanks, Tonya," Sarah said. "You're a doll."

"Don't tell anybody." Tonya winked. "I'll see ya'll later."

"We'll try to make this as brief as possible, Ms. Jennings," Mike said.

"Call me Sarah."

"Thanks, Sarah. How did you and Daran Hamid come to know each other?"

She took a deep breath. "A few months ago, I was shopping at the International Market. I had already paid for my groceries and was on my way to the door when I lost my grip on one of the bags. I had two pretty full bags and my purse. They still use brown paper bags there. The bag hit the floor hard. My large jar of tahini broke and the sesame oil that sits on top went everywhere.

"I sat down my other bag and my purse and tried to gather up the things that weren't broken. I guess I must have stepped in some of the oil and when I reached for a jar of chick peas, I slipped and started to fall. The chick peas went flying and shattered when they hit the floor. I was reaching out behind me, flailing my arms around like a crazy woman trying to catch myself and just as I was doing this windmill act, Daran came into the store. He caught me under both my arms, saved me and stood me up."

She stopped. Her face filled with emotion and she fished through her pocket for another tissue. "I'm sorry."

Norm grabbed a box of tissues from Detective Vega's desk and held it out.

"Thank you."

Norm smiled his compassion as he thought of the Hallmark card.

"Daran was such a gentleman and a gentle man as well." She blew her nose, gathered her emotions and continued.

"He grabbed another grocery bag, dropped to his knees and helped me pick up everything that wasn't damaged or covered in sesame oil and chick peas. I remember laughing while we were picking things up, and saying to him, 'So much for my hummus.' The thick sesame paste oozed from the broken jar and was now slowly chasing the oil across the floor. It was such a mess. As soon as we collected all the usable items, Daran said, 'I'll be right back.'"

"He told me later he'd been a frequent customer of the market for over six years. He asked the manager to replace my damaged items. The manager must have approved and also agreed to clean up the mess I'd made. Daran went around the store collecting replacements for the items I'd broken. He helped me out to the car with my bags and wished me success with my hummus. He was so nice.

"I remember, while he was putting the bags in the car he asked if I had ever tried making hummus with purėed hazelnuts in place of tahini. He said, 'It is awesome.' I laughed at the way he said it, and told him I would give it a try.

"I asked him his name, and I gave him mine. I remember saying, 'maybe I'll see you again, Daran Hamid.' He smiled that beautiful peaceful smile and said 'I hope so, Sarah Jennings.' That gave me a little chill. I knew it meant something."

Sarah sniffled and grabbed more tissues.

"All the next week, I thought about how nice he was and how few men like that I'd met. I decided to call the market and ask the manager when Daran usually came in to do his shopping. He told me and the next time, by coincidence of course," Sarah smiled, "I was there shopping when he came in. I spoke to him and we talked for a while. I guess we never stopped—until today."

Sarah paused to wipe her eyes.

"He was a great friend. I was always comfortable with him, and I always felt safe. I was pretty sure our relationship was about to ... improve."

"Improve?" Mike said.

"Romantically," Sarah again grabbed for more tissues.

"I see," Mike said.

"I fell in love with Daran. I'm pretty sure he was feeling the same." She suddenly laughed through her tears; she held the tissue to her mouth and her whole body shook as she continued to sob. After a moment, she struggled to explain. "Last week we made hazelnut hummus together. It was awesome."

Mike gave her a few moments before he continued his questions.

Norm knew now what he had to do with the Hallmark card once the criminalists were finished getting the sample of Hamid's handwriting.

"Do you know of anyone who may have harbored hostility for Daran?" Mike asked.

"Only one." She didn't stop to think about her answer.

"Who?"

"Jimmy Dan Mullins."

"Who is he, and what makes you say that?" Mike said, acting as if he knew nothing.

"I used to see him before Daran."

"You dated?" Mike asked.

"Yes. Unfortunately."

"Why do you say that?" Norm asked.

"He started out acting like a decent man, but the true Jimmy Dan soon came out."

"What do you mean?" Mike asked.

"When we met, he was 'acting'; acting like someone he wasn't, but I didn't know. He did a pretty good job of it. He was trying to get my attention and he knew in order to do that he would have to become someone else. In reality, he was nothing but another intolerant hate-filled redneck. It took me a while to see through the snow storm."

"What cleared up the picture for you?" Norm asked.

"We were on our way to dinner one night. He said he wanted to stop off at a liquor store and get a bottle of good cheer for after our meal.

He was checking his money as he got out of the car to go in, and when he looked up there were about a half dozen of what I realized were his drunken friends whom I had never met, nor heard about. They were all over him like long lost family. He kept looking back at me in the truck and trying to act like he didn't know them. I rolled down my window enough to hear what they were saying. They were calling him by name and asking if I was the hot piece he had been telling them about. He jerked his head around to see if I was hearing this. That lit my fuse and clarified for me what had been going on with Jimmy Dan's alter ego."

"What happened then?" Norm asked.

"He came back to the truck and needless to say, we did not go to dinner nor did we have any good cheer. I demanded he take me home immediately, and I did not speak another word. I do, however, remember giving him some sign language as I slammed the door on his pickup."

"So, was there a confrontation or a threat between Mullins and Daran?" Mike asked. "Did they meet face-to-face?"

"I don't know of a direct one-on-one confrontation between the two of them. Daran never spoke of one that may have occurred when I wasn't with him.

"Daran worked long hours and the only time we could see each other was during his breaks, so sometimes I picked up dinner and ate with him and his cousins. Jimmy Dan used to follow me, stalking me."

"You saw him?" Mike asked.

"Oh, yes. A few weeks ago, he followed me into a building the guys were cleaning. We had begun to eat when he made this dramatic entrance and ranted that I had no business spending time with a bunch of 'camel jockeys.' I know this had to hurt their feelings. It made me furious. Daran stepped forward and told Jimmy Dan to leave, that he was on private property and was not wanted there. Jimmy Dan told Daran to shut the hell up before he sent him to a place a lot hotter than the big litter box he came from."

Norm looked at Mike. "Sounds like a threat to me."

"Then what happened?" Mike asked.

"Billy, the building security guard, walked in. He stopped everything and escorted Jimmy Dan out of the building. When we finished eating, Billy walked me out. Daran told me the next day Billy also walked out with them when they finished cleaning that night. Daran said they didn't see Jimmy Dan again."

"Did Daran mention Mullins making any other threats after that?" Mike asked.

"Daran never told me if he did," Sarah said. "Yesterday I had to borrow Daran's car because mine was in for service. I was at Hickory Hollow Mall. When I returned to the car, Jimmy Dan grabbed the door before I could get it closed. He scared the hell out of me. I tried to slap him, but he blocked it. I screamed at him to leave me alone. He stood there telling me to hang on, to wait a minute. I stopped screaming at him and told him to say what he came to say and then go away.

"He told me if I didn't stop seeing Daran, *he* would stop it. He said I was embarrassing him. He said I had gone from dating him to seeing a rag-head, and he was not going to tolerate that. He sounded serious to me.

"After that, he slammed the car door and walked away. I was afraid he had damaged the door. Daran was so persnickety about his car. I hated that I had to borrow it. I was scared I would have a wreck or ..." Sarah stopped. "That reminds me. While we were having lunch at the capitol today, Daran told me that he had an accident this morning when he went to Mustafa's to order the food. He said he was leaving the parking lot when a man hit his rear bumper and scratched it."

Mike looked up at Norm who was making a note to check into the accident.

"Did you tell Daran about Mullins' threat?" Mike asked.

"Yes, but he told me not to worry. He told me Jimmy Dan was jealous and just a lot of hot air. I explained I was worried about him and that Jimmy Dan had a lot of ugly friends. I think Daran was concerned himself, but he was trying to prevent me from being scared."

"Do you think Mullins is capable of killing Daran?" Mike asked.
Sarah nodded. "I'm afraid so."

# Chapter 30

*Easy Street Tavern*
*Nashville, Tennessee*
*Tuesday Late Evening*

"You shoulda seen that sucker's face," Jimmy Dan Mullins bragged. "That burrito didn't know what hit him. I bet he didn't even wake up til the next day."

"What was he doin', JD?" Ralph Hemphill asked.

"He was busy tryin' to get up off the asphalt after I saw him swing his door into the side of my truck."

"Did he do it on purpose?" Ralph asked.

"I don't give a damn why he did it. I saw him do it, so I dropped him."

"What the hell did you hit him with, JD?" Bobby Maddox said.

"My damn fist. Look."

"JD, It mighta been an accident," Ralph said.

"Tough shit. He shoulda been more careful," Jimmy Dan said. "Man, my freakin' knuckles are raw. I hope I don't catch no disease."

"JD, if you start orderin' Coronas, I'm outta here." Bobby laughed.

"Now that's funny." Ralph snorted.

"Uh-oh." Bobby's laugh was interrupted.

"What?" Ralph said. His head rotated in both directions.

"Gestapo at my two o'clock," Bobby said.

"Ga-what?" Ralph turned around to see three uniformed MNPD officers talking with the club manager. "What do they want?" Ralph asked.

"Who knows?" Jimmy Dan said, still staring. "Chill out."

Jimmy Dan and Bobby kept their eyes on the cops and continued to empty their longnecks. Ralph couldn't resist looking over his shoulder to see what was happening.

The manager called over the club's bouncer and head bartender. One of them nodded toward the trio and the cops started for their table.

"Oh, shit. Now what?" Bobby said.

"Keep it cool," Jimmy Dan warned them. "Keep it cool."

"Which one of you is Mullins?" the largest officer asked, while the other two took up positions on either side of the big man.

The beer guzzlers looked at each other like they weren't sure who was who. Then Jimmy Dan said, "Well, if ya'll ain't gonna own up to it, I guess it's me."

"Do you have some ID?" the big officer asked.

Jimmy Dan fished out his driver's license.

"We'd like you to come with us," the officer said handing the license back.

"Whoa. What's this about?"

"We were asked to escort you downtown to discuss anything you may know about a crime."

"What crime?" Jimmy Dan asked, puzzled.

"They don't tell us everything," the officer said, stretching the truth.

"Maybe it's a murder," Ralph said, excited by the possibility.

"What murder?" Jimmy Dan asked, thinking this would be a good time for him to be the wrong Mullins.

"You'll find out what the crime was when you get there, I'm sure.

They just want to talk. Can we go now?"

"I'd rather drive my truck," Jimmy Dan said.

"Mr. Mullins, you've been drinking. Based upon what the bartender told us, you may want to accept a ride rather than have us follow and then arrest you for DUI. What do you say? Let's do the smart thing. We can bring you back when you're done. Okay?"

"Jimmy Dan reached for his beer to finish it off, but before he could get it to his mouth, the big cop placed his huge black-gloved hand over the bottle and Mullins's hand and pushed them both back down to the table with a loud bang.

"You won't need that." The officer kept his hand over the mouth of the bottle.

"I paid good money for that beer," Jimmy Dan said, his misguided confidence convincing him his complaint might change the officer's mind.

"And I'm sure your good buddies here will be glad to finish it off for you. Shall we go?"

Jimmy Dan pushed back from the table shaking his head.

"Call Harlan Norris," Jimmy Dan said, as he tossed his keys to Bobby.

"Don't worry JD," Bobby said. "We got your back, man."

# Chapter 31

*Criminal Justice Center*
*Nashville, Tennessee*
*Tuesday Late Evening*

"Which room is Mullins in?" Norm asked.

"Luxury suite number seven," the sergeant said.

Norm pushed open the door to the interview room. This room was furnished with four modest, but comfortable, club chairs positioned facing each other around a low table in a casual setting meant to create a relaxed interview atmosphere. Number seven was normally used when speaking with victim's families. Mike followed Norm in.

"Mr. James Daniel Mullins?" Norm asked.

"That's my name." Mullins kept his seat.

"I'm Detective Norm Wallace and this is Detective Mike Neal. Can we get you a soda?"

"Nope. Got one."

"Good. Mr. Mullins," Mike said, "may I call you Jim?"

"I go by Jimmy Dan or JD."

"Sure. Jimmy Dan. We're investigating a crime and we'd like to ask you some questions to see if you might know anything that could help us. Will that be okay with you?"

"I guess so," Mullins said, knowing it would be in his best interest to cooperate and keep his comments short.

"We appreciate you coming down to talk with us, Jimmy Dan. I'm terrible at trying to take notes and talk at the same time and I can't read Detective Wallace's handwriting," Mike said, reaching into his jacket pocket and starting the digital recorder before he removed it, "so if you don't mind I'd like to record our conversation. That's all right isn't it?" Mike laid the recorder on the table between them.

"I guess so." Jimmy Dan looked at the recorder, and then back at Mike.

"Thanks, Jimmy Dan. I'm told you live out by Percy Priest Lake."

"That's right."

"Are you a sportsman? You hunt and fish?" Mike asked.

"Sometimes. Can we get to the point of all this?"

"Sure, Jimmy Dan." Mike paused for a moment. "Do you know a young lady named Sarah Jennings?"

Mullins hesitated. "Yeah."

"Do you see her socially?" Mike asked.

"Not any more."

"But, you used to?"

"Yeah. Is she is some kind of trouble?"

"No," Mike said, and left it at that.

"What do you know about a man named Daran Hamid?"

"I know he's a camel jockey and he's been seeing Sarah. That's all I want to know. What difference does it make?" Mullins said, unashamed of his bigotry.

"Where were you this evening between four o'clock and seven?"

"What's this about?"

"Just answer the questions," Norm barked with authority.

"I got off work at four o'clock, and I went home." Mullins looked from Mike to Norm and back.

"Where do you work?" Mike asked.

"I work on the dock at Collier Freight Lines."

"Is there anyone who can confirm your whereabouts during that three hour period?" Mike asked.

Mullins shrugged his shoulders and held out his hands palms up. "I don't know. I live alone."

"Did you— "

"Hey. Wait a minute," Mullins interrupted Mike. "I stopped at a market on Old Hickory Boulevard for a twelve-pack. That little blond girl ought to remember me." Mullins pointed his index finger at Mike.

"What time was it when you stopped?" Mike asked.

"I don't know." Mullins glanced up. "I talked to one of the city truck drivers for a while before I left, Bobby something." He thought for a moment. "It may have been four-fifteen, four-thirty?" He shook his head and turned his hands palms up.

"What did you do after stopping at the market?" Mike asked.

"I went home—checked the mail—took a shower and watched some TV. I downed a couple of Buds. Then I got ready to go out with the boys."

"What time was it when you met them?" Mike asked.

"I met 'em—bout ten o'clock. We had a couple of long necks, shot the shit for a while, and that's when your blue soldiers entered the picture."

"The officer who escorted you stated he talked with you and your friends at about eleven fifteen."

Jimmy Dan nodded. "That sounds about right. What's the big deal?"

"Daran Hamid was murdered today."

"What? Murdered?" Mullins processed Mike's statement. "Whoa. What—you think I did it? You gotta be kiddin me."

"He was murdered in a very violent way," Mike said. "His throat was cut and he was stabbed in the back. Do you own a knife, Mr. Mullins?"

"Gimme a break." Mullins leaned back in his chair. "I had nothing to do with it. I haven't seen that freakin' rag-head in weeks."

"Mullins," Norm shouted. "Do you own a knife?"

"Yeah, I own a bunch of knives; dozens of 'em. My granddaddy was a butcher and I've got his old Victorinox and Wilkinson knives. I kill a hog or two every winter. So what?"

"Whoever killed Mr. Hamid demonstrated a significant amount of rage in the method they chose," Mike said. "This normally reflects a degree of passion—anger. We have witnesses stating that you threatened Mr. Hamid on more than one occasion."

"Time freakin' out. Hang on. I did not threaten that asshole."

"You told Sarah Jennings that if she didn't stop seeing Daran Hamid, you would stop it," Mike said.

"That was just ... " Mullins shook his head. "I didn't— "

"And we have three witnesses," Mike interrupted, "that state you told Mr. Hamid," Mike referred to his notes, "he needed to shut up before you sent him to a place a lot hotter than the big litter box he came from."

"Listen, I—"

"Jimmy Dan," Mike held up his hand. "Threats of this nature are considered particularly serious by the District Attorney. I suggest—"

The door to the interview room flew open. Brash attorney Harlan Norris, in his typically dramatic manner, exploded into the room.

"Good evening, gentlemen," he said in a loud voice intentionally interrupting any conversation that might be taking place.

Jimmy Dan chuckled at Norris's bold manner.

"Detective, is my client under arrest?"

"No. We're just having a friendly discussion."

"Did you Mirandize Mr. Mullins?"

"There was no point. He's not in custody," Mike said. "Like I said, we were just talking; it's non-custodial."

"Friendly or not, the discussion is over," Norris declared. He extended his arm toward Jimmy Dan and said, "Mr. Mullins."

Mullins stood, smiled and walked to the door.

Once his client was outside the interview room, Norris raised his index finger briefly between his face and Mike Neal's like a professor quieting his class. Then, in a discreet, almost whispered, speech he said, "Detective, just because a man has a minor history of dislike for foreigners, doesn't mean he's going around killing them. As a responsible American, this young man has every right to be concerned about what illegal intruders are sucking on our government's teats, draining his tax dollars."

Mike strained to hold his tongue, wanting to remind the infamous attorney he was not currently in front of a jury.

"You must understand something, detective. This beautiful and dynamic city, as well as this incredible country of ours, was not founded by, nor built by, Mexicans or Arabs or any other entitled minority. They were forged, formed, and fought for by white men—freedom-loving, God-fearing white men. And if you think we're through fighting for them, you're dead wrong."

Norris's serious expression changed abruptly and he gave Mike a self-satisfied smile. He reached for the doorknob and turned back.

"Thank you for your time, detectives. If you'd like to speak with my client again, you need to plan on calling my office for an appointment." He looked at Mike, then at Norm. "Good evening."

# Chapter 32

*Criminal Justice Center*
*Nashville, Tennessee*
*Wednesday Early Morning*

"With Hamid's wallet missing," Norm said, "his pockets reversed and the contents of the glove box and console all over the carpet, it looks a lot like robbery."

"Or, someone wants us to think so?" Mike said.

"That's a possibility."

"Why the brutality of both the stabbing and the slashing of his throat?" Mike asked. "There had to be some source of rage. I'm not sold on a simple robbery generating this brand of passion."

"Why not?" Norm asked. "There could be rage involved in a robbery more difficult than the ass hole expected. Maybe Hamid fought back—pissed him off."

"Where are all the defensive wounds?" Mike asked. "His right hand showed only a couple of cuts."

"Maybe Hamid didn't have all the money he wanted and the killer got pissed," Norm suggested.

Mike groaned. "I don't know."

"Maybe, he knew the killer," Norm said. "Maybe the killer had to take him out so he couldn't ID him."

"Plausible," Mike said. "Who did Hamid piss off? It had to be recent. He seems to have become pretty comfortable seeing himself as an American. There are folks around who may not have been ready for this much comfort coming from a Middle Eastern man."

"Hate crime?" Norm asked.

"Maybe." Mike considered.

"Based upon the information from Ms. Jennings and Mullins himself, *his* hate seems strong," Norm said. "Having a man, who he considers less than human, with his girl may have been more motive than he could resist. My money is on Mullins."

"He's a definite possibility," Mike said, still not sold.

"Okay," Norm said, "so what are the pieces, so far, pointing in Mullin's direction?"

Mike read from his notes. "He is a known white supremacist. He has shown animosity for minorities, specifically toward the victim. He dated Sarah Jennings who has been seeing the victim for the last few months, so jealousy could be a factor. He threatened to send Hamid to 'a place a lot hotter than the place he came from.'"

"Without a doubt, he's a threat. Don't forget," Norm said, "he was witnessed by law enforcement trespassing at the workplace of the victim, and he had to be escorted from the building."

"And Mullins, as yet, has no solid alibi for the estimated time of death," Mike said.

"That's a lot of pieces," Norm said.

"I understand. But, we've got to have a lot more than this before the D.A. will even take our phone call, much less indict. All of this is great supporting evidence as long as we have something firm for it to support—but we don't. Maybe tomorrow we can get the Captain to push TBI on the prints. The DNA, if there is any, could take those folks forever."

"I still say it's Mullins," Norm said. "He had the means, the opportunity and an abundance of motivation. The evidence shows this was almost certainly a hate crime and Mullins made it clear; he hated Hamid."

"I understand. But, let's not get in too big of a hurry to classify this as a hate crime. We don't need the feds involved in this. This one is ours. Let's solve it."

"You're right," Norm said.

"I feel like there's something here we can't see yet," Mike said. "Nothing is conclusive. I understand the killer leaving behind a scene which appears to indicate a robbery, and it may be Mullins. No problem. But, at this point I'm not ready to stop looking elsewhere until we have something more convincing."

"Gotcha," Norm grunted.

"Hamid didn't smoke and all the ashtrays were pulled out. Why would someone go through the ashtrays? What was he looking for that he thought would be in the ashtrays?"

"Trash?"

"What trash?" Mike asked. "What trash was there in the floor?"

"Candy and gum wrappers. And, there was a receipt from a car wash dated yesterday. They probably came from the ashtrays."

"What could have been placed into an ashtray that would be of interest to someone?"

"Drugs?" Norm asked.

"Maybe."

"Some people keep money in the ashtray."

"Pardon me?"

"You know. Change, for toll roads and stuff."

"Toll roads?" Mike asked.

"Yeah."

"Hey, Milwaukee, where is there a toll road in the state of Tennessee?"

"Okay—for emergencies."

"Maybe, but Hamid barely had two quarters to rub together. If it was a robbery, and the suspect was going to the extent of looking through ashtrays, why didn't he take Hamid's iPod?"

"Right." Norm paused, thinking. "The iPod was still on his arm band. That is odd."

"Odd, only if it was a robbery," Mike added as he looked at his watch. "What do you say we catch a couple of hours of sleep and a shower? I'll pick you up around seven."

"Sure," Norm said. "Maybe the A/V lab can recover something usable off the tape."

Back home, Mike fired up his PC before he climbed into the shower so it would be through with boot up and ready to check email when he came out.

The first email to catch his eye was always Colonel Lee's. Mike didn't miss the CID years in Iraq and Somalia nearly as much as he missed the guys with whom he shared them. Colonel Lee's email was waiting.

*Mike, Hope you're doing well. I'm on my way to catch a flight to Baghdad for a strategy meeting. Sorry, but I've only got a couple of minutes.*

*I had to shout at you and let you know Lieutenant Colonel Vaughn read your email and has agreed to revisit Sinjar. I told you he would listen. It seems your information matches up with some new intelligence he has received from part of his group south of there. He said he dispatched a team a few days ago, but I only found out today.*

*I'll update you when I hear something. Gotta run. Take care. – Tim*

# Chapter 33

*Criminal Justice Center*
*Audio/Video Lab*
*Nashville, Tennessee*
*Wednesday Morning*

Dean McMurray pumped the wheels with his padded fingerless gloves as he rolled down the tiled hallway at top speed. Neither his wheelchair nor the senseless accident that put him in it was able to destroy his outlook or even slow him down.

"Hey, Mike. Norm. What's shakin?"

"Deano," Norm shouted. "How's life in the A/V Lab?"

"Ever changing. Some days when I'm able to uncover the evidence, I get to look like Spielberg to the Captain. Other days—well, I come up empty and I look more like that big fat guy, Michael Moore."

Norm chuckled.

"Take yesterday. Cris Vega calls wanting me to enhance a video taken at midnight by a TDOT cam that's eighty feet in the air and two hundred plus yards from the crime scene. What do you guys think I am anyway, a magician?" Dean laughed. "All I could do was apologize, but I don't think that helped her any."

Mike was amazed at the way Dean was able to maintain such a

great attitude and move on after his accident.

A former Nashville patrol officer, Dean had been a computer geek since high school; learning software and finding new ways to utilize computer technology came to him naturally. His life plan included building a laddered career in law enforcement that included the top rungs spent in a leadership role in Information Technology with the FBI.

All was on schedule until three years ago when, during a citizen assist stop, a drunken motorist slammed into the back of his cruiser. The impact pinned Dean against the rear of the disabled car just as he was attempting to remove the spare for an elderly lady. The crash effectively amputated both legs and severely damaged his pelvis. Following a year and a half of surgeries and extensive therapy, Dean was found unable to be fitted for prosthetics and became confined for life to a wheel chair.

Rather than allowing the tragic turn to destroy his life, Dean analyzed his options and adjusted his goals. He called the Chief of Police and requested a one-on-one meeting. The Chief couldn't say no to him after what he sacrificed in the line of duty.

He shared his original dream and gave the Chief his altered plan.

"I have the full use of my arms and hands as well as my mind," Dean said. "There is no reason I can't continue to make a contribution to the city of Nashville and the police department."

He explained to the Chief he could assist in the A/V Lab and begin work to expand the department's capabilities. The chief considered it and decided it was a unique opportunity for both Dean and the department. They were always backlogged in the labs and frequently limited on qualified technicians. Also, this would be a great opportunity for the MNPD to employ a disabled person. The Chief immediately approved the position, and Dean was back on track.

"Did you get a chance to look at the VHS tape from Cumberland Plaza?" Norm asked.

Dean looked at Norm like he had told a bad joke.

"I'm afraid so. That tape had been re-recorded so many times that all the images—hundreds, I'd guess—look like a horde of ghosts. The tape was so old and thin it was ready to break. I'm surprised it held together long enough for me to make a working copy on a DVD. I'm not sure how much help it'll be, but I'll show you what I was able to capture."

"We could use a miracle, but we're not expecting one," Norm said.

"I appreciate you lowering your expectations for me." Dean grinned. "Okay guys, here's what I've got." Dean began tapping keys and pushing buttons. "The dates and times here in the corner of the screen are only marginally reliable. If it wasn't for Carol Spencer providing me with a digital still taken last night from the perspective of the elevator, I wouldn't have confidence about much of anything on this video."

Dean tucked the enlarged photo under the clip to the left of his large-screen monitor.

"As you can see in Carol's photo, we've got three open parking spaces here on the left, then the white Chevy Impala, and the dark blue Denali on the near side of the victim's Acura. Across the drive there's a silver Camry, the red Mustang and these two, whatever they are."

"This dark car is a Buick La Sabre, if I remember right. It's in our notes," Norm said, pointing. "And this one is a Honda Pilot."

"Thanks Norm," Dean said. "Once all the cars are in place on the video, you will be able to make out only a small part of the rear bumper of the Acura protruding behind the SUV, so key on the positions of the white Impala, the red Mustang over here and the SUV. The Denali is the last one to arrive. Okay?"

"Got it," Mike said.

"I'm going to start the video here in the a.m. with level six empty."

"It's not empty. There's an Explorer right there." Norm touched the screen as Dean started the video, and the car disappeared. He jerked his hand back as if he'd made the car vanish.

"Like I said, there are a lot of ghost images due to the number of re-recordings."

"I can tell this is going to be crazy," Norm said.

"Give it a chance," Mike said.

"I believe this image to be yesterday morning based upon its position on the tape at the time I received it. Tell me what you think." Dean started the video.

"Wow, I think it sucks," Norm said. "How are we supposed to determine anything reliable, the way the images keep jumping? And, what are all the fuzzy lines all over the place? Hell, they're moving too."

"Yeah." Dean laughed. "Try to look past the quality, or lack of it, and key on watching for the cars in Carol's photo. It's going to be the only way we can feel any confidence that we have the right images. The blurry lines you asked about are spider webs across the camera lens moving in the breeze. I don't get the impression this building's maintenance team is all that concerned about security or the maintenance of their equipment."

"How can we tell which image is from which date?" Mike asked.

"We can't be certain. Sorry," Dean apologized. "There are too many ghost images of the dates and times overlaying each other."

"Then what good is it?" Norm asked.

"Be patient, detective," Dean said.

"You can forget that, Dean. He doesn't know how," Mike said, smiling at Norm.

"What if all these people park in the same exact spaces everyday? Then how are we going to know the image is from yesterday?" Norm asked.

Dean looked up at him. "If they do, then I'd say this is a futile exercise and we're screwed. But, let's try not to be that pessimistic."

"Let's assume that's not the case," Mike said, with a look that asked Norm to cool it.

"Thanks. I came in at 0500 this morning, and I've viewed this tape now for over three hours in order to cull out what I'm showing you. I did not see all of these vehicles in place and matching Carol's photo except during the section I'm leading up to now.

"Here's the empty garage yesterday morning. Now the people are arriving for work. See the shadows? The camera over the elevator faces south, so the sun's rising to our left on the other side of the garage. The shadows will be our only confirmation of the time of day."

"Camry," Dean pointed at the monitor. "Impala—Buick—Pilot."

"Hey, the Pilot and Buick are in the wrong spots," Norm said.

"Maybe this is where they parked in the morning," Mike suggested, looking down at Dean for verification. "I'll bet they're in the positions in Carol's photo after they return from lunch."

"Good thinking, detective." Dean looked up, smiling at Mike.

"I'm guessing these cars must belong to the hourly folks since most of them arrived within a few minutes of each other. The Mustang and Denali arrive later."

Dean increased the speed of the video and the shadows moved more quickly.

"There is the red Mustang now. Okay, it's after lunch and all the vehicles are in the same places as in Carol's photo except the SUV, and the victim's car. I'm going to increase the speed a little. Watch the shadows lengthen."

"We know the victim didn't arrive until around seventeen-hundred," Mike said.

"You'll see the Acura arrives first in the video," Dean said. "There he is. Poor guy."

As Daran Hamid walked under the camera, Dean stopped the video.

"That's him," Mike said.

The three men stared at the monitor in silence, as if to pay homage. Daran was smiling and listening to his iPod, the bright white ear buds contrasted against the dark complexion of his ears. He looked to be enjoying his new citizenship, and sadly unaware of what would face him in the next hour.

Dean restarted the recording. After a time, he slowed the playback.

Within seconds, Norm spoke up, "Denali." The big man leaned over Dean's back for a better look as the large dark vehicle passed across the screen and pulled into the space blocking almost all of the Acura from view."

An attractive blonde in a dark business suit exited the SUV carrying a black briefcase. As she walked toward the elevator, she held her keyless remote over her shoulder and pressed the button to lock the Denali. The lights flashed.

"Shit, Norm said. "She had to park that big bastard there."

Dean allowed the video to run for a few moments, then stopped it and turned to the detectives.

"I'm not sure how valuable this is. I've tried to clean it up, but beyond some tweaking, there isn't a lot I can do with it."

"I'm sure you've done your best, Dean," Mike said.

Norm slapped Dean on the back. "Let's do this."

"I'm going to run it forward to the point just before the victim gets off the elevator, then I'll cut it to half-speed. After Hamid walks from under the camera and toward his car, keep an eye here in front of the SUV," Dean pointed, "and then between it and the Chevy. Watch for a dark image that moves around the near side then behind the SUV, toward the Acura. He's real hard to see until he comes around the back of the Denali."

Daran walked into the image from the bottom of Dean's monitor screen, stopped briefly, and then he started toward his car.

The detectives watched as he fished his keys from his pocket as he walked. He moved behind the SUV, then turned and went out of sight on the other side.

"There he is," Norm said, as the hooded image moved to the rear of the Denali and then disappeared. "Was that it? I thought you said he—"

"Hang on," Dean interrupted. "When I ran it this morning, the image was jumpy. I had to record this part eight times to even get this much of an image. This is part of what you get with recycled VHS.

Sorry."

"It's not your fault, Dean. It's just frustrating for us," Norm said.

"It is for me too. On one of the passes this morning I saw something you'll want to see. I patched it here. There were two frames of it, but I captured them." Dean continued to work the keyboard as he spoke. "It's just as he comes from behind the SUV; his right hand swings out away from his side a few inches. There. That's it."

"Freeze it," Norm said.

"I did."

"Print it."

"I did, Norm."

"Where is it?" Norm said.

"It's printing." Mike shook his head. "Chill out."

"Geez. You're right, Mike. For a detective, the man has no patience."

"Yeah, bite me," Norm said, attempting to defend himself from the dual criticism.

Dean laughed.

The whirr of the color printer produced an upside down sheet while they waited. Dean pulled the paper from the tray, turned it over and handed it to Mike.

The long curved silhouette of the knife was visible as it hung by the killer's right leg before he vanished behind the SUV and used it.

"We have to see the lieutenant," Mike said. "We need the fingerprints back, now."

"Wait," Dean said. "We still haven't seen the disc from The Bakery across the street. Sergeant Hill said there was something on it. An officer delivered it a few minutes before you came in."

"I forgot all about it," Norm said.

"Give me a minute," Dean said, "and I'll have it on the screen."

Mike focused on the dark printed image. He estimated the killer's height at 5' 8", maybe 5' 9" with a medium build and about one hundred and seventy pounds. The oversized black hoody cloaked his key features and would easily disguise any blood spatter that may have caused him to be noticed when he left the building.

"Okay, I'm ready to run this DVD."

Dean tapped a few keys and then dramatically popped the enter key to finish.

"This camera is obviously suspended over the front counter facing the customer entrance. The clock says it's—1804 yesterday."

"That's good. Run it," Norm said. "At least this one is clear."

"This is copied from a digital video recording. The quality is better than the VHS technology."

Dean ran the recording and they watched the parking garage exit in the distance, visible through the window above the reversed word Bakery. No cars came out. Unexpectedly, a man dressed in all black came strolling from the first floor garage entrance as the clock showed 18:11.

"Is that him? Slow it down," Norm said. "The son of a bitch is walking? That's balls."

They all watched as the killer reached the sidewalk and stopped.

"What's he stopping for?" Norm asked.

"Who knows," Mike said.

Just then, the man looked directly at The Bakery.

"Freeze it," Norm shouted.

Dean stopped the video, but the hood pulled low over the killer's head kept his face dark; too dark to make out any features.

"He must have smelled the bread," Dean suggested.

"I lower my window every time I drive by the place," Norm said. "Clear that up some so we can see his face."

"I can't," Dean said.

"You can't?" Norm asked. "Isn't this a digital image?"

"Yeah, but this image was shot through a storefront window with a mass-produced off the shelf camera at about three hundred and fifty to four hundred lines of resolution. It's not meant to produce the kind of clarity we need at over eighty yards away."

"Well, shit," Norm said, defeated.

"That's about what it is if you're looking for clarity at this distance." Dean started the video.

The killer turned away from the camera, looked up and brushed the hood back off his head.

"Dark hair. Same build," Norm said. "Mullins."

"Maybe. Too far away to tell," Mike said.

With his hands back inside the hoodie's front pocket, the killer walked up the sidewalk and away from the camera. The man's image grew smaller on the monitor as he strolled up the hill and away from The Bakery's camera.

The video reminded Mike of how many similar suspects over the years had committed murder so easily, even violent murder like this, and simply walked away. He thought of one monster in particular and the toll that murder's actions had taken on his life.

Dean's desk phone buzzed.

"A/V Lab."

"It's for you," Dean said, offering Mike the handset.

"Mike Neal." Mike listened. "Good. Thanks, Sarge." Mike turned to Norm. "We've got our warrant."

# Chapter 34

*Vacant Parking Lot*
*Nashville, Tennessee*
*Wednesday Morning*

Cris was convinced something was wrong with Jack Hogue. He couldn't contain his passing thoughts. He was always mumbling incoherently, salted with an occasional brief outburst. Cris wondered if he might be suffering from some form of Tourette's syndrome. His attitude, as well as the quality of his thinking, had been in the toilet since Gil Murdock's retirement—now this.

Hogue's forehead rested against the passenger side glass of the unmarked cruiser as he and Cris Vega sat in the lot next to The Daily Donut Shop. Cris was reviewing reports and Hogue was staring at a beautiful young woman in tight jeans and a low-cut top as she bent over and climbed from a bright yellow Corvette. Hogue couldn't take his eyes off her. It was as if he was unaware of his surroundings. His judgment of her appearance flowed from his tactless lips.

"A woman like that could make a man harder than Chinese arithmetic," Hogue blurted.

"Hogue," Cris said. "You are such a class act. With romantic lines like that, I bet you get all the girls, huh?"

"Shove it, burrito." Hogue had to make some kind of derogatory reference to her Latino heritage.

"Wow, more stimulating conversation. I bet your college major was International Relations. *College* Hogue, you know the place you went for one semester so you could confirm that you're a dumb ass redneck who should have paid attention in high school."

Hogue gritted his teeth and pulled one of his fifty-cent cigars from his jacket pocket.

"Do *not* light that," Cris warned him.

Hogue unwrapped the cheap stogie and crammed it into his mouth to dampen the outer leaf and slow the burn. He fished his see-through plastic lighter from his pants pocket and proudly fired up the cigar, sucking out volumes of smoke and exhaling them toward Cris in the driver's seat.

Cris threw open her door and scrambled out of the car, coughing. Backing away from the smoke now floating out the door, she yelled, "Your contrary old ass is going down, Hogue. Burris told you no more cigars while you're on duty. I know he warned you. He told me he did."

Hogue opened the passenger door and climbed out. He walked around the front of the car toward Cris all the while puffing excessively. She backed away as he came closer blowing the smoke in her direction. Hogue headed for the driver's seat.

Cris used her hands to shield her nose from the smoke. "You're not driving, Hogue."

He fell into the driver's seat.

"Get out of the car," Cris yelled.

"Get in, enchilada. Let's go."

"I'm not riding with your drunk ass. I've put up with you for the last six weeks. That's all I got. This is it. Burris is gonna have to do something about you. I'm done with it. Hell, I'll go back in uniform before I'll take any more of your shit."

Staring at Cris, he pulled the cigar from his mouth and spat a piece of tobacco in her direction.

"Are you done?" Hogue asked.

"Screw you, Hog," Cris yelled.

He crammed the stogie back into his gritted teeth, cranked the engine and yanked the gearshift into drive. Both doors slammed shut as he punched the accelerator, and gravel flew from beneath the rear tires.

Cris turned her back and doubled over to keep the rocks from hitting her face.

"You son of a bitch." She pulled her cell phone from her pocket, and held down the number three.

"Burris."

"I need a ride."

"Cris? What's the matter? Where are you?"

"I'm in a parking lot next to The Daily Donut on Murfreesboro Road."

"Where's Hogue?"

"He left in the cruiser."

"And you're not with him because ... ?"

"I'm not riding with a stinking, drunken bigot."

"Two of those traits I already know about. He's drunk too?"

"Yes."

"Did you see him drinking?"

"I didn't need to. My nose still works. He's been popping peppermints for the last two days, but they don't cover the smell. It looks like he's got him a new bad habit."

"Where did he go?" Burris asked.

"I don't have a clue, and I don't give a shit. He tore out of this parking lot and sprayed me with gravel. Lieutenant, I cannot continue working with this asshole. I can't, okay? You gotta help me. This jerk has hit the wall. He's done. Trust me."

"Patience, Detective."

"Yeah. You said that before, several times if I remember. Well, I tried. This is getting old, and *I'm* out of patience. Put me with somebody else or transfer me. I can't work like this, and no one else can either. I can't believe you put me with this racist bastard."

Burris paused. "We thought if he spent more time around someone of color, he would realize there was nothing to be prejudiced about."

"Oh, so I was the guinea pig in your social experiment?"

"No, you were available, and he was without a partner. We hoped he could be saved. He partnered for over twelve years with another equally bigoted detective. They were a fairly good investigative team for most of those years. When Gil Murdock retired this year, Hogue was—well, he was like he'd lost his way. You know, we were trying to do the right thing for a long-term employee."

"Okay, I admire your sensitivity, but I won't continue in this role as his adversary. We're supposed to be partners. The right thing would be for Hogue to follow in his old partner's footsteps and go fishing."

"Maybe. I'll talk to Moretti. You sit tight, and I'll get a car to you in a couple of minutes. Hey, Cris?"

"Yeah?"

"Sorry."

"Forget it. Just get me a new partner, preferably a non-smoker who understands diversity and maybe someone who occasionally bathes?"

"Copy that."

# Chapter 35

*Eastern Davidson County*
*Nashville, Tennessee*
*Wednesday Morning*

"Isn't this near where we investigated that domestic last summer?" Mike asked. "You remember, the one where the woman got pissed off and drove over her equally drunken husband on the lawn with a John Deere tractor mower?"

"Yeah, I remember," Norm said. "She was still smashed when we got there, and he was—well, he was all over the place."

Norm drove for another half mile.

"Here it is, thirty fifteen," Mike said.

The rusty mailbox was mounted atop a piece of weathered driftwood. The zero digit was missing from the address and the mailbox door, attached only by a single small rusty bolt, was swinging in the breeze below the box. Norm turned from the pavement onto the gravel-and-weed driveway that dropped about twelve feet at a steep angle down to a small bridge. The bridge was made from four inch steel pipes and welded onto a frame of steel channels. As they drove over the structure, the gaps between the pipes shook the car like a carnival ride. Norm's reflexes caused him to hit his brakes. When he did, the officers in the patrol car behind them almost struck his bumper.

"Careful," Mike said. "Mullins must have cows or horses running in this pasture. Keep a look-out for them."

"How do you know that?" Norm asked.

"Well, Milwaukee, that was a stock gap you crossed. It's there to keep livestock from getting out of this fenced area and still allow vehicles to come and go without having to stop and open a gate."

"Well, aren't you Farmer Brown?" Norm kidded.

"No, but I did ask a lot of questions as I was growing up, and I paid attention to most of the answers. My uncle had a small dairy farm outside Murfreesboro."

"Is that Mullins, there on the porch?" Norm said.

"Looks like him. Pull over there, off the gravel drive. Richter and Scott can park behind us."

Mike and Norm opened their car doors at the same time, and the stench of cow manure rushed them like a SWAT team. Norm fell back in his seat.

"Damn." He coughed. "I need a respirator—and hazardous duty pay."

"Come on, partner," Mike said. "You're a detective. You've been around bullshit for years."

"I don't remember it taking my breath away quite like this." Norm coughed again.

The uniforms joined Mike for the walk to the house. Norm paused to pull the evidence kit from the trunk then followed the others through the rickety gate.

"What now?" Jimmy Dan shouted with contempt.

Mike held up the warrant. "Mr. Mullins, this is a search warrant granting us the right to search your property this morning."

"For what?"

"For evidence that might connect you to, or clear you of, the Daran Hamid murder at Cumberland Plaza yesterday evening."

"I told you last night, I didn't kill that rag-head son of a bitch. Besides, this is private property, detective. I have a right to my privacy and a right to keep people off my property. It's in the constitution, I do believe."

"Mr. Mullins, we're not here to debate the Fourth Amendment," Mike said. "We'll have to leave that for the lawyers. This warrant is signed by a Davidson County judge granting us access to your property for the purpose of searching for evidence in a homicide investigation. It's perfectly legal. I assure you. You can ask your attorney, Mr. Norris."

"I intend to." Jimmy Dan unclipped his cell phone. "I assure you," he said, mocking the detective. He scrolled to Harlan Norris's number, placed the phone to his ear and turned away from the detectives.

"Harlan, what the hell is goin' on? These damn detectives are down here at my house with some kinda freakin' search warrant. They're obviously wantin' to go through all my shit lookin' for some way to blame me for that camel jockey's murder. Harlan, you gotta fix this."

Jimmy Dan listened. His eyes closed and then his lips curled in.

"Yeah, that's easy for you to say. They ain't tryin' to blame you with murder."

He listened. "This *is* calm, damn it. You need to get on the phone to somebody downtown and get these people off my property, now. Are you forgettin' about somethin, Harlan? We don't need this intrusion."

Jimmy Dan was losing this battle and he knew it.

"Do what? You gotta be kiddin' me. But, I ain't *done* nothing, and I damn sure ain't been *convicted* of nothin."

It was obvious Harlan Norris was doing his best to explain why Jimmy Dan had no recourse to the warrant.

"This is bullshit, Harlan. I'm callin' Reverend Carl."

Jimmy Dan snapped his phone closed. "I ain't believin' this shit. He says you can do whatever you damn well please, and I can't do nothin' to stop you. This is America?"

"Red, white, and blue," Norm said with a smile.

"Hell, it sounds more like Russia to me."

"Let's go," Mike said over his shoulder to the others. He walked up to Jimmy Dan and slapped the warrant against his chest. Jimmy Dan caught it to keep it from falling to the ground. He started scrolling for another number.

As they crossed the front porch and entered the house, Mike gave out assignments. He pulled on his gloves and began his share of the search in the living room.

Norm stepped into the kitchen, snapped tight his XXL nitrile gloves and turned on all the lights. He scanned the room left to right before entering and his eyes caught sight of a large butcher-block knife rack next to the sink. He stepped closer to the rack and counted fifteen mis-matched wooden knife handles protruding from the deep wooden block.

"Mike."

"Yeah?"

"You might want to see this."

"What have you got?" Mike said, as he came through the doorway to the kitchen.

Norm pointed to the rack.

"Whoa." Mike came closer. "That's quite a collection of cutlery Jimmy Dan has there."

"I'd say so," said Norm. "I guess these are the knives he was talking about last night."

Mike inspected the block then pulled up one of the larger handles until it exposed the long curved blade. He looked at Norm. Both men smiled. Mike released the knife and it fell back into the wooden rack with a pop.

"Bag them all in one large bag and label it. Make sure the knives stay inside the block until the lab gets them."

"Gotcha," Norm said.

"Check the drawers. He may have more in his collection."

"Detective Neal," Officer Scott shouted from what sounded like far away.

"Yeah," Mike returned the shout, trying to determine its origin.

"You need to see this."

"Be right there," Mike said. "Where are you?"

"Down here, in the basement," Scott said.

Mike opened doors until he found a set of stairs. Scott was standing at the bottom.

"What is it?" Mike asked, as he started down the steps.

"I'm not sure. I was searching the basement," he pointed to his right, "and found nothing suspicious, only a bunch of worthless junk. I continued my search around the room and still saw nothing of concern until I went to leave. I turned off the ceiling lights with the switch here on the wall. I glanced back into the basement and saw this."

He turned the ceiling lights off. Along the floor under the workbench was a thin strip of light about three feet long.

Scott turned the basement lights back on and looked at Mike.

Mike examined the area under the bench along the strip of light, and then he asked Scott to turn the lights off again.

"Back on," Mike said. He walked to the workbench, and squatted to inspect the area beneath it.

Standing, he grabbed the front edge of the workbench and pulled. Nothing. He stood back, looked the bench over, grabbed it and shook it. Tools rattled, but nothing moved. Squatting again, he crawled under it. He took out his tactical flashlight and shined it around underneath the bench. He saw that casters had been counter-sunk and mounted behind the bottoms of each of the workbench legs barely elevating the legs off the floor.

He searched the underside of the bench, where in the front corner, he found a black button mounted to the wood. Mike pushed the button. The whirring sound of an electric motor started. The tools rattled as the workbench and pegboard began to move forward. Mike crawled quickly from beneath the workbench and watched as the right end of the bench swung out and continued to come toward him until it made a stop at a ninety degree angle to the wall behind it.

“What the hell?” Scott said.

There, behind where the wooden workbench and pegboard had been, was a black reinforced steel door with an electronic keypad lock and a five spoke handle.

# Chapter 36

*White Tail Lodge*
*Hubbard County, Tennessee*
*Wednesday Morning*

"Morning," Brad said as he knocked on the wooden door frame and stepped into Carl Garrison's office.

"Hello, Brad. How are you?" Garrison asked.

"Doing well, thanks."

"Can you give me a hand with this?" Garrison reached behind his desk and retrieved a long flat case.

"Sure. What do you want to do with it?" Brad took the case from Garrison.

"Look it over first. Tell me what you think."

"What do you mean?" Brad asked.

"Open it." Garrison pointed toward the table.

Brad laid the case on the mahogany conference table, flipped the three latches and raised the lid.

"Wow." He stared at the contents.

"I take it by your reaction that you recognize it."

Brad laughed. "Yes, like I would recognize a old friend," he said, admiring the weapon. "It's an XM21 with a 3X-9X Adjustable Ranging Telescope. It's very similar to the one I used in Vietnam in '69, except this one has a polymer stock." Brad rapped on the weapon's stock with his knuckle. "This one will weigh a lot less than my hardwood stock did." He said as he lifted the rifle from the foam. "Oh, yeah; at least three, maybe four, pounds less. The one I carried got heavy climbing those damn trees. With optics, it weighed over twelve pounds. This one would have been nice."

"It's a beautiful rifle," Garrison said.

"That it is." Brad raised the weapon's stock to his shoulder, placed his right eye at the rear lens and aimed it out Garrison's window. "It served us well in the years we relied on it. Where did you get it?"

"Oh, you're not the only one with connections. I also have some friends in accommodating places."

"I'll bet you do." Brad smiled as he returned the rifle to the padded case.

"Well, when we get back," Garrison said, "you can add it to your collection. It's yours."

"What?"

"You deserve it, Brad. You gave the best years of your young life to our country. Accept this as a thank you gift."

"I—don't know what to say," Brad said, glancing at the rifle.

"No comment required, my friend. Just enjoy it, but do me a favor? Don't use this one on the squirrels."

Brad chuckled. "Yeah, a 7.62 NATO round would leave a little larger hole than my twenty-two."

"Are you ready to go to Kentucky?" Garrison asked.

"Sure." Brad closed the case and latched the lid. He stuck out his hand. "Thanks, Carl. This is a very nice gift."

"I'm glad you like it." Garrison smiled.

As they climbed into Brad's truck and readied themselves for the trip, Brad couldn't help but wonder why Garrison would present him with such a gift so soon after they met.

Brad had known rich and powerful men before. They all had at least one thing in common: they expected something from everyone. Brad was anxious to discover what it was Carl Garrison wanted from him.

They had been driving for almost an hour when Garrison closed the book he was reading and laid it in the seat.

"Brad, I want to thank you again for your willingness to get involved and show support for our efforts. I can't begin to tell you how valuable you have been already. I don't know if meeting each other yesterday was fate or just good fortune for me. But, I do know some of our current initiatives might have had to be abandoned without your help. You're a good man and I assure you, your service will be rewarded generously."

"You're welcome, Carl."

"As I told you earlier, we at TARPA honor your past service to America and hope to provide you a few avenues where you can stay in practice and continue to serve your country."

Following a period of silence, Brad's curiosity peaked. "What were you thinking I could help with?"

"As we started to discuss last night, there are somewhere between eight and ten thousand weapons within our membership. These range from small caliber revolvers many of the women carry in their purses—or somewhere on their bodies," Garrison looked at Brad and smiled, "up to more powerful weapons such as H&K MP5s, M4s, M16s, and even a handful of fifty caliber rifles owned by our former military men.

"One member I know has a five-acre target range that looks like something the state police would construct. On a regular basis, he and about a dozen others get together at his farm and shoot their small arms as well as an old M2, a couple of M60s and some Barrett rifles. One of them even has an M134 Gatlin gun."

"Damn, that could get expensive," Brad said. "The ammo for some of those weapons, even in bulk, is between a buck and five per round."

"Believe me, they can afford the ammo. Three of those men are lawyers, one is a veterinarian and two others are partners in a successful construction company."

"I would say they can afford it." Brad nodded.

"Our men love their guns," Garrison said. "But, of our three thousand plus members who are gun owners, I'd say there are no more than a third of them who know how to properly disassemble, clean and care for their weapons.

"If we're going to be ready for the coming conflicts, we have to be sure our weapons are also going to be ready when we're called upon to defend ourselves. That's where I need you and your expertise. I need you to teach all our gun-totin' hillbillies, who go hunting and then hang their dirty weapon on a gun rack until next time, how to service and see that their weapons remain ready for a greater purpose."

Garrison let his words sink in. "What do you say? I'll pay you a competitive monthly salary to develop and teach a weapon maintenance program. I'll also pay you whatever you charge for your gunsmith work and a healthy bonus for other special tasks I need you to perform."

"Special tasks?"

"The kind of tasks which will utilize your higher level skills; the kind of tasks only you and I can talk about—ever. Covert and critical to our continued existence, they will be quite profitable for you."

Brad looked across the truck cab at Garrison. He could see the sincerity in the man's face. It caused Brad to wonder who of TARPA's adversaries Garrison was thinking of.

After a few miles without conversation, Garrison held his gaze out the front window and spoke with a menacing tone.

"There is a small group of people that, regardless of what we do, are determined to eliminate us. In the near future, we may find ourselves in the position of needing to use the same approach toward them." Garrison turned to look at Brad.

Brad wasn't sure what to say as he turned on his blinker and slowed for the exit.

"Is this it?" Garrison asked.

"This exit is where we meet him. There's a Mapco here where I'll leave my truck, and from there we'll ride the rest of the way with him."

"I assume there is a reason for such precautions?"

"Security. He was trained, as I was, to eliminate any potential threat as standard procedure. If we leave our vehicle here, he can see everything we are bringing into his world, and he'll continue to control his environment. It's the way you have to operate if you're in a high-risk business. He's an intelligent soldier."

"Impressive."

"There he is now," Brad said.

The man was leaning against his dark green Humvee dressed in camo pants, a black t-shirt and combat boots.

"Good morning," Brad said as he climbed from the truck.

"How was the drive?" the man asked in a gruff baritone voice.

"Rough on an old man's back. How have you been?" Brad extended his hand.

"I'm doing okay."

"Roger, this is Carl. Carl, Roger."

As Roger stepped forward to shake Garrison's hand, Brad could see the image of a semi-auto in his front pocket.

"A pleasure to meet you, Roger." Garrison nodded.

Roger gave a half smile and glanced at Garrison's briefcase.

Brad wondered if Garrison noted his intentional use of first names only.

"You want to pick up some coffee or get rid of some before we leave?" Roger asked.

"We're good," Brad said. "We stopped not long ago. Let's mount up. Carl, you ride shotgun."

The men climbed into the Humvee and drove northwest on the Kentucky state highway.

Almost an hour of repetitive tree-lined roads coupled with Brad and Roger catching up, gave them time to reach Roger's rural property.

At first glance, it appeared to be like all the other farms they'd seen along the highway. The white clapboard two-story house sported a wrap-a-round front porch with matching white rocking chairs. It sat near a large tin-roof barn with a hay-filled loft and its weathered wood construction declaring its age. Between the back of the house and the barn sat a half dozen out buildings.

Roger drove past the house and around the barn, stopping at a large galvanized steel gate.

He looked back at Brad. "Can you do the honors?"

"Sure." Brad climbed from the Humvee and opened the gate allowing Roger to drive past him and wait.

"It's not much farther," Roger said, as they waited for Brad to latch the gate.

Brad climbed back in the Humvee. Roger shifted into four wheel drive and continued the trip off-road.

Another few minutes of driving along fence rows and across pasture took the men over several hills and down into a valley with a large creek running along a fence row. As they climbed the steep hillside above the creek, they came to a lone outbuilding.

This building was constructed of steel and concrete block, and it looked to be built into the hillside with the pitch of the roof matching the downward slope of the terrain above it.

Roger stopped next to one of the two stretch cab pickup trucks parked near an oversized rollup door. Brad and Garrison climbed from the Humvee and followed Roger inside the building.

The three men were met by two short bursts of barking meant to identify for their masters the presence of a potential threat. The two handlers instructed their canine partners that the visitors were not adversaries and the dogs sat.

"Brad and Carl," Roger pointed at his two guests, "this is Frank and Don and their buddies on the leashes are Hoover and Doc. Hoover there is a Belgian Malinois and Doc is a Lab. These boys are trained bomb sniffers; the dogs that is."

Garrison took a step toward the men to shake hands, but Brad grabbed the back of his shirt as the dogs stood, "It might be best not to do that," Brad said. So, Garrison gave a faint wave to the handlers.

The men nodded their greetings.

"Carl," Roger said, "I don't want you to think that you've come here on false pretenses, but I can't sell you C-4."

"What? Why not?" Garrison asked.

"Because if you use C-4, it and any of your people who touch it, will be discovered by trained dogs from any police force."

"I don't understand," Garrison looked at Brad then back at Roger.

"Of all the more powerful explosives, C-4 has a detectible odor that's one of the easiest for trained animals to sense."

"I thought you told Brad you developed a masking agent to take care of that issue?"

"The masking agent is good. It works, but not on C-4. The smell is too pungent."

"So, why are we here?" Garrison asked, becoming frustrated.

"Have you heard of Semtex."

"Yeah, I think so. Isn't that what the Irish Republican Army was famous for using back in the '80s?"

"Yes, they and other terrorist groups around the world made it popular. Kaddafi's terrorists used it to bring down the Pan Am flight over Lockerbie, Scotland. Do you know why they chose Semtex?"

"No, but I'll bet you're about to tell me."

"They chose it because it was equal in power output to C-4, but a minor variation in its production causes Semtex to be nearly odorless and much less likely to be detected."

"Do you have Semtex?" Garrison asked.

"Yes. I'd suggest you consider it."

"Makes sense to me." Garrison turned to Brad who nodded his agreement. "One question though. If the Semtex is nearly odorless, why is the masking agent needed?"

"To hide the detonators—and as insurance," Roger said.

"Understood."

"Good," Roger said. "A couple of years ago I began work on a product that could hide the scent of many explosives, so that the trained dogs would not be able to detect them in the field. Obviously, if successful, something like this would be a high value item on the black market, or any market for that matter.

"This agent, when properly used, is able to confuse trained dogs so they cannot pickup and zero in on the location of explosives or detonators. It works by adequately masking the scent with one they do not know and which effectively dominates their olfactory sensors."

"What's in the liquid?" Garrison asked.

"We won't be discussing the chemical composition of the liquid. I suggest you forget about its makeup and focus on its capabilities." Roger accented his assertion with a period of pointed silence.

The look on Garrison's face said he heard the message, but he was still seeing dollar signs.

"It's been tested thoroughly. The agent will mask the scent as long as you follow the instructions to the letter. Once your device is completed and ready to be armed, you must wear protective gloves such as latex or nitrile, then mist the device with the liquid and allow it to air dry. You must mist the surface of your device on all sides. You can use a couple of small fans at a distance on low speed, but the drying process should take between two and three hours.

"Once the device is allowed to dry, you will place it into a ten mil sterilized poly bag that I'll provide. Then, using a device I will also make available to you, you will heat seal the one open side of the bag. When the bag is heat sealed and allowed to cool, you will then spray the liquid over the entire surface of the bag, top and bottom, until the bag is covered and dripping. Then using the low speed fans, you'll allow the bag, once again, to air dry. This will also take a couple of hours. At this point, you will place your bagged device, sealed side first, into another ten mil sterilized bag and repeat the spraying and drying processes as before. When completely dry, your device is ready to be concealed."

"You are going to supply *everything* we need?" Garrison asked.

"Yes, everything," Roger said, "including written instructions. That's why this turnkey package isn't cheap."

Garrison looked at Brad, then back at Roger and nodded. "I understand."

"To demonstrate what I've explained to you, I have prepared a typical device using Semtex," Roger pulled on a pair of blue nitrile gloves and reached under a table. He placed a small, but ominous looking, device on top of the table.

Garrison stepped backward tripping over Brad's boots. He would have fallen if Brad hadn't caught him.

"But, I did not insert the detonators. They are separated from the Semtex for obvious reasons, but still provide the same challenge for Hoover and Doc since they are inside the bags with the explosive. The same spraying and double bagging process I described earlier was used last night when I prepared this device for today's demonstration.

"Frank, if you and Don will take your boys outside for a ten minute break, Carl and I will hide the device and we'll call you when we're ready.

"Follow me," Roger said as he cradled the device. "We are going through this door into an area where I have set up distractions and hiding places for the device."

Brad could tell the direction they were walking was taking them into the hillside, underground.

"Brad, if you'll flip on the light switch inside on the left."

Brad opened the door, reached inside and turned on what looked to be at least twenty-five four bulb florescent fixtures suspended beneath a fifteen foot steel-decked ceiling. The lights illuminated a single room of more than 10,000 square feet.

"Good Lord," Garrison said. "How in the world did you—"

"It took a while," Roger interrupted. "Let's go over here."

Roger walked the men and the device toward the near corner of the large room where he had assembled numerous boxes, wooden crates, metal cases, a forklift, a pickup truck and numerous other distractions, all with numbered stickers on them.

"Brad, see that fridge over there?" Roger nodded in the direction of the refrigerator. "There is a tray of snacks on the top shelf. Grab that and bring it over."

Brad retrieved the tray and handed it to Roger. Roger picked a rolled up slice of ham filled with cream cheese and extended the tray toward Garrison, and then back to Brad. Both men took a snack, and Roger placed the tray on top of a stack of wooden crates. "This will be another good distraction for the pups," Roger said.

"Gentlemen, I'd like to be able to tell you I staged all this for you, but the truth is I have two other men coming in later this week for this same demo. Okay, where do we put it, Carl?"

"Let's make it easy," Garrison said. "Put it in one of the corrugated cartons. If there is a scent it'll come through the carton easily."

"Good, I'll put it here," Roger said. "One carton on top of it, and one underneath." He cross-folded the flaps and restacked the cartons. "Let's call the dogs."

Roger walked to the entrance and shouted for the men and their dogs. Everyone gathered inside the entrance to the large room for instructions.

"Gentlemen, the device has been placed somewhere in the hodgepodge of items here in this area. None of the enclosures are sealed so any scent inside can travel out and be easily detected. There are a few intentional distractions much like you could expect to find anywhere this device might be hidden. Also, the target box is not marked in any way that could attract one of the dogs or one of you, but I assure you the box containing the device is not out of sight. It is visible and accessible. If you think you've found it, stop and give me the number off the container."

"Hoover will find it," Frank said.

"Good, I like a positive attitude. But don't expect this to be easy. If this device can be detected by a bomb dog, we want to know it now. So, if your dog locates the device, he gets a twenty-four ounce Porterhouse steak."

"Hoover will like that," Frank said.

"And you," Garrison interrupted, "will get a one thousand dollar bonus in addition to whatever Roger is paying you."

"Carl. Are you sure?" Roger asked.

"I need to know now if this is going to work," Garrison said.

"Excellent," Don said, as he rubbed Doc's head.

"The dogs will be brought in one at a time and allowed to examine the area on all sides," Roger said. "Your dog should be able to detect the target box quickly if he is going to find it. So, you will get five minutes to inspect everything here. Neither you, nor your dog, is allowed to touch the containers or equipment in any way. I will tell you when the time is up. Gentlemen, if you're ready? Frank, call it in the air."

Roger flipped a quarter into the air.

"Heads," Frank said.

Roger caught it and said, "Tails. Don, you go first. Frank, if you'll step outside with Hoover, I'll call you when Doc's time is up."

"Okay Doc," Don said, "we're on duty."

The man and his dog approached the mass of containers and equipment.

"Search," Don commanded. The dog's nose went to the ground and he began to sweep left and right until he reached the boxes. His head began a series of jerky movements in all directions as he processed the multitude of scents fed into his olfactory sensors. His unceasing mini-breaths continued to pull in the room's scents.

The Labrador worked his way around the stack of assorted items then, on his second pass, he alerted and sat next to wooden crate with the number nineteen.

"Is that his choice?" Roger asked Don.

"It looks that way."

"Number nineteen," Roger said, "has a paddle holster inside."

"You're kidding?" Don said.

"Sorry."

"Brad, ask Frank to come in."

Don left the room with his dog as Frank and Hoover prepared for their search. Hoover was aggressive and Frank had to wrestle with him to keep him off the boxes. He completed his search after alerting on three of the containers. His time was up and Frank was asked which case was Hoover's choice. Since Hoover alerted on it twice, Frank chose number twenty-six.

Garrison gave Brad a big smile.

"Sorry Frank," Roger said. "Twenty-six has an empty M16 clip. I hate to tell you, but neither of the other two cases he alerted on had the device either."

"Brad, call Don back in, please."

Don and Doc joined everyone in the big room and Roger walked over to the containers. "Gentlemen, the explosive was in box number twenty-three." He opened the carton and removed the device.

Brad looked at Garrison who was still smiling.

"Sorry guys," Garrison said. "No bonus today."

"Well Carl, what do you think?" Roger asked.

"I'm sold. Where's my Semtex and the magic liquid?"

"I have it packaged and ready for you," Roger said.

"And I have your cash," Garrison said.

"That was quite an impressive display," Garrison said when they were back on the highway. "Do you feel confident I can expect the same results?"

"Yes. If you couldn't, Roger would have told us. You have to follow all the same procedures, and make sure the heat seals are intact."

"I can't help but think the formula for that masking agent is worth millions," Garrison said.

"I think Roger wants to be selective on who uses it or even knows about it. You should feel honored, and we should honor him by keeping it quiet."

"Oh, I am honored," Garrison said. "I am."

"I'm sure Roger's concerned it could get into the wrong hands."

Garrison nodded and dropped the subject.

Garrison's cell phone vibrated.

"Hello."

"Carl, it's Harlan. We've got a problem."

"It seems lately that's all you tell me. What is it this time?"

"Those two homicide detectives are at Jimmy Dan's farm with a search warrant."

"Does he still have—"

"Oh, yes."

"Damn. What are the chances they'll find them?"

"I don't know. He says the door is hidden and they can't see it."

"Harlan, are you sure he wasn't involved in the murder at Cumberland Plaza?"

"No way."

"How can you be so sure?"

"I can tell when we're alone; he's pissed off about it. He swears he would have used a gun, so he wouldn't have to touch the Arab. You have to admit, Carl, the man had access to any number of guns and suppressors. Why would he use a damn knife?"

"So, what do we do with this fiasco if they find the vault? What will the police do?"

"I'm certain Mullins will be arrested on weapons charges. If I know the Nashville police and Jimmy Dan, you can rest assured they will play him in order to climb higher on the ladder; higher, of course, being you."

"Harlan. Damn it. I pay you to deal with shit like this. That means you actually have to come up with viable solutions."

"I told you," Norris said, "when you decided to hold those weapons under his house, it was a bad idea."

"Thank you, but that doesn't help now. I had nowhere else safe to put those guns while our armory is being completed at the lodge. We filled up the other men's gun vaults first. Hell, what's stored at his house represents less than ten percent of our arsenal." Garrison took a deep breath. "What about denying we have any involvement and saying we don't even know Mullins? It's his word against ours. We can afford to lose those guns if we have to."

"If you do that, Carl," Norris said, "he can prove relations. I'm already on record as his attorney and it wouldn't take much to uncover my relationship with you. Plus, you deny him now, and he'll talk like a parrot to the detectives and then all of TARPA will collapse."

"Okay, forget that." Garrison knew he was running low on options.

"Hang on, Harlan." Garrison took the phone from his ear.

"Brad, I've got a problem, actually a person, that's becoming unmanageable and putting everything I've worked for at risk."

Brad looked at Garrison as if to say, "And?"

Garrison returned the phone to his ear. "Harlan, let me call you back. I need to talk with Brad."

# Chapter 37

*Jimmy Dan Mullins's Farm*
*Nashville, Tennessee*
*Wednesday Late Morning*

"You can open it, and allow it to remain intact along with whatever you have inside, or we can get the bomb squad out here to blow it open." Norm offered Mullins his most serious expression. "You know, they enjoy that kind of stuff, and they don't get to do it very often. Everyone seems to always comply; then the bomb squad has to go home. It really pisses them off. Oh, by the way, if we have to blow it; anything that gets damaged is not considered our responsibility. It's true. The District Attorney considers it collateral damage due to an uncooperative suspect."

Mike sat on a stack of boxes, enjoying Norm's performance.

"And," Mike looked around at the basement ceiling and walls, "this place doesn't look all that sturdy."

"You may want to make some plans for another place to live," Norm said, as he reached his long arms over his head grabbed the floor joists and acted as though he was shaking them, "assuming of course, your insurance covers that sort of thing. What do you say, Mullins?" Norm asked. "You don't want to open it, do you? You'd rather let us blow it, right?" Norm nodded his head feigning excitement.

Norm turned and faced his partner, acting as though he had a cigar in his fingers he raised his eyebrows several times. He elevated his voice enough that Mullins could hear. "I think it would be amazing to watch this place turned into splinters."

"Alright, damn it." Mullins stomped to the door. "Freakin' Gestapo," he mumbled.

Mullins punched six digits on the keypad and rotated the five spoke handle until the plungers were retracted. He grabbed the handle with both hands and stepped backward until the door was open.

"Damn." Norm's eyes grew large as he walked toward the open door. "You were right Mike. It is a gun vault, but it's larger than you thought."

Mullins stood to the side and watched the detectives marvel at the collection of weapons and the size of the vault. Mullins looked as though he wanted to be elsewhere.

"What is this room, ten feet by fifteen?" Norm asked.

"Twelve by eighteen," Mullins groaned, arms folded and staring at the floor.

"A Barrett M82A1 *and* an M99, look at the size of those things." Norm strolled the room like it was a sporting goods store. "Hey, Mike. Here's two fifteen-count racks full of M4s complete with M203 grenade launchers. Mullins, where the hell did you get all these?"

Mullins didn't answer.

"You've got to be kidding me," Norm shouted as he pulled open a set of large cabinet doors to expose thousands of rounds of ammunition for all the weapons in the racks and on the walls.

"Here's a rack of twelve gauge Remington 870s like ours," Mike said. "Look at this wall, H&K MP5s and G36s. What the hell is this, Mullins? Aren't you aware that many of these weapons are Class Three firearms?"

"What does that mean?" Mullins asked.

"Mullins, you're not *that* uninformed are you? What kind of gun collector doesn't know that? Class Three weapons are the full autos made since '86," Norm said, "the ones you're not supposed to own unless your last name is Government."

"What do you mean?" Mullins asked. "This is America. Check the constitution. We're allowed to own guns."

"You have the right to keep and bear arms," Mike explained. "You do not have the right to possess armament equal to America's military. There are laws meant to prevent the ownership and operation of fully automatic weapons, explosives and shortened long guns modified for concealment. Many of these weapons break those laws."

"I don't know what you're talkin' about. I'm callin' my lawyer."

"Good idea," Norm said. "He can explain it all to you before the door to your cell slams shut."

"I've also got a call to make," Mike said as he turned to go back upstairs.

# Chapter 38

*Captain Al Moretti's Office*
*Criminal Justice Center*
*Nashville, Tennessee*
*Wednesday Late Morning*

"Captain Moretti."

"Captain, this is Lieutenant Ray Samuels with the Tennessee Highway Patrol."

"What can I do for you, Lieutenant?"

"Do you have a dark blue Crown Vic Interceptor that would have been on Interstate 40 in Cheatham County about an hour ago?"

"I wouldn't think so, but I can find out. Why?"

"One of our troopers clocked this unmarked vehicle doing ninety-three miles per hour westbound outside Metro jurisdiction. We thought it was unusual for a Metro vehicle to be operating at this speed without emergency equipment. We ran the tag and wanted to be sure you had an officer operating this vehicle and it wasn't stolen. The trooper who clocked the vehicle was in pursuit when the driver lit it up. So the trooper backed off after acquiring the tag number."

"Excuse me one moment, Lieutenant."

Moretti covered the phone with his hand and shouted, "Burris."

The lieutenant came quickly. He was familiar with the tone.

"Lieutenant Samuels, you're on the speaker with me and Lieutenant D.W. Burris." Moretti was furious. His neck and head were as red as if he was being strangled. He stared at Burris with wide eyes while he asked the trooper questions that had already been answered. "Where precisely was our unmarked blue Interceptor when it was clocked doing ninety-three in a seventy?" He gave Lieutenant Burris a fierce look as he stated the speed.

After Vega's call, Burris knew who the driver was, and he suspected Moretti did too.

"Interstate 40 West between mile marker 184 and 185."

"I'm sure it was our vehicle, Lieutenant," Moretti said. "It seems we have a detective on our team who has reached the end of his self-control. He's a little past due for a new vocation."

"I understand," Samuels said. "We've seen it happen."

"Do you know the whereabouts of this vehicle now?" Moretti asked.

"Sorry, Lieutenant."

"If any of your troopers spot this vehicle, let them know they have my expressed permission to detain the driver and treat him as they would anyone else who has compromised the public safety."

"Will do, and Captain?" Samuels said.

"Yes?"

"Do us a favor?"

"Sure," Moretti said.

"See to it his new career has him driving nothing larger than a lawn mower, and if possible, doing it in Kentucky?"

"I'll recommend it. Thanks for the courtesy call," Moretti said.

"Drive safely," Samuels said.

Moretti slammed the phone into its cradle. "I am going to have that idiot's shield.

Lieutenant, I don't care how you do it, but get that dumb ass in here before he kills somebody."

"Yes sir," Burris said as he cleared the doorway of the Captain's office.

Back in his office, Burris reached for his desk phone to call Hogue's cell, but it rang before he could pick it up.

"Burris."

"Lieutenant, it's Mike."

"Yeah, what is it?" Burris said, hoping Mike could detect his sense of urgency.

"We opened the steel reinforced door in Mullins's basement. It concealed a large sophisticated gun vault with over two hundred square feet. It even has climate control and a dehumidifier."

"Where in the hell did he get all that?"

"I'm not sure, but I can promise you; this knucklehead didn't put it in. He has enough firepower in there to support the 101st Airborne Division, and doesn't know anything about Class Three weapons laws."

"Are the weapons legal?"

"Some are—most aren't."

"Get an inventory and call me back."

"Lieutenant."

"What?"

"That's not all we found. He also has dozens of cases of color brochures, pamphlets, enrollment forms and assorted other propaganda for an organization called The Alliance for the Racial Purification of America."

"I've heard of these subversives. A madman named Garrison is the heir to the leadership of this white supremacist cult."

"His name and photos are prominent on all these documents," Mike said.

"These hate addicts have been around for a long time, but they've been relatively quiet over the last few years. What does Mullins say about all this?"

"He's been open with us for the entire time we've been here. Once we found all the promotional junk, he abruptly clammed up and called Harlan Norris again."

"That figures. Get me an inventory. Keep the uniforms on site, and bring him in. I gotta go."

# Chapter 39

*Mustafa's Restaurant*
*Nashville, Tennessee*
*Wednesday Afternoon*

Mike and Norm entered the small lobby of Mustafa's Restaurant. The pleasing aromas of seasoned roasted lamb and beef along with Middle Eastern music surrounded them the moment they arrived. The high pitched brass bell hanging from the top of the door frame summoned the hostess.

"Welcome, gentlemen," she said as she reached for menus.

Mike and Norm both held up their IDs in unison. I'm Detective Neal. This is Detective Wallace. "May we speak to the owner or the manager please?"

The hostess, appearing unnerved by the badges, mumbled, "Uh, one moment. I will get Mr. Mustafa for you."

Mike was scanning the interior of the restaurant and admiring the colorful décor, when he noticed Norm in his peripheral vision. His head was tilted back slightly, and he was inhaling slow and deliberate breaths; his eyes half-closed.

"What are you doing?"

"What?" Norm's eyes popped open.

"You know what I'm talking about. You were acting like you were in a trance or something."

"I was taking in the aromas," Norm waved his hands as if he was attempting to force more of the fragrance to his nose. "You know, the Middle Eastern ambiance."

"Oh, excuse me." Mike rolled his eyes as he turned back toward the sound of approaching footsteps.

A short fat man followed the returning hostess. He was attempting to remove his dirty apron from his expanded middle before reaching the officers, but was having some difficulty with the knot. Once he succeeded, he rolled the apron into a ball and threw it behind the counter. He shoved out his hand.

"Welcome. I am Mustafa. I am honored to have you visit my restaurant. What is it that I can do for you gentlemen today? May I get you something to eat?"

"No, thank you," Mike said, holding up his ID once again.

"Speak for yourself," Norm said as he followed suit. "This place smells great."

"Thank you." Mustafa's belly shook with laughter, grateful for Norm's compliment.

Mike glanced at Norm and forced himself to refrain from comment. "Mr. Mustafa, I'm Detective Neal and this is Detective Wallace. We would like to speak with you for a few minutes about an incident we were told took place in your parking lot yesterday morning."

"Sure. What incident is that?" Mustafa said, puzzled.

"I believe there was an auto accident involving one of your employees and a customer, Mr. Daran Hamid." Mike acted as if he knew very little about the wreck.

"Oh, yes. One of my servers, he was late for work, and he struck Daran's rear bumper. It was very unfortunate. I think Ahmed said a delivery truck stopped in front of Daran and he could not stop in time. Is that why you are here?"

"That's part of why we are here." Mike explained.

"Why was Mr. Hamid here so early? Were you open?" Mike asked.

"No, we had not yet opened. He came in to order food for his party last night. He was celebrating his American citizenship. But, he never came back last night to pick up his order."

"Is Mr. Hamid a regular customer?" Norm asked.

"No. Another one of our regular customers, Mr. Zaid Zebari is Daran's employer. He owns Z.Z. Maintenance and recommended us to Daran for his party."

"I see. Mr. Mustafa, Daran Hamid was killed last night."

"What? No," Mustafa said. "What happened?"

"He was murdered as he left his work at Cumberland Plaza to come here," Mike said.

"Oh, my. He was such a nice young man. This is so sad." Mustafa looked from Mike to Norm.

"Can we speak with your employee, Mr. ..." Mike asked, waiting for Mustafa to fill in the name.

"Ahmed, Ahmed al-Zubaidy. I am sorry. It is Wednesday and he works our dinner on Wednesdays. He does not arrive until four o'clock. You are welcome to come back, but I would ask you to please speak to him before work or during his break. You see, we are very busy at dinner and my staff is limited."

"Yes, I see. Do you have Mr. al-Zubaidy's home address?"

"Yes, I will get it for you. The little man waddled off toward the kitchen."

Mike turned to Norm, "Looks like he's been sampling his own creations."

"I'd like to try some myself," Norm confessed. "It smells fantastic."

When he returned, Mustafa was carrying a white paper bag. It contained samples for Mustafa's newest fan. He handed the bag to Norm and smiled.

"Here you are detective. Enjoy, compliments of Mustafa's."

"Thank you, Mr. Mustafa." Norm smiled. "You're very kind."

The manager had a grease-stained file folder under his arm. He began to thumb through it. "Let me see, his application is in here somewhere."

"How long has he been with your restaurant?" Mike asked.

"Oh," He stopped and touched his head with his thumb and forefinger as if this would conjure the information. "He came here about three, maybe four months ago, I think. A restaurant where he worked in New York City recommended him highly."

"Which one?" Norm asked.

Mustafa turned over the application. "It was called Karim's Baghdad in Manhattan. I remember, I called them, and they gave him an excellent reference."

"Do you still have the number for the restaurant?" Mike asked.

"Yes, it is here." Mustafa handed Mike the application and pointed to the number.

"Did he say why he was moving to Nashville?" Norm asked while making notes on his pad.

"Oh no, I do not question my people about their personal lives. I feel it is their business and not mine. As long as they come to work and do what I need, that is all I require."

Mike stepped back into the lobby and called the New York phone number on his cell. After several rings, the voice that answered said, "Message Number 142: The wireless number you have reached is no longer in service."

Mike closed his phone and immediately received a voicemail announcement left while he was on the phone. Mike called for the voicemail.

"Mike," Burris said on the recording, "TBI called. Some of the prints from the Hamid scene came back from the state's AFIS. They belong to a Marcus Dalton. He's an ex-con, sent up for dealing coke here in the city. He was released a couple of months ago and is currently employed at a car wash on Charlotte Avenue called Details-Details. The shop is run by another ex-con, Henry Boudreaux who went straight several years ago. See what you can find out. They're still working on the other prints."

Mike knew there was a possibility that Hamid was killed for money by some drugged up freak. There were tens of thousands of them in the TBI's Automated Fingerprint Identification System, but his gut was screaming at him that this killer knew his victim and he had a grudge.

He turned to Norm. "The New York number was a disconnected cell phone. I suppose al-Zubaidy's Nashville address will also turn out to be bogus."

"Who was that on the phone?" Norm asked.

"Burris. TBI has a match on some of the prints from the parking garage."

# Chapter 40

*Hillcrest Apartments*
*Nashville, Tennessee*
*Wednesday Afternoon*

"Yes," Ahmed said.

"I cannot talk long. Mustafa will hear me."

"Jamil? What is it?"

"The police were here."

"When?"

"They left, just now."

"What did they want?"

"I could not hear well, but they were talking with Mustafa out front. He was playing the submissive Iraqi the entire time. He makes me sick."

"Jamil, why were they there?"

"I saw Mustafa pointing to the parking lot. I heard him say your name. He told them what time you come to work today. Later, I saw him take a file folder and some food to them. One of the policemen made a phone call, and then they left. That was all I saw."

"Who did the policeman call on the phone?"

"I could not hear him speak to anyone. After he finished his call, I heard him say to the other policeman, 'I suppose his address here will also turn out to be bogus.' What is bogus?"

"Never mind that. How long were they there?"

"Maybe twenty minutes."

"Jamil, do not say a word to anyone."

"I will not talk to anyone but you, Ahmed."

"Good. Thank you, my brother. Allah shall reward you for your service."

Ahmed closed his cell phone.

"Who was that?" asked Abdul.

"It was Jamil, one of the cooks at Mustafa's."

"What was he talking about?

"The police were there, asking questions; detectives asking about me." He looked up at Abdul.

"When?" Abdul asked.

"He called as soon as they left the restaurant. The dog, Mustafa, must have his tongue removed."

"What is happening here, Ahmed? I told all of you to keep to yourselves. What is this about?"

Ahmed shook his head. "I bumped a car in the parking lot at the restaurant."

"What do you mean you bumped a car?"

"This man stopped suddenly in the parking lot. I could not stop. My car slipped in the gravel, and I hit the rear of his car."

"Idiot."

"It was an accident. It was hardly scratched."

"An accident? You are putting the plan and all of us in jeopardy with your thoughtless ways. Do you not understand? Look at all this." Abdul waved his arm. "This is a pig sty. You have all become a disappointment to Farid, to Allah, and to me."

"It was an accident. It could not be helped."

"It could have been helped if you were thinking about what is at stake and driving properly."

"You weren't there. You do not know."

"I did not have to be there to know you are reckless," Abdul shouted. "What happened with this other driver?"

"He got out of his car and looked at the bumper. He was upset. He kept saying 'no, no, no, not today.' He looked at his watch and said, 'I do not have time for this.' He acted like he had somewhere he had to be in a hurry. He asked me for my driver's license and proof of insurance card. He gave me his license and another card. I did not know what it was. Then he wrote down the information from my driver license and the number from the license plate on the car."

"You do not have an insurance card," Abdul said. "Only Sajid has that card."

"He did not know that. I told him I had lost my insurance card. He asked who my insurance was with. I did not know what to say, so I told him it was the same company as his."

"That is when he handed me my license and asked me when I was working."

"Why did you tell him you worked there?" Abdul asked.

"I didn't." Ahmed shouted. "I had on my uniform."

"I told him when I would be there, and he said he would see me later to discuss the insurance company paying for his car. He said he didn't have time to call the police and wait. He said he would report it later."

"What are we supposed to do if he contacts the police and gives them your numbers?"

"That will not happen."

"How do you know it will not happen?" Abdul shouted.

"He will not contact anyone," Ahmed said defiantly. "He is dead."

"Dead? Tell me you did not kill this man."

"I had no choice. He would have exposed us and ruined the plan."

"You idiot. You could have paid him off; given him money to repair his car, even more money than he would need to repair the car."

"I took care of the problem. It is over."

"You took care of the problem? You took care of nothing. You *are* the problem."

"What did this Mustafa at the restaurant tell the police?"

"Jamil said he told them about the wreck, and the little he thinks he knows about me. They want to talk to me. Jamil said they would be there tonight when I arrive for work."

"Ahmed, why do you have to be so careless? I cannot believe this. You continue to put the entire plan at risk. You have jeopardized all our work; our plans as well as our future rewards. I cannot believe you have failed at such a simple task."

"Relax. Everything will be alright."

"No, everything will not be alright. These police will not stop until they find you." Abdul paced the floor smoking, all the while knowing precisely what had to be done. He continued to pace the floor making al-Zubaidy even more nervous with each frustrating pass. Suddenly, Abdul stopped behind him. He grabbed Ahmed's hair and jerked his head backward. "You are unworthy!" The razor sharp dagger completed its task and was held dripping at Abdul's side.

Al-Zubaidy's throat was sliced through with such force the only thing stopping decapitation was his spine. As his heart continued to pump, blood gushed from his neck like water from a spigot. His head fell forward onto the table and into the overflowing ashtray before him. Sajid and Karim gasped, then stood frozen, staring at Abdul.

Abdul spat on the man's motionless head. "Karim, Sajid collect everything; all your possessions and his, anything that could connect you to this apartment. Do it now. We are leaving this place."

"What about the plan?" Sajid asked.

"Ahmed's stupidity has altered the plan."

Sajid looked at him with a questioning stare, but he knew better than to challenge him a second time. The reason was evident and lying slaughtered like a goat on the table in front of him.

"Empty his pockets. Remove his wallet, his cell phone and all his personal possessions. We will take them with us."

The two young men were still moving in slow motion, dumbfounded by what they had witnessed.

"We are leaving, now. Do you understand?"

"Yes," Sajid mumbled.

"Then move!"

# Chapter 41

*Details-Details Car Wash*
*Nashville, Tennessee*
*Wednesday Afternoon*

Marcus Dalton grabbed a towel, moistened with leather conditioner, from a bucket marked *Interior*. In one graceful motion, he opened the door and fell into the driver's seat of the Lexus 430 as it rolled from the drying bay at the end of the wash line. He yanked the shifter into gear and pulled the black beauty into Detail Station 3.

As always, Dalton kept a casual eye out for Henry Boudreaux while wiping down the car interiors. Henry, the owner of Details-Details; was an ex-con. Convicted in 1990, he served six years in Riverbend for armed robbery and car jacking. While inside, Henry met a man with Christian Prison Ministries who spent time with him and helped him to see a different side of life; one worth living without all the anguish that put him there.

For five years, Henry had been hiring ex-convicts to work at the car wash. He was doing his best to help turn them from their criminal ways. Some made it and moved on to higher paying jobs and productive lives. Others, for various reasons, couldn't make the transition; they returned to their old habits and then back to prison. Henry Boudreaux received a tax incentive for employing each of them, success or failure.

Dalton swapped places with Razz Pitts who had finished cleaning the inside of the rear windows. As soon as Dalton climbed into the backseat, he began wiping down the backs of the leather front seats with his right hand while his left hand performed a more profitable task. He pulled open the backseat ashtray at the rear of the console and removed the tight roll of U.S presidents. In the same motion, the plastic bag he had been palming, dropped from his hand into the ashtray. He closed the ashtray, finished wiping down the rear seat interior and exited the car.

The three men who had been drying the exterior now moved to the White Pearl Escalade parked in Station 2.

Dalton craned his neck to see into the waiting area. He was trying to capture the attention of the Lexus owner. The man stood. Dalton raised his rag into the air and rotated it, signaling the interior detail was complete. The owner walked to the front of the car, made eye contact with Dalton and handed him the pickup ticket confirming he had paid for the wash. Dalton knew the man had paid. He also knew the man had received some extra fine cocaine in exchange for his payment.

"We appreciate your business, sir." Dalton smiled flashing his gold tooth. "Have a nice day."

Dalton's system included paying each of the men at the car wash a fee for helping to cover his enterprise, keeping it from Henry and allowing them all to make a little change on the side. The success of the group relied on the silence of each member. Their solidarity was formed and supported by their common experiences as former inmates of the Tennessee State Prison System.

Dalton knew he was putting himself at risk of returning to prison, and for a much longer visit this time, but he couldn't quit selling. The money was too easy. He couldn't get another job and he couldn't make enough money at the carwash to support his lifestyle. He had to sell the dope in order to make enough to get by.

"Besides," he always said, "there ain't no way Marcus Dalton is ever gonna work a straight job. Hell, the only reason I took this shit job was so I had another avenue for distribution."

Marcus wasn't like everybody else. According to Marcus, he was unique.

"Yo, Ty," Coop said, as he wiped the beaded drops from the hood of the Escalade. "Sup with dat bitch you been seein, man?"

"Man—I dunno. She a freak," Ty said. "She always wantin' to change me and make me into sumpthin' she wants."

"She's hot," Coop said, "but, it ain't worth all dat."

"Ain't dat da truth," Ty said. "All dem bitches think dey be changin' ya. Shit gets old, man."

"Yo, cuz," Coop said to Razz in the SUV's backseat. "Who da suits?"

All the men's heads turned, searching.

"I dunno," Razz said. "Dey look like cops."

Dalton was stretched out inside the SUV wiping down the dash. He lifted his eyes enough to see through the bottom of the passenger side window.

"Shit. They is cops," Dalton mumbled. "I seen enough cops in my day. Hell, I can see da bulges in their coats from here."

Dalton continued to wipe down the interior as he slid out the drivers seat and down to the pavement. The suits were still talking to Henry and repeatedly looking his way. As soon as they looked back at each other, he bolted for the rear parking lot.

He heard one of the cops yell, "He's running. Get the car."

Dalton was making plans as he ran. He knew there was an eight foot chain link fence he could climb and use to slow the pursuing cop. He hoped these two were donut connoisseurs and would find it hard to match his speed. He knew the big one didn't have a chance, but the other cop looked fit. Unfortunately, he was the one tailing him. He might be a problem.

As Dalton approached the fence, he could hear the cop closing on him. He tried to stretch his stride into a higher gear. At about five feet from the fence, he left the pavement. Reaching out, he grabbed the chain links below the twisted barb top. He pulled up hard, all the while digging with the toes of his second-hand Nikes and climbing up the diamond shaped openings in the galvanized fence. His feet reached one of the horizontal supports giving him a sturdy point from which to push off. He jumped and cleared the fence.

*He* cleared the fence. His baggy jogging pants caught on the twisted barbs along the top and remained there when he fell to the pavement. He scarcely avoided landing on his head. He turned with the intention of grabbing the pants and their high-value contents, but the cop was already making his leap to the fence. Dalton changed his mind and instead sprinted down the sidewalk behind the building next door.

Dalton slowed as he approached the blind corner of the building. He planned to turn right at the corner and get out of the sprinting cop's line of sight. As he rounded the corner, something grabbed him at the throat.

Dalton had run into the big cop's huge left hand. The collar of his jacket and his ability to breathe were now under police control. His eyes were staring into the business end of a Glock Model 22 appropriately backed up by the enlarged eyes and sweaty red face of a three hundred pound pissed-off detective.

"Freeze, asshole," Norm said. "That's right. Your ass is mine. You made me run, Marcus. I don't like to run."

Norm's size alone was enough to make anyone whimper, but a close-up view of the exit end of the .40 caliber Glock was enough to weaken a person's bladder. Norm pulled Dalton toward him lifting the man onto his tiptoes.

"Marcus, were you going somewhere?" Norm looked down at the man's bare legs. "Forget something, Marcus?"

Everything Dalton tried to say was unintelligible.

"You got him?" Mike asked as he rounded the corner panting.

"Do I have you, Marcus? Detective Neal wants to know."

Dalton nodded his head.

"Oh, I'd say I got him." Norm twisted the jacket tighter. The ex-con's facial coloring was beginning to resemble a plum.

"Detective Neal, would you be so kind as to cuff Mr. Dalton while I recite to him his constitutional rights as a citizen of our city who has been placed under arrest?"

Mike removed the cuffs from his belt and secured Dalton's hands behind his back.

Norm quoted the Miranda then lowered the Glock and eased the twist on Dalton's collar. Dalton gasped for air. The imprint of the barrel tip remained on Dalton's forehead giving him the appearance of having a third eye.

"What happened to his pants?" Norm asked.

"He left them hanging on the fence," Mike said.

Norm looked at Dalton's colorful underwear. "Man, you got some kinda serious package going on down there, don't ya? Or, is that not your manhood, but maybe your inventory dangling there?"

Still gasping for breath, Dalton refrained from comment.

The sirens were approaching from all directions. "Let's join the cavalry, shall we?" Norm took Dalton's arm and marched him toward the arriving patrol cars.

Norm turned Dalton over to the uniforms for transport to booking and asked them for Mike's handcuffs.

"Check his pants hanging on the fence back behind the carwash," Mike said to the officers, "and be sure to examine those drawers. I inspected the jacket when I cuffed him, but I don't think the bulge in those fancy panties is all manhood."

"Put him in the backseat of this patrol car and search him," Sergeant Arnold told officers Norton and Van Horn.

"I'm gonna unlock the cuffs," Officer Norton said, as he positioned the cuff key in his gloved right hand, "and then you need to drop your drawers so you can be searched. Understand?"

"Drop em? Right here? In the car?"

“If it was up to me we’d do it standing out there in traffic, but I think the Sarge meant for us to do it with a little respect for the citizenry. We wouldn’t want to embarrass all the men in Nashville by showing off your obviously superior toolkit.”

“So,” the other officer said reaching into his pocket, “you want to be able to wear ‘em again or not?” He pushed the chrome release button on the six-inch switchblade. It flew open and locked with a solid click. Dalton’s eyes widened at the sight of the shining blade.

“Okay, okay. Damn. I’ll drop ‘em.” Dalton looked up at the officers. “Now?”

“No, later this afternoon, dumbass,” Van Horn said, still holding the switchblade at his side. “Get ‘em off.”

Without taking his eyes off the knife, Dalton hooked his thumbs into the elastic waistband on each side, and as he pushed down on the floor of the patrol car with his feet he elevated himself off the seat. He slid the briefs down his legs and four small plastic bags of white powder dropped to the seat and onto the carpet. Dalton closed his eyes and tightened his lips. He was headed back to prison, and he knew it.

“Well, looky here, Nate. I think our man Dalton took a drug dump.”

“Yeah, it looks like it, but I don’t think this dump is gonna make him feel any better. Get your hands on top of your head, now and keep ‘em there.” Van Horn folded the knife closed and pulled out his cuffs.

“Hey, Sarge.” Norton shouted. “We got something to show you over here.”

Back at their car, Mike walked up to Norm. "Buddy, I haven't seen you move that fast since the last time we ate Mexican for lunch." Mike smiled.

Norm usually laughed at Mike’s rare humor, but he didn’t look so good. With his breath still labored, Norm leaned back against the car and wiped the sweat from his face with his jacket sleeve.

“What’s the matter, partner?” Mike said. “You look whipped.”

Still having trouble breathing, Norm began to rub his chest from side to side. “My arms, they’re so heavy.” Norm winced, barely able to speak. "I feel pressure—in my chest."

"Get in the car, now." Mike opened the passenger side door and forced Norm into the seat. He ran around the car and jumped into the driver's seat. He reached across the big man and pulled his seat belt until he could latch it. Mike accelerated the cruiser as he lit it up.

Norm was leaning against the door and the head rest, looking up at nothing and blinking his eyes. His arm was across his chest, then it dropped to his lap.

"Norm! Norm! You okay?" Mike asked trying to watch both the traffic and his partner.

"Yeah—I guess." Norm grunted. "I'm—a little scared."

"Me too, buddy. Me too. I'm driving as fast as I can," Mike shouted over the siren. "Hang on. We'll be at Saint Thomas in less than five minutes."

# Chapter 42

*Saint Thomas Hospital ER*
*Nashville, Tennessee*
*Wednesday Afternoon*

Mike jumped up when Cheryl came through the double doors from the Emergency Room. He met her in the middle of the waiting room with extended arms. Her face was a mixture of sad eyes and a tired smile. She hugged him so tight it hurt.

"Well?" Mike said, returning the hug.

Cheryl sniffled. "He's going to be okay, thanks to you."

"Oh, thank God. That's great news."

"He did have a heart attack, but you got him here soon afterward and the doctors were able to mitigate the damage. He's in the Cath Lab getting a couple of stents to open his arteries up. One was ninety-percent blocked."

"Geez. Are stents going to fix that?"

"Yes. He'll be fine once I get him home for a few days. I'm going to have to whip him into shape so he doesn't end up giving *me* a heart attack worrying about him. You saved his life, Mike."

"No, they saved him in there. I only drove fast."

"What happened anyway?" Cheryl asked.

"I'm not sure. He did some running to catch up with a suspect, maybe a hundred yards? When I got there, Norm had him covered. He did a great job. It was textbook. The guy was frozen in front of Norm's Glock.

"I thought he was just taxed because of the run. Then he reached for his chest. I rushed him here as fast as I could."

"Thank you." Cheryl smiled. "You did the right thing." She pressed her palms against Mike's cheeks, leaned forward and kissed him on the lips. "Now you have to help me get him to drop some weight so we don't lose him."

"I'll help you. Tell me what I need to do."

"Thank you, Michael. I owe you."

"I'll take my payback in your Italian cooking, now that the big one can't eat it." Mike grinned.

"Deal. Norm gets the salad and he'll have to watch you eat the Italian." Cheryl hugged him again. "I've got to go back."

"When can I see the big lummox?"

"Later, I'll call you. Okay?"

"That's fine," Mike said. "I'm so glad he's okay."

"Me too," Cheryl said as she walked back toward the ER. She turned back and waved as the double doors opened for her.

"Tell him I said to hurry up and get well. I need my chauffeur back." Mike smiled.

# Chapter 43

*Charlotte Avenue*
*Nashville, Tennessee*
*Wednesday Afternoon*

Karim drove Ahmed's car into an open spot at the side of the adult bookstore and left the keys in the ignition. Before the night was over, the car would be stolen, stripped and likely burned. But most importantly, it would not be able to be linked to them. Abdul pulled the SUV close behind the car. Karim removed the rear license plate from Ahmed's car and got in the SUV. As they drove away, Sajid continued to follow the SUV in his car.

"Where will we go? Karim asked.

"I am not sure yet," Abdul said. "I must think." He drove a while without talking, and then he said, "Thanks to Ahmed, the plan is in jeopardy. If we fail, Farid will be furious, and those who have employed us will ruin us. We will be disgraced."

"I know someone who can help us with a place to live."

"Who?"

"Hasan. He and his brother have a house in an area called Donelson. It is only a few miles east of here. They have a basement apartment.

Several weeks ago he asked me to move in with them to share the rent. I told him I could not due to the lease agreement where we were living."

"Karim, we cannot go just anywhere. Do you know what I have in the back of this car?"

"Yes. I know."

"Do you understand the significance of this jihad? This conference gives us multiple targets in the same place at the same time. This attack will be felt by hundreds and remembered by all. It will show the impertinent Americans and the independent Kurds that they are defenseless against Allah's will."

"We understand more than you know," Karim said. "If we did not, why would we be here, prepared to sacrifice everything? Like you, we are committed to Allah's will. Trust us. You will not be disappointed. I intend to honor my father's memory. It is all I have left to do. I am almost Ahmed's size, and I am willing to wear the device."

Abdul looked at the young man, now ready to be a martyr. He continued to drive. "Are you sure you know what you are saying?"

"I am sure." Karim looked into Abdul's eyes. "Let me call Hasan. I am certain that he will be willing to help us. I have spent much time talking with him over the past months. He is a good man of strong faith, and I am sure he will be anxious to serve Allah's will."

Abdul glanced back at Karim, and then stared at the road ahead. He contemplated the suggestion knowing their options now were few.

"Call him," Abdul said. "I will agree to meet with him and consider the use of his home. However, he is to know nothing—*nothing.* Do you understand?"

"I do. I will tell him there was a plumbing problem above us in the building, and it flooded our apartment. There were no other apartments available, and we have nowhere else to go."

"Tell him the three of us will be there only a few days while we look for another home, and I will pay him well for his trouble. All this will be behind us soon, Karim."

"I will tell him," Karim said.

"Also," Abdul added, "tell your friend to make sure this basement is clean, or I will not be able to stay there with you."

"I understand."

# Chapter 44

*Lieutenant Burris's Office*
*Nashville, Tennessee*
*Wednesday Afternoon*

"Hi. Are you waiting, too?" Cris sat next to Mike.

"One of my most polished detective skills," Mike said, thumbing through his notes.

"You seeing the lieutenant?" Cris asked.

"Yep. You?"

"He's a popular man," Cris said.

"That he is," Mike agreed.

"Sorry to hear about Norm. He seems like a great partner. Is he going to be okay?"

"Sure. He's strong. He likes to be the center of attention, but I will have to say, this is the first time he's done anything this dramatic."

Cris laughed.

"How is *your* partner? Sorry to call him that, I couldn't think of another term for him that didn't include the word *ass*."

"You'll get no argument from me," Cris said. "I think he stays up nights studying how to be a bigger jerk. Does anyone like him?"

"I heard his mother can almost tolerate him," Mike said.

"I'm surprised."

"Cris, Mike. Come in," Burris said, standing in his doorway.

"Ladies first," Mike held out his hand.

Cris stopped in her tracks, looked at Mike and shook her head. "Not on duty."

"Good." He stepped into the lieutenant's office ahead of her.

"I was on the phone with Norm's doctor," Burris said as he pulled his desk chair under him. "The angiogram confirmed two arterial blockages. The stents should fix him up."

"They're not going to do surgery?" Cris asked.

"The doctor said it wasn't necessary; he said Norm was young and a good candidate for the stents. He's looking at maybe a one week recovery.

"He's a tough nut," Mike said.

"Okay, this brings us to this. He held out both hands; one toward each of the detectives. As of today, and until further notice, you two are partners."

"Yes!" Cris said in a controlled shout as she punched the air in front of her. "Sorry, Lieutenant." She looked over to Mike with a hesitant smile.

Mike glanced at Cris with a blank look on his face. She was smiling like a nun with four aces.

"You okay with this detective?" Burris asked Mike. "I think I can speculate on Vega's take."

Mike answered slowly, trying to appear concerned. "I'm not sure. It may take me a little while to get used to a new partner."

"Oh, my guess is you can handle it. Listen, I need you two to talk to a uniform at the South Precinct," Burris said. "His prints were all over the dark blue Denali next to Hamid's car at Cumberland Plaza. His name is Kurt Newsome and we have no record on the log of his presence at the crime scene. I want some answers on why his prints are all over that SUV. He is supposed to be meeting you two at the

South Precinct in," Burris checked the clock on his desk, "about thirty minutes."

"We've got it," Mike said.

"They also matched up another partial set from the driver's side of Hamid's car."

"Really?" Cris said.

"James Daniel Mullins," Burris said, smiling.

"We expected that one," Mike said calmly.

"What do you mean you expected it?" Burris asked.

"Sarah Jennings told us last night. He put his hands on the car when he approached her and made the threat about Hamid. She was using his car to run errands while hers was in the shop."

"Damn," Burris said. "I've got a meeting. You two have any questions?"

"No sir," Cris said.

The new partners left for the South Precinct and their meeting with Officer Kurt Newsome.

"So," Cris said after they were on their way, "I hope you don't mind, but I was asking around about you, and I heard you lost your sister to homicide."

"Who told you that?"

"I don't remember; one of the detectives."

"Yes," Mike looked straight ahead. "Connie was killed in '94."

"Sorry. It's tough losing a sibling," Cris said.

"She was my only sibling."

"That had to be tough on the whole family."

"My Mom had already passed when it happened—breast cancer."

"Geez, Mike. That's terrible. I'm sorry."

"Connie's death caused a rift in what was left of our already small family," Mike said.

"I understand the rift, but as a rule, it's not events that cause them," Cris said, "people do."

Mike thought about Cris's statement for a moment and began to feel defensive. "You have a degree in psychology?"

"No. Like you unfortunately, I have experience."

"Oh?"

"My brother Joey joined the Marines right out of high school. He was eighteen at the time, so he didn't need my parent's permission. Mom went crazy. She raised eight kinds of hell for the entire time between his enlistment and the day he left. I thought the poor kid was going to move out to get some peace during his last weeks."

Cris looked out the windows, scanning the area as they drove, and recalling the experience.

"Anyway, she fought her best fight to get Dad to convince Joey to change his mind. My father wasn't about to try to influence Joey. He acted like he agreed with her to keep the peace between them, and Joey knew that.

"He wouldn't admit it to her, but Dad was so proud of Joey he could bust. The day Joey came home after signing up, he went out to the garage and told Dad first. Joey said Dad cried. He didn't cry because he didn't want him to go. He cried because he was looking at a man, a man who was prepared to make his own life decisions and deal with the consequences. They were proud of each other."

"That's got to be a good feeling," Mike said, wishing he knew how either side of a loving father-son experience might feel.

"Joey was killed in Kuwait in '91 in a non-combat accident. Mom didn't speak to Dad for almost a month. Finally, a friend of hers helped her get out her grief. She started to come to grips with Joey's death and more so the fact that Dad and I were still there.

"Dad was a cop in Houston. He was an officer for twenty-eight years; made sergeant after eighteen years of beating the hot streets. His buddies had a hell of a time getting him to put in for the test. He didn't want to leave the streets. He knew the streets of Houston like he knew our backyard. It was something he was very good at. I think he was fearful he couldn't be as good at something else.

"They convinced him he would still be out there, but instead of trying to do it all himself, he would be supporting and training new officers to learn what he had learned. He was hard-headed, but he knew they were right."

Mike smiled at Cris and said, "Cop commitment."

"Yep. He's my role model. When I was born, he wanted another boy. He had already picked out his son's name, Christopher like my mom's father. But then I popped out. Uh oh, change of plans. What about Cris?" She laughed. "My Mom said he got used to the fact they had a little girl real fast."

"When I signed up for the academy without talking to him first, he got pissed. We argued for weeks before I started. I knew why he had a problem with it; he was worried about me and worried about whether I would be there for Mom when he was gone. If anything happened to him, I would be all she had left.

"I promised him I would be careful, and I would be there to take care of Mom no matter what. He gave in a little, remembering I was as bull-headed as he was. He could tell I was determined, and I think that actually gave him a sense of pride to go along with his worry. He told me, 'If you have to do this, be the best you can be.' I reminded him that's the way I was raised."

Cris paused and ran her finger across the corner of her eye. "When I graduated second in my class, he cried. So did I."

Cris sat without talking for a few minutes. Mike knew she wasn't finished.

"When they found the tumor, I was in my second year as a detective. He began to have some serious headaches, and he occasionally missed work. He never missed work.

"He called me. He asked me to confirm I would take care of Mom and myself. He was scared. He never wanted his little Cris to be a cop."

"Did he ... ?" Mike stopped.

"No. He's still here; well he's still in Houston. He's retired. They operated and said they got it all, but we still wonder. He has these—moments, but we still have him, and he still worries about me.

"So," she straightened in her seat, "here I am, four years a detective; almost half of one in homicide and now partnered with the best. Dad is so proud of me."

Mike laughed, "Oh, he may not be so complimentary of your new partner."

"He would admire your skill and your dedication like everyone else does."

"Everyone else?" Mike questioned. "I'm not so sure you could gain a quorum for that vote."

"I didn't realize you were modest," Cris said, smiling.

"Actually, I'm not trying to be." Mike paused. "It's just that we have a few detectives who seem to think my sole aim in life is to make them look bad. My objective is to do my job the best I can, and to try and help the people of Nashville to find some type of closure to the ugliest chapters of their lives. It's bad enough to lose someone like you lost Joey. But, to lose a loved one to a violent homicide is .... It's worse, trust me."

Mike pulled through the gate into the fenced area at the rear of the South Precinct.

"You might be surprised at the respect you have within the section."

"I would be pleasantly surprised," Mike admitted.

Mike and Cris entered the precinct and showed their shields to the sergeant.

"We're here to talk with Officer Kurt Newsome," Mike said. "Do you know if he's here?"

"Yeah, he came in a few minutes ago," the sergeant said. "I think he's in the break room."

"Do you have an interview room available?" Mike asked.

"Yeah, number two is open. Do you know where the rooms are located?"

"Yeah," Mike said. "Thanks."

Mike and Cris walked the hall toward the officers' break room. Mike scanned the name tags of the three men getting coffee and talking.

"Officer Newsome?" Mike asked.

"I'm Kurt Newsome."

The other officers left the room.

"Can I assume you've been briefed on the purpose of our visit?" Mike asked.

"I was told my prints were found at Cumberland Plaza. I'm not sure what that's about. I don't think I've ever been to Cumberland Plaza."

"Let's step in here. I'm sure you understand I need to record our discussion?"

"Sure," Newsome agreed.

Mike placed his recorder on the table.

"Officer Kurt Newsome and Detectives Mike Neal and Cris Vega at the South Precinct, April 16th. Officer Newsome, your prints were taken from a vehicle parked on the sixth floor of the Cumberland Plaza parking garage," Mike said. "Were you in that parking garage recently?"

"No. Sounds like it may be a vehicle I stopped for a traffic violation," Newsome suggested.

"We thought the same thing," Mike said, "since you were not on duty in the area at the time, and your name wasn't on the crime scene log."

"I'm sure that's what it is. I stop quite a few vehicles each day." Newsome smiled at both detectives.

"We're no longer so sure that's the explanation," Cris said.

"What do you mean?" Newsome turned toward Cris.

"We pulled your records and found you did indeed pull this vehicle over for a rolling stop," Mike said.

"I knew it would be something like that."

"Eight months ago," Mike finished his sentence.

"From the spotless appearance of the vehicle, I can't help but think it may have been washed in the last eight months," Cris said. "What do you think, Kurt?"

"What's the make and model?" Newsome asked, becoming

concerned about the detectives' facts.

"It's a dark blue GMC Yukon Denali," Mike said.

Newsome's eyes closed, and his chin dropped slowly to his chest.

"You seem to be familiar with this vehicle?" Cris said.

Newsome nodded his head. "Yeah."

"Who is the owner?" Cris asked.

"I'm sure you already know the answer to that."

"Answer the question, officer Newsome," Mike said.

"The vehicle's owner is Vanita Joynor," he said. "She's an attorney. She works at Cumberland Plaza."

"Mrs. Joynor is the owner," Cris said, "and yes, we knew that. We also suspect you and she have been seeing each other for months, possibly since her citation."

Newsome sat quietly looking at Cris.

"We also know she is married—like you," Cris said. "You have two young girls at home?"

"Leave them out of it," Newsome said, wrinkling his brow. "They're none of your business."

"When we pull numerous fingerprints of yours from a vehicle parked less than four feet from the brutally murdered body of a young man, everything is our business," Mike said. "It is also the business of the District Attorney, who is working hard to determine who was wielding the blade used to commit this monstrous crime. Officer Newsome, do you own a knife?"

"Wait a damn minute. Don't do this," Newsome said. "I haven't killed anyone, and I'm pretty sure you know that too. I was nowhere near that area of town yesterday. And, when I touched the SUV last, I was nowhere near that building."

"Officer Newsome, we deal in facts," Mike said. "What we know is, your prints are on a car that was in close proximity to an extremely violent murder, and we're looking for suspects. Until we find sufficient reasons to eliminate you as a suspect, you will remain on the short list of potentials."

Newsome's fear was beginning to surface.

"Now, how about you start providing us with some viable reasons to eliminate you as a suspect?" Cris said.

Newsome appeared defeated. He looked like a man who wished he was somewhere else, and someone else.

"What do you want?" Newsome said.

"We want to hear the facts; the truth," Cris said. "You can start anytime."

"Okay, full disclosure." The cop leaned back in his chair, closed his eyes and rubbed them aggressively with both hands. He let out a brief guttural groan, then sat up.

"I wrote Vanita Joynor a citation last year for failure to stop. She was hot, very hot. I was—at the time, doing without. My wife and I weren't getting along. I took down Vanita's information and hooked up with her the next week. We've been sorta seeing each other off and on since then. That's it. That's everything; the entire story."

"The entire story?" Cris asked.

"Yeah. That's it. You may find my prints on the inside of the SUV as well. Look, can we keep a lid on this? I got those two little girls at home, and I'd like to get past this without any further damage." His initial confidence appeared shaken.

"That's not gonna be up to us. We have a job to do," Mike said.

"We could get into some deep shit here," Cris said. "The fact your prints are found, prominently and in large numbers, at a crime scene you're not assigned to. Well, that's between you and the powers that be. We can't jeopardize this investigation or *our* jobs to save your unfaithful ass."

Mike's look suggested to Cris she might want to curtail her judgmental tone.

"Okay, what *can* you do?" His head moved from Mike to Cris and back. "Why can't you say I gave her a citation and leave it at that? Why does all this other crap have to come out?"

"We have to pursue all leads. This is, above all, a homicide investigation," Mike said, trying not to destroy the man's hope.

"I'm screwed." Newsome dropped his head into his hands. "Damn it. Why did she have to be so beautiful?"

"Newsome," Cris said, "why don't you try blaming yourself a little for this? Mrs. Joynor did not pursue you."

Newsome sat thinking and staring at the table between him and the detectives.

"Hey, talk to your sergeant now before the facts all come out," Cris said. "Explain it all to him. It will lessen the impact on everyone."

"He'll can my ass."

"Maybe not," Mike said as he stood. "Honesty helps."

"Yeah," Cris said, "honesty will probably help you a lot more before the facts come out than it will after everyone has made their assumptions and blown it all out of proportion. You owe those two little girls better than that."

Newsome dropped his head into his hands.

# Chapter 45

*Criminal Justice Center*
*Nashville, Tennessee*
*Wednesday Late Afternoon*

When Carol caught sight of Mike, he was standing outside the door to Lieutenant Burris's office talking with a tall blonde woman. She was maybe mid-thirties, sporting a tailored and expensive navy blue suit over her well-toned form. Her long legs and stiletto heels put her eye-to-eye with Detective Neal.

*This woman is not a cop.*

Carol could see the woman had Mike's full attention even before she casually unbuttoned her jacket. The shiny folded lapel of her white silk blouse fell part-way open when she pushed back her jacket and rested her fist on her hip. She never broke pace with her dialogue, acting as though nothing had happened. The intentional increase in the exposure of her lace camisole appeared to draw Mike in. The dance had begun; she was leading. She occasionally looked around the Homicide Unit while she talked so Mike might take the opportunity to enjoy her show.

*She has to be a lawyer.*

What perturbed Carol most was that Mike's awareness of this woman's plan, like his resistance, seemed to be non-existent. Mike stood smiling, nodding and holding his notebook in front of him.

*At least he's keeping his hands busy.*

The woman must have said something funny. She leaned forward and laid her hand on Mike's bare forearm. They both laughed out loud.

*Could this bitch get more obvious?*

"Who *is* this woman," Carol said aloud, without realizing it.

"Vanita Joynor," a voice behind her replied.

Carol turned quickly to see Detective Cris Vega standing at her desk. Carol wasn't sure what to say.

"She's an attorney," Cris said. "Her SUV was the blue one next to Hamid's Acura at Cumberland Plaza."

"Oh—okay." Carol relaxed a bit, now that she knew why the woman was here.

As Carol and Cris stood watching, Mike looked up. Over Joynor's shoulder, his attention appeared to freeze on Carol. Carol dropped her eyes to the photos in her hands, and turned away. She resisted her desire to look back at Mike and his new lawyer friend.

"See ya, Carol," Cris said, as she stepped toward the copier.

After a moment, Carol allowed a couple of photos to drop from her hands and she bent to pick them up. During her squat, she stole another look in Mike's direction. The two of them were gone. She stood, scanned the Unit, and then turned back to her photos. Mike was standing behind her.

"Hi," he said.

"Oh—Hi, Mike. You scared me."

"When?"

"Just now," Carol said.

"Now, or a few minutes ago when I was talking with Mrs. Joynor?"

"What do you mean?"

"You had this ... look on your face," Mike said.

"No, I didn't."

"Yeah, you did. Carol, she was flirting; pretty obvious too, huh?"

Carol shrugged her shoulders. She waited, and then nodded at Mike.

"Hey, she's married, and she knows that we know she's been having an affair. She needs us to keep that fact quiet, so she wants to be our friend."

"Okay."

"By the way, I'm still thinking with this head." Mike tapped next to his ear.

"Good. Okay," Carol said, confirming her embarrassment.

"See you later," Mike said.

"Yeah. Later."

"Hey, Cris," Mike shouted. "You ready to meet with the lieutenant?"

"Sure. I'll be right there."

Mike walked toward Burris's office. Cris came back to her desk to drop off her copies. Carol was still thumbing through her photographs and wondering how stupid she must have looked.

Cris picked up her writing pad, stepped close to Carol and whispered, "Don't give up; you've got him on the ropes." Cris winked and then walked to Burris's office.

"Okay, guys. I talked with the Captain, and he said the Chief wants you two dedicated to the Hamid case until it's cleared."

"Wow," Cris said.

"So, bring me everything else you've been working on so I can dole it out. This one is top priority. The Chief said the Mayor wants this case cleared before the Kurdish Conference on Friday."

"You gotta be kidding," Cris said. "What about the graffiti artist?"

"I'll reassign it," Burris said. "Just focus on this one for now. The powers want it cleared."

"Hmm," Cris said.

"Listen," Burris said. "You need to understand. The political implications here are huge. We've got hundreds of international dignitaries and politicos coming into the city over the next few days, not to mention all the VIPs from Congress and around the U.S.. The Mayor doesn't want the positive press for Nashville to be overshadowed by the negative coming out of this case. If the victim wasn't Kurdish, it wouldn't be quite as bad."

"We gotcha, Lieutenant." Mike stood. He knew if they had a prayer of clearing this case by Friday, they had to get back to it.

"Cris, you collect the other casebooks and get them to Lieutenant Burris. I'm going to go see the Medical Examiner. Surely some of her backlog has been cleared by now."

# Chapter 46

*Criminal Justice Center*
*Nashville, Tennessee*
*Wednesday Late Afternoon*

Captain Moretti was standing, actually pacing, in his office. Jack Hogue was trying not to look at him.

“If it wasn’t for your tenure here,” Moretti said, “I wouldn’t even be talking with you today.”

Moretti stopped in front of Hogue.

“Jack, we can remember the past, we can learn from it, and we can even relish it, but it's not somewhere to live. The world is constantly changing, particularly our part of it. I have to have someone in your job I can trust to do the things that have to be done by a seasoned detective and who will do them with the best interest of the department and the citizens of Nashville foremost in their thinking. I would like this person to be you, but based upon your actions over the past couple of months, since Murdock’s retirement, you are proving to me that this is not possible.”

“Captain,” Hogue said. “This is all a big misunderstanding.”

“I’ll agree that it’s big, but it’s no misunderstanding. Your taking the cruiser, leaving your partner standing in a parking lot then driving outside our jurisdiction at over ninety miles per hour after you'd been drinking was not a misunderstanding. Jack, that's what's called irresponsible and thoroughly dumb ass."

Hogue sat slumped over.

"So tell me, how is it the blood test showing the alcohol level in your blood at 0.04, is a misunderstanding?"

Hogue kept his chin on his chest and said nothing.

"Your actions have limited my options. You have embarrassed me, yourself and the Metropolitan Nashville Police Department for the last time. As of today, you are suspended pending an Office of Professional Accountability investigation into your most recent reckless behavior, including drinking on duty and driving while drinking on duty. You'd best prepare for the end of your career and pray you won't lose your pension over this."

"Captain, I didn't drink while on duty."

"Oh, really? I'll concede no one saw you take a drink while on duty, but you came to work after you'd been drinking. It's the same damn thing, Jack. According to the trooper who finally got you to pull over, your breath smelled of alcohol. Granted, with a pocket full of mints in you, you smelled more like peppermint schnapps, but we know you'd been drinking. The blood test confirmed it.

"Trust me, the best thing you could do for yourself right now is to glue your tactless lips together and buy yourself a subscription to a fishing magazine. Now get out of my office and report to Lieutenant Burris. I don't want to see or hear about you again until I get the results from the OPA. Understood?"

Hogue nodded.

# Chapter 47

*White Tail Lodge*
*Hubbard County, Tennessee*
*Wednesday Evening*

"Where is Mullins being held?" Brad asked.

"The county jail," Garrison said. "Harlan thinks the best opportunity we'll have of getting to him is during a move."

"Can you find out when and where he might be moved?"

"I'm sure Harlan could find out. He told me today that Jimmy Dan is scheduled to give his deposition on Friday, and we don't need that to happen. I know that boy will tell everything he knows to save his ass."

"He's in a good position to bargain knowledge for a reduced sentence," Brad added.

"If he's successful, I'll be thrown under the bus for the guns at his house, the ones in the armory at the lodge and then into prison for the rest of my years. Most importantly, TARPA and all our goals for the future would be thrust into turmoil. I just can't let that happen."

"Let's focus on step one," Brad said. "Where is the deposition to be held? Do we know yet?"

"Harlan said he suspected it would be in the Kefauver Federal

Building on Broadway," Garrison said. "He has contacts that say they can find out things."

"Then we've got to get busy." Brad stood. "That's less than forty-eight hours away. I have to know the time of the deposition; the sooner you can tell me the better."

"I'll get it from Harlan. They have to tell him. The problem is they may not tell him until Friday not long before the deposition," Garrison said.

"That's not good, but it's all we've got. Call my cell the moment he tells you. Okay?"

"Trust me. I will."

Brad pulled his truck from the shadowy woods surrounding the complex and out onto the highway. He headed home to pick up a few things. If he was going to consider doing this and collect the generous compensation Garrison promised him, he was going to have to find an elevated position where he could get the angle on the Federal Building.

# Chapter 48

*Hillcrest Apartment*
*Nashville, Tennessee*
*Wednesday Evening*

Jorge Alvarez, resident manager at Hillcrest Apartments, made his facility rounds nightly between 8:00 and 9:00 p.m. He didn't look for trouble or expect to find it, but he made sure he always carried his .380 Ruger semi-automatic in his hand, concealed in his pocket, as he walked through the sixty-five unit complex. Seeing the apartments at night gave him a different perspective on the facility. The darkness somehow made the aged place seem more capable of hostility.

As he approached Building 10, he remembered that earlier in the afternoon he received a call from his assistant manager who'd spotted one of the building's tenants packing an SUV. Since the three men living in the apartment had moved in only a few months earlier, the assistant told the manager he was suspicious of what appeared to be a move-out.

Alvarez intentionally made his pass close to the door of the darkened apartment. His curiosity, as well as his concern for his cash flow, forced him to knock. He stepped back from the door, placing himself in front of the peephole and under the light so he could be identified. He waited. Receiving no response, he knocked and stepped back again. Still no response.

He stepped to the door. "Manager," he announced, prior to knocking a third time. He waited again. With still no response from inside the apartment, he reached for his master keys. He didn't like entering residents' apartments without prior notice, but under the circumstances, this was called for. He located the key and pushed it into the lock.

"Manager," he yelled even louder this time, making sure he was following his own rules for entering occupied apartments.

His twelve years as an apartment manager taught him to be respectful of his tenants, but his instincts were driving his actions tonight. He sensed these renters were gone. As he pushed the door back, he remained outside the threshold. He reached inside and flipped the light switch. The typically messy sight he had seen so many times over the years, and that he expected to see following any move-out, would have been pleasant compared to this.

In all his years as an apartment manager, in Nashville and even in Guatemala, he'd never experienced a scene like this.

It took only seconds for him to make the call to 911, but he knew that it would take years, if it was possible, to purge from his memory what he had seen. Before the emergency operator answered, he had already turned out the light, closed and locked the door. None of his residents needed to see this.

He paced the parking lot outside the entrance to apartment 10-D, his hand was on the Ruger and his mind was on how much it was going to cost to clean up the dreadful mess inside.

# Chapter 49

*Davidson County Morgue*
*Nashville, Tennessee*
*Wednesday Evening*

Dr. Elaine Jamison was a home grown product of Nashville's public school system, Vanderbilt University and its Medical School. And, she was exhausted.

She knew she should be at home nursing a cool glass of Chardonnay and attempting recovery from the five autopsies she'd completed since 05:30 this morning. But, that wasn't an option. Sadly, the workload for the Davidson County Medical Examiner was keeping up with Nashville's population explosion. For some reason, Dr. Jamison's operating budget was losing the race.

The morgue was at half staff, and she had been pulling double shifts since Monday. The draining sixteen-hour days were beginning to catch up with her.

Mike pulled on his scrubs, gloves, shoe covers and safety glasses. He was positioning his mask over his nose and mouth when he pushed open the door to the large autopsy theatre.

"Dr. Jamison," Mike scarcely got her name out before the twin stench of death and formalin seized his nose and tried its best to turn his stomach. He had breathed this foul-smelling mixture on too many occasions and each time it took him back to the nauseating night in '94 when, on the way home from the airport, his Dad asked him to identify Connie's body. His Dad couldn't do it. Mike wished he could get to the level where the smell didn't remind him of that night—fat chance.

She looked up from the corpse currently under her knife and eyed Mike through her face shield. "Hello, detective. How are you?"

"I'm okay I guess, considering." Mike walked closer to the stainless steel table where the M.E. was harvesting organs. "I took Norm to St. Thomas Emergency this afternoon with a heart attack."

"No." She stopped with both hands inside the deceased man's thoracic cavity.

"I'm afraid so." Mike nodded. "He's doing okay though. They gave him a couple of stents. I guess he'll get an extra vacation this year."

"If you want to call it that." She continued to work as she spoke. "I hate to hear that, Mike, but I'm sure he'll be fine. St. Thomas has some of the best cardiac teams in the world."

Mike followed her movements, and considered the irony presented by the dead man's motionless heart in her hand while she sang the praises of the cardiac physicians. She laid the organ in the scale pan, stated the weight into the microphone and set the organ aside for dissection. Mike tried his best to keep his eyes up, and not look too closely at the doctor's work.

"I heard you're about to hang a 'No Vacancy' sign out front."

"That might become necessary," she said, "if we can't get a few light days where the people of Nashville take a break from killing each other."

"Believe me, we could use some of those days in Homicide too."

"My assistant is back from bereavement leave tomorrow and the autopsy assistant will be home from her Cancun vacation on Monday. Maybe then we'll get caught up."

"I wish you luck."

"So—you're here to talk about which of my guests?"

"Daran Hamid. He's the young Kurdish man who was stabbed and his throat was cut."

"Oh yes. I completed his exam a short while ago."

Dr. Jamison peeled off her gloves, removed her face shield and snatched a file folder from a rack of similar folders.

"I'll be right back," she said over her shoulder as she pulled the handle and swung open the large stainless steel door to the cold room.

Moments later, as Mike was focused on anything that would keep him from looking into the open chest cavity of the doctor's current project, the gurney with the body of Daran Hamid separated the plastic strips of the cold room curtain, and Dr. Jamison trailed it into the autopsy room.

"I sent prints and nail clippings to TBI. You should have the prints back in a few weeks, but the DNA will likely take months. As you know, TBI is still backlogged, particularly with all I've been sending them lately."

"That won't help us. The Chief wants this one cleared before Friday."

"Friday? Good luck. He'll have to pull some strings."

"I think that's what he's doing now," Mike said. "Do you think we'll ever have our own crime lab?"

"Keep praying detective."

She began to read from her report. "The right hand showed two significant defensive wounds and the left had scratches. I would assume the victim was taken by surprise and killed rather quickly, before he could offer much resistance."

"Yes, the VHS tape we retrieved from the garage confirmed that."

The M.E. lifted the sheet and pulled it back to expose the upper half of Hamid's body.

"I'm sure you noticed that Mr. Hamid lost most of his blood in the car," she said. "The throat laceration was quite deep, severing the right carotid seventy-five percent and the trachea almost completely. This was the most severe of his injuries and the chief cause of death due to the resulting accelerated exsanguination."

Mike looked at the throat wound. After years of examining serious wounds, he still became queasy.

Dr. Jamison retrieved her camera from the shelf. "I haven't had time to print these yet, but as you can see here in these digital shots I took prior to opening Mr. Hamid's chest, there was some bruising across his upper chest that I believe to be consistent with the height of the upper door jam of the victim's car." She held up the digital camera's viewer as she tapped the button to scan through the images. "That's a guess, and I'll have to defer to you for confirmation of that measurement."

"I'll verify it," Mike said.

"Help me turn him onto his side."

Mike helped the doctor roll the body.

"The stab wound to the victim's lower right side was executed with a significant amount of force. The hilt bruise was substantial. The wound was deep; 22.8 centimeters and the entry was 6.9 centimeters across. Based upon the pointed ends of the wound and the significant width, it is characteristic of a wound from a sharp double-edged knife. A single-edged blade can produce a wound with two pointed ends, mimicking an injury from a double-edged blade. But, I have seen few wounds like this one in my years that turned out to be single-edged.

The internal damage indicated the blade was curved between twenty and thirty degrees from hilt to tip."

"That part is a match," Mike said.

"Oh?"

"The security tape from the garage allowed us to see what we feel certain was the murder weapon. The wound you described is consistent with the shape of the weapon we saw on the tape."

"That's good."

"Yes, but your analysis suspecting a double edge is inconsistent with our findings at the home of our suspect. He owns a number of large knives, many with curved blades. These curved blades are butcher's knives; the kind they use in meat markets for de-boning and such."

"Okay."

"We found none of them with double-edged blades."

"None?"

"No."

"Hmm. Sorry, Mike."

"Well, until coming here, I hadn't thought about it. But, your opinion together with seeing the stab wound, reminds me of a weapon I saw while I was in the Middle East."

"Really?"

"Have you ever seen a Jambiya?" Mike asked.

"I've heard the word. Remind me what it looks like?"

"Jambiya is Arabic for 'dagger'. The ones I saw in Iraq and Turkey all had around seven to ten inch double-edged blades. The blades were curved upward to differing degrees, some dramatically, and they had a central rib along both sides of the blade from the hilt to near the point."

"Interesting," Dr. Jamison said. "You *could* be describing the murder weapon."

# Chapter 50

*Murfreesboro Road*
*Nashville, Tennessee*
*Wednesday Evening*

With his cell on speakerphone so Cris could also hear, Mike asked Lieutenant Burris, "What makes you think they're connected?"

"This victim is also Middle Eastern," Burris said. "His throat was cut in the same manner as Hamid's. According to the officers at the scene, this victim's neck was laid open with considerable force. There's more than enough similarity to suspect the same killer."

"Sounds like you may be right," Mike said.

"This is all we need," Cris said, "a serial killer targeting Middle Easterners right before this high profile conference."

"That's why we have to end this now," Burris said. "I've already called Mathis and Rains. They were assigned this case and they are at the scene now. I told them if you also feel the two homicides are related, then they are to relinquish the lead on this one to you and Cris. But they're to remain on board to assist you in whatever way they can."

"Thanks. We can use the help," Mike said. "We'll be in touch when we know something."

The cruiser groaned into a lower gear as it climbed the inclined drive to the Hillcrest Apartments. The scene was already approaching chaos. The hilltop complex offered moderate parking space for the tenants. Spaces were limited to two per unit, and at this hour on a weeknight, most everyone was at home.

"I hate arriving late to a crime scene," Mike said. "So much is at risk from so many people who don't get it. Mathis and Rains are good. I hope they've been able to control access to the scene."

Emergency equipment was parked in all directions near the entrance to apartment 10-D. Red and blue strobe lights illuminated the complex. The fire trucks, ambulance, and at least a half-dozen patrol cars filled the drive blocking all access to and from the apartments located behind the crime scene. If not for the excitement of the crime, the tenants' temporary inability to come and go could have been a major problem, but at the moment, they were focused on the events on their front doorstep.

Mike pulled the cruiser as close to the apartment as he could. As soon as he stopped, a TV remote broadcast van pulled in behind him. He walked to the rear of the car, looked at the six or so inches between the bumper on the van and the car's trunk. As he stared through the windshield at the van's driver, Mike pushed his sports jacket back and put his hand in his pocket exposing his shield and Glock. The van rolled backward three feet. Mike opened the trunk, grabbed a few pairs of gloves and Tyvek shoe covers, and handed some to Cris. He took his notepad and started for the apartment.

The tape for the outer crime scene perimeter blocked the inquisitive tenants and the media from getting close to the apartment. Every time one of the emergency responders opened the apartment door, camera flashes went off like automatic weapons. So far, it was the closest thing to access the hungry reporters had to whatever was creating this spectacle.

Mike and Cris approached the tape and after signing in at the command table, they pulled on their gloves and shoe covers. They stepped up onto the stoop, and as Mike opened the apartment door he could tell the unit had long been deprived of fresh air. It reeked from the smell of rotting food and heavy cigarette smoke. A large ashtray sat on the dining room table partially filled with, and completely encircled by, what must have been pints of thick reddish-brown blood that hours ago had been pumped onto the table until the man's brain notified his heart to stop. The victim's face occupied the middle of the blood pool.

Cris grunted to herself when she saw the body. "Wow. He pissed off somebody."

Mike pulled his digital camera from his jacket and began his personal attempt to document the scene. As he made his way toward the victim, Mike could see the bloody gash. It was so long that even though the victim's head was face down on the table, the wound was visible on both sides of the man's neck.

Mike was careful not to step in the blood that had dripped from several points around the table and pooled onto the short-pile carpeting. Through a doorway to what appeared to be a small bedroom, he spotted Detective Mathis making notes. He heard Rains talking to a crime scene tech in the kitchen.

With Cris in his wake, Mike stepped into the kitchen area.

"Learned anything yet?"

"Hey, Mike. Only that this unit was occupied by three men over the last few months who were believed to be of Middle Eastern decent. The victim is believed to be one of those three, and the whereabouts of the other two is still unknown. One of the manager's crew told him he saw the other two and an additional man loading their belongings into a large dark SUV today."

"What time was that?" Cris asked.

"The manager said about fourteen hundred."

"Did you get a description on the men?" Mike asked.

"Mathis has it. Hey, what's this I hear about Norm?"

"He had a heart attack this afternoon."

"That's what Mathis told me. Is he okay? Where is he?"

"He's at St. Thomas with a couple of stents in him. They say he's gonna to be okay."

"Wow. That's scary," Rains said. "He's younger than I am."

"Yeah, and a hundred pounds heavier," Mike said. "What's the status on our techs?"

"The photographer is finished. He got here just after we did. The sketches are being completed and prints are being collected now. The lieutenant called a little while ago. He thinks this may be related to your Cumberland Plaza case, huh?"

"Yeah," Mike said. "I think it may have too much in common not to be."

"So, are you assuming lead investigator?" Rains asked.

"Yeah, but don't let that numb your instincts. We're still going to need all the skills we can summon if we're going to solve these two by Friday."

"Friday?"

"Yeah, that's the task," Mike said, "straight from the Chief and the Mayor."

"Wow, no wonder he wants us all on this. Hmm. Okay. What do you want me to focus on?"

"Right now let's make sure we get all the evidence that's here. The place is a mess and that means sloppiness on the part of the suspects. So, there should be plenty of chances for prints, trace and DNA. Make sure we get some of those uncontaminated butts from the ashtray on the table. The brand looked familiar."

"I thought they were all Arabic," Rains said.

"They are. Remember, the more data we get from here, the better our chances to find a parallel with the Cumberland Plaza case. I'm going to find Mathis and see what he's discovered from the manager. Cris, why don't you check with the print tech and make sure we are getting *all* surfaces printed and not just the easy ones."

"Got it," Cris said.

Mike almost ran into Mathis as he was coming out of the bedroom. He was still scribbling; his mind on his notes.

"Hello, Mike. How's Norm?"

"He's okay. He'll be back in a few days."

"That's good to hear."

"What did you find out from the manager?"

"Mr. Alvarez said these three signed a one year lease about four months ago. He said they're students at TSU. They drove a maroon four-door Nissan Sentra, early nineties model and they had another old car, but he didn't recall the make or model. He didn't know the plates. He said one of them, the tallest of the group, was the only one he ever spoke with. His name was Aziz. He always paid the rent on time, and he paid with cash."

"What was his take on all this?" Mike nodded toward the body.

"He wasn't much help. He said they were quiet. He never heard anything strange coming from the apartment. For the most part, at least until the abrupt move-out, they were model tenants."

"What about this new guy the manager's employee saw today?"

"He said his assistant told him the man was dressed well in a dark suit, not like the students," Mathis said. "He said he was older, late thirties, early forties, but did not appear old enough to be their father."

"Middle Eastern like them?"

"Yeah. He said he thought so," Mathis said.

"What about the vehicle?"

"A dark SUV; maybe black," Mathis said. "He wasn't sure of the year or make."

"That narrows it down; a nice looking well-dressed man in a dark SUV. Not too many of those in Nashville," Mike said facetiously. "We gotta catch a break from somewhere."

"Mike."

"Yeah, Cris."

"I talked with the manager outside, and I asked him if he'd ever noticed what time these three came and went. He said they usually left in the morning around o seven hundred, presumably for classes. Then, they came home in the afternoons and left again around sixteen hundred most days."

"Did he know where they were going?" Mike asked.

"Not until he and Mrs. Alvarez were having dinner a few weeks ago and saw two of them working at Mustafa's."

"Interesting," Mike said. "What else did he tell you?"

"He said—I was beautiful," Cris said, proudly with a smile.

"You're kidding?" Mathis said.

"What's that supposed to mean?" Cris asked, offended.

"Nothing," Mathis said, wishing he'd thought twice before speaking. "I ..."

"You what? Cris asked.

"I didn't mean anything," Mathis said. "I thought it was a strange thing for him to say."

"He said I reminded him of his daughter in Guatemala," Cris said. "He hasn't seen her in six years."

"That's sad," Mike said.

"Truly," Cris said.

Mike's cell phone rang.

"Mike Neal."

"Detective Neal, this is Hoshyar."

"Hoshyar. How is your family?"

Cris turned to watch Mike, interested in what Daran Hamid's cousin had to say.

"We are still hurting. Have you arrested anyone yet?"

"I'm sorry, no. We're working on it."

"You asked us to call you if we thought of anything that might be helpful to your investigation."

"Yes. Do you have something?"

"I called to tell you Zena found something I think could be important for you. I am not sure."

"Great. What is it?"

“It is a piece of paper, maybe—like a receipt.”

“Okay.”

“I think it is the receipt from Mustafa’s when Daran ordered the food for his party.”

“Where did you find it?”

“There was a bag in the refrigerator; a white bag. Zena opened it and saw that it was baklava; the baklava Daran told her Mustafa gave to him as a gift when he ordered his food. The paper was inside, stuck to the bottom of the plastic container.”

Mike immediately recalled Norm with his head stuck in the bag smelling the baklava. “Why do you think the receipt might be important?”

“There is writing on the back,” Hoshyar said. “It is Daran’s handwriting.”

# Chapter 51

*Mustafa's Restaurant*
*Nashville, Tennessee*
*Wednesday Late Evening*

"Welcome to Mustafa's," the hostess said. "Oh. Hello, detective. Will you and the Mrs. be having dinner with us this evening?"

"No, thank you," Mike said. "Detective Vega and I need to speak with Mr. Mustafa."

Cris continued to hold up her shield.

"Sorry," she said looking at Cris. "I will get him. Can I get you anything to drink while you wait?"

"No, thank you," Mike said. "Just Mr. Mustafa."

"I will be right back."

Mike turned to Cris and smiled.

"I'm used to living in a man's world." She returned the smile. "This place sure smells good."

"That's the same thing Norm said when we were here this afternoon. It does smell nice. Maybe we'll eat lunch here sometime."

"Hello, my friend," Mustafa announced as he waddled up to the lobby.

"Mr. Mustafa, this is Detective Vega."

"I am honored to meet you, Detective. And where is my friend Detective Wallace?"

"Detective Wallace is—unavailable this evening."

"I hope he enjoyed Mustafa's cuisine." The fat man smiled with pride.

"I'm sure he did," Mike said. We are continuing to investigate the Hamid case and some new information has come to light. It has brought us back to you."

"What information is that? Come with me please." Mustafa led the detectives to the quiet of the private dining room."

"We'll get to it shortly," Mike said as he opened his tablet. "But, I need you to tell me exactly what happened yesterday morning when Mr. Hamid was here to order his food. I need to know everything you can remember."

"Let me see." Mustafa challenged his memory then communicated everything he remembered in as much detail as he could. In conclusion he said, "I am not sure what else there is I can tell you."

"What about Ahmed al-Zubaidy?" Cris asked. "Did you talk with him yesterday morning?"

"Yes. I asked Ahmed why he was late. He told me about the collision, and that he had to exchange information with the driver. I told you this already, did I not?"

"Yes," Mike said. "We often have to cover information more than once. Please indulge us."

"What else did he tell you about the wreck?" Cris asked.

"I remember he said it was his first auto accident. I asked him whose car it was he hit. He described Daran and asked me who he was. I told him that he was a customer who had been referred to us by Mr. Zaid Zebari. Ahmed asked me how he could get in touch with Daran in order to pay him for the damages to his car. I told him I knew Daran worked for Z.Z. Maintenance Company cleaning offices here in the city. He thanked me and I think that was all he said. I assumed he would take care of the damage with Daran."

"When did you last hear from al-Zubaidy?"

"I—uh, have not spoken with him today. I guess it was yesterday when he called to say he was sick and would not be at work. He is scheduled to work tonight's dinner."

"I don't think you'll see him tonight," Cris said as she looked at Mike.

Mike pulled his digital camera from his pocket and scanned through the images until he found one that showed al-Zubaidy's face before the Medical Examiner's team took him from the apartment. He zoomed into the image until the blood and the young man's open throat were not visible.

"Would you be willing to look at a picture of him? We have no one else to confirm his identity."

"I ... I guess so."

Mike held out the camera's display screen.

Mustafa covered his mouth and gasped. He looked up at Mike and nodded. "What happened?"

"He was murdered a short time ago in one of the units at the Hillcrest Apartments." Mike returned the camera to his pocket and retrieved the receipt Hoshyar had given him.

"Is this from your register?"

"I think so, yes."

"Turn it over," Mike said. "According to his cousin, that is Daran Hamid's handwriting."

"What does it mean?" Mustafa asked.

"We believe those are the notes he took the morning his car was struck by your server. Al-Zubaidy's name, his Tennessee driver's license number and the license tag for the car that struck the Acura."

"I do not know what to say," Mustafa said.

"We're still gathering facts. This is why we need as much information from you as possible about all this."

"Detective," Mustafa said appearing shaken, "I need to know

whether or not all this will damage my assignment."

"What assignment is that?" Mike asked.

"I was chosen months ago to provide the traditional Kurdish meal for the Kurdish-American Conference on Friday at the Centurion Nashville Hotel. This could bring the wrong kind of attention to my business. I cannot afford for my good name to be a part of all this ... this turmoil."

"Honestly, I don't know if this could have any impact on that decision," Mike said. "I hope not, for your sake. With less than two days until the event, I can't imagine the conference committee making any changes."

"Besides," Cris said, "al Zubaidy only worked here. As his employer, you're not responsible for his actions or what happens to him outside his work hours."

"Yes, I understand that. But, I have worked for many years here in Nashville to build a good reputation for my restaurant and myself. Surely, you realize the obstacles we as immigrants face as we attempt to build new lives for our families here. Even our names when spoken aloud prime the pumps of hatred and fear. When we come here, at first we are forced to try and become invisible, to find a way to blend in without drawing attention to ourselves. Then as we slowly build credibility and trust, we are hopefully allowed to become hyphenated Americans; Iraqi-Americans such as my family. Later, we pray that at some point over the years we may be known only as Americans, without condition." He paused. "I fear something like these killings could destroy all I have worked for."

"Mr. Mustafa," Mike said, "we will do all we can to see these unfortunate events don't draw negative attention to you or your business."

"Thank you, detectives." Mustafa offered his hand to Mike, then to Cris. "I have been fortunate since I came to America and to Nashville years ago. I have made many friends. I was welcomed and allowed to start a new life here. I owe this country and this city so much. I hope they will allow me to repay them."

"You sound like an American to me," Cris said, smiling.

# Chapter 52

*Saint Thomas Hospital*
*Nashville, Tennessee*
*Thursday Morning*

"Morning, Milwaukee." Mike yelled as soon as he pushed back the door and confirmed there was no one else in Norm's room. "How's my favorite cheese-head?"

"Partner," Norm said with a weakened voice and a strained smile. "Hi, Cris."

"Hello, Norm." Cris walked to the foot of his bed and squeezed his toes. "How are you feeling?"

"I feel like I got tackled by Green Bay's entire defensive line."

Mike walked to the side of the bed and took Norm's huge hand and squeezed it for a moment. "You sure know how to scare the crap out of your friends."

"I was only testing your ability to negotiate the streets of our city under the stress of emergency driving conditions."

"Right. Did I pass?" Mike smiled.

"Yep, I gave you an A. The patient survived the drive. Now, if I can survive the hell Cheryl's going to put me through to lose weight."

"It's for your own good, big boy. And beware, she's recruited me to help her."

"No way," Norm said.

"Yeah, we're gonna be coming at you from both directions. The bulk's coming off, Bubba. You're too important for us to let you kill yourself."

Mike's cell phone vibrated. He looked at the display. "Excuse me a minute." He stepped outside the room.

"So, what do you think about our partner," Norm asked Cris as the door closed behind Mike.

"I think he's a rare bird," Cris said.

"Definitely one of a kind," Norm agreed. "I've never known another cop with his level of compassion for victims."

"I can believe that," Cris said.

"I don't know how much he's told you about himself, but he's had a rocky life. Over the years, he's lost a number of people close to him. It's caused him to be cautious with relationships."

"Yeah, he told me about some of it," Cris said.

"That trauma may be the reason he's as caring as he is. Rather than choosing to become hardened like some cops, they've made him more perceptive of his relationships and their value to him. I think he has a unique ability to understand other folks' pain. As I'm sure you know, in this job, he gets plenty of opportunity to practice."

"That's for sure," Cris agreed.

"Now I owe him for taking care of me and getting me to the ER when he did."

"I'd say Mike did that out of love, Norm. No favor owed."

Norm nodded.

Mike pushed the door open. "Sorry, boys and girls, but it's time to go to work. That was Burris. Moretti was able to influence the TBI. They called with results on some of the prints from the apartment. He wants us in front of him, post-haste."

"What apartment? No, don't tell me. I'll only get pissed off because

I can't go with you." Norm shook his head. "Shit."

"Easy, partner." Mike took Norm's hand. "You're still in the game. You're just warming the bench for a few weeks. Do what they tell you, so you can get out of here." Mike stepped backward toward the door. "Okay? You get well," Mike pointed his finger at Norm, "or I'll be kicking that big Yankee ass." He laughed. "I'll call you later."

Cris grabbed Norm's hand and gave it a squeeze. "Take care."

"Thanks for coming by, guys," Norm said.

The door came open as Mike reached for it. He stepped back. A young lady in dark blue scrubs entered carrying a tray with a bowl of oatmeal, a small bowl of berries, a scrambled egg white, a piece of whole wheat toast and coffee.

"Feast," Mike said when they passed the dietician.

As they paced the long hallway toward the elevators, Mike said, "I'm sure glad he's okay."

"Me too," Cris said. "He sure thinks a lot of you."

"It's mutual; I assure you."

As the stainless steel doors to the elevator separated on arrival at the first floor, the new partners spotted a wall of dark blue approaching them. Almost two dozen uniformed officers and a handful of familiar faces in plainclothes stopped in front of the elevators.

"How's he doing?" Doug Wolfe asked.

Mike smiled at their display of camaraderie as he looked across the group.

"He's going to be fine."

"We're gonna see if we can cheer him up," Wolfe said.

"You will definitely do that," Mike said. "Thanks, guys."

# Chapter 53

*Criminal Justice Center*
*Nashville, Tennessee*
*Thursday Morning*

Burris spotted the detectives from his desk as they came through the door. He waved them in.

"Good morning," Cris said.

"Have a seat." Burris stuck out both hands, each containing identical copies of the fingerprint report.

"Here's what we've received from the TBI, so far. One set of partial prints came back from the FBI's AFIS and they're being reviewed by the examiners, but they feel the point count is low and they're still working for a better match. The extra effort is being made because a valid match could put one of the names from the FBI's Terror Watch List at the al-Zubaidy crime scene. His name is Abdul Malik Kadir and he's aligned with known terrorist leader Farid al-Rishari. The FBI says al-Rishari is a confederate of bin Laden."

"Wow," Cris said.

"What's the plan?" Mike asked.

"Captain Moretti is talking with Burton Jarvis, Special Agent in Charge at the Nashville field office of the FBI," Burris said. "The probability of a connection to international terrorism is high. Hell, the feds got the print report before we did."

"Wonderful," Mike said with a sarcastic tone. I thought you said they matched two sets of partials," Mike asked.

"That's even more interesting," Burris explained. "The other partial set had only been in the database a short time."

"Really?" Cris said.

"Yeah, only since TBI checked the state's AFIS yesterday." Burris looked at the detectives for their reaction.

"Yesterday?" Mike asked, wrinkling his brow. Then he said, "Hamid's car."

"That's right," Burris confirmed. "The second group of partials was taken from the Acura yesterday. But, even though we have a match, it was still with an unidentified set of prints."

"Geez," Cris said.

Burris hesitated. "Until about thirty minutes ago."

"What?" Mike said.

"Dr. Jamison called. The unidentified set of prints from the Acura and the apartment belong to the second victim, al-Zubaidy."

"Al-Zubaidy was at Cumberland Plaza," Cris said.

"Or," Burris offered, "he touched Hamid's car during the exchange of information following the wreck at Mustafa's."

"Or," Mike said, "al-Zubaidy wasn't butchered by the same killer as Hamid. He was Hamid's killer. But, if that's true, then who killed al- Zubaidy?"

"And why?" Burris added.

# Chapter 54

*Hasan al-Fulan's Basement*
*Donelson Area - Nashville, Tennessee*
*Wednesday Late Evening*

The windowless basement apartment was no place for a martyr to spend his last days, but Karim was undaunted. His focus was on memories of his father, Allah's will and what he was about to do to honor both.

"How do you feel?" Sajid asked his friend, praying the young man remained committed.

Karim knew what Sajid was actually asking. "I am ready. Allah's will be done."

"Your treasures await you," Sajid said, nodding his head.

As Abdul watched the conversation between the two young men, he could see that Karim's face showed less commitment than his words, but Abdul had seen this look before on the faces of young soon-to-be martyrs.

Karim stood and placed his hand across his forehead. "I would like to be alone for a while. I need to take my medicine and lie down. This is not a good time for a headache."

"As you wish," Abdul said. "I have one request."

"Yes."

"I would like to see you wearing the device, so I can make adjustments and be sure it is going to be hidden beneath your clothing."

Karim looked at his watch. "I will come to you in one hour. I hope I am feeling better by then," Karim said. He walked slowly to the small bedroom and closed the door.

Abdul looked at Sajid who appeared worried about his friend. "Do you feel there is cause for concern?"

"I do not think so," Sajid said. "I believe I would feel as nervous as Karim under the same conditions."

Abdul merely stared at Sajid.

"Any intelligent man about to surrender his life," Sajid said, "would be just as withdrawn and in search of his God."

Once the hour had passed, Karim came to Abdul. Sajid held the straps as Karim carefully slipped his arms through and wrapped the device around his body. Abdul made the needed adjustments and secured the straps. Sajid helped Karim pull on his tuxedo shirt and waiter's white jacket. Abdul checked to make sure the device was not visible.

Satisfied the device would be hidden beneath Karim's clothes; Abdul checked his watch, then nodded at Karim and told him he could remove it for the wait.

Sajid helped Karim remove the device and the young martyr-to-be returned to the privacy of the dark bedroom and his prayers.

Abdul wanted his last words to Karim to be worthy of the young man's impending sacrifice, so he planned them carefully.

When it was time, Sajid and Abdul again helped Karim with the device, and his clothes. He looked good and the device was well-hidden, much better than his nerves.

When they were ready to leave, Abdul spoke to him and said,

"Karim—may Allah grant you resolve and victory today and may you find abundant riches in Paradise. For whoever obeys Him alone will enter the Garden. May the peace and blessings of Allah be upon you today as you carry out His will."

"All praise be to Allah," Sajid said.

"Allahu Akbar," Abdul said.

"Allahu Akbar," the young men repeated together.

# Chapter 55

*White Tail Lodge*
*Hubbard County, Tennessee*
*Thursday Morning*

"The schedule has the rag-heads and the politicos drinking and chewing the fat in the Coliseum Room on the first floor until twelve-thirty," Vernon McBride said. "They're to begin serving lunch in the ballroom at one-fifteen and the head table introductions begin at two o'clock, minutes before the keynote address starts."

"Do you think the timing will be that precise?" Garrison asked.

"We're assured by our contacts inside the hotel that everything is highly structured at The Centurion. Their events manager is exceptionally meticulous, and the staff has learned not to disappoint her."

"Nice of them to help us." Garrison smiled.

"Senator Raymond Westbrook is to be the last one introduced by the master of ceremonies," McBride said. "He's scheduled to begin his final tolerant immigration policy address ten minutes before he gets screwed. We're all set to go at two-fifteen, about the time Westbrook is hitting his bleeding-heart liberal stride."

"Screwed?" Garrison laughed.

"The package is wrapped in five pounds of wood screws." McBride smiled. "Ouch."

"Excellent. Who's taking care of getting the package into the hotel?"

"Hightower and Dixon."

"When is it going in?"

"It's there now."

"Already?" Garrison asked, surprised.

"It's on the top floor, outside the ballroom. Our men were there this morning and took it in behind the florist when they made their delivery of all the fresh flowers this morning. They blended in nicely." McBride said, with a proud smile.

"Good job," Garrison said.

"Hightower and Dixon will finish the placement," McBride looked at his wristwatch, "about an hour from now. I should get a confirmation call once it's in place."

Garrison looked at his watch and then at McBride. "Five hours until the border starts closing?"

McBride nodded. "Five hours."

"Call me at home when it's done," Garrison said as he stood. "I'm going to be working on my next letter to the good people of TARPA. This statement will be made even more compelling by today's explosive message."

# Chapter 56

*The Rutherford Hotel*
*Nashville, Tennessee*
*Thursday Morning*

"Good morning, sir. Welcome to The Rutherford. How may I help you?"

"Hello," the middle aged man smiled. "I have a reservation; Dr. Arthur Springfield?"

"Let me check, sir." The smartly dressed young woman tapped a few buttons on her keyboard. "Yes, I have it here. Will you still be staying with us through the weekend?"

"Yes. That's my plan. I requested a special room."

"Yes, sir?"

"My wife and I—we came to Nashville. We spent our honeymoon here, back in 1988. Elizabeth passed away last year and I ... I wanted to come on our anniversary and stay in the same room we shared back then. I asked the young lady when I called. She said she could get it for me; I don't remember her name. She assured me." He smiled a painful smile.

"I'm sorry to hear of your loss, Dr. Springfield. What was the room number?" The clerk appeared concerned about whether or not she was going to find the request honored in the hotel's computer system.

"Room nineteen fifty-two. I remember, we laughed. The room number was her birth year. She decided it was a positive omen."

The desk clerk smiled.

"We stood at the window, toasted our future and then watched the lights and the tourists downtown." He dragged the back of his bent index finger across the corner of his eye.

"Here it is. I have a note. Yes sir, it is being held for you," She confirmed.

"Thank you," he said. "Thank you, so much."

"It's my pleasure, sir." She gestured to the bellman. "Okay, sir. I have room number nineteen fifty-two on the nineteenth floor. Here is your room key. Is there anything else I can do for you?"

"No. I think that will be it. Thank you for arranging the room. It means so much."

"It's our pleasure, sir. Please call the desk if there is anything else you need, and thank you for choosing The Rutherford."

"Thank you," he strained to look at her name tag and smiled, "Bonnie."

"You are quite welcome. I hope you have a pleasant stay with us."

Dr. Springfield turned to see the bellman placing his bags on a brass cart.

"Thank you. Please be careful with the golf clubs," Springfield requested. He leaned closer to the bellman and whispered. "My game sucks enough already."

The bellman smiled and patted the hard shell golf club case and said, "Yes sir. I'll take good care of them."

The two men shared pleasantries during the elevator ride. Once in his room, Dr. Springfield turned to the bellman and gave him a five dollar bill.

"Thank you, sir. Enjoy your stay."

After tossing his jacket across the back of a club chair, Brad loosened his tie and laid the golf club case across the bed. He unlocked it and opened the latches. Pushing aside the partial set of clubs, he removed the long polymer case from amidst the graphite shafts. He opened the slim case and removed the telescope from the protective foam recess along side the rifle.

He pushed back the drape sheers enough to unlock the sliding window and pull it open the full four inches before it struck the steel bar. The bar was apparently in place to allow fresh air into the room, but prevent any distraught hotel customers from using the building as a launching pad for a nineteen-story Music City suicide.

He'd walked the south side of Broadway on Wednesday night in his cowboy hat, the western shirt that Julie gave him and his dancing boots, looking like any other curious tourist snapping photos of the downtown architecture. He was focusing on the view of the Rutherford Hotel from the entrances to the Kefauver Federal Building. The zoom lens on his digital SLR camera allowed him to select a group of rooms that would provide him the needed angle on all entrances the marshals might use to bring in Mullins for his deposition.

A late visit to the hotel along with a few hat-tips and 'Howdys' got Brad onto the elevator for a stroll down the upper level hallways confirming that even-numbered rooms offered windows facing the downtown action. Luck and a phone call last evening to a sentimental reservationist obtained him an acceptable room for his task.

He focused the eyepiece; certain now the distance to the target would be no more than three-hundred and sixty yards. It was less than half the accuracy range of Garrison's generous gift.

"This should be simple," he said to himself as he again lifted the telescope to his eye.

He was scanning the areas around the front and sides of the Federal Building when his cell phone vibrated on his belt. He pulled it from the holster and checked the display.

"Hmm. I wonder what *he* wants."

"Hello." Brad listened to the caller.

"What was he thinking?" Brad asked, rhetorically. He pulled the phone away from his ear to reduce the volume of the answer. "Okay. I understand. I'll call you."

Brad closed his cell phone and looked out the hotel window.

"Well, Jimmy Dan, I guess that was your reprieve. Whatever revenge you'd intended for TARPA—is now yours. " Brad grabbed his jacket and his bags and abandoned his original plan.

# Chapter 57

*The Centurion Hotel*
*Nashville, Tennessee*
*Thursday Afternoon*

The Centurion looked more like a hotel in Kurdistan than in Nashville. There were hundreds of visitors inside the building and milling about the grounds; the majority of which were of Middle Eastern heritage. Nashville was being honored as host of the Kurdish-American Conference and the Kurds' celebration was on.

The growing Kurdish community in Nashville was a patriotic group; as proud of their new Tennessee home as they were of their homeland. Kurdish flags alternating with Old Glory and the Tri-Star Tennessee flag encircled the lobby and the hotel entrance. Outside, flags mounted every ten feet waved in the light breeze as they ran from the portico to the street welcoming the limousines and taxis arriving with their VIPs.

Many of the international visitors had arrived in advance so they might experience the Music City they had heard so much about. Local tourist venues were readied with their southern hospitality and pervasive country music.

The official registration and welcoming event for the two-day conference began in the hotel's first floor Coliseum Room. Esteemed leaders from across the Middle East were mingling with heads of local and national groups, seeking common ground. It would not be long before the dignitaries would be invited into the seven thousand square foot ballroom for seating. Everything was ready.

The Centurion's Event Manager, Teresa Maxwell, knew she had been a pain in the ass for the large kitchen and serving staff throughout the last few days. Juggling all the dining and social issues, while fending off irritated hotel employees and dodging police dogs, had served to heat up her blood pressure to just short of vaporizing.

All this seemed trivial at the moment compared to her current challenge: acting as the unofficial International Intercessor between the hotel's audacious French chef and the quiet people from the odd little Middle Eastern restaurant chosen to prepare the traditional Kurdish meal for the conference.

Gerard De Lorme, the hotel's head chef, was livid.

"Police dogs in my kitchen?" The Frenchman was about to blow a gasket. "I cannot endure this."

"I understand, Gerard," Teresa explained. "I feel the same way, but the police said they have to make a sweep of this floor once each hour and it's almost time for the last one before the VIPs enter the ballroom."

"Sweep my floor? My kitchen does not need to be swept."

"No, Gerard," Maxwell said. "They walk through looking for suspicious things like explosives or—or whatever else it is they sweep for."

"Explosives?" Gerard's eyes were the size of canapés. "The only thing about to explode in my kitchen is me."

"Gerard, please. Try to understand. We have many very important people with us today. It is crucial they feel safe here, so they will want to return to Nashville and to The Centurion."

With arms folded and a wrinkled brow, he looked down at the

small woman. "Oh, all right," Gerard let out a huge breath. "One more *sweep*."

He began to walk away, but turned back quickly to face her. "Isn't it enough," he said, "I have to tolerate these—these—*people* here in my kitchen?" He waved his arm like a king surveying his stainless-steel kingdom. "Was I not good enough to prepare the culinary fare for your VIPs?" He spat the letters.

"Gerard, we've been through this—"

He cut her off, throwing up his hand. "I have received over thirty awards for my creations. Is Gerard De Lorme no longer good enough for The Centurion?" He pointed his Gallic nose in the air and was still able to look down it at the mute event manager.

Maxwell knew it was pointless to elaborate further, and besides, she looked at her watch, she was supposed to be downstairs greeting the honored guests in five minutes. She wasn't about to miss this.

"I have to go, Gerard. Everything will be okay. Trust me." She turned, rolled her eyes and left before he had a chance to whine further.

She had not been gone ten minutes when one of the maintenance men, who was replacing light bulbs over the elevated speaker's platform, swung his ladder and knocked over one of the large potted palms located near each end of the head table.

The maintenance man returned the plant to its position and attempted to clean up the mess, but with its fronds askew, it no longer matched the other palm. Another maintenance man joined him and they removed the plant from the ballroom, returning with another palm which appeared to match the one at the other end of the speaker's table. Everything was back to normal.

"Where did you get that palm?" The head waiter asked as he approached the men.

"I saw it at the end of hallway outside. It matched that one," the maintenance man said, shrugging his shoulders and pointing to the other palm.

The head waiter looked at both plants, and then back at the man.

"Thank goodness Maxwell wasn't here. We'd have to listen to another twenty-minute tirade on safety and why we should pay more attention to what's going on around us."

The maintenance men finished cleaning up the dirt, and were leaving the ballroom with their ladder as a young waiter, on his way to the beverage station, passed by them carrying a large tray of coffee cups and saucers.

The maintenance man clutching the back end of the ladder was distracted on his cell phone and almost collided with the waiter as he passed.

"Vernon. It's me. Everything's ready. Yeah. We're out of here." The maintenance man returned his phone to the pocket of his coveralls and shared a smile with his partner at the other end of the ladder.

Once the waiter arranged the clean cups at the beverage station, he retrieved a tray filled with dirty cups and silverware which had been used by the policemen and security teams. Balancing the tray on his shoulder, he started for the kitchen.

While working at the beverage station, the waiter caught the attention of Bart, one of the police dogs who silently sniffed the air stirred in the man's wake. The K-9 tugged on his leash and attempted to follow the waiter. Officer Larry Parker responded to his partner and the two quietly closed on the waiter from the rear. As the dog came within a few feet of the man, he alerted Parker by sitting behind the waiter. The officer reached for the microphone attached to his epaulet, turned away from the waiter and quietly radioed for immediate backup.

Within seconds, six .40 caliber semi-automatic pistols were drawn and leveled at the waiter's center mass.

"Freeze," Parker shouted.

The waiter stopped. He slowly rotated his body with his tray still balanced in his left hand and steadied with his right. His eyes were enlarged, but he did not appear to be afraid.

"I said freeze!" Officer Parker's voice boomed.

"Bart, guard." Bart stood less than three feet from the waiter, flexed and ready.

Several other people within earshot stopped dead still upon hearing the officer's command, not knowing for sure at whom it had been directed.

"Keep your hands where I can see them," Parker said. "Do not move, and the dog won't bite you."

The waiter looked back and forth at the officers and the vigilant K-9. Acting as if he couldn't understand Officer Parker's command, he smiled and mumbled something in Arabic. Still balancing the tray with his left hand, he took his right hand from the edge of the tray and began to reach toward his left lapel nodding and saying, "Green card? Student visa?"

"Bart."

In half an instant, the German Shepherd sprang from his guard position and locked onto the waiter's wrist with vice-clamp jaws. One hundred and fifteen pounds of writhing aggression pulled the man's arm down to the dog's level and caused the tray and dishes to go airborne. Cups, saucers, and spoons bounced and broke as they crashed onto the floor and each other.

"Aaaah!" The waiter screamed as he tried to reach inside the same lapel with his other hand, but before he could do so, his left arm was hooked by the arm of Officer Gary Kirby. Both men and the dog slammed into the floor. Blood spurted from the man's wrist as Bart's large canine teeth ripped open his forearm.

"Twenty-one. I need Med-Com in the ballroom, now." Lieutenant Brian Cole yelled into his mike and then again toward the entrance to the ballroom. Blood was squirting onto Bart, Officer Kirby and the floor. Back to his feet, Bart still had the waiter's wrist in his teeth. Within a matter of seconds, eight hands secured the bleeding man and Bart was called off.

The waiter's hands were pulled together, cuffed and held secure in front of him so pressure could be applied to the wounds and the blood flow controlled. Officer Wesley Stephens placed his knee in the waiter's crotch and held the chain between the cuffs, so he could not move his hands from that position.

"I think I found the reason for Bart's alert," he said as he patted next to his knee which was resting on the crotch of the waiter's pants. "Let's get his pants down," Stephens said.

One of the officers helped Stephens unfastened the man's pants and pulled them down.

"No man has that kind of bulge," Cole said.

Grateful for his nitrile gloves, Stephens grabbed the waistband of the waiter's briefs with his left hand and removed a small Beretta semi-automatic pistol with his right. He held it up for Lieutenant Cole to see.

"How the hell did he get that in here?" Cole asked.

"He didn't bring it in today; that's for damn sure," Stephens said as he released the magazine and ejected the bullet from the chamber.

"He had to have it hidden somewhere on this floor," Cole said. "We've been sweeping the place for two days."

Officers secured the waiter's ankles with plastic cable ties and one of them placed his knee on top of the restraints between the waiter's feet to prevent any movement. Gloved hands prevented the man from moving any part of his body more than an inch.

The EMTs arrived and began to work on closing the waiter's wounds.

He was screaming something in Arabic, but the officers didn't know or care what he was saying. They simply wanted him to stop his attempt to free himself. With all the officers in place to keep the man secure, there was barely room for the EMTs to work.

Cole shouted into his mic, "Twenty-one. Get an interpreter up here now, grand ballroom."

The conference organizers knew an international function of this size was likely to present multiple opportunities for interpreters, so a group of multi-lingual Tennessee State University students had been employed to assist the hotel and the police during the conference. One of the male students from Kuwait was on the ballroom level and was rushed to the scene of the scuffle.

"What is he saying?" shouted Cole.

The young man listened. "He is praying to Allah," said the student, "begging forgiveness for his failure."

"Failure of what?"

The young man spoke to the waiter in Arabic.

The waiter mumbled.

"He said for his failure to execute Allah's retribution."

"For what?"

"Failure to—"

"I heard you the first time," Cole said. "What the hell does that mean?"

"Do you want me to ask him?"

"Yes, damn it. Ask him."

Before the translator could speak, the waiter screamed at him in Arabic.

"What did he say?" the Lieutenant asked.

The student hesitated. "He cursed me. He called me a traitor to Islam and a whore."

"I've been called worse," Cole said.

The waiter's screaming banter was becoming a distraction.

"Damn it," Cole said to the EMTs. "You guys got anything to shut that crap up?"

"Gladly." One of the EMTs reached into his kit, tore open a packaged syringe, grabbed a small bottle and inserted the needle. He withdrew some of the clear liquid and after a couple of thumps to the syringe he provided the waiter with a reason to sleep for a few hours.

Officer Stephens continued to pat the man down. As he reached under the waiter's arm he felt a variation in texture that caused him to pause. He checked under the other arm and found the same firmness. He pulled the clip-on bowtie from the shirt collar and unbuttoned the top button of the waiter's shirt. With both hands, he slowly popped each button on the shirt to expose what appeared to be some sort of strange contraption which, under the circumstances, convinced all the officers—it was a bomb.

"Oh Shit," three of the officers said in harmony as they leaned back from the unconscious waiter without releasing their hold on his extremities.

Cole immediately shut down his radio, formed his hands around his mouth and shouted across the large room, "Signal Sixteen. Signal Sixteen. Shut off all radios, now. Signal Sixteen. Pass it on."

All officers switched off their radios.

"Listen up," Cole turned to Sergeant Hughes who was standing nearby. "I need the bomb squad in here now, Signal Ten. Keep it quiet. I don't want a panic."

Sergeant Hughes pointed to a young officer who said, "Ten-four, I got it," then broke away from the group and sprinted for the elevator.

International occasions such as this were rare in Music City and the MNPD prepared for just about anything. Officers from the Bomb Squad had been assigned to conference security and were on-site with their equipment at the rear of the hotel.

"And clear this top floor of all civilians and non-essentials, immediately," Cole said. "I want a controlled evacuation of this entire hotel beginning with the ballroom and working down floor by floor from the top."

The officers huddled around their Sergeant for instructions.

"You guys about through?" Cole said to the EMTs as he returned to the sleeping suspect.

"We have the bleeding stopped, but he needs to be transported soon."

"Okay, you two get out of here. If we need you again, I'll send for you."

"Yes, sir," the senior EMT said. "He'll be asleep for a while."

"Good," Cole said.

It took less than five minutes for Sergeant Rob Smolinski from the

MNPD Bomb Squad to arrive on the top floor and begin to examine the contraption.

"Lieutenant, I don't think this is a bomb," Smolinski said.

"Great news," Hadley said.

"Maybe not."

"What do you mean?" Cole asked.

"My guess is this device, whatever it is, may be more dangerous than if it was a bomb."

"What the hell does that mean?"

"I can disable a lot of bombs. This thing is different. I've never seen anything like it. There appears to be no timer attached to these—things."

"Is this good?" Cole asked.

"Not really," Smolinski said. "If there was a timer, we'd know exactly how long we have to deal with this thing. As it is, it could go off any second."

"Smo, you're not making us feel any better about this," Stephens said.

"Sorry. Just telling it like it is. One other thing."

"What?" Cole asked.

"I'd keep this asshole asleep if I were you, at least until I can get this thing off him and into our containment vessel. If he wakes up, he'll likely attempt to trigger it, now that he knows he's caught."

Cole brought his hands to his mouth, getting ready to shout again.

"Lieutenant," Smolinski interrupted.

"Yeah?"

Smolinski stood and leaned toward Cole. "Let's get the Hazardous Devices Unit up here."

Cole motioned for one of the officers to come to him and instructed him to see his Sergeant and get the HD crew in the ballroom immediately.

In less than ten minutes, officers from the Hazardous Devices team and the Bomb Squad began removal of the strange vest from the waiter. As they cut away his jacket and shirt, they were careful not to compromise any part of the mechanism. Once the device was exposed, the officers looked it over in order to be sure there was no booby-trap.

Convinced they were safe, they snipped the straps holding the mechanism in position against the man's body. Extending upward from the canister on the man's left side was a plastic ring mounted to a short strap which ran to the back of the unit. This was undoubtedly the trigger to the release valve for whatever variety of death he planned to distribute to the unsuspecting conference attendees.

Two of the officers elevated the sleeping waiter's upper body so the other two could remove the device and place it into the containment vessel. Once it was clear from his body, they secured the mechanism, closed and vacuum sealed the vessel.

A loud noise surprised the officers until they realized it was applause coming from the other officers watching through a cracked door to the ballroom entrance. The four officers smiled. They gathered their equipment and with one man on each side of the containment vessel, they carried the heavy container from the ballroom with the apparatus securely inside.

While the officers from the Bomb Squad and Hazardous Devices Unit were receiving their appreciation in the hallway as they waited for the elevator, Hadley and Stephens helped the EMTs load the impotent terrorist onto a gurney. Following transport to Metro General Hospital, he would be placed into strict quarantine until he was examined and determination could be made as to his threat level and ultimate disposition.

Once the device was removed from the ballroom, Lieutenant Cole gave the okay to allow the ballroom staff back into the hotel. A group of officers, who were waiting in the hallway, began to return in order to help ready the ballroom for the hundreds of thankfully oblivious guests on the first floor.

Officer Parker squatted near the rear of the ballroom to reward his K-9 partner once again with some well-deserved attention.

"Good job, Bart," the officer said as he scratched behind his partner's ears. Parker checked his watch. It was almost 14:15 and Lieutenant Cole had just asked all the K-9 teams to make another full sweep of the ballroom and kitchen while the hotel staff was being gathered for return to their work stations.

As Bart and Officer Parker approached the kitchen, they were suddenly lifted from their feet and hurled toward the rear of the ballroom. The impact from the explosion had such force it tore through the room tossing dark blue uniformed bodies and furniture about like toys. All the windows, as well as the glassware and china throughout the ballroom, shattered from the shockwave.

Parker found himself lying on the floor and up against the wall. He tucked himself into the fetal position and held his ears in an attempt to halt the ringing and the pain. He saw dozens of officers rushing into the room searching through the smoke and the mist from the sprinkler system for any of their friends who needed medical attention. Parker waved off one of his fellow officers who came to his aid.

"Help someone else. I'm okay," He tried to say. His voice sounded to him like he had his fingers in his ears.

Parker called for Bart and squinted trying to find him through the haze. He couldn't hear anything except the incessant ringing. He called for the dog again and began to feel around along the room's perimeter thinking he would have been also thrown against the wall. Searching in the dust and broken glass, he could tell his hands were bleeding, but he didn't care. He finally grabbed a handful of fur and called to Bart again, but he didn't move.

"Bart," Parker yelled. "Bart."

Parker put his hand on Bart's chest. He could feel a slow swell telling him his partner was still breathing. Bart's hesitance to respond to his voice caused Parker to fear the dog's sensitive hearing could be damaged.

He prayed to God his partner was okay. He had grown to love this dog as much as any of his human friends, even more than some. There was a bond there which was hard to explain. He was his partner; his other half.

"Bart. Come on boy. Talk to me, Bart."

Bart at last raised his head enough to look up at Parker's face, then as if no longer able to support it, his head dropped back to the floor. Parker knelt on one knee beside his partner, slipped his hands and arms beneath the dog's body and picked him up. He staggered, and then fought to stand with the large dog in his arms.

"I need Med-Com," Parker shouted as he stumbled toward what looked like the ballroom entrance. "I need Med-Com, Signal Ten," he screamed. "Officer down!"

# Chapter 58

*Near Downtown*
*Nashville, Tennessee*
*Thursday Afternoon*

Mike stopped talking mid-sentence and turned up the volume on the radio. He looked at Cris and then back at the traffic before him. He checked his mirrors, flipped on the emergency equipment, then accelerated out of a U-turn in the middle of Eighth Avenue.

The dispatcher called for available units in the vicinity of The Centurion Hotel. They were a couple of miles from the hotel, but Mike knew they could be there in minutes.

"Forty-six," Mike said.

"Forty-six, go ahead."

"ETA to Centurion is two minutes." Mike confirmed their intended response to dispatch.

"Ten four, Forty-six," the radio squawked.

The fact they were close had nothing to do with Mike's response to the call. The Kurdish-American Conference was opening today at The Centurion and the homicides of the two Middle Eastern men remained unsolved. This sudden disturbance at the conference was surely no coincidence.

As Mike listened closely to the radio for more information, his cell phone interrupted.

"Damn." He dug the phone from his pocket, looked at the display and flipped it open. "Yeah, Lieutenant."

"Mike, where are you?" No doubt, Burris could hear the siren.

"We're on Eighth approaching Division; about a minute from The Centurion."

"Listen. I know you've heard already about the disturbance at the hotel. You need to know they captured a man in the ballroom; he was dressed as a waiter. He had some type of device strapped to his body."

"A bomb?"

"What?" Cris said.

"They're not sure yet what it is," Burris said. "The Bomb Squad is there and they've called in the Hazardous Device team. They say they have him secured, but I don't want you two near the ballroom until they have him out of there and the threat neutralized. Do you understand?"

"Lieutenant?"

"I mean it, Mike. You both stay out of it until they remove him and the bomb from the hotel. I need you investigating, not policing. And I damn sure need you in one piece."

"Who is this asshole? Do we know which group of crazies he represents?" Mike slowed for a traffic light as he and Cris searched for cross traffic.

"We don't know much of anything yet," Burris said. "They told me the suspect was speaking Arabic. So far, it's all I know. They've locked down the ballroom. Hopefully, you'll be able to evaluate what, if anything, this fanatic and his intentions may have to do with your two murders. My gut is telling me he's involved—somehow."

"Okay. We'll wait outside until they bring him out. I'll need you to keep me posted so we're not the last ones to get in there."

"Count on it," Burris said. "Stay off your phone. If you need to make calls, use Cris's phone. I'll get back to you shortly."

Mike slowed the car as he put away his cell. He crossed West End Avenue under a green light and pulled halfway onto the sidewalk across the street from the hotel.

Mike and Cris grabbed their Kevlar vests from the trunk and were still tightening the Velcro straps when they started their dash across the street.

The deluge of shattered glass from the top floor windows followed the deafening blast from the explosion. The detectives' self-preservation instincts caused them to stop, flinch and raise their arms to shield their faces.

"Damn it," Cris shouted. "He blew the bomb."

"Let's go," Mike yelled.

As they approached the hotel entrance, glass from the ballroom windows was still striking the cars parked near the building.

They ran through the evolving chaos outside the hotel and fought their way into the lobby. Mike was confident, as he cleared the hotel doorway; his pledge to Burris had been voided by the explosion. Cris tried her best to keep up with Mike, but the crowd was thick and his strides were more than her short legs could match.

Mike made his way through the mass of people. He reached the bank of three elevators only to be stopped by a sergeant who had seized the lifts and was already rationing their use to EMS teams and officers evacuating the injured from the ballroom level. Cris caught up in time to hear Mike.

"Cris," Mike shouted. "The stairwell is back there where we came in." He pointed. "Are you up for fifteen flights?"

"Hell yes," Cris said, hoping she was right.

"Come on."

As he entered the staircase with Cris on his heels, Mike heard a high-pitched alarm coming from the upper levels of the building. He climbed the metal and concrete steps fearing the explosion may have caused a fire, and a fire within a crime scene was the adversary of any detective trying to put together the already disjointed pieces of a homicide puzzle.

The detectives kept to their right as they fought their way up the flights, facing the flow of kitchen help and servers escaping the top floor along with guests from the upper floors who felt the shock or heard the alarm.

When they reached the fifth floor level the alarm went silent. Mike knew it had to be a good sign.

On the ninth flight they came up behind a Nashville Fire Department team that had obviously been assigned event duty at the conference. They were carrying a backboard and emergency medical kits. Cris was thankful the pair were slowing her climb, but wasn't about to let it show. She hung in behind Mike and used the opportunity to catch her breath. As soon as another mass of hotel employees passed by, Mike moved left to overtake the gear-laden team. Cris hesitated, summoned her strength, and followed him.

Less than a full flight later, Mike slowed again to acknowledge an injured officer being supported by a fellow policeman as he made his way awkwardly down the stairs. His left arm and hand appeared hastily bandaged and he looked dazed.

The smell of blood was in the air. As they climbed, Mike and Cris passed several more officers and hotel employees with minor injuries. Each was being escorted down the stairs by others who appeared unhurt.

As he approached the fourteenth floor, Mike could hear muffled shouting from above him.

"I need some help over here."

"Hold on, Damn it. This man needs to go now."

Mike stepped onto the fifteenth floor's half-flight landing and looked back to see Cris pulling herself up with the handrail.

"We're almost there."

"Good," Cris gasped.

As he finished the exhausting climb, Mike grabbed the stairwell door and pulled it open for another young EMS team who had just passed Cris. As he and Cris followed the team in, he was struck by the chaos, the noise, and the sight of so many injured people.

They walked the hallway dodging gurneys and emergency teams who were working their way toward the elevators with the injured.

Mike spotted a stretcher against the hallway wall with a large German Shepherd lying on it. Blood was drying as it seeped from the dog's ears. He was receiving oxygen through a mask made for humans and occasional medical attention from an EMS tech nearby. The tech's time was split between caring for the K-9 and a small group of officers with minor injuries. One officer was sitting next to the stretcher with his hand securing the oxygen mask in place and stroking the dog's motionless head. Even without the K-9 arm patch, it would have been obvious; he was the dog's partner.

Mike and Cris entered the ballroom which looked more like an Iraqi war zone. They could see EMTs, as well as police and fire department teams, attending more than two dozen officers. Mike never saw or smelled any sign of fire, but the soggy carpeting and the collapsed wet ceiling tiles confirmed the sudden increase in air pressure from the explosion had blown out some of the thin glass bulbs in the sprinkler heads. The resulting spray of hundreds of gallons of water further reduced the chances Mike and Cris had of collecting meaningful evidence. With Nashville Fire Department personnel already on site, someone had wisely shut down the flow to the sprinkler system soon after the explosion, once the threat of fire was eliminated.

"The water and this number of people are going to destroy most of the evidence," Mike said.

"What the hell?" Cris bent over to pick up a half dozen of the thousands of small steel screws from the wet carpet.

"They must have been in the bomb," Mike said. "Look." Mike pointed to numerous screws implanted into the room's drywall.

"There had to be some folks severely injured with these things flying around," Cris said.

"Looks like it," Mike said. The folks we saw in the stairwell, I'm sure, were some of the minor injuries."

"Mike," someone yelled from across the ballroom.

Mike turned and moved toward the voice. As he came closer, he realized it was Sergeant Rick Hughes. Rick and Mike survived the MNPD Academy together.

"Hey, Rick."

"Are you two working this disaster?" Hughes asked.

"We're gonna try, if there's any evidence left." Mike scanned the room looking at the activity. "We suspect this mess may be related to a couple of homicides we're already working."

"Well, in case it's any help, I was in here when Parker's K-9 took the Arab bastard down."

"Great," Mike said, as he pulled out his note pad and pen. "What can you tell us?"

Sergeant Hughes explained the sequence of events as he witnessed them.

"Where was the bomber at the time of the explosion?" Cris asked.

"He was right there on a stretcher being transported." Hughes indicated. "He was unconscious after the EMT's injection. Lieutenant Cole and the two officers stayed with him until Smolinski got here from the Bomb Squad. The contraption he was wearing was already off him and hauled out by the Bomb Squad at least five minutes *before* the explosion."

"Before?" Cris asked.

"Right. I saw Smolinski leave with it. Then the bomb went off over there next to the speakers' platform." He pointed to the four-foot diameter hole torn open in the ballroom floor.

"Where were you when it detonated?" Mike asked.

"I was walking back into the room through that door." Hughes pointed. "There were about twenty uniforms in all. We all went down. Glass, furniture, flesh, blood and screws all over us." He looked down at his wet uniform and picked at something still hanging from his shirt. It was a screw, caught in the fabric of his shirt. "My ears are still ringing," Hughes said.

"Hadley and Stephens were hauling his sorry ass out on a stretcher with one of the EMTs." Hughes pointed again. "The blast ripped him and our brothers to shreds," Hughes pinched his lips together with his teeth and looked down. He took a deep breath, "not to mention the damage, physical and otherwise, it did to the officers coming back in with me. We were going to help get this place back in order for the conference." Hughes paused, looking around at the destruction. "This is wrong. It's so wrong."

"I'm sorry, Rick," Cris said, touching his arm.

Hughes nodded.

"Where in the hell did the bomb come from?" Cris asked, "and why didn't the dogs pick it up?"

"I don't know," Hughes said.

"Well, we've got to find out," Mike said. "Did you see any cameras in here?"

"None inside the ballroom," Hughes said. "I've already looked."

"Thanks, Rick," Mike said. "Have you been checked out by the EMTs?"

"I'm waiting until they get through with those guys." He nodded toward the injured officers.

"Make sure you let them check you too," Cris said.

"I will," Hughes said.

"Cris, let's get busy," Mike said. "We need to get statements from the others before they're gone."

As Mike and Cris were approaching a couple of officers receiving medical attention, Mike's phone rang.

"Mike Neal."

"Mike."

"Yeah, Lieutenant."

"We received a call from a man who said the bomb at The Centurion was Semtex."

"How does he know?" Mike asked.

"He says he's the one who sold it to the bomber."

"Did he also tell us who the bomber is?"

"Yeah. He said he sold the Semtex to Carl Garrison yesterday."

"Carl Garrison? *The* Carl Garrison, our favorite racist cult leader?

"The same."

"So, I'm sure the caller identified himself, right?"

"Negative," Burris said.

"How do we know this jerk's credible and not a disgruntled cult member trying to nail Garrison and his redneck camp? And how does he already know about the bomb anyway?"

"It's all over the media," Burris said. "Everybody in the city knows by now. The caller was on long enough for us to determine he was calling from a pay phone off the Interstate at a gas station in Logan County, Kentucky. He said he was in the demolition business and had access to the Semtex. He said Garrison came to him and made him a cash offer he couldn't turn down. Garrison told him the Semtex was for clearing a large beaver dam on his property in southern Tennessee. He told him the beavers were causing a creek to flood his pasture land."

"Bullshit," Mike said.

"When this guy heard the news media break into regular programming he said he put two and two together and figured it must have been Garrison. He said if he knew Garrison was going to kill police officers with the Semtex he wouldn't have sold it to him. He said he felt terrible and wanted to do the right thing."

"So, he's turning himself in?" Mike asked.

"He wasn't *that* interested in doing the right thing."

"Figures. Did we get any other usable information from this honorable and concerned citizen? There couldn't be a camera in the vicinity of the pay phone, could there?"

"No. I already called Kentucky State Police," Burris said. "No cams."

"Prints?" Mike asked.

"Phone was wiped clean."

"Damn," Mike said. "He did the right things, all right. Have we picked up Garrison yet?"

"Tennessee HP and the Hubbard County Sheriff are on their way to his home now. We called, but there was no answer. We got his machine. If he's not there, we'll get him at the lodge."

"Mike," Cris shouted, interrupting his call. "Jason says he's bagged some body parts. One is a severed forearm with most of the hand still attached. The arm is partially burned, but he says he's got at least three good fingers. He said the skin color looks dark."

"Lieutenant, hang on." Mike lowered his phone. "Jason."

"Yeah, Mike?"

"I need prints. I need them *now*."

"I'll have them for you in ten minutes."

"Lieutenant," Mike said. "One of the criminalists found a hand. Looks like it could belong to the waiter."

"Get the prints scanned and sent to TBI immediately. I'm calling them now to give them a heads-up so they can rush them through the state's AFIS and the FBI's nationwide."

"I'll call you when Jason sends them over," Mike said.

"Thanks. Hey, Mike?"

"Yeah, Lieutenant."

"While Jason's working on getting those prints, I'd like you and Cris to come to my office for a few minutes. I need to discuss something with you."

"Right now?"

"Yeah."

"Seriously?"

"Now. It's important."

"If you say so."

# Chapter 59

*Hubbard County, Tennessee*
*Thursday Afternoon*

"He's dead," Brad said as soon as the phone was answered.

"Good. I told the thieving bastard to leave it alone," Roger said. "You'd think he would have picked up on the fact that I'm not the type of man you want to screw over."

"I warned him too," Brad said. "Money makes folks do stupid things. Garrison must have gone straight to the lab as soon as I dropped him at the lodge."

"I'm sure he planned to make a fortune, but trying to steal my formula was a bad idea. His attempt to use a laboratory which is one of the same ones I've worked with for over five years, was a supremely bad idea; no—a deadly idea.

"I've known the lab's owner, Al Bryson, since the '80s. He told me he thought he recognized the scent when his technician brought him the sample. Al called me when the analysis came off the gas chromatograph."

"What did Garrison tell them when he ordered the analysis?" Brad asked.

"He gave them some bullshit story about having a partner in a chemical firm who he believed was attempting to rob him of his share in a potentially substantial discovery. He said he needed an independent third-party analysis of the sample to protect his interests.

"When Al called me, I told him to feed Garrison some bunk about the chromatograph acting up in order to delay the feedback on the sample."

"I'm not sure what made him do it other than greed," Brad said. "I don't know about his financial situation, so I can't speak to that. But, I know he was building up his racist army for some major hostilities. I apologize for getting you involved with him," Brad said. "There will be no fee for this."

"That's not necessary. You were hooking us up for what you believed was a mutually beneficial exchange. You had nothing to gain and you didn't know this asshole Garrison was a thief."

"No, I didn't. He did make a comment on the trip back from Kentucky, and maybe I should have picked up on it then. He said he thought the formula for the agent must be worth millions. I thought, at the time, he was simply impressed by your ingenuity. I guess I missed his true intentions."

"Forget it, Brad. It wasn't *your* intention. Are you okay?"

"Sure."

"Was he a friend of yours?" Roger asked.

"No. I met him a couple of days ago through a friend. Garrison had money. I wanted money. He had connections to help me find justice for Julie. It looked promising for a while. Garrison was a silver-tongued devil. That's for sure. He had those folks at the lodge ready to go to war on his signal. It was sorta scary, now that I look back on it."

"Well, I don't think his cult is going to be able to escape the attention of law enforcement officials for a while."

"Oh?"

"His army took a big first step today, but I'm guessing it'll also be their last one."

"What do you mean?" Brad asked.

"They blew the bomb at The Centurion less than an hour ago."

"No shit?"

"Yeah. When I heard about the explosion, I called the Nashville Police and confessed to selling Garrison the Semtex."

"You did what?" Brad said.

"I didn't identify myself, and I didn't place the call from here. I may have told a few lies, but only enough to get them interested in Garrison's little club."

"Payback can be painful," Brad said.

"Very true, but I will say I'm grateful to Garrison for one thing."

"What's that?"

"Getting that bomb past the heightened level of security that was in place at The Centurion today provides me a better testimonial than I could possibly pay for. Garrison's efforts today may very well make me the million dollars he predicted my formula is worth."

"That's ironic," Brad said.

"Where is the body, anyway?" Roger asked.

"Still at his desk in his study, I guess. His house is just a few miles from the lodge."

"How did you arrange that?"

"I didn't have to," Brad said. "After you called, I made a call to the lodge. They said he was at home. I'm just glad he liked to work with his windows open in the spring. It made it much easier to line him up. You remember how accurate the XM21 was in Nam?"

"Yeah, I remember all you shooters took care of those rifles like they were female."

"Garrison gave me one yesterday as a gift," Brad said.

"You are kidding?"

"No. He told me I earned it with my service to America, and I should consider it a thank you gift."

"Now *that's* ironic."

# Chapter 60

*Nashville International Airport*
*Thursday Afternoon*

He found an isolated row of seats away from the other waiting passengers. Buried behind his newspaper and his natural do-not-talk-to-me scowl, he was biding his time until the call to board.

Abdul glanced at his wristwatch to see how long before he would be airborne and away from this soon-to-be city in turmoil.

*Less than a half-hour until the flight and only a few more minutes for Allah's glorious retribution. Karim will honor his father, complete this jihad and achieve his reward today in paradise.*

*By now, Sajid has left the city in the SUV, and is on his way north.*

Suddenly, Abdul's newspaper collapsed from his hands onto his lap. "What the ...?" He jumped from his seat, prepared to defend himself.

As he stood, a foam rubber football fell with his paper from his lap onto the carpet. The six-year-old boy, who missed the errant pass from his brother, fell in front of Abdul, but not before he stepped on

Abdul's Italian loafers.

Two small boys stood before the enraged man frozen by his angry face.

"You two need a beating," he said aloud in Arabic before he realized he was speaking. He looked around to see if anyone witnessed his reaction. He kicked the football and jerked his paper up from the floor. Returning to his seat, Abdul straightened the paper and spread it in front of his face convincing himself he did not care who may have translated his rant.

*These American dogs should teach their offspring more respect for other people.*

"Ladies and gentlemen," a pleasant female voice came over the public address system. "Welcome to Nashville and American Airlines. It is now time for us to begin boarding our Flight #2976, service to New York City with a brief stop in Washington, DC."

Abdul gathered his newspaper, stuffed it into his carry-on bag and walked to the boarding line that was forming from the gate. He could not leave this place fast enough.

He didn't notice the attractive CNN anchor on the monitor hanging from the ceiling until she interrupted regular programming. "We have breaking news from The Centurion Hotel near downtown Nashville, Tennessee where hundreds have gathered for the Kurdish-American Conference."

Abdul's eyes widened and he turned toward the TV. The screen displayed a live aerial shot of the hotel with people fleeing through the exits like bees from a hive. He checked his wristwatch, then turned his attention back to the monitor suspended over the waiting area.

Assuming Karim had triggered the device, he mumbled to himself in Arabic, "No! Karim, you fool. It is too early."

# Chapter 61

*Criminal Justice Center*
*Nashville, Tennessee*
*Thursday Late Afternoon*

"What do you think this is about?" Cris asked, as Mike parallel parked outside at the Criminal Justice Center.

"He didn't say, but I've got an idea," Mike said. "And, if I'm right—it's gonna top off an already seriously shitty day."

"What do you mean?" Cris asked.

Mike turned off the ignition and turned in his seat to face Cris.

"Okay. As guilty as Mullins looked initially, the video from the beer market confirmed his whereabouts and saved his red neck from a murder charge.

It appears al-Zubaidy must have killed Daran Hamid. His prints were on the Acura, too many for casual contact. I figure al-Zubaidy feared the potential for his exposure and decided to take Hamid out of the picture to protect the plan to attack the conference."

"Okay," Cris agreed.

"Burris told us this morning, the FBI's AFIS kicked back partial prints suspected of belonging to a known international terrorist named Abdul Malik Kadir, who the FBI's Counterterrorism Division says is aligned with Farid al-Rishari. This madman is linked to bin Laden and al Qaeda. Obviously, these discoveries tie both al-Zubaidy's and Hamid's murders to Kadir and therefore to al-Rishari."

"The apartment manager at Hillcrest stated there were three young Arab-looking men living in the apartment where we found al-Zubaidy's body," Cris said, "and Mustafa admitted all three worked for him at the restaurant."

"Yes," Mike said, "and I believe the body of one of the other two young radicals is now splattered across the Centurion's ballroom and his soul is searching for his divine reward. I would like to think Jason could tell us which martyr got the assignment when he pulls the prints from the severed hand he found, but prints of young terrorists are not normally found in anyone's AFIS."

"What about the other Arab, and Kadir?" Cris asked.

"I don't know, but now that their attempt at jihad has failed, I'd say Kadir and whoever else was left from his cadre of young impressionable fools, has moved on to their next holy war. Kadir is obviously too high up the chain to stick around and endanger himself."

"So, you think Burris is going to pull us?"

"Not by his choice. Burris won't like this any more than we do, but he has a job to do which includes following orders. The jurisdiction on known terrorists, international or otherwise, always falls to the feds."

Mike got out and stood at the front of the car, waiting for Cris to join him.

"My guess is, Burris will take us to Moretti, where there'll be suits waiting there with him. They'll all stare at us without saying much, confident we're sharp enough to know why they're here."

They walked toward the entrance.

"Moretti will introduce them. We'll get the bad news. Then, all our work from this week will be turned over to them and we'll be back on the streets tomorrow with our vinyl binders, looking to make some sense of our fellow citizens' attempts at mutual destruction in Music

City."

"What about Hadley and Stephens—and the EMT?" Cris asked.

"The feds will allow us to stay involved to investigate their deaths if only to appease the Chief and the Mayor. We'll have limited access to the scene and the facts. The investigation will be cumbersome at best."

"And that's it?" Cris asked.

"Will it help any—if I *want* to be wrong?"

Cris shook her head.

Having their fill of stairs for the day, they entered the building and took the elevator to Homicide.

As Mike opened the door, he could see Burris waiting at his desk, with a funeral face.

"Moretti's office?" Mike asked, before he reached Burris's doorway.

"Burris nodded with an apologetic look. He stood and joined them for the short walk."

The glass panel next to Moretti's door was filled with charcoal gray. The two men stood as Mike and Cris walked in.

"Mike—Cris," Captain Moretti said, "I'd like you to meet Special Agent in Charge, Burton Jarvis of the Nashville field office and Special Agent Hal Pennington with the FBI's Counterterrorism Division Ops II."

Mike looked at the two men, nodded and turned back to Cris, "Sometimes I hate being right."

# Chapter 62

*Mike Neal's Home*
*Nashville, Tennessee*
*Thursday Early Evening*

Mike tossed his keys on the counter, walked to the bar, and wrapped his fist tight around the neck of what was left of a fifth of Jack Daniel's. He looked at the bottle, and wished he had been able to do the same to the necks of Carl Garrison and the damned Arab maniac who caused the deaths of two fellow officers and an EMT.

Mike jammed a highball glass into the refrigerator's ice dispenser hoping his friend Jack Daniel could help him get his mind on something else.

He walked to his desk and punched the power button on his desktop PC. He was headed for the bedroom to change into his workout gear when his cell phone rang.

"Mike Neal."

"Mike. You okay?"

"Oh, I'm just peachy. How about you, Cris?"

"I'll get over it. I thought you might want to know the TBI lab was able to analyze the contents of the vest."

"How'd you hear so fast? Wait, don't tell me. You're dating one of the lab techs."

"No way," Cris said. "You underestimate me."

Mike chuckled.

"I'm dating the lab *manager*."

"I knew it," Mike said.

"It was Ricin."

"Seriously?"

"Yeah. If he had been able to release that junk," Cris said, "we'd have a hotel full of dying Kurds and cops tonight."

"And a locked-down city inundated with feds by morning."

"We may have that yet. The Center for Disease Control already has The Centurion under quarantine to be sure none was released."

"I'll bet that's great for business," Mike said.

"It could have been a lot worse."

"Burris called me on the way home," Mike said. "He told me they'd relocated the conference to the Convention Center. Maybe they'll be able to salvage their meeting after all."

"I'm surprised the Convention Center was available. Hey, before I forget, my friend at the TBI lab told me about a job opening they have for an experienced crime scene photographer."

"Are you thinking about taking up photography?"

"No, but I told him about Carol," Cris said. "And, I told her about the job. Was that okay?"

"Oh—sure. Maybe she's interested," Mike said, looking for a way to change the subject. "Hey, Burris brought up the graffiti artist shooting on Interstate 65. That was yours, right?"

"Yeah, mine and the Hog's. I guess you and I will inherit that one."

"It'll be one of the first challenges for our return to the real world."

"I guess so," Cris said. "See you at seven?"

"Yeah, if not before. Cris, you did a good job today."

She hesitated for a moment. *"Gracias, socio."*

"*Socio* means partner, right?" Mike asked, always unsure of his negligible Spanish skills.

*"Si."*

*"Buenos noches,"* Mike said with an insecure smile on his face.

Cris laughed at Mike's mis-pronunciation as she closed her phone.

By the time Mike returned to his computer, the desktop was loaded. He fell back into his chair, pushed the mouse across the pad and clicked the ISP icon to bring up his email. As per normal, he scanned first for email from Iraq. He wasn't disappointed.

> *Hey, Buddy. Hope all is well in Nashville and you're kicking some serious criminal ass.*
>
> *Well, my friend, I'm gonna make your day. As I told you earlier in the week, I forwarded your email about Sinjar Mountain to Lieutenant Colonel Rob Vaughn. Initially, he said he believed you may be enjoying a little too much sour mash back there in Tennessee.*

Mike held up his glass, and swirled the ice around in a salute to Jack Daniel.

> *But, after Rob read it all the way through, he called me.*
>
> *His investigative teams discovered villages south of Sinjar City along the Wadi Al-Tharthar River, with people who have exhibited some serious symptoms that eventually resulted in a number of deaths.*
>
> *Rob sent in a medical team who began testing the blood from hundreds of the people living along the river. They also tested sources of their drinking water. They found Anthrax spores right there in their damn water.*
>
> *This river is the main watercourse running from Sinjar*

*Mountain southward for about two hundred kilometers to the Tharthar salt depression. The Army has already flown in an alternative water source for the people.*

*Rob said the environmentally hardy B anthracis spores are heat resistant, and can survive for decades in soil; and in some cases, water. Can you believe that?*

"Amazing." Mike took a swig of Jack and kept reading.

*He dispatched two Haz-Mat teams in an attempt to trace the tainted water back to its origin. They followed the river into the mountain. The farther they moved northward, the higher the concentration of the toxin. They reached the point where they believe the water was leaving the mountain, and tested the water there. They found levels of Anthrax in excess of three-hundred parts per million.*

*Yesterday, one of the engineering teams on the northern slope radioed, stating they found spills of cement exposed near the base of what appeared to be a rock slide. When they pulled the rock away, they exposed a solid wall of rock and concrete.*

*The impact echo told them the wall is approximately twelve feet thick. Sometime in the next twenty-four hours they plan to drill a two inch hole, install a plug, and seal it until the atmospheric probe arrives from the United States. The probe will capture a gas sample from inside the wall, and tell them what dangers await them.*

*The Iraq Survey Group asked me to extend to you their thanks for your suspicions and your doggedness, but most especially for your continued service.*

"Hooah!" Mike shouted.

*I'll send you an update in a day or two. Keep your fingers crossed. This could be huge.*

*- Tim*

Mike's pride swelled as he considered the possibility of the Iraq Survey Group uncovering weapons of mass destruction in the location he had been describing for years as Saddam's closet. But he was more moved by the idea that he may have had a hand in saving hundreds, maybe thousands, of people from serious illness or death.

# Chapter 63

*Davidson County Court House*
*Nashville, Tennessee*
*Thursday Early Evening*

"Manuel Avila."

The gang banger turned to see who had spoken his name. He had just met with his public defender and was out of his element around the courthouse. Having someone recognize him could mean trouble. Even though he rarely wore gang colors any more, his tattoos made him easily recognizable to numerous unfriendly people. He'd learned to wear long sleeves and remain conscious of his surroundings at all times.

*"Como estas?"* the well-dressed man said as he stood up straight after leaning on the black Porsche Carrera. "I'm Trent Delaney, attorney with Miller, Ramirez and Hart," the man said using excellent Spanish. Delaney extended a hand with his business card and took a step back so as not to create apprehension in Avila.

Avila accepted the card with his left hand and squinted at it. He remained in a defensive mode. He did not know any whites that he trusted. His right hand remained formed into a fist and poised behind his thigh.

"I won't take but a few minutes of your time. I know you don't know me, but I know about your case. Vehicular homicide is always a very serious matter. The fact that the deceased, Mrs. Julie Evans, had terminal breast cancer will play on the jury's sympathies and weaken your case. But, I want to share with you something I'm certain can help you get through this without a long prison stay.

"About ten years ago, our law firm began a practice of extending legal services to members of the Hispanic community at no cost. That's right," Delaney nodded. "Free."

The word free elevated Avila's attention, but he had learned long ago that nothing in this life was ever free.

"In legal circles, it's known as *pro bono*. We began this service after one of our senior partners, Luis Ramirez, brought to our attention the growing need for this service in the expanding Hispanic community here in Nashville. I understand that you have a public defender representing you. Is that right?"

*"Si."* Avila nodded, hesitant to say anything else and determined not to respond in English.

"I'm not sure if you realize it, but these public defenders are severely over-worked and grossly underpaid. On occasion, they are attempting to represent up to twenty or more clients at the same time. Have you had trouble trying to contact your attorney on the phone, or to set up meetings?"

Avila nodded again with a disgusted look.

"We all know no one can serve that many clients at once and give each one adequate, much less appropriate, representation. As a large successful law firm here in Nashville with ties to the Hispanic community and over twenty attorneys on staff, we can offer you a much improved level of accessibility and representation. You can see how this would improve your chances in court, right?"

Avila paused, shrugged then answered softly, *"Si."*

Delaney looked at his watch. "Hey, I've got a couple of hours before

I need to be anywhere. What do you say we run over to Las Cervezas del Mundo, grab a couple of drinks and talk about your case? Have you ever had *Jose Cuervo Reserva De Familia*?"

"No," Avila lied.

"It is the best tequila ever." Delaney smiled. "Let's grab some shots and talk. What do you say? My car is right here." Delaney extended his hand toward the Porsche.

Avila hesitated briefly, and then stepped toward the car.

The two men dropped into the low riding seats of the sleek sports car, and Delaney talked about his favorite tequilas for the five minutes it took to reach the restaurant.

Delaney ordered their tequila and Avila lit a cigarette.

For the next forty-five minutes, Delaney talked about pro bono services and what Avila could expect from Miller, Ramirez and Hart. The *Jose Cuervo* seemed to loosen Avila, and he became more talkative.

After four shots worth of Avila's banter about his public defender, Delaney's cell phone rang. He checked his watch and said to the caller, "I'm sorry. I forgot. I'll be right there, honey."

"Manuel, I forgot I promised my wife I would take her to dinner tonight. Are you married?"

Avila wrinkled his brow. He painfully recalled an agonizing chapter from what he referred to as his *former life*, and shook his head.

"If you were, you would understand." Delaney laughed. "Where can I drop you?"

*"Mi coche,"* Avila said, and then drained his beer.

"No problem," Delaney said.

As the two men walked toward the Porche, Delaney stopped.

"Damn. I forgot to leave a tip. I know the owner here, and I have to leave one. He's a client of our firm. I'll be right back." Delaney hurried toward the restaurant reaching for his wallet.

Avila turned and continued to walk across the parking lot. He pulled his cigarettes from his shirt pocket, shook one out and grasped it with his lips. He stopped, cupped his hands and spun the flint wheel on his Zippo. The lighter closed with a sharp metallic click as he pulled deep into his lungs a mouthful of smoke from the unfiltered cigarette. As he leaned his head back and enjoyed the rush from the nicotine, he recalled the day this *circus of legal bullshit* had all started—when he was following the gangster that had the balls to pull a gun on Manuel Avila.

*Then, that bitch had to get in the way, and wreck my damn car. Maybe this smooth-talkin' jerk can make it all go away, so I can stop worrying about everybody else and get back to my life.*

The smoke was escaping his nose and open mouth when his head jerked sideways less than an inch. His eyes flared briefly. His body buckled, and he hit the pavement, hard.

When Delaney returned from the restaurant, he saw Avila stretched out on the parking lot near the Porsche and a small crowd standing over him. One man was attempting CPR.

Delaney knelt beside Avila. "What happened?"

A man said, "He just dropped to the pavement."

"There's blood." A woman pointed to Avila's head.

Delaney checked for a pulse. He saw the phony business card he had given Avila protruding part way from his shirt pocket. Acting as though he was checking his breathing, he palmed the card as he asked the crowd, "Has anyone called 911?"

"Yes," Someone said.

"Thank you."

The sirens grew louder. The Nashville Fire Department was first to arrive with a huge red truck. The crowd stepped back and gave room to the men who were trained to save lives. This one, however, would not be saved.

Delaney decided to sit in his car, watch the scene and wait for the detectives to arrive.

He spotted the black Crown Victoria as it rolled up close to the scene with its blue strobes flashing. Delaney decided not to wait for the detectives to find him. As a fellow detective, he wanted to appear interested and willing to assist with the investigation in any way he could.

He explained to the detective who had climbed from the driver's seat that he was a private investigator, and that Avila had approached him at the courthouse after overhearing him talking with another Hispanic client. "He told me he was uncomfortable with his current representation and would feel better with someone who spoke his language and who could understand him. I explained to him I did investigative work for three local law firms who frequently worked in the Hispanic community."

The detective scribbled on a small pad as he nodded his understanding.

"He wasn't sure how pro bono worked, so I explained it. He asked how he could be considered for it. I told him about the procedures, and he was interested. After we talked a while, he suggested we come here to have a drink and discuss his case."

Delaney told the detective he was not sure what happened, since he was not with Avila at the time. He told him that after talking with Avila here at the restaurant for quite a while, he had reason to believe the man was a member of a local gang and his death could have been related to his violent lifestyle.

"I was about to take Mr. Avila back to the courthouse to get his car when I found him like this. Did anyone say they heard anything, or saw anything?"

The detective had several more questions, but Delaney found him predictably unwilling to answer any of his. When asked for his business card, Delaney made sure the detective received the real one.

"It's okay for you to go." The detective handed Delaney his MNPD card. "But, stay close to your phone. There may be more questions."

"No problem," Delaney read the card, then looked up. "Detective Neal, I'd be glad to help any way I can."

The Carrera's four hundred plus horsepower whined as Delaney accelerated from the restaurant parking lot and moved through a half-dozen gears. He flipped open his cell phone to view the message that had vibrated his phone during his discussion with the detective. It read, Missed Call: Brad Evans.

He pushed the send button to return the call.

"Hello."

"Nice shot. Thanks for missing my car."

"You're welcome."

"Do you feel better?"

"No," Brad paused, "I'm not sure that's possible. But, at least I feel some damn justice has finally been done for my Julie."

# Chapter 64

*Las Cervezas del Mundo*
*Nashville, Tennessee*
*Thursday Evening*

Mike was unsure about Delaney's version of the facts. Most of his suspicions were driven by his past experience with private investigators that weren't old enough to have come from the seasoned ranks of Nashville's, or any other city's, police department. Delaney looked to be a rich pretty boy who was stroking his ego by carrying a P.I. license and a gun, and relishing an inflated opinion of his novice investigative skills.

Following his discussions with some of the restaurant's patrons, Mike snapped digital photos of the body, the crime scene and its surroundings. He assessed the buildings near the site which could provide cover for a person interested in killing Avila.

No one at the restaurant had admitted hearing or seeing anything helpful, other than Avila suddenly collapsing to the pavement. Witnesses remembered Delaney drinking and talking with Avila at one of the patio tables, but they all said that neither Delaney, nor anyone else, was near Avila when he collapsed.

Gang bangers were well-known for executions of competing gang members, but they were not known for sniping. On the contrary, they were famous for the in-your-face execution. They wanted their prey to know who was cancelling their ticket. Very little in the gangster world was meant to be covert, outside of their money-making ventures and any clandestine relations with the police.

Mike stepped toward the cars parked along a wall that provided the perimeter to the restaurant parking lot and the backdrop to the crime scene. He had just started to inspect the vehicles when Cris joined him from behind.

"Looking for this?" She pointed to a small hole in the plastic bumper on the rear of a black Honda Pilot.

Mike squatted for a closer look. "Good eye." He rotated his body so he could look from the area of the bullet hole up through a calculated point where Avila's head would have been at the time. He snapped a photo. "Assuming Avila was walking toward the spot where Delaney's Porsche was parked, this gives us a broad-spectrum possibility of the bullet's point of origin. We know the bullet passed through Avila's head left to right and after who knows how much deflection, it hit the Honda. Your thoughts?"

"Sounds logical," Cris said, "based upon the limited intuitive data we have at this point."

Mike looked up at Cris. "Now that was about as politically correct an answer as I've heard in a long while. You should be promoted in no time."

Cris folded her arms across her chest and faked a frown.

"Sergeant," Mike shouted for the crime scene supervisor. "I'd like you to have your officers check the roof tops and any spaces with windows on this side, within these two blocks." Mike gestured using both arms. "But have them work mostly in these three buildings here." Mike pointed at the structures he thought offered the most likely chance of discovery.

"Will do," the sergeant said, then turned and grabbed his epaulet microphone.

"What is it with the long-distance shootings lately?" Cris asked. "First the graffiti artist out on Interstate 65 and now this?"

"I'm not sure yet, but I'm guessing they're connected. Did you see Avila's tats?"

"Yeah," Cris said. "He's got enough ink on him to print the Tennessean."

"Does it tell you anything?"

"Los Punzados," Cris said.

"Right. Black and gold. What kind of cap did you say the artist was wearing?"

"Steelers—black and gold."

"Circumstantial? Maybe," Mike said. "But, my gut is telling me they're related."

Cris nodded her head. "I just spoke with one of the waitresses who's worked here for four years. She recognized Avila when she walked out onto the patio earlier. She said he used to hook up with one of the girls who waited tables here a few months ago."

"Did you get the girl's name?"

"Nia, but the waitress couldn't remember her last name. I asked the manager on duty and he thought the girl was talking about Nia Gallegos. He said she worked here for about eight or nine months. He also said she quit one night after her boyfriend went off on the bar manager, threatened him and caused several customers to leave."

"Sounds like that could have been our tattooed friend here," Mike said.

"He gave me a copy of the application they had in Gallegos's employee file. I'm going to run her through NCIC and then assuming she's still in the area and I can find her, I'll set up an interview."

The FBI's National Crime Information Center offered federal, state and local law enforcement agencies 24/7 access to criminal record historical data.

"I'm going to learn everything I can about Mr. Avila this evening,"

Mike said. “Maybe his past can tell me something about his recent activity and net me a list of who might have wanted him dead.”

# Chapter 65

*Criminal Justice Center*
*Nashville, Tennessee*
*Friday Morning*

The background checks Mike ran on Manuel Avila produced a number of the expected results. Mike was amazed to discover that Avila was an American citizen, and had been since his birth near Las Cruces, New Mexico in 1972. Mike suspected that his pregnant mother, like so many others, had come to the U.S. from Mexico with the hope of giving birth to a child who would be an American citizen and who would have a chance at a better life.

Mike was also surprised to find that Avila had virtually no criminal record until eight years ago at which time he appeared to have fallen into a pit of crime following his honorable discharge from the U.S. Army. Since that time, Avila managed to get himself arrested fourteen times for everything from DUI to assault and possession of stolen property.

Avila's association with Los Punzados was first a matter of record in the fall of 1996 when he was arrested along with three other members of the gang for assault, disturbing the peace, and resisting arrest after they beat up two members of a rival Nashville gang.

When Mike learned of Avila's most recent clash with society stemming from the automobile crash and subsequent wrongful death lawsuit filed by the husband of Julie Evans, he knew it could be helpful to talk with the deceased woman's husband.

Mike ran checks this morning on Brad Evans in order to learn as much about him as he could prior to scheduling an interview. The only arrest of record for Evans was dated September, of 1971. This appeared to have taken place less than a month after his honorable discharge from the U.S. Army. Evans was arrested for public intoxication and assault & battery. It appeared the judge must have shown compassion based upon Evans recent military service. He imposed a $500 fine, and six months probation. During that probation, Evans began working for a local gunsmith.

Mike learned that at the time of Julie Evans death, she and Brad had been married almost thirty years. During that time, the couple lived on eighty acres of farm land south of Nashville in Hubbard County.

He discovered some other facts about Brad Evans that concerned him. In addition to being a gunsmith, Brad's military records showed he was a former Army sniper in Vietnam. Mike knew these associations with guns alone did not convict Evans of Avila's murder, but they brought considerable attention to him as a man with the skills needed for such a task. And this, along with almost any supporting evidence, would push him past *person of interest* and paint him as a potential suspect.

"Hello."

"Brad Evans?"

"Yes."

"Mr. Evans, my name is Mike Neal. I'm a detective with the Nashville Police Department."

"Okay."

"Mr. Evans do you know a man named Manuel Avila?

After a moment, Brad spoke, "I know who he is. Why?"

"Is he the driver that struck your wife's car in December of last year?"

Brad hesitated, wanting to be careful with his answers. "Yes, he is the man that killed my wife."

"Mr. Evans, I'd like to speak with you about your wrongful death suit against Mr. Avila and about any interactions you may have had with Mr. Avila since the accident."

"I've not had any interactions with the bastard, and I don't intend to. Why do you want to see me?"

"We need to know what you know about Mr. Avila."

"I don't know *anything* about him, except that he killed my wife. Why don't you just talk with my lawyer? He filed the wrongful death suit. He has all the facts."

"Mr. Evans, Manuel Avila was murdered last night outside a Nashville restaurant and we're in the process of checking all the leads we can generate to hopefully determine who killed him." Mike concentrated in order to hear everything Brad said and didn't say.

There was a brief silence on the phone as Brad crafted his response. "Seriously?"

"Yes." Mike waited before continuing. "Most folks don't realize how much they know, and how much they can help until they sit with us and talk. Mr. Evans, can you visit with me for a few minutes and do what you can to help us with this case. We'd appreciate your input."

"Okay. I understand. When do you want to talk?"

"Now would be good, if you're available."

"Well, it'll take me a while to get there. Maybe a couple of hours."

"Do you know where the Criminal Justice Center is downtown?"

"I think so," Brad said. "James Robertson Parkway, isn't it?"

"Yes. Ask for me at the guard's desk."

Mike was reexamining the notes from his interview with Brad

Evans when Cris returned from her meeting with Avila's former girlfriend.

"Hey, how'd it go with Evans?" Cris asked.

"His responses were all pretty typical. He said he was at home alone on his farm at the time of the murder. He didn't offer up anything momentous and not much we didn't already know. He did tell me that the morning before her death, his wife Julie was diagnosed with stage-four breast cancer. She never got to tell him."

"How sad," Cris said.

"What about your interview with ..." Mike tried to remember the girl's name.

"Nia Gallegos. It went better than I expected. She was withdrawn at first, but opened up a little after I started speaking Spanish and distracting her with small talk. She wasn't very interested in talking about Avila. I found out later, she has lots of reasons and lots of bad memories.

"I think speaking in her native language made her more comfortable, and helped to keep her talking. I tried to discuss things early that didn't involve Avila. She is still scared of him."

"You did tell her he's dead?"

"I'm getting to that."

Mike made himself comfortable and gave Cris all his attention.

"We met at Centennial Park, by the lake. When she first got in the car, I could tell she didn't want to be there. She sat with her head down and focused on the baby."

"Baby?"

"Yeah. She has a baby."

"Avila's?"

Cris nodded. "I found out later the reason she kept her head bowed was because she has an ugly scar down the left side of her face. She tries to hide it with her hair. The night he cut her, she had threatened to hit him back after he punched her in the abdomen."

"Bad idea," Mike said.

"Once the hospital released her, she ran. She never told him she was pregnant."

"As we talked, she was careful not to say anything that might piss off Avila if it was repeated to him. She told me what he'd shared with her about his past. She said he came from a hard life."

"And he caused several other lives to be hard as well," Mike said.

"She said he ran away from the orphanage in San Salvador when he was nine years old and he's been on his own since."

Mike squinted his confusion wondering which of Avila's histories was really his.

"He told her about his youth. She said he told her he grew up begging, stealing and picking pockets to survive. She heard him tell some other gangsters that when he was young he used to slice men's rear trouser pockets with a straight razor, steal their wallets as they fell out, and then run like hell."

Mike was beginning to feel confident that the American Manuel Avila, born in New Mexico in 1972, was another person altogether and long ago deceased. Most likely, the real Mr. Avila's identity was stolen by this creative criminal years ago, and whatever his real name was, he was now residing where his chosen lifestyle had deposited him, the Davidson County morgue.

"When I first told her he'd been killed, she didn't believe me. She was adamant that she'd been told of his death several times before. In the end, he was always alive.

"I listened. I let her talk. She pulled her long hair back from the left side of her face to show me the scar. After we talked a while, she realized I was being honest with her and she asked me if he really was dead. I assured her he was. She broke down. I don't think it was sadness."

"More likely relief," Mike said.

Cris nodded. "I gave her some time, some tissues; I comforted her and allowed her to let it out. Once she regained her composure, she started telling me the kinds of things I wanted to hear. I think she loved him at one time, but he scared the hell out of her too many times. I asked about whether he ever talked to her about the wreck that killed Julie Evans or any crimes he'd committed in his past. She stared out the side window for a while. I explained that no one knew she was talking with me and that as far as I knew she was not a party to any of his crimes, and she had nothing to worry about.

"I pointed out that this was her chance to gain some justice, without any threat of retaliation. She listened and finally told me he had never talked to her directly about any of his criminal past, but she used to overhear him bragging about crimes, beatings, armed robberies, and such with his fellow gangbangers.

"She sat quietly for a minute, then told me about overhearing him talking with three of his fellow drunken gangbangers who were at the apartment playing poker. They were bragging about who had committed the most brazen crime. She said one of the other bangers told about a Confidential Informant for the MNPD who he and another guy followed to a movie theater. They sat behind him and then used a length of wire wrapped around two short pieces of pipe to garrote him, and then they changed seats and watched the rest of the movie before leaving."

"Emilio Pineda."

"You knew him?" Cris asked.

"No, but I knew who he was. He was a CI for our Narcotics Section."

"Nia said the entire group displayed their admiration for the grizzly crime. They all ended up laughing, saying the informant would not be informing on anybody else.

"Nia said she watched Avila lift his hand and interrupt the others. The entire room fell quiet. He told them when he was in the Army, he came home to find his wife had left with another soldier who'd gone AWOL. Nia didn't know Avila had been married. She said he told her once when he was drunk that he started dying that day he came home from deployment, and he just wasn't through yet."

"He is now," Mike said.

"She said Avila told the bangers he got wasted and took his rage out on two young couples who were irritating him with their loud talking and laughter at some country and western bar. He said he was more pissed off then he had ever been in his life. Everything was falling apart and he wanted revenge.

"He admitted to raping the girls and killing all four of those kids that night at some old rock quarry."

"He what?" Mike leaned forward in his chair. He wasn't sure of what he'd just heard.

"He killed all four kids," Cris repeated.

"Where?"

"A rock quarry."

"No, in what city?"

"He was stationed at Fort Campbell at the time, so I'd say somewhere near there."

Mike froze. His face turned pale.

"Are you okay?"

His head dropped, and he stared at the floor.

"Mike, are you okay?" When she asked him the second time, he finally looked up as if he was going to say something, but only swallowed hard and looked back at the floor with his head in his hand.

"Cris put her hand on his shoulder. "Is there something wrong? What is it?"

"What else did she say Avila told her about the four killings?"

Cris thought a moment. "Nia said he was bragging about how easily he took them all by surprise, cutting the boys throats, raping both girls and then killing them, too."

Mike's breathing became faster as if he'd been chasing someone. His face reddened and his brow furrowed. He stood.

"Mike, what's wrong?"

He looked at Cris, squinted and before he could explain, he saw the realization as it hit her.

"Oh, my God!" Cris grabbed her mouth with her hand as her eyes bulged. "Mike, I'm sorry. Oh, shit. I didn't realize."

Mike looked at her with a face burdened by nine years of emotion.

"Oh, Mike. It didn't register. I'm so sorry."

Mike walked toward the door. "I'll talk to you later."

"Where are you going? I'll come with you."

"No. You stay here in case something else surfaces."

"Mike, let me come with you."

"I have to do this myself," Mike said, without turning around.

# Chapter 66

*Hubbard County, Tennessee*
*Friday Late Morning*

Mike checked his notes for Brad Evans's home address. On the long drive to Hubbard County he had considerable time to think about Connie, about the last nine years searching for her killer, and about the fact that her killer had finally received his due. Even though Mike didn't dole out the justice himself, he knew it was delivered by a man who was equally motivated and similarly wronged.

Looking back, Mike was grateful that with the way things had turned out, he'd not been tempted to violate his oath nor jeopardize his career. Many times over the past nine years, during moments of extreme grief, Mike had decided, "When he's captured, if the evidence against him is conclusive, he will not make it to trial."

Mike spotted the Evans mailbox and turned onto the gravel drive. He drove the long road up to the front of the white Victorian style house. The home's front porch with its decorative brackets and balusters wrapped around three sides of the spacious home and was decorated with four ornate rocking chairs and a large swing suspended from the ceiling on two chains. The old home reminded Mike of his numerous childhood visits to his uncle's farm southeast of Nashville.

As Mike exited his car and scanned the rolling countryside, a part of him was envious because of the beautiful place Brad had built. But, Mike knew that Brad hadn't built it for himself, and this country utopia surely didn't mean the same to him now.

The screen door slapped the door facing as it closed, forcing Mike to turn toward the house.

"Did you forget something?" Brad stepped down the concrete steps and out to where Mike had parked.

"After you left," Mike said, "I met with the other detective who is working this case. She spoke at length today with Manuel Avila's old girlfriend, about him and his past. He lived a life very different from most of us."

"I'm sure," Brad agreed. "I doubt you and I would call it much of a life."

"The young woman told my partner about some of the things Avila had bragged about over the years to his friends."

Brad stared at Mike, appearing interested.

"She overheard him at times when he was drinking and telling his fellow gangbangers of his criminal exploits."

Brad leaned against Mike's car, crossed his arms and said, "What's all this have to do with me."

"Actually," Mike looked Brad directly in his eyes. "It has to do with both of us."

"Both of us? What do you mean?"

"In 1994, Manuel Avila was an E-3 stationed at Fort Campbell. Yes, he was a U.S. citizen. At least his identity said he was. He'd been deployed for about a year when he returned to Campbell to find his wife had left him with another soldier who'd recently gone AWOL."

Mike told Brad all the horrible facts surrounding the deaths of the four young people and subsequent unsuccessful investigation into their murders.

"One of the girls that were murdered that night ... was my little sister, Connie. My only sibling; she was seventeen."

"Oh, man. I'm sorry," Brad said. He rubbed his forehead with his hand and closed his eyes. "Damned animal."

After a few minutes of silence, Mike said, "Brad, it's obvious that you are the prime suspect in Avila's death. Your skills provided the means that matches the method. Your personal loss provided more than enough motivation and your inability to supply us a verifiable alibi ... well, to a great extent, it closes the gap."

Brad looked at Mike without comment.

"I don't know whether to shake your hand for doing what I had considered myself, or slap cuffs on you."

Brad stared silently at his house. He finally turned back to Mike and said, "Can we take a walk?" Brad gestured toward the hillside at the rear of the barn. "I'd like to show you something."

If it had been anyone else, Mike would have declined, but when he looked at Brad, he saw a lot of himself. They were sharing much of the same pain today.

"Sure," Mike said. He followed Brad through the steel gate that accessed the pasture.

Brad was quiet for several steps. "Are you married, detective?"

"No."

Brad nodded. "My Julie was everything to me."

Mike listened.

She was the reason I got up in the morning. Brad chuckled. I used to sit at the kitchen table drinking my coffee and wondering what I had ever done to deserve such a caring and beautiful partner. She was everything I wasn't, and never really wanted to be. I thought I was supposed to be the tough guy."

Mike let him talk.

"She was my best friend." Brad gave a weak smile. "Actually, she was better than a best friend."

Brad looked ahead of them across the rolling field as he spoke. "She was the source of most of the good that was ever in me. I guess that's why since she's passed, I've not been the same. I can feel it. I no longer have her to balance me." Brad looked at Mike and shook his head. "I've looked for the good," he said. "It's gone. I lived a rough life before I met her—probably nothing like Avila's, but pretty rough, none the less.

"After 'Nam, and all the killing I had to do," Brad spoke slowly, "I was empty. No emotion. I came home drained, classic withdrawn PTSD. Then I met Julie and I felt myself start to change—to heal. Our life together was something I'd never felt before. Julie was like a friendly-fire mortar round that hit me and knocked me back into life. Now ... I feel like I don't care again, a lot like just after 'Nam."

The two men stood only a few feet apart, gazing into the distance and only occasionally at each other.

Mike, always the detective, said, "What about the shooting on Interstate 65."

"What do you mean?" Brad asked.

"It was almost a carbon copy of Avila's shot, only from a different angle." Mike looked at Brad, waiting for his response.

Brad wavered and started to walk again.

"It wasn't the same. The artist's shot was directly into the medulla oblongata—instant death. He had on the gang colors. I thought he was one of Avila's gangbangers." Brad blew out a huge breath. "I really screwed up."

"Avila's shot was from the left side. He was alive maybe a second or two afterward. With his lifestyle, he may have realized he'd been shot—but honestly," Brad shook his head, "I doubt it."

They walked some more without talking. Mike didn't want Brad's current thoughts or his confession to be interrupted.

"Did you know Carl Garrison?" Brad asked.

"The racist? I know who he was."

Brad stood facing Mike. "He was a bad man. And one who thought of himself as some kind of sanctified shepherd to the world."

"I take it you knew him?" Mike asked.

"Briefly," Brad said. "For two days, I knew him. He tried to use me."

"Use you?"

"He wanted me to take out one of his cult members gone astray. One of them was about to blow Garrison's empire apart in order to save his own ass. Garrison said he couldn't allow that."

"Mullins."

"Yeah," Brad admitted. "How'd you know?"

"Lucky guess."

"Right." Brad was beginning to like this detective.

"And?" Mike asked.

Brad stopped walking and turned toward Mike. "I didn't do it. When Garrison double crossed both me and a friend of mine, I ended up delivering *his* well-deserved karma. This man was a hate merchant, pure and simple. Much like Avila, in the end, he deserved everything he got."

Mike listened.

"But ... not the artist. That was a really bad mistake, driven by my out-of-control hatred for Avila." Brad bent down, pulled on a long stem of orchard grass and began to break the shaft into pieces.

Mike let Brad's confession hang there between them as they looked at each other. "As much as my own personal loss helps me to understand what you've experienced and motivates me to have compassion for you, Avila's murder is just as much a homicide as Garrison's or the artist. You took the lives of three people. You know that you'll have to answer for that."

Brad continued to move toward the crest of the hill. From their elevated position atop the knoll, Brad stopped and looked out over his acreage.

"Julie and I used to get up before daybreak and come up here to watch the sunrise ... and talk. This was her favorite place on the farm." He squinted and closed his eyes pushing tears down his face.

"I've done all I can to obtain Julie's justice. Without her, I no longer have an interest in life."

Brad turned to face Mike. That's when Mike saw the compact pistol in Brad's right hand, hanging at his side. Mike drew his side arm and aimed it in Brad's direction.

"Brad, don't do this. I'll do what I can to get you help, but this is not the way to deal with these issues. You *can* get through this."

Brad shook his head. "No. There's no way I'm going to be able to deal with the consequences from all of this."

"After all you went through in Vietnam; you're obviously not the kind of guy who kills himself."

Brad stared at the ground in front of him. "No ... but my Julie's waiting." Brad lifted the pistol and aligned the sights toward Mike.

"Don't!" Mike shouted as he dropped to one knee.

Brad squeezed the trigger and fired a shot over Mike's head.

Mike returned fire. He had no choice.

# Epilogue

*Mike Neal's Home*
*Nashville, Tennessee*
*Friday Evening*

It had been months since Mike had drawn his weapon while on duty and almost two years since he'd fired it outside the department's North Nashville target range. In Mike's years as a Metropolitan Nashville Police Officer, he had only witnessed 'suicide by cop' on one occasion. Fortunately, prior to today, he hadn't been involved.

The shooting of Brad Evans was under investigation just like any other officer-involved shooting. The Sig Sauer P250 found next to the body was registered in Brad Evans's name. It was established that the weapon had been fired, and the gunshot residue on Brad's right hand confirmed that he had fired a weapon recently. Mike was confident his use of deadly force was justified, and that following the investigation, he would be exonerated.

Mike had a couple of days off and decided to pay some important people a visit. He pressed six of the seven numbers and then stopped for a moment before the last one.

"God help me." He pushed the button. The phone began to ring.

"Hello."

"Dad?"

There was a considerable pause. "Michael?"

"Yes, it's me. How are you?"

"Oh ... I'm okay I guess, all things considered. It's been a while since you called."

Mike's feelings of regret made it difficult for him to talk. "Yeah, I know. Sorry it's taken so long."

"That's okay, son."

"We found the guy who killed Connie," Mike said.

"What? You found him?"

"Well, we found him after he was killed."

"I don't understand."

"That's okay. I'll explain it all later. I was wondering. Are you busy tomorrow morning?"

Mike's father hesitated. "I don't think so. Why?"

"I ... I was planning to visit Connie's grave and uh, tell her that we found him. And, I was hoping maybe you would want to come with me."

"Uh. Well." He thought about it for a moment. "Sure. Yeah. I can do that."

"Can I pick you up around nine?"

"Yeah. I'll be ready."

"Good. I'll see you tomorrow."

"Michael?"

"Yeah."

Mike's father took a moment to prepare his words. "Son ... I'm sorry. And, I'm glad you called."

Mike closed his eyes. "Me too."

## Acknowledgments

To my good friend Dew Wayne Burris, who throughout the writing of this novel provided helpful feedback and encouragement at all the most critical times. Thank you. Your untiring efforts helped to keep me on point.

To Sergeant Patrick Postiglione of Nashville's Homicide and Cold Case Investigations Units, whose thirty-plus years of dedicated service to our city have been filled with numerous high-voltage investigations that he and his team have skillfully resolved for the citizens of Nashville. Thank you for your support and for sharing your priceless experience.

To Lee Lofland, retired detective and author, whose capable counsel through conversation and print has proven to be a lifesaver. Thanks for all you do on behalf of our passionate crime, mystery and thriller writers.

To Dr. Zaid Brifkani, one of the many proud and dynamic Kurds who make their home in Nashville. Your willingness to help with this project is appreciated.

To the members of The Murfreesboro Writers Group, where I found encouragement, meaningful critique, and a great way to spend Wednesday nights. Thanks.

To my wife Sandra, for thirty-five happy years, for your undying support, and especially for patiently believing in me. Thank you.

## Author Bio

Ken Vanderpool is a life-long fan of Crime Suspense and Thriller fiction who began to write his own in 2006 following an eye-opening medical procedure and an intimate encounter with his mortality.

Ken is a graduate of Middle Tennessee State University with his degree in Psychology and Sociology with a concentration on Criminology. He has also graduated from the Metropolitan Nashville Citizen Police Academy and the Writer's Police Academy in Greensboro, North Carolina.

He is currently at work on his second novel in the Music City Murders series, FACE THE MUSIC.

Ken has spent his entire life in Middle Tennessee and proudly professes, "There is no better place on earth." Ken currently lives near Nashville with his wife Sandra and their Cairn Terrier-ist, Molly.

CPSIA information can be obtained at www.ICGtesting.com
Printed in the USA
LVOW100513180313

324691LV00003B/11/P

9 781937 937003